Heart Thief

"I loved *Heart Thief*! This is what futuristic romance is all about. Robin D. Owens writes the kind of futuristic romance we've all been waiting to read; certainly the kind that I've been waiting for. She provides a wonderful, gripping mix of passion, exotic futuristic settings, and edgy suspense. If you've been waiting for someone to do futuristic romance right, you're in luck, Robin D. Owens is the author for you."
—Jayne Castle

"The complex plot and rich characterizations, not to mention the sexy passion . . . make this a must-read . . . I just wish Robin D. Owens wrote faster. I hope she's got a huge pile of ideas for future Celtan stories, and I for one can't wait to go back."
—*The Romance Reader*

"Owens spins an entrancing tale . . . Although the setting is fresh and totally captivating, it is the well-developed characters, both human and animal, that make this story memorable. Crafty villains, honorable, resourceful protagonists, and sentient pets drive the plot of this fast-paced, often suspenseful romantic adventure. As have others before her (e.g., Anne McCaffrey, Marion Zimmer Bradley), Owens has penned a stunning futuristic tale that reads like fantasy and is sure to have crossover appeal to both SF and fantasy fans."
—*Library Journal*

"Owens has crafted a fine romance that is also a successful science fantasy yarn with terrific world-building."
—*Booklist*

"A tremendous science fiction romance that affirms what many fans thought after reading the prequel (*HeartMate*): that Robin D. Owens is one of the subgenre's giant stars. The story line is faster than the speed of light, but more important is this world's society seems so real that psychic powers feel genuine . . . [a] richly textured otherplanetary romance."
—*BookBrowser*

Heart Duel

"[A] sexy story . . . Readers will enjoy revisiting this fantasy-like world filled with paranormal talents."
—*Booklist*

"An exhilarating love story . . . The delightful story line is cleverly executed . . . Owens proves once again that she is among the top rung of fantasy romance authors with this fantastic tale."

—*Midwest Book Review*

"With engaging characters, Robin D. Owens takes readers back to the magical world of Celta . . . The characters are engaging, drawing the reader into the story and into their lives. They are multilayered and complex and grow into exceptional people."

—*Romance Reviews Today*

Heart Choice

"The dialogue is brilliant . . . Terrific writing with incredibly detailed visions of this mystical world, coupled with a very realistic and sensual romance, make *Heart Choice* a fantastic read . . . intense, exciting, and magical. Don't miss it."

—*Romance Reviews Today*

"The romance is passionate, the characters engaging, and the society and setting exquisitely crafted." —*Booklist*

"A wonderful book to lose yourself in for a while! I'll be anxiously awaiting the next book in this wonderfully imaginative series." —*Romance Junkies*

"[A] well-written, humor-laced, intellectually and emotionally involving story, which explores the true meaning of family and love in a nontraditional setting." —*Library Journal*

"Robin D. Owens's world of Celta fascinates and intrigues me . . . I thoroughly enjoyed the entire book from beginning to end. Robin D. Owens can lure me into her Celta stories any time she sees fit." —*ParaNormal Romance Reviews*

"All the passionate, magical, and powerful characters you have come to expect from an Owens novel are on full display in this electric tale." —*Romantic Times*

HeartMate

Robin D. Owens

BERKLEY SENSATION, NEW YORK

THE BERKLEY PUBLISHING GROUP
Published by the Penguin Group
Penguin Group (USA) Inc.
375 Hudson Street, New York, New York 10014, USA
Penguin Group (Canada), 90 Eglinton Avenue East, Suite 700, Toronto, Ontario M4P 2Y3, Canada
(a division of Pearson Penguin Canada Inc.)
Penguin Books Ltd., 80 Strand, London WC2R 0RL, England
Penguin Group Ireland, 25 St. Stephen's Green, Dublin 2, Ireland (a division of Penguin Books Ltd.)
Penguin Group (Australia), 250 Camberwell Road, Camberwell, Victoria 3124, Australia
(a division of Pearson Australia Group Pty. Ltd.)
Penguin Books India Pvt. Ltd., 11 Community Centre, Panchsheel Park, New Delhi—110 017, India
Penguin Group (NZ), Cnr. Airborne and Rosedale Roads, Albany, Auckland 1310, New Zealand
(a division of Pearson New Zealand Ltd.)
Penguin Books (South Africa) (Pty.) Ltd., 24 Sturdee Avenue, Rosebank, Johannesburg 2196,
South Africa

Penguin Books Ltd., Registered Offices: 80 Strand, London WC2R 0RL, England

This is a work of fiction. Names, characters, places, and incidents either are the product of the author's imagination or are used fictitiously, and any resemblance to actual persons, living or dead, business establishments, events, or locales is entirely coincidental. The publisher does not have any control over and does not assume any responsibility for author or third-party websites or their content.

HEARTMATE

A Berkley Sensation Book / published by arrangement with the author.

PRINTING HISTORY
Jove mass-market edition / December 2001
Berkley Sensation edition / August 2006

ISBN: 0-425-21240-8

BERKLEY SENSATION®
Berkley Sensation Books are published by The Berkley Publishing Group,
a division of Penguin Group (USA) Inc.,
375 Hudson Street, New York, New York 10014.
BERKLEY SENSATION is a registered trademark of Penguin Group (USA) Inc.
The "B" design is a trademark belonging to Penguin Group (USA) Inc.

PRINTED IN THE UNITED STATES OF AMERICA

10   9   8   7   6   5   4   3   2   1

To all struggling writers.
Never quit.

Acknowledgments

This book would not have been realized except for:

Those who first believed in my talent, Victoria Dann (Glenn), Morgan de Thouars, and Kay Bergstrom.

My long-time critique buddies who stuck through three books before Celta: Sharon, Steven, Judy, Anne.

My other critiquers: Liz R., Sue, Pam, Leslee, Teresa, Janet, Peggy Sue, Alice, Debbie, Anita, Michelle, Kathee.

Everyone else in Rocky Mountain Fiction Writers, Novel Critiques, and Romance Writers Unlimited who gave me their support.

With thanks to Cindy Hwang for her belief in me, and to Lisa Craig who developed my website: *www.robindowens.com*.

And to the cats: Diva, Mistral, Muse, Maddox, and Black Pierre.

Mistral and Diva, your stories are coming, stop whining!

One

⚜

Today you will meet your HeartMate. Rand T'Ash's blood thrummed in his temples as he stared at the divination dice that he'd just rolled.

The polished blue-green stones gleamed in the light, the symbols incised on them showing off deep red veins, looking like blood. He didn't quite believe the glyphs carved in the twelve-sided pieces of bloodstone, and the prophecy they foretold. He'd throw again, to be sure.

The deep emanation of his Flair—his psi power—pulsed through his blood. A few years back he'd created the dice, first choosing the bloodstones, then chiseling and shaping them.

He let the swell of his emotions flow through and from him. A tingle of premonition shivered up his spine. He focused his will and mage power. With a flick of his wrist, he threw the dice again. They rolled, spun, stopped.

Today you will meet your HeartMate.

Excitement surged, and an overwhelming tide of triumph.

His heart picked up beat. Shimmering tension embedded in his nerves.

T'Ash sat and gripped his half-empty caff mug between his palms. It was oversized, made by a mage-potter to fit his hands.

The ebb and flow of his preternatural Flair had changed over the last few days, he now realized. The daily divinations had foretold something unusual, signs that he'd overlooked. TwinMoonsday—*Enjoy the moment, for it will pass;* Midweek—*Prepare yourself;* Quert, yesterday, *Restructuring is necessary.*

He stared at the dice once more. *Today you will meet your HeartMate.*

How long he had waited! He was thirty-seven. The sole member of a GreatHouse, the highest rank of Celta. There were only thirteen GreatHouses. His was a colony FirstFamily, the House of the Ash. By the grace of the Lord and Lady, he'd escaped the destruction of his Family by a rival House when he was six years old. By sheer will and determination he hid and lived as a boy in the slums of the worst part of the city—Downwind. He grew strong first to survive, then for vengeance.

Only in the last few years, after he'd reestablished his GreatHouse and started his shop, plying his Flair for magegems instead of fighting, had he been able to live life with deliberate ease.

After tomorrow he would never again be alone. An exhilarating, but disturbing, thought.

His caff was cold. The pungent scent no longer wafted through the air. He looked around his home workroom. The large desk of gleaming reddwood stood in sharp contrast to the scarred workbenches. On the far wall, behind a protection spell, were his gems and precious metals. In the corner, hidden by deep shadows, was his walk-in vault. It was built large to accommodate a man of his size and magical ability. The vault held a smaller safe containing his most precious possessions, including the necklace. His HeartGift.

T'Ash rose and walked to the vault. After disarming the door with a routine spell Word, he went inside.

His HeartGift. An item created in three days after his last

Passage, seventeen years before. It was the third and last Passage that gave mastery of psi powers—rather than just confirming the Flair, then releasing it. And it was the final Passage that indicated HeartMates. In the delirium of that Passage T'Ash's Flair had spiraled to bond with his Heart-Mate, though he'd never felt the link since.

He placed his palm on the safe and muttered an opening spell. He reached for the velvet case. The moment he touched it urgency swept through him, the HeartGift's power. He grabbed the case, slammed the safe shut, strode out, and armed the vault. He set the round-cornered box in the middle of his largest worktable, positioned in the sunlight.

T'Ash watched with disbelief as his hands trembled when he opened the box. Hands that had firmly swung a broadsword, hands that had steadily fixed tiny jewels in a tracery of delicate chains—still, his fingers shook.

Energy, power, magic streamed from the necklace, driving him back. He raised his hand and felt pulses from the piece. The sexual potency of a virile twenty-year-old man imbued the HeartGift; a man who had spent three days in an erotic delirium of a Passage that finally freed his psi power. T'Ash had focused all his creative, carnal energy on fashioning the necklace. Seventeen years had passed, and it still radiated.

Sexual tension washed through him and lodged, tingling his nerves, warming his muscles, pooling in his groin. He'd feel the pressure until he took his mate. The tautness was disconcerting, pleasure bordering on pain. Anticipation.

T'Ash sucked in a breath and looked at the necklace again. Now he saw only how it was fashioned. He frowned. The strands of silver, gold, and redgold wire weren't uniformly thin, but showed lumpy nodules in places. The gem mountings were often clumsy.

One side of his mouth quirked. When his hands hadn't wavered from sexual arousal, they'd shaken from exhaustion. He didn't remember eating or sleeping during the days he created the necklace—forging the metal, twisting the wire, setting the gems. The final jewel was a large roseamber pendant he'd spent septhours shaping. With the energy pouring through him, he wouldn't have been surprised if it had ended up in the shape of a phallus.

He'd made a heart.

Zanth, T'Ash's cat and Familiar, strolled in. *Fish again,* he projected telepathically to T'Ash. He carried his muscular fighter's body with grace. He'd attached himself to the child, Rand Ash, the first week in Downwind. The cat had announced he was Rand's Fam and demanded an Ash Family name. T'Ash's crate in the slum had been barely big enough for them both. Zanth had made the move into T'Ash Residence as if it were his due, though he looked every inch the Downwind tough. The cat was huge, two-thirds of a meter long. Irregular black blotches dominated his white fur.

A red tongue caught a stray bit of food from his whiskers. *You hear? Fish again! Oily. Me not like and don't want any more.*

Zanth's comment grounded T'Ash. "I'll speak to the chef."

Zanth went to the workbench and stared up at the necklace. *That thing. From long ago.* His pink nose wrinkled. He opened his muzzle and curled his tongue to use his sixth sense—a combination of smell-taste. *Don't like it. It's feral you. Too much you and not enough Me. Take it away.*

"I'll take it with me to the shop tonight. I'm running the store. Majo, my manager, is on vacation for Discovery Day."

Col-on-ists in spaceships found Celta on Dis-cov-ery Day.

"That's right."

Ships were down to few Cats. Good to party. You go on vac-a-tion, too.

"Not tonight. Maybe tomorrow." When he had his Heart-Mate. He could arrange a wedding on Discovery Day, then a long honeymoon. He grinned.

The gleam of a gem caught his eye and he looked again at the necklace and *saw* it, beyond its inherent power and the skill that fashioned it. He saw the style and the color of the gems. In that moment he knew who the woman was. His mate.

He had never seen her, but he knew of her. Majo had told him how often she visited the store. *Today you will meet your HeartMate.* Not today, but tonight. For the first time in several years he had to man his exclusive shop in CityCenter.

In the last few months he'd been playing a subtle game from a distance with an unseen customer, teasing her with his creations. She'd buy the charming and the whimsical, and preferred roseamber and redgold. All the jewelry she'd purchased had been at the least expensive end of his line. The pieces had also been some of his most original—and sensual.

He wished he knew her name.

From his pocket he pulled a long silver chain set with oddly shaped beads, and slid it through his fingers. It was designed to suspend a personal amulet. Some of the beads were round, some stone nuggets, and some faceted crystal. A simple piece with a small price, yet it was significantly superior in craftsmanship to the HeartGift.

Zanth hopped up on the worktable and swatted the chain.

T'Ash obligingly swung it. "The necklace is my gift to a mate, radiating my essence, and will draw her to me. We will have a woman living with us tomorrow. What do you say to that?"

Zanth looked past the swinging chain and narrowed his jade-green eyes at the necklace. *Mate prefer mouse.* He turned his back on the HeartGift. Snagging a claw in the chain, he brought it to his mouth. *This female. You play with her. Give toys.*

"Yes, I make her jewelry." T'Ash dropped the end of the chain. It rattled to the desk.

Zanth tangled his paws in the chain and glanced sideways at T'Ash. *This bauble was for her. She not take it.*

T'Ash shrugged. That he couldn't consistently predict her taste intrigued him. Several pieces that he'd made especially to tempt her had been bought by others, or remained unsold—so Majo said.

T'Ash had not asked her name. Instead it had been an increasingly enchanting game.

A game once, but not now. She'd visit the shop tonight. He knew it by his sharpened senses and the deep expectation humming in his bones.

Zanth snuffled. He'd picked up a sinus infection prowling the alleys of Downwind that T'Ash had been unable to treat.

Zanth was not amenable to nosedrops in each nostril three times a day. *Female.* He looked at the necklace. *Female's scent improve it.*

T'Ash winced at his cat's blunt remark.

Females are soft laps. Will accept one in My domain. Pro-vis-ion-al-ly. With that, Zanth gathered some of the beaded chain in his mouth and hopped from the table. The chain skittered on the floor as he turned and exited, tail high.

T'Ash didn't care to dwell on the thought of soft laps. He glanced at the HeartGift one more time and left it on his workbench. He needed more caff.

The power from the necklace swirled around him. He felt it, and so would she, the passion that heralded a lifelong love, the deep yearning for one special person. The necklace would attract and affect only her. The vital sexuality as well as his basic nature portrayed in his HeartGift would snare her, and he would take her home. Simple. Easy.

He had built a new Residence, a luxurious palace, after his final act of vengeance. Now he would have someone to share the echoing rooms with—a woman, a wife, a HeartMate.

A fierce smile curved his mouth. Having a mate would be satisfying, as satisfying as the orderly life he'd so carefully crafted after long struggle.

Today you will meet your HeartMate.

With a sweep of his hand, he gathered the dice on his desk. Two bounced and fell to the floor, one cracking. He bent and his fingers stilled. *Blaser rays surround a vulnerable woman.* He picked up the die showing the woman.

It fell to pieces.

A woman in danger.

His heart pounded like a hammer on an anvil. His Divination set, ruined. His lady, threatened. He'd put the violence—and the man he'd become seeking vengeance—behind him, but now his lady was endangered.

*D*anith Mallow sidled to a corner of the elegant shop T'Ash's Phoenix. Here a table draped in beige damask held a lovely china caff set. After selecting a mug, she picked up the t'pot, keeping an eye on the man behind the U-shaped counter. She was accustomed to the friendly Majo, the slight salesman who usually staffed the store.

This man—it wasn't just that he wore black, both shirt and trous, or that he had long midnight hair. Or that he was so big.

He stared at her.

His sky-crystal blue eyes looked shockingly light under his heavy brows and against his olive skin. Eyes as potent as blaser rays. His very presence was a dark, intense force in the bright, jewel-glittering shop.

Her smile faded. The man was too dark. Too solid. Too brooding. And she was alone with him.

Her eyes widened as she saw his sleeve cuffs—ash brown with embroidered green ash tree leaves. T'Ash himself!

She set down the hot t'pot before a stream of golden liquid wavered from her half-full mug.

She liked his designs. She could even afford the simple ones, but she'd never expected the mage-crafter to be so intimidating. Who'd expect a jeweler to look like an outlaw?

Glancing up from mixing her tea and sweet, she saw he still stared at her. He dipped his head, then turned to look pointedly at a necklace displayed on a black velvet easel sitting on the long part of the counter opposite the door. When his scrutiny returned to her, she shivered at the power, then lifted her chin.

Again his gaze touched the necklace and moved back to her. "Perhaps you would be interested in the necklace." His voice sounded as dark as the rest of him, with a rasp that should have roused fear, but somehow seemed to stroke her skin.

"No, thank you." She held her warm mug of tea, both as a prop and a comforting drink.

He scowled. A spark of anger flared in his eyes. Who'd expect the man to be so sensitive about his work?

His eyes narrowed. He angled the display stand facing the door directly toward her. With one large finger he delicately traced the stones of the necklace, touched the roseamber heart. A tingle ran up her spine.

"You'd like the necklace." The undertone in his voice was darker still, tempting, almost decadent.

"No," she lied. She'd seen the piece the moment she entered. Well, *seen* wasn't quite the right word. *Felt, been drawn to,* or even *enchanted by* were more apt. As with all of his jewelry, something about it satisfied her on several levels. But she knew at a glance that the value of the stones alone put it far beyond her modest budget. Why, the roseamber heart itself was a good four centimeters. She blinked and leaned forward for a better view. In the center of the gem glowed a golden flaw in a shape she couldn't quite make out.

"Come look."

"No, thank you." Danith couldn't afford the thing, and if she saw it close enough to really desire it, she sensed it would haunt her when she left. There were many things beyond her grasp in life, and this was simply one more. Besides, the necklace was only a few handspans from the man.

"Come. Look." He didn't coax now. He demanded.

"No."

T'Ash made her uncomfortable, his aura and his rank. Sooner or later she might succumb to the pull of the necklace, or curiosity, or his intent stare, and find herself trying on the piece. She didn't need one more unattainable thing in her life, one more lost dream.

She slid her gaze to T'Ash. He continued to stare at her. She made a show of glancing at her timer, set her tea down, and sent him a false smile. "Sorry, I must go." She headed for the door. A hum sounded. She pulled on the knob and nothing happened.

Whirling around, she glared at him. Her heart thumped with a mixture of wariness and anger. She chose to show the anger. "You locked the door. Open it, now."

He smiled. The flash of his white teeth didn't lighten his face. "Promise to look at the necklace."

"You GreatLords think you can flout the rules of conduct—"

A dark cloud seemed to coalesce around him. The atmosphere in the shop dimmed and grew thick. For the first time, Danith felt alarmed. She groped for the red firepull behind her.

"Don't." He made the word soft and persuasive. "Please, GentleLady—"

"Miz," she snapped. "Simply, miz."

"Stay. Look at the necklace."

"Open the door."

With each moment the silence between them changed from strained to something quite different. The intensity of his blue-silver gaze mesmerized her. His evident power, not only magical but his essential male vitality, enveloped her.

And it wasn't menacing, but sheltering. It quieted her breathing, calmed her fears, and impressed an elemental fact upon her. *He would never harm her.* Even so, she didn't feel quite safe.

A short hum buzzed loud in the silence. She touched the doorknob behind her. It turned under her fingers.

The light in the shop was suddenly too bright. She closed her eyelids, shutting away the gleaming brilliance of the jewels and shining metals, none of which were as dazzling as his light blue eyes.

A soft, whispery noise made her open her lashes. T'Ash pushed the velvet stand down to the short leg of the counter, across from the caff set, then he retreated to the middle of the glass case opposite the door and her. He stepped back until he was against the far wall and put his hands behind him. No doubt it was supposed to be a reassuring gesture, but the black shirt outlined his impressive biceps and chest.

"Look at the necklace. Try it on."

She glanced at it, finding its charm even more heady than before—just the sight of a glimmering sapphire pulled at her. And the golden amber flaw in the heart tantalized. She jerked her gaze away only to meet his considering expression. Irritation welled up in her. She compressed her lips.

"Try the necklace on," he urged quietly.

"I. Can't. Afford. The necklace." Not in money and not in peace of mind.

Now *he* blinked. His heavy, dark brows arched slightly, and he smiled. "Yes, you can. Easily." The lilt of his words caressed her.

Danith stared at him with suspicion.

He set his hands on his lean hips. "I am T'Ash. I, no other, set the price on my work. And the necklace"—his lips curved again as he nodded to it—"is one of my earlier efforts. You will find that it doesn't have the quality of the other pieces you've given a home."

Her eyes narrowed further. She was about to reply when the bells hanging on the door behind her jangled. She moved from the doorway, her steps instinctively going to the comfort of the tea—but also toward the necklace.

Four laughing women entered, and Danith instantly felt scruffy, unsophisticated, and exactly what she was. Common. They were all nobles: one GreatLady, then two GrandLadies and a lesser GraceLady. They wore long gowns with colorful embroidered patterns in shining metallic thread, or long ankle-length tunics cut up the sides to the hip to show billowing silkeen trous of contrasting colors. Their hair was arranged in intricate designs.

Danith glanced down at her plain blue knee-length tunic over her narrow-legged trous. She placed a hand on her hair, which had escaped its simple tie, and sighed. Definitely common.

"T'Ash!" the GreatLady exclaimed, holding her hands out over the counter in greeting. "It's so rare we see you. Not since the FirstFamilies Council last."

FirstFamilies Councils and GreatHouses had nothing to do with Danith. She had never envied nobles or aspired to their status. The titles carried too much formality and responsibility. Still, it wasn't often she could see them up close. She reached for her tea mug, studiously avoiding the necklace. Yet, in directing her gaze from the jewelry, her glance focused again on the man. She watched T'Ash from under her lashes as she sipped her delicious but now tepid drink.

"D'Birch." T'Ash grazed one of the GreatLady's hands with fingertips, then reverted to brooding. He'd never make a salesman.

"You have such Flair, such lovely things," D'Birch gushed.

The other women agreed and spread throughout the shop, gravitating to the cases where the most expensive jewelry was.

"Excuse me, I'm quite parched." One of the GrandLadies smiled at Danith and reached for the cocoa carafe. Danith looked at the embroidery on the Lady's sleeve—a spindle, signifying her name.

"GrandLady D'Spindle," Danith acknowledged the older woman.

D'Spindle poured a mug of cocoa and offered the carafe.

Danith smiled and shook her head. "No, thank you anyway." She stepped back until she bumped against the glass case. When she turned, the sight of the necklace dazed her. Something huge wrenched inside her. Her mug clattered to the counter as she pressed a hand to her breastbone.

"Are you all right?" D'Spindle left her cup and hurried over.

Danith gasped. Her gaze locked on the necklace. Wave after wave of hot sensation captured her pulse. Heat rose to her cheeks. "The necklace," she panted.

"The necklace?" D'Spindle patted Danith on the shoulder and looked around distractedly.

Without thought Danith reached for the incredible piece of jewelry but managed to fist her hand before actually touching it. "The necklace."

"Hmmm?" D'Spindle peered beyond Danith's fist. "Yes, there does seem to be something there, but it's of no matter, my dear. What can I do to help you?"

"A cold drink." Heat and more uncoiled from her very core. Desire stirred, a deep sexual yearning she'd never experienced. And she knew exactly the man responsible. She dragged her gaze from the necklace and shot a look of pure fury at him.

T'Ash nodded and smiled smugly. "The necklace."

Anger boiled in Danith. A seduction spell. He'd put a filthy seduction spell on the jewels and no doubt considered a common woman like her fair game to test it on, to see if she would come trembling with lust to his bed. She felt cheapened and oddly betrayed.

The commotion drew the others to Danith's end of the room.

"Yes," D'Birch said, "it is a necklace. I think." She peered at the radiant thing. "Though I must say the spellshield on this piece is faulty. I can barely see it." She sniffed. "There is a nice bit of roseamber, about thirty thou?"

Taking a cold tumbler from D'Spindle, Danith gulped ice water with a tang of mint. She'd known she could never afford the necklace. Now she knew the price would have been too costly in more ways than one. Nausea rose at the idea of playing the sextoy for some jaded noble.

"It can't be only thirty thou gilt." The little, beak-nosed GraceLady squinted at the necklace. "It has a rare flaw of golden, looks like a fish. Sixty minimum. Just for that stone."

Danith finished her water and clinked the tumbler next to her mug on the glass counter. Everyone's words sounded crazy. No one acted rationally. She had to get out. She smiled at D'Spindle. "Thank you, but I need some fresh air."

Danith strode to the door but jumped aside as a man hustled in. Slightly younger than T'Ash, exquisite embroidery graced his cuffs—from it she identified the man as Holm, the Heir of the Hollys, another GreatHouse. My, she was mixing with exalted company this eve. The whole night's events made her mind spin.

"T'Ash, I need you. My brother's life's at stake! A weapon and a calming spell—" Holm demanded.

Danith caught the door before it swung shut and slipped out. Through the glass panel she saw T'Ash vault over his counter and head for her.

"Stop!" he shouted.

She ignored him, and before he could take a step farther, Holm Holly grabbed fistfuls of T'Ash's shirt. "You owe me from the time I helped you find and bring your Family's killers to justice—your vengeance stalk. I'm claiming my boon."

Danith couldn't resist one final glance into the shop. An aura of power surrounded the bright stones of the necklace, placed at an angle where she couldn't really see it. How disappointing. Though she shouldn't want another glance at it, she did.

She also felt compelled to look at T'Ash. He inclined his head to her, and his fiery blue gaze seemed to issue a promise. A promise cloaked in danger.

She broke eye contact. He was too disturbing, too big, and

too powerful—both in Flair and in rank. She looked at her timer again and sighed.

The evening was slipping away and she still had a namegift and four Discovery Day tokens to buy. The namegift was for Claif, her current gallant. Not an intimate present, but one of serious intent—she was almost in love with Claif, he was exuberant and masculine and uncomplicated. She *did* love his large, cheerful, and welcoming family. Something special for Claif, perhaps a generation alemug with a touch of magic. . . . Planning her future, a comfortable middle-class future, she turned and walked away.

T'Ash watched his *HeartMate* stroll up the street. Frustration burned inside him. He'd followed her with his gaze every instant she'd been in the shop, and now she was gone. He had never known how to treat a woman, and had obviously been too impatient, pushed her too hard.

She hadn't touched the HeartGift, let alone him. She hadn't accepted the necklace willingly and without knowing it was a HeartGift, which was necessary by law for him to claim her. She wasn't going home with him tonight, something he had expected and anticipated.

He glared at Holm Holly, who'd ignored T'Ash's obvious outrage and continued to make demands. T'Ash didn't want to risk ruining the shop by fighting with Holly.

T'Ash craned to see out the window, up the street. Before he could move, she'd hopped onto a public carrier that trundled along the twisting street of luxurious shops.

"I'm speaking to you," Holm said.

T'Ash dragged his attention back. He owed Holm a debt of blood and honor, and Holm was claiming it. Now, at the least convenient time. Naturally.

T'Ash set his teeth. Small problems. Minor things he could and would handle. They would not be allowed to wrinkle the smooth fabric of his days or ignite the wildness that lived in his center.

Removing his shirt from Holm's grip, he went behind the counter, putting distance between them and forcing his anger into the grounding mat beneath his feet. "I hear you, Holm."

"Listen!" Holm raked a hand through his silver-blond hair. It fell back smoothly, not a hair out of place. "I need a weapon for my brother, something longer than a dagger and shorter than a sword—a main gauche, and with a very powerful but subtle calming spell."

T'Ash's mouth twisted. Holm wanted impossibilities. "When?"

"As soon as possible." He fisted the elegant fingers T'Ash envied, pounding hard enough on the case to shiver the glass.

"You know how long it takes to forge a quality spellblade," T'Ash said.

Holm met his stare with a dark gray one. He put both palms on the counter and leaned forward. "We followed your vengeance trail day and night until it was . . . done."

T'Ash jerked his head in a nod.

"It looks as if my brother's Passage will coincide with Discovery Day. Passages for a Holly always involve death-duels. Remember my own when I found myself in Downwind and you saved me? I want a spell to help Tinne keep his head, dampen his emotions and impulses. I want the best magic for him. Only you can make an object strong enough to handle such a potent spell and splendid enough that he would wear it all the time with his blaser gun."

A small warmth suffused T'Ash at the words praising his skill, but it wasn't enough to quell his simmering frustration.

"I need the blade and I need it in just a few days."

"That will take most of my time, strength, energy, and Flair." T'Ash smiled grimly. He wanted to pursue his Heart-Mate, not forge a main gauche.

Holm's expression hardened. "With Passage, the bloodlust will come. Imbue the weapon with calm, disciplined emotions. I can trust you for that, too." His restless fingers drummed on the glass.

"You have called in your debt of blood and honor."

"My brother, Tinne, is very impetuous."

"Like all the Hollys."

A humorless smile flashed across Holm's face. "My brother is even more rash than I was."

"Than you are."

Holm lifted a brow. "*Was.* However, Tinne, being the second son, believes he has more to prove to the world than I. He seeks duels to demonstrate his honor and manhood. And since I was drawn Downwind during my Passage, no doubt he, too—"

"A bellicose, arrogant Holly with something to prove. I shudder."

Holm snorted. "I wouldn't want him to meet you in a Downwind alley."

T'Ash's face froze. He'd spent too many years, had too many experiences in the slum for it to be an amusing matter, even now.

Holm's eyes widened, but he slid over the moment with the ease of a gregarious talker. "I have some ideas. I want the main gauche to be a gift, but don't want Tinne to realize that it's more than it seems. I have an ancient heirloom." He drew out a black hilt and half a blade.

A shaft of pure pain speared T'Ash, but he kept his face impassive. His Family, his Residence, all his line's treasures and possessions, all his own small belongings, had been destroyed in the huge voracious fire—except the ring he'd worn and the book he'd carried.

He remembered weapons owned and used by his forebears, books to fill two libraries, furniture and paintings commissioned and carved for his Family over generations. All gone.

Holm tapped an elegant finger on the fancy engraved scrollwork on the knife's hilt. "Tinne has always been particularly fond of this dagger, because of the pattern."

From under lowered brows, T'Ash studied the piece. The weapon dated from two centuries before. Beauty combined with function and melded with sculpted grace to make the dagger a work of art.

He glanced around the shop, noticing that D'Birch and the other noble ladies had departed, probably to spread gossip about Holly business. Someone had tidied up the counter and caff table. T'Ash put the dagger down and left Holm to serve some waiting customers who were either enjoying the conversation between Holm and himself or were too awed by the GreatLords to interrupt.

Even with the hustle and bustle of the shop, no one gave the necklace more than a passing glance. Nor did Holm. But a HeartGift was only easily visible to himself and his Heart-Mate if he was not concentrating on it.

After taking care of the shoppers, T'Ash returned his attention to the ancient blade. Reverently he lifted it to scrutinize the smithing. He felt the tingle of old power in the hilt, indicating a once formidable spell. This dagger was not as strong as the weapon T'Ash could craft, but Flair had grown more powerful in two centuries. Now it was far beyond the puny psi-gifts of the original colonists, even the twenty-five FirstFamilies who had commissioned the starships so they could find a new home and develop their Flair. They'd left Earth and journeyed to Celta to be able to live without fear of persecution.

The feel of the hilt, the echo of Flair sparked inspiration. T'Ash pulled a sketchbook from behind the counter. With a few quick lines he drew an elegant main gauche with a pattern reminiscent of, but more modern than, the one on the old dagger.

"Yes. Exactly!" Holm pinched at the drawing as if he could actually feel the thing. His smile deepened until a crease showed in his cheek. T'Ash remembered that look, usually saved for the exuberance of a fight. "In fact, I'll commission three. One for myself and my father, also."

T'Ash frowned and took the papyrus from his friend. "Your brother's main gauche first, as soon as I can manage. Have Tinne come tomorrow night to test the preliminary balance of the blade. Your nameday is three twinmoons phases from now, your long dagger will be finished then. Your father's will be ready by the anniversary of Holly GreatHouse."

Holm's fingers made another tinkling tattoo on the glass counter. "No sooner for the others?"

T'Ash straightened and matched Holm's height. He leaned forward, emphasizing his Ash bulk. "I have other priorities now. You called in your blood debt and I will honor it. The rest must wait."

Both of Holm's winged silver-blond eyebrows rose, and a wicked smile graced his lips. "Personal business." He rubbed his hands, touched the handle of his short-barreled blaser at his side. "Fighting?"

"No."

Holm sighed and looked at the sketch again. "Pity. You have grown positively staid of late."

"My vengeance is over. It had to be pursued but now is done. I can concentrate on rebuilding my line and shaping my life."

A hint of envy flickered in Holm's eyes. "You have no Family to pressure you, no bonds of obligation to anyone else. You can live life as you please."

"No Family. No ancestral home." T'Ash tapped the dagger. "No generational possessions. Only myself and my hopes alone. Only a Residence that echoes with newness. Only possessions I have purchased or made."

Holm inclined his head. "I understand. And despite all those lacks, you still have the duties, responsibilities, and rituals that all FirstFamilies and GreatHouses must observe."

"Indeed." T'Ash didn't want to think of the void still in his life, particularly since his HeartMate had rejected him. With a drawtool he began detailing a complex bit of the hilt on his design. The commission would keep his mind off his problems, at least until the shop closed. "You know, this main gauche far exceeds a Discovery Day trinket."

Holm waved a hand. "Leave the explaining to me."

T'Ash looked up and met his friend's eyes. "As I did when I heeded your advice to quit spilling blood and deliver the last of my enemies to the FirstFamilies Council? As I did when I let you 'explain' our—my—duels of vengeance to the Council?"

"The Holly ability to 'explain' is only excelled by our ability to fight." Holm winked.

T'Ash smiled. The Hollys deeply believed that motto of theirs. He gripped Holm's shoulder. "I don't know if I ever thanked you for those little speeches, but know that I am grateful. Beyond the debt of blood and honor."

Holm hunched his shoulder, then glanced out the window. "I'll leave you to your craft, then. Pretty ladies are strolling the avenues this eve."

T'Ash withdrew his hand and followed Holm's gaze out the window to a well-rounded blonde. A pang of yearning spurred him. His own small HeartMate of the chestnut hair and hazel eyes had escaped the range of his senses some moments before.

T'Ash turned to the line of customers and boxed up small charms in the shape of starships before he once again spoke to Holm. "I can keep the dagger to study?"

"Yes, yes," Holm replied absently, flirting with the lady outside.

T'Ash watched unspoken messages pass from Holm to the woman and wished for his friend's suavity. "You should invite her in and purchase a bauble for her."

That broke the spell. Holm laughed. "My friend, you do excellent work and are well rewarded for it. A creation from T'Ash's Phoenix should not be wasted on a mere passing fancy."

"Thank you. You'd best hurry, I think she's moving on."

Holm adjusted his embroidered cuffs. "I'll see you soon."

"Remember, have Tinne come in so I can fit the main gauche to his hand and charge the blade to his energy."

"Yes, of course," Holm said with a nod. "Merry meet."

"And merry part," T'Ash gave the traditional reply.

"And merry meet again," Holm said and strolled out the door.

T'Ash nodded, then his gaze fixed on the antique dagger once more. The spiral engraved on the pommel . . .

He spent the rest of the evening in the first flush of inspiration and grudgingly handled sales. The shop was far busier than he recalled. Perhaps he should give Majo a higher percentage. That thought was the last T'Ash had of the store until he noticed the shop was vacant. So was the street outside, lit by nightpoles and the weak light of two waning twinmoons.

Sighing, he opened his cramped hand, stretched it, and rubbed his fingers. Before him lay three pages of drawings, one for each main gauche. T'Ash felt satisfied that the weapons would be exceptional and capable of holding mighty spells.

He shuffled the papyrus drawings together, then started to close the shop. His memory flashed on the beginning of the night. His HeartMate had left him. His previous disappointment crashed down on him like a physical blow.

He swung the black velvet display around. His heart lurched. The necklace was gone!

Two

❦

*H*is *HeartGift, gone! The realization jolted. His* stomach clenched and his skin turned clammy. How could this be? Only he and she could see it and handle it. And she had not returned.

With carefully controlled movements masking his dread, he searched every millimeter of the shop. He turned out the lights, slowed his breathing, and sent his mind down a labyrinth of meditative paths until he could focus on the necklace. He reached for it with his senses and all his Flair.

Nothing. Gone.

He had to have the HeartGift. Without it, he couldn't win her. He wanted to tear the city apart. Hunt. Kill.

He couldn't. He was bound by vows to forge a main gauche for Holm. Tinne Holly's life hung in the balance.

Cursing under his breath, T'Ash stirred the water in his scrybowl to initiate its inbuilt spell, then let the liquid settle. He formed a detailed mental image of the guardbuilding and vized the Council Guard, projecting both sound and a holo of himself.

The guard who answered promised immediate service.

T'Ash waited in the gloom, standing on the grounding mat to expend the churning tide of red anger. The anger he'd channeled so well when stalking his Family's killers. Anger, an emotion that could turn him into a feral beast.

A man tapped on the glass door, and T'Ash reluctantly gestured the lights on and the door open. As befitted T'Ash's rank, the guard who entered was a mature man of forty or so. His cuffs showed the embroidery of a GrandHouse son.

He scanned the shop, and T'Ash felt some relief at the man's keen gaze and the flow of his searching Flair. He nodded to T'Ash. "Winterberry of Hazel, on special assignment to the FirstFamilies. You have a missing necklace."

"More." T'Ash gritted his teeth, still unable to grasp how this had happened. He could barely form words.

"More items than the necklace?" Winterberry walked through the shop, examining the placement of the jewelry as if for gaps, angling his head as he sensed the shieldspells.

"More than just a necklace. A HeartGift," T'Ash ground out, angry, too, that he couldn't control his Downwind short-speech. He'd started mending his speech patterns immediately after he'd reclaimed his heritage, and hadn't lapsed for years. But then he hadn't been embroiled in such a provocative situation in years. Somehow he didn't think things would get better.

Winterberry had stilled at T'Ash's revelation. The guard raised an intent hazel stare to T'Ash. They weighed each other in silence.

"T'Ash. You have a reputation. . . ." He left the sentence hanging, but T'Ash knew he'd referred to the results of his vengeance—the duels, executions, and banishments.

"Justice." T'Ash lifted a heavy hand. He didn't care about the past, not now, not when his future had been stolen. "That is done."

Winterberry nodded and again prowled the shop. "You have exceptional security and a reputation as a fighter. A necklace stolen from your presence—"

T'Ash growled, "HeartGift."

Winterberry stopped and stared. "HeartGift—" He pressed his lips together, nodded shortly. "What value would you place on this piece?"

"My HeartGift! It was forged long ago. I'd give my fortune, my skill, my Flair, my blood—"

"Calm." Winterberry raised a hand, palm out. A wave of soothing placidity washed over T'Ash, and he accepted it, used it to regulate his breathing to a more even pace.

The guard hesitated at the end of the counter across from the caff set. He shaped the air with his hands. "It was here. The emanations are still very strong." He glanced at T'Ash with a crooked smile. "And very male."

T'Ash jerked a nod.

"The HeartGift wasn't protected by a spellshield?"

"To lure my HeartMate." He drew in a deep breath and shifted on the grounding mat. His feet were hot with the energy of his wrath. "No need for a spellshield. Only she and I could see the necklace, some others with Flair if I focused on it."

Winterberry nodded. Silence grew. When the guard asked no more questions about his HeartMate, some of T'Ash's tension eased. The last of his temper sizzled through his soles. He studied the guard again. Though the man wasn't his size, an aura of intelligence and sheer Flair surrounded Winterberry.

"You didn't sense when it was stolen?" The guard's question was mild enough that it didn't offend.

Blood heated T'Ash's neck. "The effects the necklace had on me consisted of an—ah—increasing and uncomfortable sexual need. I didn't notice when the ache ended, just became more—relaxed."

"I see." Winterberry drew in a deep breath and stepped close to the counter where the HeartGift had rested. He jumped back, his brown hair ruffled.

"Null," he said flatly.

"Null?"

"A Null is very rare, unable to use Flair and unable to have Flair used against him. He wouldn't have been blinded by the innate Flair of a HeartGift, but would have seen an unprotected necklace. We have a disinherited GreatHouse renegade Null abroad. He can be very unobtrusive. It must have been a challenge, to lift a HeartGift from under the nose of the formidable T'Ash. How much could he sell it for?"

T'Ash checked renewed anger. "If he split the stones up, a hundred thousand gilt, a hundred thirty. The necklace itself, as jewelry I crafted, two hundred thousand. It's a dramatic piece, created during my last Passage—"

"And ransom?"

Surprise flickered through T'Ash, along with relief. "Ransom? The HeartGift delivered to me for payment?" His lips curled into an unholy grin, he slowly fisted and unclenched his hands.

Winterberry shot him a stern, repressive look. "Leave this to me, GreatLord. You are of the twenty-five FirstFamilies, even more, your Family is one of the thirteen GreatHouses; you have a duty to be an example to others."

T'Ash snorted.

"You can't afford any more blood on your name," the guard continued.

T'Ash slitted his eyes. He wouldn't let this man take his rightful prey. He'd only called the Council Guard so they could discover the bastard while T'Ash was otherwise occupied.

"And what would your HeartMate say to another death?" murmured Winterberry.

A blow. So hard it locked T'Ash's knees. He didn't know his lady. But her body, presence, and aura had been soft and generous. Her features had been fine and her frame delicate. Her Flair had been subtle. She chose only exquisite pieces from his hands and Flair. She would not appreciate crude acts. Damn.

Winterberry raised his hands and a breeze swept through the shop. T'Ash smelled, tasted, and sensed the Flair of those who had been in the store. Bold Holm. Greedy D'Birch. Kind D'Spindle. His lady—he strained for her fragrance, her essence, but like her it swirled just out of his reach. He stomped more heat into the grounding mat.

"Approximately sixty people were in here tonight. All of them approached the counter, forty purchased something," the guard stated.

"Mostly Discovery Day starship charms," T'Ash said.

Winterberry's stream of force riffled T'Ash's drawings, reminding him of Holm's commission. Another blow, now to the gut. T'Ash owed Holm a debt of blood and honor. Honor—long ago Holm had believed a ragged young Downwind man claiming to be the sole survivor of a GreatHouse. Holm had stood by him in fights, in explanations to the Council, and in urging punishment for the men who destroyed GreatHouse T'Ash. Blood—both in the duels with the murderers they'd fought and killed, and in the blood spared from T'Ash's hands as Holm convinced him to let the Council punish the others.

T'Ash could not hunt and kill the Null. Yet.

T'Ash kept his gaze steady. "My own concerns will keep me from pursuing this Null for an eightday. Then I will hunt."

Winterberry looked at him coolly. "He will be found and your HeartGift returned by then. And if you receive a ransom note?"

T'Ash smiled.

Winterberry took a viz button from his guardjacket pocket and flipped it to the counter. His scry locale imaged on the air. "Viz me."

T'Ash picked up the spinning disc. "Perhaps."

Winterberry stared at him, then opened the shop door.

"Grrr," Zanth rumbled as he walked in. He flicked his whiskers in dismissal at Winterberry.

The guard's eyes narrowed at the sight of the massive, battered cat.

"My Familiar, Zanthoxyl," T'Ash explained.

Winterberry glanced at him and then the cat. A ghost of a smile lightened his expression until Zanth sneezed twice on his polished black boots. Winterberry frowned at the cat, then looked up to T'Ash. "Merry meet."

"And merry part."

"And merry meet again. Blessed be." He left.

Your turmoil woke Me. Zanth lashed his tail, then sauntered around the shop. *Long time since Me here. Not enough Me-smell.* He rubbed the glass cases containing rich gold and jewels, kneaded scent into the opulent Chinju rugs, and then hopped on each luxurious chair.

T'Ash sighed. Zanth was a companion, but T'Ash now realized he wanted, *needed,* a great deal more. Even with Zanth here, T'Ash felt empty and alone. The advent of his

HeartMate had primed his expectations of a lover, of rebuilding his Family.

He had only felt this empty and alone twice before in his life. Once, when the wild rage and grieving for his slain Family had subsided and survival in the warrens of Downwind had been mastered. The second time when all his Family's killers had been punished, and all his own fury drained away by the hard fight.

Zanth jumped up to the counter and settled his large self squarely in front of T'Ash. *You disturbed. Not tend Me. Stroke Me. NOW!*

T'Ash did as he was bid. Zanth's deep purr hardly differed from his growl. Though his hair was coarser than any purebred, pampered cat, it still felt soft beneath T'Ash's calloused fingers.

Life is good. We have dry, clean, soft sleep place. Plenty food. We hunt when We please.

True. T'Ash shuddered at the memory of the conditions he'd endured in Downwind. That was past. After he'd won back his Family's estates, he had realized he alone could rebuild the GreatHouse T'Ash. And whatever he built, for good or ill, would be the measure of himself, in his own eyes and the world's. An overwhelming task, yet he had done it. He had a great palace, an enviable reputation, all the wealth and more from the old Ash assets. But he was still alone.

What more?

T'Ash's mouth thinned, "My woman."

Rrrrmmm. Mating time.

"Most definitely." He rubbed the thinly furred, scarred skin before Zanth's flat ears and chuckled in irony. Why had he thought that something he wanted would come easily to him for once in his life? Only the last few years had been serene, deliberately so. Even as a child, as the third son of the Ash, he'd been in trouble, sporting a rebellious streak that often put him at odds with his parents and his FatherSire.

His mouth twisted in a wry smile and he shook his head at the splendid things displayed around him. Wealth alone had come easily to him. Not his Flair, nor his vengeance, nor retrieving the Ash concerns, nor refounding his House.

Nor his HeartMate.

Where's female?

"She's gone."

Was here?

"Yes."

Zanth lifted his nose and sniffed delicately. *Many scents.* His nose wrinkled. *Much fake flower stuff.* He sneezed. *One very excited smell. Male. Taking. Winning.*

"Don't talk to me about that."

Another flare of cat nostrils. *One really good smell. Most ex-cell-ent smell. Warm. Soft. Flair.* He walked around the counter until he reached the black velvet necklace display. With a swipe of his paw he knocked it to the floor. *Grrr. Men smells. You—young, feral. Other—winning. Last—hunting.*

He jumped across to the caff set and nosed at the mugs, setting up a clinking until he found what he sought. His large muzzle disappeared as far as it could go into a cup.

Cat slurps. Yum. Me like smell. Flair female. Loves Cats. Will adore Me.

She had drunk from a mug. Her fragrance and taste and very essence would still linger in that cup, should T'Ash care to torment himself. He decided he did.

He vaulted over the short counter. "She's my woman, and that's my mug." He picked up the heavy cat and dropped Zanth on the floor.

Zanth gave a regal stare, then turned to walk a few steps, sit on his solid rump, and groom droplets from his whiskers.

T'Ash smiled with the first genuine, undimmed pleasure of the evening. Before, when she'd been here, he'd been so tight and aroused, burning with anticipation, that he had no iota of simple pleasure.

He lifted the mug to his nose. Bracing himself, he inhaled deeply. Scent of Zanth, then her fragrance teased his senses elusively—like just ripened apples. He pulled it into himself and it whipped through him to lodge in his bones, to echo in his blood, to shiver just under his skin.

His muscles tensed and his manhood hardened. His arousal returned, an ache on the dagger-edge of pain.

He turned the cup until his lips pressed against the precise place where hers had touched. Finally he tasted her.

Small. Rounded. Generous of spirit, of heart. Sensual, but unsophisticated. Lighter in spirit than he, more optimistic.

But an emotion from her reverberated inside him—she was lonely. Alone, like him.

Zanth stopped licking his paw. *You with Me. And she has Cat. Neutered,* he ended with revulsion. He shifted as if verifying his own sex remained intact.

"I am your person, but she is my mate. It's not the same."

Zanth's loud purr rasped. *Ex-cel-lent smell. Ex-cel-lent taste. Perhaps sa-tis-fact-ory. She must adore Me.*

"I will have her."

T'Ash glanced down and saw remnants of the fine tea leaves whirled around the cup. His brows lowered. Wasn't there a method of divination for tea dregs? Which of the Great or Grand houses practiced that Flair?

With a whispered breath he melded the leaves to the cup and coated the inside with a spellshield to keep anything from disturbing it. The cup could still break from the outside, since he hadn't protected that, but T'Ash couldn't bear to be without some lingering touch of her—her fingers on the handle, her lower lip on the outside rim.

You took drink dish. Me get something else. Zanth jumped back to the counter and paced around the U, peering down at the jewelry displays.

T'Ash grunted and returned his attention to the drink dish—the mug. A whiff of tea remained. She liked tea. Not caff and not cocoa. T'Ash picked up the t'tin and looked at the label. The tea was the best, Majo saw to that. But surely there would be more than just this one type. Perhaps Majo would know that, also. It struck T'Ash that Majo, having served the Miz over several months, might know a great deal about her.

The t'tin label stated, "Tea from original Earth plant lines, no hybrids, grown, harvested, and blended by the oldest and most experienced Family in tea, GraceHouse T'Tea."

Original Earth plant lines with no hybridization? Tea must be one of the few native Earth species to thrive on Celta. Interesting. GraceHouse T'Tea. Odd name, that. He'd have to lay in supplies of tea for his HeartMate.

Mine. Unsheathed claws clicked on glass. *Mine. Mine. Mine.* Zanth grinned at him.

T'Ash frowned. The cat sat directly above his most expensive and elaborate jewelry.

Mine. Come give to Me.

T'Ash put down the tin. Zanth stretched out on the case and purred, framing the item under the glass with his paws.

Collar. Sparkles green. Color of My eyes. No damn bell. He jerked his head to the side and a cheap tinny bell rang.

"Green jade is the color of your eyes; you would be better complemented by it than those emeralds."

Claws skittered across the glass again. *Mine.*

T'Ash sighed. Six "mines." Zanth was determined. If T'Ash didn't give him the emerald collar, a collar elegant and costly enough for a GreatHouse child, the cat would screech. Zanth's screech would literally shatter glass. Then Zanth would snag the collar anyway.

T'Ash would have a broken case, bills, and a cat that had been insulted.

And the emerald collar wasn't as valuable to him as the mug, after all. T'Ash reached in and plucked the collar from its white silkeen nest. Placing his other hand on Zanth's head, he rubbed his Familiar behind his ears. Zanth purred. T'Ash gathered his strength and meshed it with the love between them for a protection spell.

Zanth's present collar held a small guarding spell, but a cat wearing a fortune in emeralds needed more than just a simple spell. Particularly when that cat liked to hunt in Downwind. As a further deterrent, T'Ash added a furious holo of himself to be activated upon touch. He still had a reputation Downwind.

T'Ash replaced the old collar with the new.

Zanth purred in delight. *Nice.* He jumped from the counter and tried to prance to the door, yet continued to move like the tough scrapper he was. *Time to hunt. To show My collar. Life is good.*

T'Ash opened the door for him. The cat slid into the shadows and disappeared.

Returning to the counter, T'Ash carefully wrapped his drawings around the mug and placed them in his satchel.

He swept the room with one last glance, stopping again on the necklace display, a black square lying fallen against the colorful Chinju rug. Caustic disappointment scourged his heart.

This morning his carefully constructed life had been proceeding in an orderly and serene manner. This night his life was a shambles. His grip around the hide strap of his bag tightened until the edges hurt his hand.

His outstanding honor and blood debt to Holm had been called due.

His HeartGift had been stolen.

His HeartMate had rejected him.

She was a woman surrounded by blasers. Danger threatened her.

And he didn't even know her name.

*D*anith wearily palmed the opening spell to her rented cottage. It sat in a small grassyard overshadowed by crowding two-story buildings. The rent was low because the neighborhood wasn't the best. Still, she'd invested in good spellshields. She juggled several bags and entered. Gentle, welcoming purrs from her long-haired gray tabby cat greeted her.

She dropped her packages on a chair and went to feed Pansy, murmuring reassurances. The search for the right gifts had taken much longer than she'd planned, and the last rays of Bel, Celta's sun, had faded into night. Further, she felt inexplicably depressed.

Danith collapsed on the softly pillowed settee that was too small for her to stretch out on. She toed off her shoes and wriggled until her head was on a pillow she'd made and her feet propped up on the far arm. The nightpole shone yellow light between the shutter slats, the twinmoons were crescents in the summer sky, giving little light. Danith groaned and crooked an arm over her eyes.

Silence hung in her rooms except for the drip of a faucet, the small clink of Pansy's tags, and Danith's own soft breathing.

She didn't like the quiet. Her whole life had included

noise. Noisy children in the orphanage, and later, efficient sounds at the office. But here, trapped in little rooms, the silence coalesced thickly, and the only noise was that which she or Pansy made.

Where had this melancholy come from? She'd started the day with exuberance. Her accounting work had been more than routine, and time had passed quickly. She had forgotten her job as soon as the Week'sEnd Bell had rung, and she'd left the office with the anticipation of spending a summer evening on the avenues.

Ha! The shop, T'Ash's Phoenix, that was when the whole night began to deteriorate. The thought of the disturbing man and the immoral, illegal seduction spell on the necklace still made her feel cheap, and common, and that she'd never amount to anything.

That was the crux, of course. She had struggled to make her life as full as it was, yet her efforts were far short of what she had hoped.

Claif's laughing image came to mind and she smiled, particularly when she widened the vision to include his large and boisterous family.

Yes, she decided.

When he proposed, as was traditional on Discovery Day—a day of new beginnings—she would answer yes. She yearned to be part of his extended family, who had so welcomed her. She would quit her job and accept a position with her in-laws in the family furniture manufacturing firm.

Time to finally bury stupid, futile imaginings and face life as it was. No use dreaming of discovering a great Flair in herself. The tests at Maidens of Saille House for Orphans had been irregular and superficial, but despite all Danith's longing, not one smidgen of extraordinary Flair had been revealed in her.

Pansy came and sat next to the sofa with a small mew, asking if she were allowed to sit on her person. Danith sighed and picked her up. Pansy had been abused before Danith had bought the cat with her first paycheck. That such a sweet-natured animal had been hurt infuriated Danith. She stroked the soft, long fur, and Pansy purred loudly.

Danith felt constricted by her clothes, and she squirmed to

get comfortable, bringing her feet down, curling into the soft pillows of the settee, and adjusting herself around Pansy. Sleep beckoned.

Yet as she slid into it, she recalled the large, muscular form of T'Ash and his brilliant blue eyes set in an olive complexion. His hands had been large and blunt, but had touched that wretched necklace with the utmost delicacy. He was an obviously complicated nobleman with Flair and dark shadows in those amazing eyes. A lone wolf with no morals.

She really shouldn't find him attractive.

After leaving the shop, T'Ash went home, changed into a loincloth, and worked at his forge on his estate.

As he heated the steel, he looked at the flames enveloping the first welds of the laminated nickel-steel blade. He'd had to learn to overcome his fear of fire. He had learned to work with it as long as it was confined in an enclosed place, but he still had trouble with pit fires and went out of his way to avoid alarms screaming of a burning building.

He pulled the weapon from the forge, placed it on the anvil to hammer, and glanced at the timer. The middle of the night was no time to viz Majo, but T'Ash needed to learn the name of his lady.

Majo hadn't been at his parents' house an hour before. T'Ash was sure the older Plantains would not appreciate one more call from him. They might be polite and nervous, as they had been on his previous calls, but there was such a thing as courtesy. T'Ash admitted gloomily that he had never been solidly grounded in the finer points of manners and etiquette.

A timing bell rang, and he strode to the magical trough that was now the perfect temperature to harden the blade. He studied the laminations carefully. With the aid of his Flair, layers would be forged and welded again and again before the next evening, when Holm's brother, Tinne Holly, would come to have it customized. He slid the weapon point down in oil to quench and harden it.

Sweat rolled off T'Ash. Flair was not always easy, but always demanded a price. The strength and the energy needed to forge the powerful spellblade would drain him for days, not to mention the plain physical labor and short nights. He'd lose several pounds.

He had to get the job done so he could pursue his Heart-Mate. And a debt of honor demanded the utmost effort, so he'd push himself to the limit. A life hung in the balance.

Splat! An awful stench pervaded the forge. Zanth swaggered in, leaving his offering of a huge sewer rat at the threshold.

Good hunting tonight.

The rat wasn't the only thing that stank.

"You've been rolling in Downwind filth again. I just brushed you yesterday." He still had the long scratch on his arm where Zanth had caught him when T'Ash had tugged too hard.

Zanth sniffed, reminding T'Ash that he should have a Healer instead of a vet examine the cat. But Healers hated treating animals, truthfully saying that their Flair was not for Fams—Familiars—but people.

Bell rings. Time for more fire. Me like hot metal smell.

"It's certainly better than your smell." T'Ash studied the thermal gauge of the hot box and magically augmented the fire. He took the blade from the quenching trough and placed it in the coal forge.

Zanth jumped on the workbench and nosed the various metals and jewels T'Ash had taken from his vault to use in the hilt of the main gauche. The assortment contained everything from sheets of platinum to common red glass beads.

Zanth knocked a bead to the floor and followed it down to chase and bat it around.

"Hey!"

Zanth planted a paw on the rolling bead and looked up at T'Ash. *You have much stuff. Never leave any pretties behind. Small room full of stuff. My bead. Mine.*

"I might need it."

Not for this knife.

"Maybe in the future," T'Ash muttered. Zanth was right. T'Ash's design for the pommel didn't include that particular bead. And the vault was full of materials for his work. He hadn't been able to part with a bead, gem, or a sliver of metal except in the creation of his jewelry, since the destruction of his GreatHouse.

With a hard slap Zanth sent the bead careening across the floor, waited for it to bounce off a wall, then pounced.

T'Ash selected a roughly carved, heavy smoky-crystal to set in the pommel of Tinne's main gauche. Turning it over in his hands, he planned how he would embellish it with symbols of T'Holly GreatHouse.

He'd bought the stone early in his career in a box of old jewelry at an estate sale of a vanished Family. Humans still hadn't quite adapted to Celta. Even after four hundred years the population was sparse, and Families had to be vigilant in keeping their numbers up and watching for sterility or genetic paths that led to extinction.

Another reason for marrying a HeartMate was that such unions invariably had more children and a stronger line than other, more prosaic unions.

A bell dinged and T'Ash drew the blade from the flames and put it on the anvil. As he pounded and shaped the metal, he sent his energy and a protection spell into the nickel and steel with each blow.

He turned the weapon over and worked the other side. This time he imbued the long dagger with caution.

When he finished and immersed the piece again in the quench, Zanth demanded T'Ash's attention with a meow. The cat sat, tail curled around his paws, waiting.

"Yes?"

My collar dull.

"It sparkled when it left the shop."

Dull now. Fix.

T'Ash smiled slowly. "We've had a variation of this conversation before. You stink. If you want me to come near you, I'll have to use the de-stench spell on you. The one you hate. You decide if you want dazzling emeralds."

Zanth turned his head to stare out the open wall of the forge at the rest of the Ash compound and the Residence across a groomed field. The tip of his tail twitched. *Do not care to smell this way.*

It was the closest the cat ever got to a civil request. T'Ash clapped his hands together. Zanth hunkered down, furling the tips of his horizontal ears inward.

Slowly, building a cat-sized force-field between his palms, T'Ash walked to Zanth. He slipped the magical atmosphere over the cat and listened to Zanth's squeal of rage as every hair on his body stood straight out. T'Ash smiled, then said a Word. The smell and grime vanished.

"Grrr." Zanth straightened and licked down a patch of hair on his shoulder.

While Zanth groomed, T'Ash ran his finger over the gems of the collar and murmured a standard brilliant-cleaning spell, using a spurt of small energy to send the charm over every facet and into every corner. Then he held up a sheet of glisten, a reflective iridescent metal native to Celta, for Zanth to preen.

"Grrr." *All My hair on end!*

"Your collar looks great."

Zanth gave another look in the metal mirror. *Yes. Mine.* He turned his head back and forth. *Easier to see in than Downwind night puddles. Collar is Me.*

T'Ash snorted and put the glisten down.

Zanth sent him a sly glance. *Much nicer than old necklace.*

T'Ash gritted his teeth.

Zanth pricked his ears and made a fussing noise. *Still upsets you. Make another.* He continued slicking down his hair.

T'Ash stared at him.

Zanth gave one last swipe with a paw and sauntered to stand over the glisten. Though he smelled much better, and the dirt was gone from his hair, his paws left muddy marks on the metal. *Ex-cel-lent.* He turned his jade eyes back to T'Ash and T'Ash was touched to see concern in them.

Make new toy.

"HeartGift."

"Yessss." Zanth vocalized only when he was extremely serious.

"I don't think I can. I made it during Passage."

Zanth snorted. *You can. New toy will show you now, not you then. Much, much more magic.*

It was an idea. Perhaps even a good idea.

Zanth jumped down from the workbench and started toward the open wall. *Play with dice. They will say yes, too.*

"They're broken."

Zanth flicked his tail in dismissal. *Use old ones.* He wheezed his odd cat-laugh. *Old dice and new toy. Nice.*

The notion did have a certain irony to it. T'Ash had the first set of Divination Dice that he'd made, all crude angles and broken corners and rubbed-down glyphs, in his safe. "Maybe."

Make ear toys. Ears are very beau-ti-ful. Zanth swished his tail and headed for the open wall. He sniffed lustily at the sewer rat. *Life is good.* He strolled toward the Residence.

Earrings! Pain shot through T'Ash. How could the cat have known? His HeartMate had worn earrings that he had fashioned, small redgold Celtic knots. But he could make her something better, and imbue it with all the essence of his current self—his wealth, his station, his Flair, and his desire for her, only her.

Was there a way to force Passage? And should he do it?

His scrybowl trilled just as he heated the forge one more time. T'Ash went to the scrybowl and saw Majo. "Here. I need the name of a customer."

"Ah, the small Mizzz." Majo chuckled. He looked cheerful and more than a little drunk. His flushed face weaved from side to side in the water.

T'Ash scowled. "Her name."

"Wondered how long you'd hold out. A nice morsel." Majo smacked his lips.

"You are speaking of my HeartMate." When the words rasped, T'Ash realized he was gritting his teeth again.

Majo's eyes went wide and jaw dropped. "Whoops," he said, disappearing. *Thump!* "Lost m'balance."

"This is confidential." T'Ash projected his voice. He thought of the shop manager as his friend.

"Of coursh," Majo's voice echoed eerily, as if he were beneath the sea.

Fingers gripping a table showed in the scrybowl, then tousled straw-blond hair, then Majo's amiable visage. "A Heart-Mate. How ni—nish—nice for you. Have you considered that you'll ackshually have to get emoshunally close to her? Most likely lose y'r famous control?"

T'Ash had already lost control. The structure of his life lay in ruins. He hated it. "Enough maudlin psychology. Just give me her name. You must know it."

Majo beamed. "Know 'lot, m'friend. Not only do I have her name, but I have her scry image at the sh-op."

T'Ash sucked in a breath.

Majo nodded. "Yep. She ordered a sh—chain once and I vized her when it came in. Got her name and her scry and her addresh. Yep. Gonna like wash—watchin' you take the lovefall."

"Give me her name."

Majo chuckled. "She's gotta gallant, too."

T'Ash froze. The heat of the forge vanished as ice crackled in his veins. He pushed down a sick feeling.

"He came in the sh-op with auntie and three shi—sisters. Must be from one-a tho-sh rare lines that don' have low birth rates. Middle-clash, v'ry easy manner, v'ry ex-troverted, young but sh-solid finanshully." Majo's grin widened. "Happy-go-lucky fellow, rather like m'self." Majo slid his gaze over T'Ash. "Nothin' like you."

"Her name!"

"Awright. Awright. Name"—Majo lifted a finger—"one Danith Mallow. Common name. In accounting at some little firm. Address on the shabby end of Johnswort. Her address and viz locale on her viz disk at the shop." He vanished with another thump. " 'Night."

T'Ash cut the spell with a sharp gesture. She had a gallant! There was no choice now. Despite the danger, despite his low reserves of strength and energy, he'd have to attempt a Passage.

The night wore on and T'Ash worked and brooded. He used energy from frustration and trepidation to channel strong spells of protection and discipline into the main gauche for Tinne Holly. When the metal couldn't take more work without harming it, he put it aside and cleaned his forge.

T'Ash trudged to his Residence and up the long back stairs to the master bathroom, where he stripped off his loincloth and stepped into the showeroom. He ordered the waterfall on high. Soaping his chest, he touched the small ring that hung from a chain around his neck.

The ring was wrought gold, engraved with his station as ThirdSon of T'Ash. He had been wearing it when he'd escaped the blazing destruction of his Family and home. The memories came again, hot and hurtful. T'Ash stood under the waterfall until it pulsed long and cold, cascading down on him, dousing all images of fire.

Wrapped in a thick fleece robe, he went down to his vault and retrieved an old frayed pouch containing the first Divination Dice he'd made, then took them to the reddwood desk.

He opened the Pouch and eight dice fell into his palm. He sighed. They felt small and awkward, with erratic power.

He threw. *Danger. A man with a bloody sword. A woman surrounded by blasers. Three threats. You will lose or win all.*

He shuddered. The power of the dice was inconsistent, that was all. He sat for some moments and held the dice, letting them once again take his emotions, his dreams, his essence.

Breathing deeply, he threw again. *Danger. Passage. HeartMate and HeartGift. A woman surrounded by blasers.*

He grabbed the old dice and put them away.

T'Ash closed his eyes and rested. When he opened his lids, the empty, oiled expanse of his reddwood desk reminded him of a scry surface. His thoughts went to his lady. His HeartMate. Danith.

He couldn't resist. For the first time in years he gave into impulse and summoned the viz disks from the shop to his home. They landed on the desk with a small rattle. He found the disk with her viz locale, a large one for those with ordinary Flair—combining technology and magic. The disk detailed a two-dimensional image of a small blue scrybowl painted with pink mallow blossoms on the inside. The bowl was set on a maroon mat and the mat placed on a table.

Only wanting, not thinking, he set the scry spell humming.

Three

❦

Seconds *later a sleepy voice came through Danith's scry-*
bowl. "Here. One moment."

Her very voice sent ripples of sensation through T'Ash,
causing a deep yearning and quick arousal.

Her face loomed over the bowl, showing half-closed
brownish-green eyes, a high-necked, faded, and rumpled
yellow commoncloth cotton nightshirt, and tumbled chestnut hair. Her pinkened cheeks were creased and her sensual lips parted in a yawn. "Sorry," she said. "Who's
there?"

With a flick of his fingers, T'Ash disconnected. He sat
stiff and straight. Damn. He banged his fist on the reddwood
desk. Damn. Damn. *Damn.*

What was he thinking, calling her? His HeartGift was his
best chance. What with surviving Downwind, prowling the
vengeance stalk, and establishing his life, he knew nothing
of women except slaking his sexual needs with tavern
wenches. He'd never had any sort of relationship, never
squired around a girl, a woman, a lady. And he didn't have
time to learn. He had to forge the main gauche, force Passage to create a new HeartGift, retrieve his necklace.

He scowled at the scrybowl. How clumsy he had been.

And the glimpse of her had been far too tantalizing. He ached for her in his body and his mind.

She hadn't looked in danger. She'd looked lovely, content, and he'd wanted to return to the mussed bed with her.

He shook off the thought. Closing his eyes, he fashioned a strong mesh of golden forcelines. With an exhalation and a Word, he sent it to protect her. Any assault on the spellshield would alert him. The spell would weaken as his power and energy drained, but by that time, he would have her HeartBound.

He would guard her, no need to worry her by telling her she might be in danger.

A HeartMate. His pulse picked up pace with excitement, but wariness touched him, too. Majo was right. A HeartMate would demand emotional intimacy, a closeness he'd forgotten how to give. He hadn't loved a person in a long, long time.

A HeartMate would want more than lust; she'd deserve love. He would give his heart to her, such was the nature of bonded HeartMates. His parents had been HeartMates, and T'Ash remembered the love between them. His mother had chosen to perish with his father rather than live without him.

But in giving Danith his heart, T'Ash would be incredibly vulnerable. More vulnerable than a sheltered six-year-old boy lost Downwind. A HeartMate would discover all of him, things he hid from others, even things he hid from himself.

She could destroy him. A stranger held his heart and his future in her small, delicate hands.

*D*anith *blinked drowsily at the scrybowl. For an in-*stant she'd thought she'd seen the glint of sky-crystal blue eyes. No. Positively not. That GreatLord T'Ash had not vized her. What she saw had been merely an image slipping from her dreams.

She frowned. He hadn't belonged in her dreams, either. He'd been sexy but disturbing, settling the necklace over her head and gently drawing her to him with it, tracing the stones and the skin they lay on until he reached the pendant between her breasts. . . .

She tromped back to her bedsponge and flopped down on

the thick, springy mattress of Celtan permamoss. She'd had
erotic dreams before. They just hadn't been about a specific
man. It must be the necklace spell. That necklace had been
the most beautiful piece of jewelry she'd ever seen.

Pansy gave a small purr of delight when Danith burrowed
back into the covers. Danith smiled. Her cat, a shield against
loneliness.

Cats weren't as rare as dogs, but Danith couldn't have
afforded Pansy if the petstore manager hadn't believed the
young cat was dying.

Danith stroked the soft fur of her cat. There was nothing
wrong with Pansy; she'd thrived under Danith's doting. A
pity Pansy had been spayed in an effort to save her life.

Near sleep, Danith felt a warmth envelope her, as if a thin
blanket had been folded around her to keep the cool of the
summer night at bay.

A raspy yowl came from outside. Danith smiled again.
She loved cats and left a bowl of food for the strays that
were allowed by law to roam free.

The cat cry came again; ringing with triumph. Danith
yawned. She could almost have sworn it sounded like
"Yessss."

Smoke suffocated him, pressing hard on his chest, clogging his lungs. The big book he clutched was almost too
heavy for his six-year-old arms.

Flames licked at the Residence, showing orange inside
the windows. Rand's pounding heart squeezed all the breath
from him.

Bad men were in the Residence. They had plunged
through the french doors, shattering glass in the very room
where Rand was reading. He'd ducked behind curtains.
They hadn't seen him as they ran through the ResidenceDen.

One had stopped at the doorway. "I'll wait here. Set the
firebombspell in the CoreHall. That will destroy just the
Residence. I want the property untouched."

No alarms sounded. The spellshields didn't hold.

Rand stumbled outside, away from the men. Now the

flames, mere flickers an instant ago, swallowed the whole first floor in hungry orange fire.

Screams.

His brothers.

Rand stood stiff, couldn't make a sound.

Tears ran down his face. His mind flailed in a torment of confusion and denial.

He saw his mother's wavery outline in the LordSuite window and screamed himself, dropping his book to lift his arms to her. Crying again and again for her. She glanced at him, then vanished deeper into the fire. Her last shrieked words pummeled Rand's ears—"HeartMate, Nuin, *NUIN*."

With a terrible whoosh, fiery flames engulfed the Residence, imprinting the image forever on Rand's brain.

A man came running, sword blade gleaming, blaser pulled. He grinned at Rand, an evil, feral grin.

Rand stumbled over the big, leather book he'd dropped, then snatched it up.

He ran and ran and ran, knowing he ran for his life. Wild blaser fire arrowed next to him, barely missing, until he knew the blaser was discharged. Pounding feet followed him. Rand's sweat mixed with tears. His side stitched and he ran limping. He bolted to a place where he'd often hidden, a place just outside the fascinating, forbidden district of Downwind.

Footsteps clattered behind him, the clank of a blade on stone. The walls would nick the blade, ruin it. His papa would never do something so stupid. His papa—A new rush of tears blinded Rand.

"I've got him!"

A hand grabbed his shirt, and Rand squealed, a high caught-animal sound. Papa had taught him a Word, and Rand shouted it.

A bright flash lit the dark. Behind Rand, the man cried out in pain.

The energy of the Word cost Rand. He slipped, fell. More steps hammered down the street. Rand glimpsed a small hole in front of him, a crack between two decrepit buildings.

Pushing the book before him, the way made easier by slime, he slithered inside the tiny shelter.

"Where is he?" asked a smooth voice with a Noble accent.

"I lost him."

"We'll hunt him and get him," a third man's rough voice said.

"He will rue the day." The first man chuckled evilly.

"I get tired of that play on my name," the highborn one said. Rand could see his gaudy boots. One toe tapped impatiently and caught Rand's eye. The etched brass toeguard looked like the suit of clubs on playing cards. He recognized rue leaves.

"Sorry." Evil Voice didn't sound like he was.

"Leave him for now. With luck, he'll be dead by morning, a casualty of Downwind. How badly was he burned?"

"Don't know."

"It doesn't matter, one of the properties of that fire is that it will eventually consume all. If a cinder landed on his skin, it's burrowing through the kid even now."

Rand shivered and shivered again. Even at six he knew only strong magic could have torched the Residence like that. He felt himself for any touch of smoldering fire, but he was cold, cold, cold.

"It'll look like an accident," the son of Rue said. "Flame-tree promised me. Everyone knows the second boy, Gwidion, has—*had*—a Flair for fire and problems mastering it. Let's go. You can come back tomorrow and hunt, keep a sharp eye out."

The feet disappeared and Rand huddled in his hiding place. He trembled with cold, and knew no awful fire burned him. He was too scared to sleep, and when he shut his eyes, images of flames outlining the Residence, stone breaking, black timbers crumbling, scored his eyelids.

He cried until he was emptied of tears, cradling the book and rocking. Finally an exhausted sleep took him.

T'Ash groaned and thrashed awake from the nightmare, the one he'd hoped was gone forever. Memories were enough without reliving them in his sleep.

Zanth extended his claws to T'Ash's chest as he tried to

sit up. No wonder he felt suffocated, the Fam had decided to honor him by sleeping on him. T'Ash carefully detached the claws and pushed the cat away.

Me warm. Not ready to move, Zanth protested.

T'Ash staggered from bed. He needed caff, hot and strong. And heated by magic, not by fire. He gave his orders to the chef via the scrystone intercom.

Walking through his Residence, he looked neither left nor right. He didn't dare. It had none of the feeling or the hominess of the old T'Ash Residence. The walls were bare, the rooms sterile. Furniture was functional, not aesthetic. Some chambers stood empty. The library was minimal and the ResidenceDen austere.

The fire had taken so much from him. In a frightening few moments the GreatHouse of the Ash Tree became a ruin of ashes.

Only the HouseHeart, the most ancient spiritual place of T'Ash Residence, had survived behind the mightiest spellshield. T'Ash had returned a few days after the fire and squirmed through the rubble to hide the stairs down to the inner sanctuary. He made sure the primitive stones forming the ancient, circular pattern of the Rainbow Serpent were untouched and still vibrant with magic. He hid the HouseHeart both physically and with a short, easily memorized chant that all the Ash boys knew.

Years later T'Ash had been at a loss to decorate his new Residence, though the building itself was a modern architectural gem of swooping curves combined with pointed angles. He remembered vaguely what some furnishings looked like, had purchased a Chinju rug or two that echoed his recollections. But he had been too busy and too unsure of his taste, with the overlay of hard Downwind living, to make the new Residence a home.

The lingering images of his nightmare, of rooms of wealth and gracious style, mocked T'Ash and his efforts. He'd had a Residence designed and constructed, but it was as hollow as his life. He'd expected his HeartMate to make the house a home, he now realized.

You gloom. Gloom. Gloom. Gloom. Zanth said as he trotted by T'Ash. *Life is good.* Zanth headed to the kitchen where he could terrorize the chef, a prospect that never failed to please the Fam. T'Ash had negotiated that the cook would stay as long as Zanth was allowed in the kitchen only at breakfast. Consequently, Zanth was always in exuberant spirits in the morning.

He dropped the beaded chain in T'Ash's path. *Play with toy.* Then the Fam whisked around the corner to the back stairs.

T'Ash picked up the inexpensive piece of jewelry and ran it through his hands. It showed marks of tooth and claw. He smiled a moment before he nodded in decision. He needed his HeartMate.

A HeartMate could decorate his Residence.

She could make it a home.

A HeartMate would be a companion.

He would not wake alone.

He'd have to visit T'Ivy for the drugs to induce Passage, and GraceHouse Rose for hints on love. This HeartMate business wasn't easy. And it wasn't going to be cheap.

*D*anith stirred in her sleep. *Dreams flowed around her,* through her, transforming into shapes and themes she'd never had before. She wriggled, settling once more against the long, soft fur of Pansy.

A wave of determination washed over her, surrounded her, feeling both comforting and threatening with its utter intensity. Possibilities opened inside her and something deep in the core of her being altered. Forever.

*T*he last pink streaks of *Bel's rise streamed across the* blue-purple sky when T'Ash presented himself at the gates of the T'Ivy estate. He knew it was early for calling, but he could not wait another moment. Not after remembering what Majo had told him.

Danith Mallow. *She had a gallant.*

The gallant, in fact, was everything T'Ash wasn't and could never hope to be. He hadn't actually asked whether

Danith and this rival were lovers, but the question tormented him.

He needed a Passage, a forced dreamquest in which he could create another HeartGift. And to do that he would need the help of GreatLord T'Ivy or GreatLady D'Ivy. They were the craft masters of mind-altering drugs.

Though it was early, GreatHouse Residences supposedly were always open to GreatLords. T'Ash had dressed in full regalia. Shirt, trous, and boots in the finest silkeen of ash brown, embroidered at all cuffs with the most delicate stitches money could buy. His GreatLord cloak was of glass green, also embroidered with taste and style. He wore his blaser on one hip, a sword he had forged himself along his other thigh.

He tugged the bellpull with a dangle shaped in the form of a mass of ivy leaves. In the far reaches of his mind he heard a response. He stood in front of the greeniron gate scrystone connected to the one in the Residence.

The Ivy household was efficient. The gates were opened and T'Ash was formally greeted and led to the Residence within a few moments. He waited in the ResidenceDen for the master.

T'Ivy entered from a side door, a man just past his prime, beginning to fade in physical strength. He studied T'Ash warily. T'Ash knew T'Ivy had never forgotten the young T'Ash who'd stood over a heap of captives before the First-Families Council with blood on his blade and hands, smelling of singed blaser fire.

T'Ivy nodded regally as T'Ash rose. "Please, sit. You have business with me?"

T'Ash returned to his chair. "Yes, sir. I have a request."

T'Ivy sank into a throne-like chair behind a massive desk. He steepled his fingers. "I believe this is the first time since your Initiation as T'Ash that you have approached one of the FirstFamilies for an alliance."

"An exchange of Flair," T'Ash said evenly. He hated being in anyone's debt, anyone's power. T'Ivy was one of the thirteen GreatLords, of the twenty-five FirstFamilies. And those Families were the most powerful on Celta—in status, wealth, and Flair. "Yes, this is the first time."

T'Ivy nodded, dispelled a powerful shield, unlocked a safe in the lower wall, and pulled out the T'Ivy box of Testing Stones.

T'Ivy muttered words of opening, and the case lid lifted. The Testing Stones nestled like eggs in the box, tools to measure and define the Flair of the House of Ivy.

Before T'Ash knew it, he'd drawn the case away from a surprised T'Ivy. Without conscious volition, T'Ash's fingers danced over each stone, feeling the power, caressing the polished rock.

"T'Ash!"

He stopped and withdrew his hands.

Too late. Every single stone glowed with mage power.

T'Ash compressed his lips. He'd not been so completely fascinated by stones since he'd been a child with his Flair beginning to bud. Then, he'd been unable to keep his hands off the T'Ash stones despite several whippings. None of the T'Ash stones survived the fire.

He looked up and kept his face impassive as he met T'Ivy's hard glare, deciding to rationalize his actions. He gestured to some dim stones. "Some of your stones need to be recharged with the proper energy." He pointed to three. "These should be replaced with more efficient stones; the lattices within are not quite correct to hold and funnel power. I can handle both responsibilities for you, as partial payment for my request."

T'Ivy still stared at him, face set in harsh lines.

T'Ash continued. "And the sky-crystal—" He clamped his fingers together to stop from touching the exquisite stone that radiated incredible magic. "The sky-crystal is close to shattering. Its structure is too weak for any further use."

T'Ivy cleared his throat, but when his voice emerged it still grated. "The sky-crystal has been the prime testing tool for our Family since Landing."

T'Ash breathed deeply. "Sir, to use the sky-crystal further will kill it. I could reshape it into several jewels for your Flaired Family members. That way some of its power would remain and it would still be useful, decorative, and cherished."

T'Ivy's eyes blazed as blue as the sky-crystal they were

speaking of. "Large quality sky-crystals that will hold power for generations of Ivys are scarce."

T'Ash scanned his memory of each and every such stone that had crossed his path. "Southeast, two days from here by glider, Gael City has a merchant that deals in fine gems. He has several great sky-crystals. I would travel there to choose one for you, and shape it. Again, at my own cost, for your expertise now."

T'Ivy's steel gray brows rose. "You would do that? This business means that much to you?"

T'Ash leaned forward. "Yes."

T'Ivy nodded.

"My situation must remain confidential."

T'Ivy slapped a palm on his desk at the insult. "Do I look as if I tattle of GreatHouse business? You question my honor?"

T'Ash inhaled. "No, of course not. But my circumstances are—difficult. The matter I come to you about concerns the survival of my House and is of the gravest importance. More important than my vengeance."

Now T'Ivy's brows knit. "I see." He met T'Ash's eyes once more, then his lips moved in a small smile. "A veiled threat. I can't recall when someone last warned me. It is almost refreshing." He shook his head. "Ah, the young. I will tell only my wife. She is my HeartMate and a discreet woman. Your—request—will go no further."

"A HeartMate?"

Now T'Ivy raised his brows in slight correction. "You left GreatHouse training when just a lad. No matter what you think, the FirstFamilies believe in wedding HeartMates more often than arranged marriages. It is only logical. With HeartMates, troubles are met and overcome, marriages bind the House and Family together, and are not a cause of concern or strife. It has also been realized that the merging power of HeartMates increases the magic and Flair of the House."

T'Ash nodded. He had paid precious pennies to be taught by an old GrandLady who lived in a shanty Downwind, but she'd had no stories about honorable GreatHouse marriages. He took a deep breath and plunged into the story.

A few moments later T'Ivy looked stunned. "A Null." He shuddered. "Lady and Lord, a thieving, GreatHouse Null. Horrible." T'Ivy shot a sharp glance to T'Ash. "The guard didn't give you a name?"

T'Ash felt a feral smile twist his lips. "You jest."

T'Ivy stared. "No, of course he wouldn't." He touched the T'Ivy sky-crystal as if in reassurance, then met T'Ash's gaze again. "Perhaps we should put a little pressure on him—"

"Winterberry is a good man. He agreed to keep the nature of the necklace confidential, and I don't want any pressure that might cause leaks."

"You will actually wait for him to return it?"

T'Ash waved a hand. "No, that is why I am here. I intend to force another Passage and create another HeartGift, more in keeping with the man I am now."

T'Ivy's face stilled. "That is very dangerous."

"But necessary."

T'Ivy scowled. "Perhaps." He measured T'Ash with penetrating eyes. "You are not at the height of your energy or power."

T'Ash shuttered his gaze. "I have a demanding commission."

T'Ivy glanced at the still glowing Testing Stones ironically. "No need to validate your Flair, or the strength of it." He clicked the box shut and manually locked it with an ornate key. "But you must be at your peak when you take the herbs that will stimulate another Passage. Finish your work for HollyHeir, then come to me after resting three days."

"So long?"

Smiling, T'Ivy shook his head. "Youth. I'd imagine you didn't like Holly's immediate demands, either."

T'Ash simmered. He stood. T'Ivy also rose. T'Ash inclined his head, one GreatLord to another.

T'Ivy hesitated, then spoke. "My wife will prepare the potion—harvest and grind the herbs, and make the infusion. She will need an object imbued with your vibrations."

T'Ash frowned. "I have a ring I wore as a child." Reluctantly he pulled it from his shirt and took it off the chain. He held it out to T'Ivy. It glittered, tiny and precious on his large palm.

T'Ivy opened a drawer and placed a square of dark blue velvet on the desk. "Put it there. I can feel the emanations, strong and vital. My wife will deal with it."

Rising and bowing formally, T'Ash thought that he'd somehow manage to obtain the potion as soon as the main gauche was finished. "Merry meet."

"And merry part," T'Ivy replied.

"And merry meet again." T'Ash inclined his head and left.

As soon as he was outside the gates, he teleported to his shop. At T'Ash's Phoenix he put up a sign in the window that he would not open until evening. The first day of the weekend, Playday, was one of his best business days, but forging the main gauche was too important to delay, not to mention courting his lady. He didn't have enough septhours, not even enough microns in the day, to accomplish all he needed to do.

He smiled ironically. Lord and Lady, *when* would he get her?

*D*anith *stepped into her small back grassyard with dry* food for the stray cats' breakfast.

Sitting tall, tail wrapped around his haunches, was one of the largest cats she'd ever seen in her life. It looked as if it was genetically descended from a regular domesticated— no, a battered alley cat. But it was more the size of the hunting cats being bred by some of the GreatHouses, at least two-thirds of a meter long.

It was undeniably male. The size alone told her that, but also the attitude. Somehow it—he—managed to swagger even while sitting. As she shook her head in near disbelief, the bag of food rattled in her hands.

He swiped a long red tongue over his whiskers. He didn't run at her appearance like most of the feral cats that fed at her back porch.

Of course not.

She dumped food in the heavy ceramic bowl and stepped back to the porch stoop.

He sauntered over to the food and noisily crunched a few bites.

Danith smiled at his enthusiastic appetite.

He sat back and licked his paw to groom his whiskers.

Danith grinned. The action was too delicate for his appearance—flattened, tattered ears, splotchy black and white coat, crooked tail.

Danith sat down on a step. "Greetyou."

He looked at her and his whiskers twitched. Then he ambled over and butted her hand with his scarred muzzle.

She rubbed his head. It was far larger than her hand and almost perfectly round. A rusty purr rolled from the tom.

"Look at you. A real pussycat, aren't you? How huge you are. What a nice cat."

He flopped on his side and offered his belly to be scratched.

Danith giggled and obliged. "What a lovely tomcat."

He was one of the ugliest cats she had ever seen, but that made no difference. She had a little syllogism that she adapted from her early lessons in geometry. Danith loves all cats. Tom is a cat. Therefore Danith loves Tom.

"What a big guy." She saw the glint of something around his neck. "You have a collar?"

She bent close to look, but the cat wriggled from her grasp to run a few feet and jump to the crosspiece of the fence. He perched there, his bottom too large for the small beam. Discomfort passed over his face before it settled into a haughty expression. That was spoiled by a sneeze.

Danith laughed. She walked over, knowing from experience to stand outside paw reach. He bobbed his head. She took a couple of steps to him and lifted her hand. He sniffed. Once more she rubbed him, this time above his pink nose and along his jaw.

"Rrrow." He stood and walked along the fence crosspiece, turning to face her at the corner. "Rrrow," as if it were good-bye. He blinked, then, with a gracefully muscular jump, disappeared on the other side of the fence.

*G*rand*L*ady *D'Rose*, all fluttery, with a plethora of gushing, unfinished sentences, led T'Ash to her Residence-Den herself. "My dear boy. Lady and Lord, so good to see you." She looked up at him, her soft, round face beaming. "How very large you are. Quite like your father. Yes, dear me, quite. I had a most *wonderful* flirtation with that man. Yes. Indeed. Before he met your dear mother, of course. Poor things. Poor, poor things."

T'Ash tensed. One of the reasons he limited his contact with noble society to the compulsory rituals was that he was so at a loss to deal with such sentiments.

GrandLady D'Rose was just the sort of woman that most discomfited him, making him aware of his rudimentary manners. At least he'd waited until a decent hour—late morning—to call.

She led him to a seat and went to the caff table. With short, efficient Words, she brewed caff as T'Ash stared at the ResidenceDen around him. It swam with flower patterns—wallpaper, paintings, holos, tablecloths, furniture coverings. They all seemed to fit, which puzzled him before he decided it was his lack of knowledge of the decorative arts. Still, all the fussiness and flowers nearly made him dizzy.

Or perhaps it was the pungent scent of roses. For some reason, Earth roses flourished on Celta. They grew large and profusely, and most incredibly, with heightened scent. As the smell of caff began to overlay the roses, T'Ash inhaled deeply, glad of the slightly bitter aroma.

"Here we are, now." She offered him a small cup. He took it, but it looked fragile in his hand, and he hoped he wouldn't break it.

She settled her nicely padded self on an equally padded divan. "Now, what can I do for you, my dear boy? I am pleased, nay, honored, that you come to me for advice." She preened a little, patting her auburn curls with a plump hand.

"Ahem." Heat crawled up his throat. Why hadn't he planned what he wanted to say before now? Because the whole errand made him deeply uneasy. "HeartMate," he muttered.

She merely stared at him with raised little brows plucked like arrows. She didn't seem to have heard him.

He refrained from fiddling with the peacebond chain on the blaser at his hip.

He gulped the caff. It burnt his mouth. That didn't make his tongue any more facile.

Clearing his throat since she still gazed at him expectantly, he nerved himself. "I found my HeartMate. I have no manners. No finesse. I need—"

He knew that he spoke in short Downwind sentences. He knew what he needed, or the result he needed, but he didn't know how to ask.

GrandLady D'Rose leaned over and patted his hand.

He jumped.

"Now, my dear. Don't carry on so." She tilted her head a little, and though her expression remained placid, her amber eyes sharpened until T'Ash felt they saw deeply into him, measuring every last little bit of him.

"The Ash Family has never been known for its charm. Of course not. You must leave that to the Hollys, the Spindles—others." She waved a hand. "HeartMate, you said?"

T'Ash nodded.

"Why, then, nothing could be easier."

T'Ash thought handling red-hot steel with his bare hands would be easier.

"A HeartMate will be predisposed to value all that you can offer." She frowned a little. "But I must admit, you might, just *might* need a little polishing."

He needed more than a little polishing. T'Ash knew he was more than a gem in the rough. He needed to be broken from the rock. He needed to be cut and faceted. More, he needed a brilliance-spell. Too bad it didn't work on humans.

D'Rose tapped a forefinger on her lips and again looked him up and down. She smiled brightly. "But such potential! Yes, indeed, I swear, in nine twinmoons cycles, I'll—"

"Three days."

Her eyes bulged. She fell back against the divan, a hand placed to her impressive bosom. "Dear me, dear me, dear me."

"HeartMate."

"Yes, my dear boy, I know, but—"

"A HeartGift—"

"The very thing. A HeartGift, yes, indeed. To attract and bind her to you. For quick results, just the thing."

He nodded.

She sat up straight again and wagged a finger at him. "But you know the laws. The HeartGift is not to be revealed to the prospective mate, and must be accepted freely."

He nodded.

"How soon did you think to make this HeartGift? Perhaps in the meantime—"

"Soon."

"Ah, yes, well. Regarding your manners, perhaps you might want to *consider* a little polish—"

"No time for lessons."

"Oh." She wrinkled her brow. After a moment she tapped a small china bell with a fingernail. Though the sound was clear, it was short, soon swallowed up by all the plush fabrics of the ResidenceDen. Yet T'Ash knew a daughter or son of the House of Rose had heard.

A young woman came in with two books, handed them to GrandLady D'Rose, and left.

D'Rose pouted a little. "A distant cousin. Not quite a Rose yet, in manner. We got her late. But I have high hopes—"

"The books?"

"Ah, yes. Now, personal lessons would be much more appropriate, much more effective—"

"The books look handmade."

She caressed the quilted covers. Again rose scent filled the room. "Yes, they are. Family books. We don't have too many copies of them, and none have been allowed to pass from this House, but under the circumstances—"

T'Ash took the books and lifted her to her feet so he could bow over her hand and get out.

"My dear, I must advise you—"

"Thank you very much." He pulled a large, deep-red ruby cabochon from an inner pocket. It was the most valuable he had and was sculpted and buffed with exquisite precision to appear like a real rose bloom. The gem displayed mesmerizing color with flashing red highlights.

"Oh. Oh!" D'Rose exclaimed.

T'Ash bowed and shoved the jewel into her hand.

She clutched it, eyes wide. "My dear boy, this will make a perfect Flair Aid—"

"Yes. Thank you."

"My dear, such generosity, such style." She gazed at the stone, then looked up to beam again at him. "You have nothing to worry about, nothing at all! Blessed be!" she called as he hurried down her CoreHall to the door.

Once outside her gates and back on the street, he looked at the books. There was *The Manual of Manners for the Gentleman of Noble Background,* and *The Successful Courtship: Skill, Style and Ritual.*

T'Ash shuddered.

T'Ash inspected his new treasures during lunch, then took them to his workroom. From *The Successful Courtship: Skill, Style and Ritual,* he concluded that a gift of flowers seemed appropriate for Danith. The book advised starting with a single bloom and escalating to posies, bouquets, small arrangements in elegant vessels, large arrangements in valuable vases.

T'Ash grumbled when he saw that such offerings were to be interspersed with personal contact. He had no time for personal contact, except—he looked at the scrybowl. Calling. He could call, when he mustered enough nerve. He flipped through an appendix that listed topics of conversation and opening lines and smiled. He would practice a little.

The section on HeartGifts made him slam the book shut.

He ordered the delivery of a single white rose edged in pink from a shop D'Rose had recommended.

Then his thoughts spiraled back to the evening before, and he glanced at the tea mug he'd placed on his desk. "ResidenceLibrary, request for Information: Individual or Family with Flair for Divining Tea Vestiges."

The scent of tea swirled on the air. A disembodied voice, as much like his Mother's remembered tones as he could make it, answered. "Prophecy in reading tea leaves are as follows: D'Ceylon, second daughter of GreatHouse Vine, head of her own household, accuracy 96 percent. Nilgir, first son of—"

"Cease listing. Supply information on D'Ceylon Heraldry, preferred stone."

"D'Ceylon preferred stone is flawless dark amber."

"Provide viz image of D'Ceylon scry locale."

A clear quartz prism suspended above T'Ash's desk flickered an image of an elegant white scrybowl on a straw mat, filled with a golden liquid. T'Ash grimaced. The liquid was probably tea. Some people took themselves too seriously.

He was sure he didn't want to speak with D'Ceylon, a woman who had been raised a GreatHouse daughter. No doubt she'd be aristocratically proper and sneer at his manners.

"Produce collection box symbol and dimensions," T'Ash asked.

The image changed to a fancy, intricate coat-of-arms on a large collection box.

T'Ash grunted. Pulling a tray of stones from his shelves, he selected several. "Provide cost of a priority tea reading."

"Ninety gilt."

T'Ash chose a three centimeter stone of flawless dark amber, wrapped it in a softleaf, and placed it in the tea mug. Cupping his hands around the top of the mug, he added a glow message requesting the reading and a report as soon as possible. He couched a polite but dire warning that the mug be returned to him intact. He visualized the collection box symbol and 'ported the mug.

"Residence scry cache, hold messages from D'Ceylon only if there are questions, refusal of the job or payment, or information regarding delay. Delete any other messages, such as acknowledgments." Or any gushing female stuff, any curiosity inquiries into his business.

"Instruction noted."

T'Ash rubbed his head. One task completed, the communication with another noble house successfully concluded. Now on to another, much more satisfying endeavor. He began to design his new HeartGift.

Two hours later Zanth pranced into T'Ash's workroom, a large cat-smile on his muzzle and rumbling a purr. *She beau-ti-ful.*

"Good," T'Ash said absently, turning the redgold over. The piece had once been a marriage cuff, but was so old that the figures in relief were almost worn down to the background, the inscription long gone, the metal flat. The echoes of strong emotions were still there, fading but solid, something that could be built upon.

He was a master at rebuilding. Yes, this cuff had been crafted with love, given in love, worn in love, and passed down through generations with love. Perfect for his new HeartGift, a set of earrings.

Zanth, still smugly purring to himself, jumped onto the redgold. *Me. Me too in toy.* He kneaded at the metal. *Me. She loves Me. Toy must include Me. ME! We FAMily.*

T'Ash narrowed his eyes and crossed his arms. "You were saying?"

She loves Me already. He sprawled on his side across the bench. *Beau-ti-ful. Soft hands. Nice touch. Warm. I approve.* "Yesss."

"You are speaking of my woman?"

Your HeartMate. Pink. All pink. She pink, just like you royal-blue-to-indigo. Pink like stone in center of round window.

"Her aura is pink."

Said so.

T'Ash pulled a chest of stones from his open vault and set a number of pink-colored gems on the workbench. Zanth sorted through them, finally placing a paw on a faceted jewel. *Mine. Mine. Mine. Mine. Mine. Mine. My gift to FamWoman.*

"That is a pink diamond. It must have come from Earth itself, since it doesn't resonate like anything on Celta. It belonged to one of the colonists that came to Celta four centuries ago in one of the three spaceships."

Mine!

"It is very rare—"

Only one pink person.

T'Ash shut his mouth on his words and scrutinized the cat. "Repeat that, please."

Only one pink person. No others.

"I see."

No, you don't, Zanth teased. *You don't see colors except stones. You don't hear tones except stones. You don't feel vibra-tions except stones. You don't smell—*

"Enough! That little bauble you have under your big, fat paw is very, very expensive. If you want it for a gift, your gift, then you must pay for it." T'Ash readied himself for dickering.

Four

❧

Zanth narrowed his eyes at T'Ash and sniffed, but it was a small one, not his usual loud snuffle, almost as if his sinuses were actually drying. He lifted his common, round head like the pointed-jaw royalty of a Siamese and moved the jewel close to his belly behind his paws. *Yes. My gift. Fifty sewer rats.*

"Thank you, no."

The tip of Zanth's tail flicked back and forth. *Three kittens.*

"One Fam and my lady's cat is enough—kittens? Don't tell me you have a female with a litter on the way?"

Zanth smirked. *Kittens come soon. Big bunch, three. You can have all,* he offered generously.

"Are we talking about a Downwind stray or a GreatHouse purebred?"

Purebred Persian. GrandHouse T'Spindle. Female Fam-Cat, queen. Me, Tom. Ex-cell-ent kittens.

"Then I'm sure the queen has promised them already, or GrandLord T'Spindle or GrandLady D'Spindle."

My kittens.

"No kittens."

Zanth twitched his whiskers. *Last word. Big purple stone in old fountain on hill.*

T'Ash frowned. "A purple stone from a fountain on a hill?" He thought hard, every stone that might fit the requirements flickering through his mind.

Purple stone in fountain with stone black woman.

"The old T'Blackthorn estate? The fountain of the Dark Goddess?" He stared at Zanth, eyes widening at the memories.

We slept there two nights. You screamed.

T'Ash didn't like being reminded of that. "I was only six! And the twinmoons were full. That place is haunted. And they say the stone is cursed."

You liked stone.

It had been the largest, most beautiful lambenthyst he had ever seen. It still was.

Zanth looked at him slyly. He lifted a forepaw and began to lick it casually. *You best with stones. You stop curse.*

The Lord and Lady preserve him from a clever Fam! Zanth knew all T'Ash's weaknesses. "Straif T'Blackthorn might have something to say about your taking the lambenthyst from the fountain."

Zanth settled solidly on his rump. *He's gone long time. Your Family dies, you stay. His Family dies, he goes.*

T'Ash shuddered. He didn't like to think of Straif, either. As Zanth had said, their circumstances were too much alike. The last he'd heard, Straif was making his way in the world as a mercenary—a fate T'Ash had narrowly escaped.

T'Ash glanced at Zanth, who still guarded the pink diamond. The cat's eyes glowed like radiant jade.

"Done. The Dark Goddess lambenthyst for the diamond."

My gem now. Zanth picked it up in his mouth.

"Yes. I'll give you until a cycle of Cymru and Eire twinmoons to obtain the lambenthyst. Be careful. If you have problems retrieving the stone, we will discuss another price."

Zanth ignored T'Ash's caution. *We go to shop. I show you how to make My gem into good toy.*

T'Ash thinned his lips. Now he was taking a commission from his Fam. Where had his steady, rational life gone?

He muttered a few moments before glancing at his wrist timer and scrying the flower shop. The manager assured him the rose had been delivered. As T'Ash paged through the courtship book, Zanth jumped up and nosed at the volume, lifting his lip at the heavy rose smell.

T'Ash looked at the posies and frowned. Zanth plopped a paw on a button, activating a three-dimensional image. *Pansy. FamWoman's cat once female. Is named Pansy.*

T'Ash stared at Zanth. The cat rippled his back in the equivalent of a shrug. *Not Pansy's choice. Cat has funny face, looks like flowers. Would rather be called Princess.*

Zanth preened. *Cat loved My collar.*

T'Ash smiled. "Is that so? What color are her eyes?"

Zanth went over to a workbench and clawed through some yellow gems, then picked out a piece of citrine. *Use this. Pansy has no taste, not like Me.*

T'Ash looked at the other gems. "What jewel on this table is closest to the shade of her eyes?"

Cat is unsexed.

T'Ash raised his eyebrows. He wouldn't want his pet termed an "it," even if the animal was a neuter. He was sure that both Danith and Pansy would be offended at labeling the cat an "it."

One of the few lessons he recalled from his mother was that if he was offended by something—such as having a muckworm crawl around and slime his bedsheets—he should also expect his brother Gwidion to take offense. Even if Gwidion was five years older and should have controlled his temper. But a black eye had been worth seeing Gwidion, the precociously Flaired one, jump screaming from his bed-sponge and climb the bedpost.

T'Ash smiled. Odd, he'd long forgotten that incident.

Zanth whipped a paw at the stones, demanding his person's attention. T'Ash caught several gems as they shot off the worktable. "Nevertheless, we will refer to Pansy as a 'she.' Now, what color are her eyes?"

Zanth looked guileless but flexed a forepaw. T'Ash picked up the paw and plucked the EarthSun away from the Fam.

Zanth growled. *EarthSun too valuable for Pansy.*

"Perhaps so."

Told you.

"EarthSuns are more precious than those emeralds you wear."

Zanth turned his head away.

"I will make her a collar of matched citrines, varying in color from pale yellow to dark orange. And someday, perhaps, give her an EarthSun pendant. But for now I'll merely put the citrine on a breakaway chain."

Pansy not ad-ven-tur-ous. House Cat.

"A breakaway chain. Just in case she chases you from her territory."

Insulted, Zanth sat straight up. *Pansy knows who Me is. Me Fam and Noble. Pansy common Cat.*

T'Ash scrutinized Zanth. Cats didn't get any more common looking than Zanth. From Zanth's manner, T'Ash was willing to bet that Pansy was one beautiful cat.

He looked at the citrine, the images of flowers in the courtship book, and stirred the scrybowl. He ordered a posy of pansies to be delivered at once.

T'Ash noted the time and started stripping, ready once more to work in the forge on the main gauche for Tinne Holly. After another couple of hours T'Ash could order a bouquet. Later, a small arrangement in an elegant vessel. He wondered exactly what constituted an elegant vessel. He shrugged. He'd have that delivered just as twilight became night, he decided.

He pondered whether to continue the gifts during the night, since he'd be up. No, by that time, he would have practiced enough to call. And he would scry her, just a couple of times. He nodded, a good plan.

Tonight flowers, tomorrow gems.

*L*ate in the afternoon Danith waited in her best friend's workshop behind Mitchella's showroom. Mitchella Clover, a gifted interior designer, was out charming a customer into changing his mind from draping his bedsponge in scarlet to encasing it in an elegant celtawood frame. Danith smiled at the overheard conversation. As cheerful as her brother Claif, Mitchella's Flair included a subtle charisma that made her an especially good saleswoman. And she was genuinely interested in people.

On the shelf of Mitchella's desk, Danith caught sight of a

deck of divination cards. The images drew her and she picked up the pack. She leafed through the flexipapyrus cards. She liked the colors, and the modern drawings were exquisitely detailed.

She glanced at the name of the artist on the cardbox and nodded. This was the controversial set crafted by the recently discovered Downwind artist who, disdaining botanical names, called herself Painted Rock.

Danith stared at the Heir of Wands—a blond young man flying across a fertile plain, highlighted by a shaft of golden sunlight from between grayish clouds. The soft voluptuous clouds formed curves of a woman, full in breast and buttocks.

The sensuality of the card reminded her of T'Ash's jewelry. She shivered. She'd accessed the small amount of information available about him from PublicLibrary. He'd come late to his heritage and had a Downwind background.

Slipping the cards though her hands, she scanned them rapidly. Some images were quite disturbing, some almost viscerally erotic, yet they spoke to her.

She closed her eyes and concentrated on the deck. There was no echo of magic that even a person with the least amount of Flair could feel. Mitchella obviously hadn't had the cards keyed to her vibrations by a Diviner. The pack was pure.

Danith squared the cards between her palms and focused, not asking for anything more than a hint of her future. She cut the cards then spread them in the ancient pattern—Cross of Present, Past, Future; Lady's Crescent-Bowl of Family, Prosperity, Career, and Love; Lord's Staff of Feelings, Obstacles, Assistance, and Final Outcome.

As she stared at the images, a blossom of disquiet bloomed inside her.

Mitchella, a tall, curvy redhead, walked in. "Ah, I see you've found my Discovery Day gift to you. An interesting pack, isn't it? And an old-fashioned two-dimensional deck instead of three. I don't care for the pictures but knew that they'd appeal to you. Let me know which Diviner you want to tune them, and we'll go together, my treat—" She stopped as she saw the spread.

"Ah." She cleared her throat and followed Danith's gaze

to the Heir of Wands, the card closest in temperament to Claif, Mitchella's brother and Danith's gallant. The card was placed in Danith's immediate past.

Mitchella sighed. "I was going to speak to you about that."

"Oh?" Danith said, her voice higher than she wanted. She met Mitchella's emerald gaze.

"I love you like a sister, I really do. But I don't think Claif is the right man for you."

Danith's heart started thudding low and heavy. She froze the expression on her face, hoping it was pleasant and not showing too much hurt.

She had been rejected before. Several times. When child-less couples came to the Saille House of Orphans and adopted other girls. When the childhood playmate who had shared her dreams married another. When the Seekers of Flair shook their heads at her eager requests. When Maiden Brigit had told Danith she must depart Saille House. She'd hoped rejection would hurt less now. "I think I should leave."

"No. No!" Mitchella reached out and took her hands. "I do love you. And I like you better than Claif. He isn't good enough for you. He's not . . . not *substantial* enough for you."

"I don't care."

"But you *should*. I don't think he could ever give you the deep love that you need."

"I won't ask for that."

Mitchella sighed more gustily and rolled her eyes. "You need love, you deserve it, and Claif simply isn't the right man for you, not this twinmoons-phase, probably not ever."

The conversation ripped at Danith. Now she knew that Mitchella would never approve of a marriage between her best friend and her brother. Another illusion shattered. "I'll be going now," Danith said.

"No, you won't." Drawing herself to her full inches, Mitchella was a head taller than Danith. "I love you. The family loves you. I would welcome you as a sister. The family would welcome you as a daughter. But Claif is not the husband for you."

"Goodbye." Danith didn't even try to smile. She just wanted to go home and hide. She started past her old friend.

Mitchella stepped in front of her. "You're not *hearing* me. The family will always welcome—"

Danith bit her lip to keep the tears burning at the back of her eyes from falling as she shifted to brush by Mitchella.

Mitchella grabbed her by the upper arms. They scuffled. Mitchella slipped off-balance and her hip hit the edge of her desk. She planted her palm in the middle of an empty space surrounded by the cards.

Danith heard her gasp but hurried to the door.

"Goddess! Oh, and God, too. Danith, did you look at these cards? Other than the Heir of Wands?"

Danith made her way to the door, more slowly now, since tears started to blur her eyes. It was a good thing that she knew her way around the room crowded with furniture.

"*Dan*-ith, don't you go! What a LoveFortune you have here. You *must* see. Love, Danith. Love, love, love," Mitchella caroled, trying to tempt her.

Danith stopped to dig in her pockets for a softleaf before she stepped out into Mitchella's newly refurnished showroom. Danith found the tissue and dabbed at her eyes and nose. Behind her she heard Mitchella chuckling, her feet tapping in a little dance that she always did when extremely pleased. The sound made Danith think instead of feel. She hadn't looked at those cards much.

"Love, thrice repeated in the spread," Mitchella said. A shaft of pain stung Danith. Mitchella knew how much she wanted a family and a man. A large family, like the Clovers.

Danith heard swishings as if her friend was straightening the pattern so the cards would be perfectly regimented and neat. Some things never changed, and one was that Mitchella preferred order and tidiness. Another was Danith's love for Mitchella. Could Danith really just walk out on her closest friend in the middle of an argument, no matter the hurt? Simply because Mitchella told the painful truth?

"*And* you have a goodly amount of the GreatSuit here— the Crimsonnuts of Knowledge, the White Flower Maid, Avalon Apple Island, the StoneMarker of Fate, the Cave of the Dark Goddess—well, maybe we shouldn't speak of that. . . ."

Without willing it, Danith turned back. She wiped her eyes once more on the softleaf. The first pang of her heartache had diminished. She knew it would return again, when she was home alone, but right now it was manageable, and curiosity dulled it.

Danith sniffled. Mitchella stood tapping her finger against her lips and voicing a creaky hum. The woman could dance, but her singing endangered the ears.

Danith found herself joining her friend at the desk. Mitchella grinned at her and pointed to the Love card location. "Look at this. Who is this guy? Is there something you're not telling me?" she teased.

Surprise jolted Danith as she gazed down at the card—the Lord of Blasers, a dark man of great intensity. T'Ash's visage immediately sprang to mind and was hard to banish since the Lord on the card had a passing resemblance to the man, with long black hair, olive complexion, and sky-crystal eyes that literally emitted a blue-beam blaser ray to the edge of the flexipapyrus.

And that wasn't the only place he appeared. His GreatHouse card, Ash, the World Tree, was placed in the position of Assistance. She stirred uncomfortably.

"And see here, here, *and* here!" Mitchella crowed. "Oh, you sly one"—Mitchella's elbow nudged the top of Danith's ribs—"the near future is the White Flower Maid, a time of sensuality, eroticism, and love. I like that! Further in the future, the two of cauldrons—a marriage of *partners*. Now, that's what I'd like to see for you. And *as a Final Outcome* you have the ten of cauldrons, a HeartMate marriage!" She dramatically clasped her hands to her breasts and fluttered her lashes. "Who could ask for anything more?"

It was too good to be true. The White Flower Maid—well, Danith wouldn't be seduced by the necklace or the man. As for the rest, the love in the cards was equaled by the threat of danger.

Danith nibbled at her lower lip. Obstacles—the Cave of the Dark Goddess, such a powerful card and not a good omen. It signified destructive energies all around her, and this was upsettingly mirrored by the eight of blasers, a woman caged by red blaser lightspears. Two other cards foretold peril.

She scanned each of the cards, melding them into a flowing pattern for the future. Love, a good marriage of equal partners—she didn't really believe in HeartMates, at least for herself—a happy outcome, if she was courageous enough to overcome her own faults, fight for her wishes, and survive destructive energies.

Her gaze went naturally to the card in the Family placement, the position she always considered of the utmost importance. She frowned at Coll the Hazel Tree, the Crimsonnuts of Knowledge. What an odd place to find it. Usually she read the card as intuition, but now she searched her memory for alternative meanings.

Slowly it came to her. A channel of creative energy, especially in increasing potential for others, a catalyst or transformer. Now would she be the catalyst to increase the Family of others, perhaps the Clovers? Or would a catalyst appear in her own life?

"Six of stars for Prosperity, that's some money coming in. And the StoneMarker of Fate in Career," Mitchella enthused on. "The power of truth and recognition of your worth. I always said you had unplumbed depths. Well, what do you think?"

Danith's eyes were drawn once more to the harsh countenance of the Lord of Blasers. "I want some ice cream. Cocoa."

*W*hen Danith returned home an hour later, a rose scent lingered in her rooms. Pansy stropped Danith's ankles in greeting, then went to sit in the kitchen near her bowl while Danith opened the collection box. Inside was a fragrant white rose, its petals edged with the faintest of pinks, gorgeous in its simplicity. Eagerly she reached for the card. Maybe it was from Claif, though he wasn't usually a man for romantic gestures—but if it was, then perhaps he was willing to ignore Mitchella's opinion of their marriage.

The small card was bordered in gold. In elegant penmanship, it read "T'Ash." Danith narrowed her eyes. The slime.

First he had set a seduction spell on a necklace to lure her against her will to his bed, then a heavy-handed proposition, now a measly rose. Perhaps he was interested in a common woman as a mistress before he worked himself up to the nobility for a wife.

She didn't want to be seduced and cast aside. She couldn't think of anything less appealing. Danith took intimacy seriously. Affection, passion, and love were too precious.

And she didn't want a man like T'Ash, who once moved in tough Downwind circles, and now rich noble circles. He was too different than she. Too intense. And too alone.

She wanted a man easy to love, a man who would give her many laughing children and a large family of in-laws. A man she could understand and anticipate, a man willing to vow a solid marriage. Her emotional life had been hard enough as a child; why shouldn't she want something simple now?

Pansy mewed and Danith went to the kitchen. The flower was too beautiful to throw away so Danith put it in a glisten vase. The iridescence of the metal complemented the simplicity of the white rose. It would look nice in her mainspace.

As she fed Pansy, Danith thought of Claif. She knew what she wanted, and she wanted him. She didn't care if Mitchella believed it would be a poor marriage. Danith would work hard to make a good life for both of them. Mitchella or not, Danith would accept Claif when he proposed on Discovery Day.

The collection box played the short melody announcing a delivery. Danith opened it to stare down on a little bunch of pansies charmingly set in a silver holder.

Again she hoped they were from Claif. Again the card said "T'Ash." Simply T'Ash, nothing more, not one word why he would send flowers or what he wanted in return. He would want something as payment. The man she saw last night would never do anything without motive or reward.

She set her chin. She had told him she wasn't interested in his games yesterday evening, and she hadn't changed her mind. He hadn't looked dense. Just exactly what was his game?

"*I'm glad to see you,*" *T'Ash* muttered. Bang! He swung his hammer to thin the edges of the main gauche on the anvil. "I'm glad to see you." Bang!

He stopped and wiped the sweat from his brow with a rag. He'd been practicing the words for his scry call to Danith for half an hour and he still had only one sentence. This was going to be harder than he'd thought.

He critically examined the blade. It was looking very, very good, and there was power in it, lightly shielded from Tinne Holly, T'Ash hoped. He'd done a fine job in setting the spells for protection and discipline, and would complete the next portion of the ritual Words later.

The ritual Words! His eyes widened. This last half-hour he'd been concentrating on the dagger edges, not the spells, and chanting his first line to Danith. "I'm glad to see you."

He touched the hilt. Those words were in the weapon, all right. Damn.

Then he threw back his head and laughed. The Hollys were such fighters that they were glad to see any challenger, and perhaps T'Ash could work that into the spell.

He tossed his sweat rag aside and picked up a magic cloth to wipe down the blade, giving it a bit of brilliance-spell at the same time. Now, those were easy Words. Easy to create, easy to remember, not even taking much power or energy. Why was the formula for Danith so awfully important?

Because she was.

Zanth loped in. *Go to shop now. Make My gift to Fam-Woman.*

T'Ash glanced at the timer. Zanth was right. T'Ash needed to clean up and open his store, where Tinne Holly would come to check on his new weapon.

"The shop will be very busy tonight. Three days from now, Mor, is Discovery Day. I'll have many sales. Also, Tinne Holly will be by to have his main gauche attuned. You will have to wait until after that before I can spare time for you."

Zanth flicked his tail. *Me patient.*

That was a lie.

Will sit in corner velvet chair. Look at toys. Think of per-rrfect toy for FamWoman.

T'Ash was afraid of that. It wasn't that he didn't trust Zanth. He did. He trusted Zanth to be Zanth. Perrrfectly capable of scratching some female customer cooing over him. Perrrfectly capable of spitting at Tinne Holly. Perrrfectly capable of disrupting the shop.

FamWoman come tonight?

T'Ash hoped so. She should have gotten the two offerings of flowers by now; perhaps she'd come to thank him. He smiled.

He wondered if the HeartGift spell had influenced her at all, if she was even slightly enamored of him. If she wanted him as much as he wanted her. Perhaps the HeartGift only needed time to do its job and she was waiting at the store. Nice thought.

FAMWOMAN COME TONIGHT?

T'Ash sighed. "Perhaps."

Me approve. We go. First you dress. Look like Downwind feral.

"Right. I'll meet you at the shop. Do you want me to take or teleport the pink diamond there?" He hadn't seen the stone since Zanth had glommed onto it.

My stone. Me take. Zanth rose with dignity and left the forge, crooked tail waving.

T'Ash glanced at the timer again. He'd have to leave the choosing of an attractive bouquet to the florist. He exhaled with relief.

Z*anth curled and overflowed the small velvet corner* chair, watching customers come and go through slitted eyes. T'Ash had to admit that his Fam wasn't calling any attention to himself and was behaving well.

An hour after the store opened, Tinne Holly entered. He walked with more swagger in his step than his older brother Holm. T'Ash measured the youth. T'Ash had judged correctly, the main gauche should be proportional to the young man's stature.

Tinne was seventeen and, from the power and Flair emanating from him, more than ready for his second Passage.

T'Ash shuddered as he remembered his own second Passage. It had been triggered by the young Holm Holly, caught in Downwind during his Passage. Holm had been bouncing erratic energy, Flair, and emotions all over the place. T'Ash first got caught in the tide, then swept into the whirlpool, shooting into a raging inferno of fire and lightning that sundered all his beliefs, large and small. Passion had seared him, passion for living and for vengeance.

It had ripped him apart emotionally, nearly driven him insane.

Holly had fought almost every hour. Passage brought deathduels for Hollys. Now the danger menaced Tinne.

T'Ash continued to study Tinne from under lowered eyelids and suppressed a sigh. The silver-haired youth could not stand still for two microns.

He prowled the shop, looking at the wares and waiting until T'Ash finished ringing up sales. A mannerly boy.

He didn't look stupid, and he didn't look as if he would appreciate a weapon imbued with strong disciplinary and protection spells. He might need a little distraction when he tested the main gauche for balance.

T'Ash wanted no argument with a hotheaded Holly if Tinne discovered spells in the blade.

Finally the last customer ready to purchase something was served and Holly approached the counter.

"Greetyou. I'm Tinne Holly, my brother said you wished to see me about a weapon?"

T'Ash offered his hand. The FirstFamilies were often superficially friendly and quietly cutthroat, but Holm Holly was T'Ash's friend and nothing in Tinne's demeanor said he'd be any less honorable. Less stable, less dependable, less sensible, but equally loyal.

Tinne's eyes widened and he clasped T'Ash's hand. Wild, hot energy surged up T'Ash's arm. He didn't let the shock show.

"Your brother commissioned a main gauche for you." T'Ash brought the long dagger from under the counter and handed it over.

Tinne took it, jerked a little, and squinted down the fuller groove of the blade.

Distraction needed. "Tell me, Holly. What would you consider a good opening line for a scry to your beloved?" T'Ash asked casually, congratulating himself for combining two purposes at one time. He was diverting Holly from testing the weapon with his Flair, and was getting some masculine advice.

Tinne shot a surprised gaze at T'Ash, then grinned. Tinne had the Holly charm, in abundance.

Tinne placed the main gauche carefully on the glass case, but traced the gold wire in the shape of a holly branch along the main gauche's hilt to the smoky-quartz pommel.

He looked deeply into T'Ash's eyes and lowered his own lashes in a sensual look T'Ash didn't think he'd be able to master in a few short hours.

"Darling delight," Tinne purred better than Zanth, "did you miss me?"

T'Ash didn't think that would work for him. "Try something else."

The young man's smile flashed again, revealing a dimple. Damn but these Hollys had life, and women, easy. Tinne fondled the pommel of the main gauche. "Compliments on eyes or a smile are always good."

Pleasure filled T'Ash at the thought of Danith. "My lady *is* beautiful."

Tinne blinked. "A Lady? You?"

T'Ash's face froze.

Tinne took a step back, two, his expression no longer lighthearted. He raised his hands in a placating gesture, then formally bowed his head. "I apologize. You are worthy of any Lady."

Now T'Ash fiddled with the blade. He noticed customers sidling quietly to the door. With effort he summoned a smile. He nodded in return. "Forgiven."

Tinne smiled quickly, young and confident enough to be so simply reassured. "My thanks." He looked at the long dagger on the counter. "I would hate to forfeit such a magnificent treasure. Particularly since my brother is paying for it."

"You like the design, then."

"Perfect."

"Please, try the balance. And as with all my weapons, it must be attuned to the unique vibratory band of your Flair."

Looking interested, Tinne approached. He closed his hand over the blade, hefted it.

Those customers not fascinated by the show again slid toward the door. T'Ash sighed. Majo would be most unhappy if business did not stay steady. Not to mention the fact that T'Ash had his pride. He wanted to show his manager that he was equally adept at sales, even though he'd had to close for most of the day.

"Come behind the counter. There is space enough here to match the main gauche with your resonance."

Tinne nodded. With a wave of his hand, T'Ash dissolved the spellshield between the counter and where he stood.

T'Ash positioned the young man on the grounding mat. "Hold the weapon loosely in your left hand. Gauche means left. The long dagger is meant to complement your blaser or your sword. Stand still. Breathe and clear your mind of all thought."

Now the customers crowded to watch. T'Ash quietly rang up sales, pleased at the trade. He kept his senses focused on Holly until he felt Tinne had achieved the proper contemplative state.

When T'Ash looked at Tinne, his heart contracted. The Holly was so young. Had he, himself, ever been that young? Not since he was six. But he remembered Holm Holly, looking very like the youth before him, some twenty years past. Now, beyond the vow of blood and honor T'Ash owed Holm, T'Ash would do his best to let this young man live and mature into a good man.

After a quick glance around the store to ensure no one needed help, T'Ash went over to stand before Tinne, cupped one hand over Tinne's right shoulder, and curved his other hand around Tinne's left one, clasping the weapon. T'Ash matched his breathing to Tinne's and felt the waves of Flair between Tinne and himself and between Tinne and the blade.

T'Ash increased the cadence and shortened the waves of his own energy, to raise and empower Tinne's.

A mental touch.

A Flair twist.

Done. The blade was tuned to the young Holly.

T'Ash stepped back, glad the sweat on his scalp was being absorbed by his hair, and not flaunted for all who watched.

He studied Tinne's relaxed stance: balanced, but still ready to act, a natural fighter, just like all his Family.

"On guard, quatre!" T'Ash commanded.

Tinne snapped into the fencing stance.

"Parry."

The blade angled.

"Riposte."

Tinne thrust, still with eyes closed.

"Good. The weapon looks well-balanced for your use."

Tinne opened his eyes and grinned, holding the long dagger tightly. "Oh, it is, I assure you. I've never had one so perfect. I usually carry a castoff. Now I have a weapon crafted just for me!" His exultant tones reminded T'Ash that there could be no better gift for a Holly. It was as if T'Ash had found a rare peridot brought long ago from Earth. The peridot was the designated stone for the Ash Family. . . .

T'Ash nodded shortly. "I guessed at your build, but the blade should still fit when you reach your full growth."

"Nice."

"Thank you."

"I suppose I couldn't take it with me now?"

"It needs some finishing touches." *And even more magical reinforcement.*

Tinne looked at it and shook his head. "I can't see that. But Holm always said you were a perfectionist." Reluctantly he handed the main gauche over to T'Ash.

Tinne placed right palm over his heart and bowed formally to T'Ash, not lowering his eyes. "I thank you. Both for the utility and the beauty of the weapon. It suits me."

"You are welcome. The main gauche will be finished the day after tomorrow."

Pleasure lit the young man's eyes. "So soon? This Ioho, Discovery Day eve? Superb." With a lilting laugh he vaulted over the counter and tipped a hand in T'Ash's direction as he walked to the door.

"Come to my estate to receive it," T'Ash said.

Tinne nodded.

Before he could leave, Zanth jumped down from the chair and went to sniff at Tinne. T'Ash wasn't deceived, the Fam's body was tense, ready to claw if threatened.

"Greetyou." Tinne smiled down at the Fam, then actually squatted beside the large cat.

T'Ash noticed with approval that Holly kept his knees together, protecting what a man prized most even from a cat. Though Zanth would never be taken by anyone to be just a common cat. His size, if nothing else, ensured that.

"My Fam, Zanthoxyl," T'Ash said.

"Rrrow." *Acceptable boy. I like. Smells really, really, REALLY good.*

Tinne quirked a brow. "Fam? Telepathic to you?"

"Very."

Tinne studied Zanth's unpreposing appearance and grinned. He scratched Zanth's head. "Nice size. I have a Fam of my own, also a cat."

Truth.

"Salesclerk. Salesclerk!" called an obnoxious female voice.

T'Ash and Tinne stood. Anger darkened the young man's eyes.

"Salesclerk, I want you now." A heavy woman puffed to the counter with several shopping bags.

"I come," T'Ash said.

"Doesn't she know—"

"Go," T'Ash ordered.

"Salesclerk! I was told this was an exclusive shop—"

"She shouldn't treat you—"

"She shouldn't treat anyone that way. Go." T'Ash sent a gentle nudge of energy to Tinne. The young man scowled, but left the store.

T'Ash strolled back behind the counter. He held himself straight and kept his face impassive, but his presence was enough to have the woman's mouth opening and closing like a fish.

She shoved a small silver charm in the shape of a spaceship to him.

T'Ash didn't touch it. He didn't like her negative energy, and the last two draining days left him extremely sensitive. He took some colored softleaves and wrapped the token, pushed it across the counter, teleported the woman's money into the till, and exhaled in relief when she left the store.

Nasty thing, Zanth said.

"Yes."

Looked at toys. Come. Zanth sauntered over to a case and rubbed his nose against it, leaving a smear.

T'Ash winced.

This one. Make My gift like this.

T'Ash knew it. Nothing simple for Zanth. Chains of silver descended in loops for three inches, finally suspending a white diamond from a twisted strand.

"Silver?" T'Ash hoped.

Glisten.

"Glisten is difficult to work with, especially in thin twists like this."

You best. He put a paw against the glass and tapped it with extended claws.

"All right. For the T'Blackthorn fountain lambenthyst."

Yes.

"But it will have to wait a while, a week or two."

When you do HeartGift?

"Tomorrow evening."

Do then.

"I think," T'Ash said carefully, "that Fams can experience Passage also. If you want me to ask Lady D'Ivy for some herbs—"

Two weeks fine. Me in your other Passages enough. Zanth crossed to the door.

"I'm touched."

Zanth sniffed.

No doubt about it, Zanth's sniff didn't sound the same, hardly punctuation at all.

FamWoman not come.

"No." She must have received the flowers by now. Soon he could make his first scry call. Anticipation tinged with anxiety climbed up his spine.

Me go see.

"As you please." T'Ash opened the door politely and his Fam slipped out.

Sewer rats await. Life is good.

There was a lull in shoppers around dinnertime, and T'Ash resolved to scry Danith. He started forming the image in his head, then changed his mind. Perhaps one more call to the florist.

"This is T'Ash."

The man on the other end of the viz bowed. "Greetyou, GreatLord. How can I be of service?"

"Have my flowers been delivered?"

The man clasped his hands and smiled. "Oh, yes, Great-Lord. A single white-blush rose, a posy of pansies. Now, you left the composition of the bouquet to us—"

"Yes."

"And we sent a mixture of seasonal blooms—"

"Did they smell?"

The man blinked. "Ah—"

"They smelled good?"

The florist smiled. "I assure you they were most fragrant."

"Fine." Now what came after bouquets? T'Ash thought for an instant. A small arrangement in an elegant vessel. He still didn't know what an elegant vessel was. T'Ash studied the florist. No doubt the florist would know. But time was wasting, and T'Ash decided not to send some piddling little thing.

"I want a large arrangement. Your best. Huge. Fancy. Immediately."

The florist gaped. "Now?"

"Within the half-septhour." T'Ash would call her after she'd been impressed with it.

"GreatLord, surely." He swallowed. "Something of a unique, elegant nature takes time. You are an artist yourself—"

T'Ash scowled.

The florist stepped back from the bowl until he looked small. T'Ash looked beyond the man's puce face, his straining waistcoat embroidered in gold, to something else. . . .

"What's that thing behind you?" T'Ash asked.

The man turned. "Oh, it's an arrangement—"

"It looks to be about a meter tall."

The florist twitched his lips in a smile. "Yes."

"I like it. Big round blue flowers, little white starblossoms, and that green stuff."

"A Discovery Day motif—"

"Send it to her."

The man started. "GreatLord. It is a banquet arrangement, hardly approp—"

"Does it smell?"

The man drew himself up. "The Guild of Airship Technicians didn't request—"

"Stick some roses in it. Maybe a pansy or two."

"GreatLord—"

"And deliver it within the septhour."

The florist compressed his lips. "I'm afraid our ground transportation is otherwise occupi—"

"Teleport it to her collection box—No, too big." But Danith's scry image included a table. "Teleport it to the scry locale, a few inches away from her bowl."

"GreatLord, my most abject apologies, but we do not have someone with such Flair available—"

T'Ash drummed his fingers on the glass counter. "I'll scry back in fifteen minutes. You should have it looking and smelling fine by then. You can give me your coordinates and I'll handle the transport from here." Not wanting to give the open-mouthed man any chance to disagree, T'Ash cut the scryspell.

Crash! The awful noise made Danith jump. She ran from the kitchen to her mainspace to see her small scrystand, her one expensive piece of antique furniture, lying battered amid a mass of flowers. Water puddled everywhere.

She muttered a curse under her breath and hunted for her scrybowl, finding it a moment later under her settee. She wiped at it with the corner of her tunic and checked it for chips. It looked whole; the extra gilt she'd paid for the protection spell had been worth it.

She steadied her nerves, cradled the bowl in her hands, and closed her eyes to check the magic. Like most residents of Celta, she had just enough Flair to use the common magical/technological items. Slowly she felt the bowl with her mind. Yes, the magic still coated it. With some new water and a small priming spell, it would continue to work.

Making a face, she stepped over the hideous blue globe-like flowers on the way to the kitchen. She had never liked spheris blooms. Native to Celta, they seemed monstrous to her. She filled the scrybowl and passed her hand over it to activate the magic. Then she went to check on her poor scrystand.

The giant bouquet looked as if it had gobbled her little elegant table. The bottom of one leg had snapped off. Danith set her chin. She'd loved that table! Even with Mitchella's discount, Danith had paid more than she could afford. The stand and Pansy had been the most expensive purchases Danith had ever made.

Pansy gurgled her sweet purr. When Danith looked down, her cat sat contentedly amidst the flowers, a leaf in her mouth. Danith picked up the scrystand and set it against the wall next to the door. It would need Flaired repair, and that would cost even more.

Danith slowly pulled the arrangement upright, and Pansy jumped from her spot. Petals, dirt, and leaves fell from the thing. So did a card. Danith picked it up. "Best wishes for your new management."

Five

As soon as the shop was empty, T'Ash locked it. He rubbed the sweat from his hands. He didn't want to look at them and see that they trembled. The big moment was upon him. Time to scry Danith. He had never spoken her name, but had thought of her as Danith since Majo told him of her.

Danith was a very pretty name. When they wed, she'd be called Danith D'Ash. He liked the alliteration; it sounded right.

Should he compliment her on her name instead of her smile? T'Ash considered. Then realized he'd never seen a real smile from her, and especially not one directed at him.

His pulse pounded in his temples. He'd actually closed the shop for a few moments to make the call.

He breathed deeply, carefully forming the image of her scry locale in his mind. For a moment the visualization wavered, then it snapped through—to a different place. T'Ash saw pale yellow walls and copper pans, but no lady.

"Here," Danith said shortly, out of view.

T'Ash took another deep breath. "I'm glad to see you."

"Who's that?" She glanced into the scrybowl with a glowering, flushed face.

His heart contracted. "Your smile is beautiful."

She blinked and her cheeks got redder. "GreatLord T'Ash?"

"Just T'Ash." The faint glow of his protection spell still surrounded her but did not hide her loveliness. He hadn't seen her in two days. It seemed like years. He *needed* to see her. His heartbeat quickened, as did his loins.

"Did you send this?" She frowned and waved a big blue bloom. It looked frowzy and ragged.

"Ah—"

She made a disgusted sound. "That florist of yours is inept."

Something was wrong. T'Ash reverted to Downwind words. "Rose?" he asked. "Pansies? Bouquet?"

Her frown faded and her eyes softened. Her eyes were beautiful, large and greeny-brown.

"Well, yes, those came through fine. Quite lovely. But this *thing*." She scowled again and brandished the massive flower that engulfed her small hand.

How could he have forgotten his first impression of delicacy and discrimination? And why hadn't he taken that into consideration when ordering the flowers? Stupid. No, weariness and inexperience. He would do better with gems.

T'Ash copied her frown. "A single rose, then a posy, then a bouquet. *Then* a small arrangement in an elegant vessel," he said virtuously. "You didn't receive a small arrangement in an elegant vessel?"

She stared at him. "What are you talking about?" She huffed a breath and shook her head. "It doesn't matter. No, I didn't get a little arrangement. I got some great hulking thing in an awful basket that broke my antique scrystand. Honestly, you would think a florist would know better than to teleport an arrangement of that sort to an obvious scrystand. . . ."

She stopped. Now she breathed deeply. It lifted her breasts and T'Ash looked at them. Round, full, and ripe, they were perfect. He ached to touch them.

She crossed her arms.

T'Ash scrambled for something to say. This wasn't going as planned. He needed a better script. "I don't work with wood in general, but—"

She waved a dismissive hand. "Not your concern. I have friends in the furniture business—"

He could imagine. But he didn't want her going to anyone else for anything she needed. He would provide her with everything she would ever want or require. She would soon belong to him. They would be a HeartMate couple, complete in themselves with no necessity for others. They would refound his GreatHouse. "Bring it to me."

"No! No." Now she flashed him the same insincere smile she'd given him at the shop before trying to leave, the only sort of smile she had ever graced him with. The small curve of lips didn't improve upon repetition. And he hated it more.

He considered. Better for him to see where she lived. "I'll come get it."

He'd like to see her home. Somehow he was certain it was a home. Perhaps he'd get an idea of how she would furnish his Residence. The thought warmed him.

Her brows lowered. "Not at all necessary."

"What sort of wood is the—the scrystand? If it's ash—"

"I'm not sure. It doesn't matter. Thank you for the flowers—" She sounded like she was going to cut the scryspell.

Desperate measures. "Forget the flowers." He lowered his eyelids and tried for the sensual look that Tinne Holly had demonstrated. "I have a necklace. . . ." he said huskily. It was the truth. He had many necklaces, and any or all were hers. He was just missing a HeartGift, temporarily.

Her cheeks reddened again and fury flashed in her eyes. "No necklace."

For a moment he was distracted by her lovely appearance. "Perhaps some earrings. You're wearing some of mine." Delicate fashionings of the twinmoons and a couple of dangling stars.

"No. The sort of man that puts a filthy seduction spell on something is low. Low. Lower than a Downwind scruff—" The stars in her earrings whirled as she pulled them from her lobes. She tossed them in the scrybowl.

Call disconnected.

T'Ash stood, stunned. "Lower than a Downwind scruff." Did she just insult him? His HeartMate? He rubbed his chest. It hurt inside.

A soft tapping came on the glass of his shop door. Winterberry stood outside.

T'Ash opened up the shop for the guard and some customers.

Once again T'Ash canceled the shieldspell between the display cases and the public area, invited the man in, and replaced the barrier. T'Ash gestured Winterberry to the far corner.

Winterberry's eyes scanned the shop, and the quiet use of his Flair raised the hair on T'Ash's nape. He got the impression that the guard could describe each change in the store, which pieces had been sold and which were newly displayed.

"Our thieving Null has disappeared. Word went out on the streets that he made a major mistake and has an item that is extremely valuable, but also cursed by the extremely menacing T'Ash," Winterberry said.

"I thought you disapproved of my reputation."

The Guard shrugged. "We use whatever works. Deduction, Flair, intimidation . . . You have customers. Serve them and I will report the results of my visit to the Null's abode."

T'Ash donned a bland countenance as he transacted several sales. The least expensive Discovery Day charms were gone, but the gold, platinum, glisten, and redgold still sold briskly.

While new customers browsed, T'Ash returned to Winterberry.

"Yes?" asked T'Ash.

Winterberry smiled and it was a male smile, a fighter's smile that T'Ash understood. "Your name makes powerful waves. I easily obtained permission to enter the Null's premises. The whole place reeked of an *absence* of Flair, a complete emptiness. Simple observation showed that our man left in a hurry. There were several old Earth machines that he abandoned. The man has a hobby of fixing them."

"The HeartGift wasn't there?"

"No."

T'Ash shifted a little. He didn't want to talk about this. He wanted action. "Currently the HeartGift is a low priority for me. I have more important irons in the fire than finding this

Null and meting out punishment. For now. You can put that message out on the streets, too."

"We *will* catch the man. I notice you have not offered a reward for the return of the HeartGift."

"Reward a man for stealing from me? Ludicrous."

"It could turn hands against our Null."

T'Ash snorted. "Perhaps you don't know Downwind as well as you believe. If the word is that the necklace is cursed, no one's going to touch it."

Winterberry inclined his head. "As you say. I do, however, know the man quite well. I'd not be surprised if he approached you."

T'Ash stared. "Me?"

"One thing you can count on with this thief—he doesn't lack guts."

T'Ash bared his teeth in a wolfish smile. "If he comes to me, I'll deal with him."

"Try to keep your sword clean and your blaser charge full," Winterberry warned. "Blessed be," he said in formal farewell.

T'Ash nodded shortly, then turned to the quiet line of people waiting to purchase his wares. Winterberry left.

After closing the store, T'Ash stopped in his home workroom before going to labor on the main gauche at the forge. He glowered at the courtship book.

He'd figured out the error in his strategy. He had followed the stupid book and sent flowers instead of going with his strengths and gifting her with gems. He had also tried some of the "personal contact" instead of simply letting his gifts speak for him.

He opened his vault and retrieved some exquisite pieces of jewelry that he only showed by appointment. He spread about thirty items on a long velvet display table in his workroom. Looking at them, he decided that was too many. When he had narrowed the selection down to twenty-five, he placed them in a velvet-lined case to take with him to the forge. He could teleport them to her collection box every time he had a break.

At the forge he carefully arranged the pieces on a large,

scarred worktable. He alternated chains with bracelets, earrings with pins and necklaces. He decided the book was correct in scaling the gifts from the simple to the magnificent. How he wished he could offer his HeartGift once more! But it was stolen and he hadn't yet made the new one. He lined the presents up in the proper order.

What toys for? Zanth jumped onto the table.

"Watch the jewelry! They are gifts for my woman." T'Ash pulled aside the next item before it got swiped by Zanth's twitching tail. He glared at his Fam. "These are my best pieces. Treat them as you do your collar, because they are as valuable."

Zanth put a paw in the first gift, a glass bowl of polished stones, some semiprecious, and cabochons of true gems.

Pretty. He tumbled them about, then, treading carefully around the rest of the items, he retreated a foot or two and crouched down, nose to table, to evaluate his artistic endeavor. T'Ash was sure Danith wouldn't be looking at the bowl from the same perspective, but didn't say so.

He visualized three stones that he often carried and teleported them from his Residence to include them in the dish. It would be interesting to discover if she'd sense those stones held a different vibration, an intimate resonance of T'Ash himself. He rubbed his hands in satisfaction. He had no doubt. They were HeartMates, and she would innately prefer the stones that echoed of him. Her Flair was subtle but powerful.

He slipped the stones in the dish, and Zanth glared at him for disturbing the mixture. Then sneezed. Then once more arranged them into some unique catlike pattern only he understood.

The next present was a charm bracelet, with a delicately detailed tiny rendition of the generation colony ship that had actually discovered Celta, *Lugh's Spear.* The silver charm was suspended from an intricately woven chain of silver, redgold, and glisten. T'Ash touched the small starship with his finger and found his jaw clenched.

Another memory resurfaced. A charm bracelet was a tradition in his Family. Though the Ashes had wealth and jewels as much as any other GreatHouse, T'Ash's father, Nuin, had often given his mother a charm to celebrate an anniversary or other special occasion.

T'Ash stroked the small charm. He would follow the Ash Family traditions that he remembered, that were written in the history book he'd saved from the fire.

And just as every GreatHouse had traditions, so did every GreatHouse have responsibilities to the FirstFamilies' rituals. Acceding to his duty, he had become integral to the ceremonies. And soon Danith, as his HeartMate, would become equally valued and essential.

Done. Beau-ti-ful. Right. Finishing his task, Zanth sauntered down the long table, stepping cautiously, inspecting the rest of the gifts, his whiskers twitching. *Nice. Good idea.*

"Are you completely finished? Can I teleport the bowl of stones to her collection box now?"

Zanth inclined his head, ignoring the sarcasm.

T'Ash visualized a single pink mallow blossom, Danith's symbol on her collection box that he'd previously memorized. With a swish of displaced air the bowl vanished. Far away the tuneful little melody of Danith's collection box resounded to T'Ash's mind.

He skinned off his clothes and donned a fresh loincloth. Then he examined the forge; everything was ready for his labor.

He looked at the main gauche, awaiting his touch. It now consisted of four hundred layers of nickel and steel, to make the blade strong and flexible. He wanted to finish the red-gold engraving, grind it one last time, polish it, and add a final spell with his hammer and his Flair.

The long work he'd put in had made him tired and slow. His magic would be sufficient. He had strength and discipline left enough for that. It was his arms and hands that might betray him.

Not see FamWoman, Zanth grumbled. *Sat on win-dow-sill. She not notice Me.*

The woman would have to be blind to overlook a cat of Zanth's bulk. T'Ash smiled wryly as he understood that the entire Ash household was annoyed from the same cause—being ignored by a particular woman. Not a pleasant feeling, and one T'Ash had never expected to experience. He'd always thought winning his HeartMate would be quick and simple.

He sighed, turned on the quench trough, and heated up the fire. "We're nothing but Downwind scruffs, Zanth."

Speak for self, Zanth retorted, lashing his crooked tail. He lifted his pink nose, but the gesture was spoiled by an incipient sinus snuffle.

T'Ash eyed him. "I am. And I'm speaking for you, too. We both have our share of scars and rough experience. *You* still hunt Downwind sewer rats."

Sewer rats best fun. ME NOT SCRUFF. Me once Downwind, now Noble. Past not matter.

That was a cat for you.

T'Ash took the long dagger and put it in the fire, watching as it turned red hot, mesmerized by the color, then shook his head. He had to concentrate.

Gloom again. FamWoman not see you?

"She saw me fine. In the scrybowl." When the temperature was right, he took the weapon to the forge and a specialized hammer to work the metal.

Water. Yuck. No good way to talk. She talk to you?

"She had plenty to say." He rapped delicately on the edges, murmuring words of restraint and discipline with each blow. When he could free his mind from the task, he ran over his abrupt conversation with Danith again. Just as he picked up his hammer, the meaning of her final words burst upon him. "The sort of man that puts a filthy seduction spell on something is low."

He stared at the blade, then grabbed it to channel the renewed energy his anger fueled. She thought he'd put a seduction spell on the HeartGift! A disgusting act. An illegal act. An act he would never have considered.

Obviously she couldn't distinguish a sleazy spell designed to incite lust and lure a woman for cheap mindless sex with a gift that was crafted with only one special person in mind, a HeartMate. A gift that reflected everything he was when he'd crafted it, down to his most basic nature.

Now the main gauche glowed bright from his Flair instead of the fire. His arm stretched straight and rigid, bunched with muscle. A new swirling spell of power exploded into his mind and he chanted it down the blade. Light coruscated around the weapon. It sang with the sound of ringing metal, future fights, and bloodletting.

STOP!

T'Ash stopped. Placed the main gauche carefully on the anvil.

Zanth crouched in a corner, glaring, tips of his flat ears folded inward.

In one last fit of fury at her blindness and rejection, T'Ash gathered up several gifts and tossed them in the air. They winked out of sight as he teleported them to Danith's home.

Knife good?

T'Ash glanced at it, small sparks still lightninged up and down the blade. He nodded shortly.

Almost ruined knife. Would have to start again. Not good. Zanth scolded. *You tired, blown. Go sleep.*

"No. I'll finish the knife—the main gauche. I have enough energy and power for that."

Zanth growled. *Stubborn. Stubborn. Stubborn. You nothing but noble scruff.* He stalked out.

Insulted by his Fam! T'Ash growled himself.

Then, as an exercise in patience, he organized the remainder of his gifts. His fingers lingered as he touched his best work. He regretted that last careless flinging of his pieces, though they would have landed gently enough in the collection box.

He'd continue with his previous tactic of sending her presents through the night.

Her words told him that she'd felt the carnal power of the HeartGift. At least he knew the HeartGift had attracted her. After a few moments his temper cooled, and he was able to smile. Not only did the HeartGift attract her, but it had stirred sexual feelings. The idea lightened his weariness.

Someday he would give her the necklace. But he was resolved that the new HeartGift would be a true reflection of himself. She would have a harder time ignoring that.

Ping!
Whir.

Urga, urga, urga, arrgh, ka-CHUNK.

In the wee hours of the morning the twiddley melody of her collection box had driven Danith mad. She'd flung a heavy pot at it in desperation. It hadn't broken the box, and it hadn't stopped the sound, merely changed it.

Now, in the first dawn light, she pulled on some clothes and dragged herself into her mainspace.

Sitting in a nest of gems, several necklaces draping around her, Pansy purred, deeply satisfied. Dark ruby beads complemented her subtly shaded gray fur.

Before Danith went to see the last harassing gift—at least The Necklace hadn't appeared—she sifted her fingers through the bowl of polished stones. A smooth wedge of green aventurine felt particularly pleasing, soothing, and she tucked it through the slit in her tunic into her trous pocket.

Pansy purred louder. She must be wearing several thousand gilt worth of jewels. They couldn't possibly be real, could they? Or perhaps they could. T'Ash was a wealthy GreatLord who could afford to spend gilt on a prospective mistress.

Danith's lip curled. She would not be seduced by a GreatLord.

Dawn filtered through her shutters. A yowl rose from the grassyard. Squaring her shoulders, Danith grabbed the foodsack and went to fulfill her duty of feeding the feral cats. She did not function well on little sleep.

Danith opened the door. On the top step sat the huge, ugly, lovable cat. He smiled an ingratiating smile.

He held *a string of beads in his mouth!*

The cat dropped it on her foot. Slobber rolled down between her bare toes. She shuddered.

Carefully reining in her anger, she picked up the string of beads. It was the worse for wear, with a few tooth marks, but she recognized it from T'Ash's Phoenix, where she'd seen it a few weeks before. It was meant to be attached to a personal amulet, but Danith didn't wear amulets.

With a questioning mew, Pansy came to stand beside her, trailing a tangle of jewels: two necklaces, a brooch, four pins, a pair of clip earrings, and a redgold chain.

The tom sniffed, then sat up straight, raising his chin. An

emerald collar worth a fortune caught the light, sparkling like nothing Danith had ever seen before. Her fingers itched to caress the collar.

The cat's rusty purr resonated.

She touched the collar. "You!" T'Ash's voice roared.

Danith jumped.

A fierce hologram of T'Ash solidified and scowled at her. "Know you that this is my Fam, Zanthoxyl. Harm him and you answer to me!"

Zanthoxyl preened.

"Zanthoxyl," Danith muttered. T'Ash's cat—Fam—of course. She should have known, they looked a lot alike. A cat bearing gifts. The wretched man had even suborned his Fam. This was too much.

And nothing she ever asked for or wanted.

Now she was going to tell him so. She'd confront him with his degenerate ideas of playing sexual games with a common woman and throw the gifts back into his face.

Yes, that would be satisfying.

She had no room in her life for decadent GreatLords.

She stomped to her bedroom, slipped a pair of weaves on her feet, grabbed the jewels at hand, thrust them in a sack, and left, slamming her door behind her and muttering the security Word.

Zanthoxyl smiled at her from her front sidewalk. She scowled at him, but his cat grin didn't slip. The beginning of a nagging headache buzzed behind her eyes. She rubbed her free hand on her temple.

Danith considered the cat—the Fam. She'd never met an animal bonded with a noble. They were supposed to be intelligent. "Take me to T'Ash."

The cat's smile widened even more. He rumbled a purr and turned to trot down the street, tail waving.

Danith marched behind him. The buzzing in her head increased, sharpening her annoyance. She grumbled. "It's Midweekend, true. But I have things to do, errands to run, and no bloody time to spend fending off some stupid, brutish scruff."

Jewels clinked musically as she transferred the sack to her other hand. Her wrist brushed her tunic over her trous pocket, and a soothing warmth startled her. She touched a lump. The stone. She should throw it away. She reached for it.

Zanthoxyl turned his head and emitted a long, rising whine. She left the stone in her pocket to rub her temple again.

The Fam picked up speed and Danith walked faster.

Half a septhour passed as Danith followed the cat. The streets had widened, as did the space between houses. Now they were in an area of large, old Noble estates. She slowed. Not a house could be seen, only hedges, or walls, or green-iron fences showing lush growth behind them. Maybe this wasn't a good idea.

She was a common woman and he a GreatLord. All the power was in his hands.

Bel completed its rise from behind the horizon, shining white-blue rays upon the empty gray stone-paved street. No public carriers traveled this area. The GreatLords had enough Flair to teleport to where they wanted, or used personal gliders.

She'd never been this deep into noble country. Perhaps she should just turn around and go back home, pretend the whole thing had been a bad dream.

She stopped in the middle of the wide street.

"Prrrp." It was a small, conciliatory-type noise, coming from Zanthoxyl.

He pricked up his horizontal ears as far as they could go, only a slight lifting, and made a series of little noises, almost encouraging her. Her head throbbed until she could barely think.

Zanthoxyl crossed to her and stropped her ankles, front and back, purring like a motor. It was the loudest sound in the large, quiet street.

Danith looked down, a multitude of coarse black and white cat hairs clung to her clean trous. She sighed and hiked the loop of the sack up her arm to her shoulder. She would have to return the jewelry, at least. And make her position as a nonmistress clear.

"Very well," she said to the Fam, and bent to pat him. Her headache eased. "I hope we're nearly there."

The cat bobbed his head and renewed his trot, checking often to see that she hadn't strayed.

Soon they came to an intimidatingly huge set of greeniron gates. The top formed curlicues, and the fence running down each side of the property bristled with wicked spikes. And worse. The whole thing positively glowed blue with a shield spell. Danith had no doubt that if she touched it, she would be shocked into oblivion, and an alarm would summon the master. Definitely time to turn around.

"Prrrp, prrrp," Zanthoxyl said.

He stood before a meter square gate, obviously designed for the Fam, next to the great greeniron ones. He touched a paw to one of the bars and the blue forcefield vanished.

"No," she said. "I am not crawling through your gate."

In a flash he was behind her, hissing.

Danith put down the bag, then placed her hands on her hips. She tapped her foot. "I am not crawling through your gate."

He did something worse than hiss, than whine. He licked her bare feet through the straps of her weaves.

She shuddered at the feel of his rough tongue and backed up. A step, two.

"Prrrp!" Warning.

She stopped. When she turned, she wasn't surprised to see herself next to Zanthoxyl's gate.

He smiled and tilted his head.

"Ping! Whir. Urga, urga, urga, arrgh, ka-CHUNK." Zanthoxyl's mimicry of her broken collection box was uncanny. It also did exactly what she suspected he wanted. It whipped up her anger once more. Her feeling of being imposed upon, harassed.

She snarled and snatched the sack. She didn't want T'Ash's gifts, and would let him know that in no uncertain terms. Descending to her hands and knees, she pushed at the gate and scuttled through an archway of thorn hedgerow on a beaten path of dirt.

The stench hit her. She gasped and took a lungful of fetid air. The path stank like something out of a sewer. She hurried forward, avoiding the worst of the trail, and her hand slipped in something slimy. She held her breath and contin-

ued to crab forward, feeling wetness seep through her tunic
and the knees of her trous. She hoped it was dew.

As soon as she was through the hedgerow, she stood. One
glance at her clothes made her decide not to examine them
closely. With two fingers she plucked a softleaf from her flat
trous pocket and wiped her hands. She stuck the crumpled
and stained softleaf in the sack.

Clang! The gate rang behind her. She turned to see Zanthoxyl standing, surveying his kingdom, tail straight up.

The metal clang of the gate was echoed by faint clangs in
the distance.

The estate was dappled in light and shadow. The sun, Bel,
had not yet touched the deep gloom near several hedges,
huge trees, and outbuildings. Only the grassy areas looked
blue-yellow with sunlight.

The grassyards, flowerbeds, and bushes were pristine, too
much so. Strict and severe. She glanced toward the green
swath of lawn and caught her breath. Though it appeared
healthy enough, it didn't look as if it was the centuries of
tended growth that holos of the other Residences sported.
She blinked. For an instant it looked all gray and black and
burned. An illusion. She blinked again.

Hadn't there been a fire? She couldn't remember. But as
she examined the Residence, she knew. The modern structure stole her breath with its beauty. Angles and curves
melted into a sensual delight to the eye, something she now
expected of T'Ash. Burnished windows of glisten-glazed
hardglass shone in the sun, reflecting rainbows on the
grassyard. Whatever stone the Residence was actually constructed of didn't show, only a smooth layer of blinding
white armourcrete.

She winced. She didn't like white. She'd paint the entire
thing a creamy-yellow.

Still, there was no mistaking it belonged to a GreatLord.
Glisten-coated hardglass windows and armourcrete. The
Residence might not loom with stone walls, towers, and
crenelations, but she'd bet it equaled or surpassed any other
Residence fortress.

"Ping! Whir. Urga, urga, urga, arrgh, ka-CHUNK," said
Zanthoxyl.

It stirred her ire again. She turned, eyes narrowed. She had words to say to the GreatLord.

The cat, now ahead of her, ran across the meadow. She ran after him, thoughts grim.

The smell of the forge came to her first. Hot metal, cold chemicals, male sweat, and pure, unadulterated, hair-raising Flair. The repetitive pounding grew louder.

Danith stopped in her tracks. She stood, stunned at the sight of T'Ash's gleaming body clad only in a brief loincloth. Her breath clogged in her lungs and her own body underwent an unusual reaction—her breasts tightened and a low ache started between her legs. Shocked at her response, she could not tear her gaze away from T'Ash.

The strengthening sunlight didn't reach into the dark swaths of blackness inside the forge. Only fire highlighted the anvil and the man. And what a man! His broad shoulders tapered to lean hips, then to taut thighs and buttocks. The muscles of his back and arms flexed as he worked, pounding at a length of sharp steel, and looking as strong as the metal. Also like the steel, his swarthy skin showed white scars from a hard, pounding life. A knot that had to be a knife wound was under his right shoulder blade, a long line twined from the nape of his neck to around the left side of his waist.

As he worked, he chanted words of Power. She stood for moments watching him, so enthralled that her breathing came in time with the rhythm of his hammer.

Though the planet Celta had been founded by those espousing Celtic traditions, the colonists had not shunned other mythologies, and every child learned about the many ancient cultures of their ancestors. To Danith, T'Ash was the living image of Hephaestus, the Greek God of the forge. At that thought her stare traveled down his solid, straight thighs, and she shook her head, coming out of her daze. He carried scars, but he wasn't crippled like the God. And Hephaestus had been the butt of jokes, not a perpetrator.

Still uncomfortably attracted to him, she tried to recapture her anger at his presumption, but failed. She sighed. The most she could summon was irritation at his harassment, and she wondered why. The man had been more than a nuisance.

His spell ended with a shouted Word that thundered past

her ears and a last, ringing blow on the metal. He lifted the shining blade, and the redgold inlaid pattern nearly seared her eyes.

She said nothing, but he whirled around. Long, tangled black hair framed his face, which looked thinner, harsher than when she'd seen him at the shop two nights before. His blue eyes were bright and piercing in their intensity. He held a lethal weapon, his stance predatory.

Fear should have swamped her, but like anger, it found no place in her heart.

He smiled and her knees weakened. The smile didn't make him look a mite softer, or even more attractive. But she sensed it was genuine.

He was glad to see her. Twisting, he pushed the blade back onto the anvil. Then he faced her once more and gave a half-bow. His smile broadened.

That smile drew her into the forge. She bit her lip, the small pain allowing her to marshal her wits. If she couldn't retrieve her rage, she could at least feign it.

She scowled. "You!" She pointed an accusatory finger at him, trying to remember her angry thoughts and put them into words. "You wretched creature. You insulting, insensitive, obnoxious—"

"Downwind scruff?" he asked, too softly. The fire that roared in the forge also sparked blue in his eyes.

Danith took a step back. She glanced behind her.

Zanthoxyl sat squarely in the middle of the long open wall of the forge, and somehow she got the feeling that if she made a run for it, he'd be faster, and pounce. She didn't like the idea.

But oddly, neither T'Ash nor Zanthoxyl intimidated her; instead they prodded her temper once more. Who was T'Ash to be offended? It was she who had been the object of his less-than-humorous jokes.

Her fingers hurt. She looked down to the sack tightly clenched in her fist.

She dropped the bag.

A flash of something like pain showed on his face.

She didn't care for the surge of pity his small reaction pulled from her.

She lifted her chin. "I'll be blunt. Somehow, I think you can only understand bluntness. I don't like feeling pressured. I don't like being harassed. I have no intention of becoming a nodding acquaintance, let alone a sex-partner. I think a man who uses a seduction spell is—"

"Low. Lower than a Downwind scruff."

He repeated the words almost exactly. She frowned. No, not almost—exactly. And used Downwind short speech to say so. She stared at him.

He activated a spellshield around the long knife, then stretched his massive body.

She gulped. Then got further annoyed that his body distracted her, that he aroused unwanted attraction in her.

He looked at her with an impassive expression that she sensed concealed a deep sadness. He rubbed his chest.

The hair on his chest was curlier than that on his head, and thinner. She would have expected a hairy pelt, but he was obviously more man than beast.

Silence draped the forge.

Danith reached for the vestiges of her anger, but it was gone again. How could a shade of hurt in sky-crystal blue eyes disarm her so?

"It wasn't a seduction spell," he said softly.

"No? Then what was it?"

He didn't answer, and now she hurt, as if for some reason she had really expected a rational explanation. "That's what it felt like." She waved a hand, groping for words. "An attraction. Something you'd try on me, like you kept trying to tempt me with that other jewelry."

The faintest smile curved his lips, before his gaze dropped to the sack. When he raised his eyes, they were once more fathomless.

She plodded on. "A cheap little seduction spell on a common, Flairless woman to incite lust and draw her to you. A little amusement for the great T'Ash. A plaything. A sextoy—"

He moved more quickly than she could follow. His huge hand manacled her wrist, his fingers overlapping.

His jaw clenched. His eyes fired once more. "No. Not like that. You are not a toy." His other hand touched her shoulder, slid up her neck and his fingers nudged her chin until she met his blazing stare. "Never. Not an amusement."

Then his hand curved around the nape of her neck, and she trembled with sensation. With ease he pulled her against his large form. The very touch of his skin sent pulsing little shocks throughout her. She drew breath to speak, and his scent acted on her like drugged wine, dizzying her beyond reason.

She saw the flash of blue eyes for just an instant before he bent down and put his mouth on hers. Kissed her. A very gentle, almost tentative kiss. His very lack of demand disarmed her. She hadn't noticed how soft his lips were. Surely the softest thing about him.

His hands cradled her head as his mouth brushed against hers once again. More than sensuality spun between them, an extra energy, a heart-threatening tenderness. And he feathered their lips together again. Pleasing, tantalizing, a small courtship.

His was the sweetest kiss she had ever known. How could the fiercest man she'd ever met give her the sweetest kiss?

She pulled her mouth from his, put a hand to her lips. "This can't be." She struggled to think, but his scent, his masculinity, scrambled her mind.

"Yes. Divination Dice foretold. Don't you practice prophecy?"

"The cards. I drew the Lord of Blasers," she blurted.

"Yes!" His gaze burned blue, just like on the card. Bespelled, she lifted her fingers and trailed them down his square jaw.

He groaned. He lowered his head once more. His tongue outlined her lips, tasting her, and she couldn't resist. She opened her mouth to let him in and plunder.

When his tongue rubbed against hers and she tasted him, fast, liquid desire enveloped her.

The kiss passed beyond sweetness, beyond passion. A layered fog closed about her. She sensed the complexity of the man, and the intensity. Both she wanted to deny, both drew her to the flame.

He explored her mouth thoroughly and she strained upward, arching her body against his. More than desire was revealed in his kiss, an echoing loneliness, a craving that would overwhelm her, claim her forever. And even more. In the depths of him was the bedrock of his powerful Flair.

His arms locked around her, lifting her from the ground. The movement collected her wits. She could never match him in strength, physical or psychic. She could never match him in status or wealth.

She pushed against him, scrabbling for words that would put an end to this once and for all. His energy, the potent electricity between them, was frightening in its power.

"Stop!"

With evident reluctance, he dropped his hands and stepped back. Danith didn't dare look down his body. She knew he was aroused. She'd felt him.

"I don't want this," she said.

"No?" It was a challenge.

Her smile felt more like a grimace. "I want an easy life, and you are not an easy man."

His eyes darkened to midnight. "True. Life is never easy. Foolish to think so."

She retreated out of the hot-iron-masculine smelling forge and into the sweet sunlit, flower-scented grassyard. "Why don't you leave me with a few illusions, GreatLord? Like, life is easy. Love is undemanding. Noble GreatLords are not predatory debauchers of common, Flairless women. Please don't scry or send any more gifts or flowers." She turned.

Before she took a step, he'd caught her hands again.

"Let me go."

"No. What do you mean, common and Flairless? Nothing common or Flairless about you, woman!"

Six

❧

Danith blinked at T'Ash's forceful tone. Laughed.

He slid his palms up and down her arms. Her laugh strangled on the flowing energy.

T'Ash raised a black brow. "You hum with Flair. Fine and complex and very, very strong." He squeezed her fingers.

She gasped at the small jolt. "That's just you."

"No."

"Just us, then."

A smile quirked his mouth, reflected in his eyes, now a dazzling blue. "Maybe. Nice, isn't it?"

She made an exasperated sound. "Let me go."

"No. You don't believe me about your Flair."

She shook her head.

His mouth hardened. "You don't believe my words about the seduction spell or about life. You don't believe in my honor or your own uniqueness and Flair."

A mew and a buzz sounded in her head.

T'Ash glanced at his Fam. "Zanth agrees. Your aura is pink. There's only one pink person, he says."

"He talks to you?"

"Another thing you don't believe? That I am not telepathic with my Fam?"

"No. I mean, yes. I believe that. I've heard of that before."
She tried futilely to break his hold. She believed in his
strength, too. He hadn't noticed her brief struggle. Inwardly
she scoffed at herself. She could never begin to match a man
who worked at an anvil and forge.

"Not many people would question my honor to my face."
He scowled at her. She stood mutinously. Banding one hand
around both her wrists, he touched her cheek. "But, then, you
are not just anyone. You're my He—You're special. A special
pink person—the color of your aura, and special to me."

His thick brows had lowered. She felt him searching, considering, doing something with his great Flair. His Flair as
great, or greater, than his physical strength. She shivered.

"Come with me. I will prove it."

"Let me go!"

"No." He glanced at her impatiently, let one of her wrists
go, but kept the other. He hauled her rapidly across the
grassyard separating his forge from his Residence. Zanthoxyl loped ahead of them.

She dug in her heels, to no avail. "Let me go!"

He stopped. Looked down at her. His jaw set. "Do you
want to walk or be carried?"

Her eyes widened. "You wouldn't."

Just that suddenly his mood changed. He grinned. Large,
white teeth flashed. "Yes, I would. I was once a Downwind
scruff. Now, as Zanth informs me, I'm a Noble scruff."

"I never meant to call you that," she said, finally admitting
the shame it caused her. "I didn't mean to insult you."

"No? Now I don't believe *you*." He snorted, then started
off again.

"At least slow down so I can keep up!"

He shortened his steps and curbed his pace. She was surprised at his action, pleased, and it allayed her anxiety. She
moistened her lips. "Prove what? Where are we going?"

He stopped. When he looked at her, his saturnine face was
the epitome of honorable nobility. It shook her.

"We're going to my ResidenceDen to use my Testing
Stones. I created them, and I'm the very best with stones.
There are no stronger, more sensitive testing tools on Celta."
His voice rang with pride.

Blood drained from her head to her feet. She felt cold. Not again. Not to fail one more time. "No."

He released her, bent down to level his eyes with hers. "I pray you trust me in this, Miz Mallow. If you cannot trust the man, or the GreatLord, please trust the craftsman's Flair. I swear by my lost Family that I would not lie to you in this."

"No. I cannot do this."

His eyes remained steady on hers, blue gaze intent. "Yes, you can." He held out a hand. "Please."

She didn't have the courage for this, but she couldn't refuse the look he gave her. She placed her hand in his. And when his fingers enveloped hers with strength, they gave her not only a shock of pleasant sensation, but a bit of courage.

He stopped before arched and glowing reddwood doors, ornamented with redgold straps and nails.

Lifting her hand, he placed it in a depression. He took a deep breath and closed his eyes. A frisson of tingling waves washed through her. She was caught close. Cherished. Released.

Her breath caught in her throat.

"The Residence Identify has memorized your essence." T'Ash bowed. "Miz Mallow, you are welcome to my home, at any time, whether Bel shines or twinmoons glow. You have only to ask and you can enter."

This unnerved her more than anything else that had happened. Except for the kiss.

An odd look of uncertainty passed over his face. "It's ugly."

"Your Residence is splendid."

"No, it's ugly. You should be prepared." Once more he held out his large palm. Once more she placed her hand in his.

Warmth and gentleness enveloped her fingers.

He opened the door with a Word, glanced down at her. "You'll remember the Word?"

Her ears still rang with it. How could she forget? "Yes."

"Good." He drew in a deep breath, then tugged her over the threshold.

Zanthoxyl awaited them. Danith hadn't seen him enter, but the Residence must be riddled with Fam doors. She was sure the place was built after T'Ash and Zanthoxyl became a Family.

The thought snagged her attention. A Family. T'Ash and Zanthoxyl were a Family, very small, very close, but indubitably a Family. She had thought T'Ash a loner.

She shook off the idea. T'Ash and Zanth were only two loners together, that was all.

T'Ash reached to a row of hooks next to the door and pulled on an ash brown silkeen robe. Long and flowing, it covered his near nudity. Danith regretted the hiding of his body as much as she felt relieved that so much stunning virility was concealed. Her unruly gaze had returned time and again to the hard delineations of his muscles.

She looked around. T'Ash was right. His Residence was ugly.

She couldn't imagine living in such a sterile place. All the walls were white and stark. Not a photo, painting, tapestry, or holo hung on a one of them.

The halls were so empty their footsteps echoed. Danith glanced down at the mellow oak flooring. It should not have sounded as lonely as it did.

The ResidenceDen, when they reached it, was no better. An octagonal room with warm paneling, the chamber should have been welcoming. It wasn't. The room contained only a desk and chair, and four straight-back chairs of no particular style. Two of the chairs sat in front of the desk. The other two were awkwardly placed in two angled corners.

T'Ash sat down behind the large desk that had seen better days. It needed to be oiled and cared for. Here and there a new chip showed lighter wood; so did the claw marks on one leg.

She frowned at Zanthoxyl.

He twitched his whiskers.

Turning to T'Ash, she said, "You should get Zanthoxyl a post to scratch in here and save the finish on your desk."

T'Ash looked up, an arrested expression in his eyes. He craned to see the scratches on the desk, then shook his head. "You're right."

He smiled, slowly, gently, and Danith found her heart

beating harder. He turned his gaze to his Fam. "I would never have thought of that. Zanth, what sort of post would you like?"

Danith rubbed her temples, her ears filled with a drone. When she looked at T'Ash he seemed expectant.

"Well?" she asked.

His gaze became no less intent, but he shrugged. "Zanth says he wants a furra hide post with a platform on top. Higher than the desk surface," T'Ash ended dryly.

Danith chuckled.

Both T'Ash and Zanth appeared inordinately pleased.

With a Word, T'Ash summoned a small tray with tea, sweet, and a mug of steaming water onto the edge of his desk near her. "Please, drink. I know you like tea."

Danith flicked a smile. "No, thank you. I'm too nervous."

He frowned, with a wave of his hand the items disappeared. He reached down and Danith heard a drawer open, stick, and open farther. It needs some wax on the runners, she thought.

Reverently T'Ash pulled out an intricately carved case.

Danith tensed.

Zanthoxyl sauntered over to her and nudged her hand with his head. With a sigh of relief, she began to pet him, rubbing the thick scars before his flat ears.

His purr roared in her head.

The top of the case rose at a spoken Word from T'Ash. An array of egglike stones radiated color and power.

Danith gasped.

She had never seen anything so beautiful.

She had never seen anything so fearsome.

She believed T'Ash now, at least about the Testing Stones. They would be the best on Celta, because, as he'd said earlier, she did trust the craftsman.

T'Ash hummed a little lilting folk ditty under his breath. Zanthoxyl purred in rhythm.

T'Ash touched the eggs, pulled several out, polished them, and repeated a Word. Each time the stone glowed a little brighter, each time his eyes dulled a little.

Danith stilled. She had always felt there was great Flair inside her, had always wanted to free it and fulfill some yearning in her soul, but since the goal was forever out of reach, so were the consequences. Flair demanded a price, paid in time and learning, energy and strength. Seeing T'Ash today, thinner and wearier, and comparing him to the man she'd seen two nights before, was her first lesson in the cost of Flair.

Her breath stopped. The next septhour could change her life. Forever.

A deep gong reverberated throughout the Residence. T'Ash lifted his head, touched a finger to an imaging crystal. In the large projected holo a man paced back and forth before the greeniron gates.

"Holm Holly," T'Ash murmured, too low to catch the man's attention.

T'Ash stared at Danith, as if weighing her.

She stiffened. Had he lied when he'd said she was special to him? Would he be ashamed for her to meet another noble?

His eyes narrowed.

The gong boomed again.

A corner of T'Ash's mouth quirked. "The Hollys don't have a minute of patience amongst them."

He raised his voice. "Heir of the Hollys, you are welcome."

The image closed in on Holly's handsome face. One silver-blond brow lifted. "I thank you, GreatLord T'Ash. Entrance, if you please. I wish to speak to you about my commission and my brother," he responded, equally formal.

T'Ash inclined his head. "Zanth will meet and escort you."

Now both brows raised. "As you please."

Pop! Zanthoxyl disappeared, startling Danith. She wondered who had teleported him, or if he'd teleported himself.

The holo, now shrunk to a few centimeters hovering over the edge of T'Ash's desk, showed both Holly and the Fam.

"I think, for both our sakes, that we should have a witness to your Testing," T'Ash said.

Even more tension settled in Danith's shoulders. Continuous quivers ran through her. Her stomach tightened at the thought of Testing again, particularly before such powerful men who were strangers to her.

The distant clang of a door came, then the sound of a cheerful male voice in conversation and various cat-speakings.

"Danith," T'Ash said.

She jerked her gaze from the closed door.

T'Ash stood, his eyes as intense as ever. "I will introduce Holm to you. You will not offer your hand."

She stared at T'Ash. Before she could reply, T'Ash uttered the entrance Word and the door opened. Zanthoxyl strutted in and stopped by her chair.

"T'Ash, Tinne told me—" Holm stopped when he saw her. "Well, well."

Danith rose.

Holm made a suave, sweeping bow.

T'Ash crossed to him and offered his hand. Holm shook it, but when he began to step around T'Ash to greet her, T'Ash blocked him.

Devilish amusement lit Holly's eyes. Oh, this was a dangerous man, all right, Danith thought. In a completely different way from T'Ash. Still, he might be easier to manage.

"Miz Mallow, may I present Holm, the Heir to Holly GreatHouse. Holly, Miz Mallow." T'Ash frowned at her, as if making sure she would follow his instructions.

"Greetyou, HollyHeir. I'm Danith Mallow," she said, tilting her head to see the rangy man behind T'Ash.

He grinned at her. "Meeting a fair lady first thing in the morning is always a pleasure, and an omen of good luck."

T'Ash snorted. "I see you peace-bonded your sword and blaser. Too bad you can't do the same with your charm."

Holly laughed.

"Miz Mallow is here for Flair Testing. Please witness," T'Ash said.

Holly bowed again. "Delighted."

"Take yourself off to a corner chair and try to be inconspicuous. Miz Mallow is nervous."

She'd forgotten to be, until T'Ash reminded her. She stared at him in annoyance, plopped into her seat, and bit her lip.

"I, inconspicuous? Impossible. No one—" Holly broke off as his gaze rested on the Testing eggs. "Lord and Lady, T'Ash . . ." he breathed with awe. "I've never seen such stones. Bless me, the sheer power . . ." He sent a speculative look at T'Ash. "How much does it cost to Test with those?"

"More than you can spare. Speak with T'Holly if you wish to arrange an appointment." T'Ash moved back to his desk.

Danith jumped up. "I can't afford this. I must be going."

T'Ash glowered at her, and when he spoke, it was in his soft, dangerous voice. "I once told you that I, T'Ash, set the price on my work. And it is not a matter of cost between us, is it, Danith? It is a matter of honor."

Danith hesitated, then nodded.

T'Ash smiled, and his eyes lit to silver-blue, and contained the sweetness that had shaken her in their kiss.

"Ah!" Holly said, the one word laden with realization and satisfaction.

"Sit," T'Ash said.

They both sat, Holly in a chair behind Danith.

"Now, Danith, relax. Breathe deeply and evenly. We will wait a few moments until you compose yourself."

Each of her nerve endings seemed to tremble. She didn't think she could relax. Zanthoxyl butted her hand, and she stroked him in the cadence of his ever-louder purrs. Soon she breathed as slowly as the cat under her palm.

"Good. Very good." T'Ash looked up and smiled at her once again, this time it was so free and easy that it made him look years younger. "Now. Your palm, Miz Mallow."

Danith put her right hand, palm up, on the desk. He placed his thumb in the hollow and closed his eyes. Once more Danith felt the cycles of his power in a tiny contact. They rippled through her.

He raised his lashes and his eyes were more brilliant than ever. He opened his free hand and a clear, smooth crystal egg flew into it. "Close your eyes."

She wanted to run. She swallowed.

"You can trust me. I've worked with those of great Flair before. Just last night I tuned a—an object to a young man's vibrations."

Danith inhaled deeply and closed her eyes. When he fit the stone in her hands, it felt neither hot nor cold, light nor heavy. It was as if she curled her fingers around air.

The room was completely quiet. She couldn't even hear the sound of Zanthoxyl snuffling or her own breathing.

"Look, Danith," T'Ash coaxed.

She opened her eyes. The stone lit the room, casting deep shadows around the furniture. Her fingers clamped over the crystal. Light seeped red from between them.

She cried out and dropped the egg. It fell to a felt mat.

T'Ash smiled. Now his gaze showed gentleness. Until he picked up the egg. His eyes went blank and a tremor passed through his large frame. As light faded from the crystal, his skin took on color. A few lines eased from his face. He set the stone carefully in its velvet-lined depression in the box.

His eyes met hers, bluer than they were before. "Energy. Your energy, Danith. You see with your own eyes that you have great Flair."

"I witness." Holly's voice rang from behind her. "Max strength was indicated. The Tester will be accepted into the Nobility upon request."

"No!" cried Danith.

Zanthoxyl put his forepaws on her knees and made a noise Danith supposed should have been reassuring. It hurt her head.

"Miz Mallow doesn't seem to have a great opinion of us." Holly sounded amused. "We are a varied class."

They weren't.

"Just look at the Fam before you," Holly continued. "Or T'Ash there, born a noble ThirdSon, with power to spare and a Downwind past. Or myself—easy, kind, honorable—"

"Time for the next phase," T'Ash said. He turned the box to face her, the eggs arranged in a rainbow from black obsidian through deepest purple, blues, greens, yellows, oranges, reds to darkest maroon. Some contained veins and speckles, some glowed with one solid color. "Touch any or all. Pick them up, and focus. They will evidence the type of your psi ability."

Danith pulled the box closer. She ran a finger down the first three. Shock! She gasped. They were strong, pulsing, full of power, and quite uncomfortable. They also reeked of T'Ash, the unique signature of his Flair. Her hands had become sensitized, she supposed, what with the jewelry she'd been purchasing over the last few months, the gifts of last night, and now this.

She took a deep breath. She hadn't completely accepted that her Flair was finally verified. But she could not stop now.

Slowly, carefully, she passed her hand above the stones. Tingles ran from them to her. The procedure worked better with her eyes closed and centered breathing. Finally one called to her, more than any other. She opened her eyes and plucked from its nest a cream-colored egg shot with varicolored streaks and glittering with flecks of gold and redgold.

"I've never seen anything like it," she said with wonder, turning it in her hands.

"Microcrystalline rock called Anifile," T'Ash said, "denoting animals. Your Flair lies with animals."

Zanthoxyl's rumble filled the room. He licked her hands and the egg between them.

"Zanth approves. Is that the only one you wish to hold?"

She nibbled her bottom lip. His gaze narrowed.

Blindly she reached into the box and took another. This one, too, fit her palm as if it had always been hers. It connected with some deep energy within her, now finally stirring and swelling to the surface. She looked down. The stone was a deep maroon carnelian.

"Yes!" T'Ash said.

"Lord and Lady," murmured Holly.

Zanthoxyl purred louder, filling her mind with his sound. She touched the stone to his nose, and he squeaked in horror and hopped backward.

She laughed and held the stones to her chest, caressing them with her thumbs.

When she looked back to T'Ash her laughter died.

His gaze burned.

She stirred warily on her chair.

He stared at her hands cradling his stones, then slid the entire box over to her. "Yours," he said. "Take them."

Danith dropped the two eggs she still held. All the peace and real satisfaction that had filled her vanished. She looked at the exquisitely carved box and the unique stones with alarm. She could never accept such magnificence and power. "No."

The man overwhelmed her once more, presenting her

with a situation that was too much to cope with. She swept from her chair and across the room to the door before which he stood, face impassive.

She bowed her head formally but kept her eyes on him. "I can never thank you enough, but please, keep your gifts." When she thought of all the things he had sent her the night before, she smiled wryly. "All the multitude of your gifts." She hesitated, hand on the doorknob. "I will scry you later."

Hurriedly T'Ash reinforced the protection spell around her, using the energy he'd previously gained from her. It hurt him to relinquish the sweet Danith-strength, but was necessary.

He watched, expressionless but yearning, as she slipped from the room.

Me follow. Guard. She tired, blown, Zanth said.

T'Ash nodded at his Fam. Zanth twitched the tip of his tail and sauntered out.

"Ah, my friend," Holm said, rising and coming to the desk as T'Ash bleakly stared at his HeartMate, who had rejected him and left. Again.

"You push too far, too fast."

"HeartMate," T'Ash said, unclenching his fingers one by one.

"I gathered that."

T'Ash brooded at the Testing tools on his desk. They contained, in most respects, the best he could ever be, fashioned over long hours and with the greatest of Flair, skill and care. They should have been as nearly irresistible as his HeartGift.

Holm hitched himself on the corner of T'Ash's desk and swung an expensively shod foot. "You know, I have heard word round noble circles that a HeartGift was stolen by a Null."

T'Ash pinned his gaze on his friend and growled.

Holm grinned. "That's my Downwind friend. You're speaking in shortspeech again."

"Nothing but a Downwind scruff."

Holm froze. He laid his hand on the hilt of his sword. "Tell me who said that, and I will be pleased to carve him into tiny pieces."

His heart aching, T'Ash looked at the door. He closed his eyes briefly. His senses told him Danith had left his estate.

"Ah, the ladies. They can prick us where we hurt the most."

"She apologized."

"Good. But about this missing HeartGift—"

T'Ash raised a hand. "No matter. I'm making another. One more reflective of me and which she can't refuse."

Holm winced. "Please be careful, my friend, and don't set yourself up for a fall."

T'Ash looked at him.

Holm started swinging his foot again. "Now, about this Null. I know you've been occupied making the main gauche for my brother, and you have all my esteem and gratitude for placing my needs over your own at this time. Tinne, by the way, was ecstatic at the gift." Holm shook his head. "I must congratulate myself for thinking of it."

T'Ash moved from his desk and took the chair Danith had sat in. Warmth from her body lingered, as did her scent of fresh apples.

Holly examined him with pewter-colored eyes. "You have been concentrating on adeptly crafting a weapon to guard my younger brother and ineptly wooing your Lady. How many septhours have you slept lately, anyway?"

T'Ash shrugged. "About four septhours."

"For two nights and two days, fifty-six septhours?" Holm whistled. "Go rest. I imagine you're nearly done on the blade."

T'Ash nodded. "It's steeping in power and magic."

"Good. I've met this Ruis Elder, this Null." He shuddered and shaped empty air with his hands. "There is no sensing him. It is as if he doesn't exist. We are completely blind to him."

"Ruis Elder." Sudden pleasure at the new information made T'Ash grin. He rolled the name around on his tongue again. "Ruis Elder." He tucked the knowledge away, for later use.

Holly matched his feral smile, then looked down, studying his fingernails. "I'll take the burden of hunting him for you."

"You relieve me," T'Ash mocked, knowing it was more sport than burden for the Holly.

Holm's smile broadened. "True. I am a noble, honorable man, and will be glad to pursue this foul thief for you. It will be a good hunt. He is clever and quick."

Holm sounded like Zanth talking about sewer rats. But then, the thief and a sewer rat shared common characteristics.

Then Holm's face became unusually serious. "I would prefer to look out for my brother over the next few days, but he would feel my emanations. He'd be enraged if I baby-sat him. A young man's pride and honor . . ."

T'Ash nodded.

"So I will occupy myself with your Null thief. It's the least I can do."

"A guard, Winterberry, is on the case of this Ruis Elder. He is trustworthy."

"Winterberry? Damn. He's a connection of ours. Hard-ass," Holm grumbled. "He'll keep the hunt to himself or bind it with laws."

Holm reached out a finger and rolled the deep maroon egg until it clicked into the cream-colored one with multicolored veins. When T'Ash didn't object, he picked up the maroon one, yelped at the power, and let it fall from stricken fingers to the felt.

T'Ash smiled. "Hard for a Holly to hold a Healing egg."

Holm looked down his straight nose. "I'll have you know, we Hollys have the utmost respect for Healers."

"Since you need their services so often."

Holm raised his eyebrows. "You are one to speak. My body is no more covered with scars than your own."

The thought struck T'Ash immobile.

Holm smiled. "Not to worry. Most women don't mind a few scars on a man. Some prefer them."

"Humph."

"Do you think she knew it was a Healing stone she chose?"

T'Ash shook his head. "She thought she was Flairless. Whoever Tested her before must have had poorly calibrated Testing Stones."

"Ah. But yours are the most powerful I've ever seen."

"True. But I felt her power from the first, strong but fine, like an exquisite diamond."

Holm smiled wickedly. "I felt it today, too. Yet I don't recall noticing it when we were in T'Ash's Phoenix last Koad."

T'Ash stiffened. "You remember her?"

"I don't often forget a female face and form. Another gift of the Hollys. Perhaps her Flair has expanded since she's rubbed up against you. Lord and Lady know that your Flair is potent enough to stir even the feeblest. I learned that when we rode Passage together. And you *have* rubbed up against her. At least once, haven't you?"

Heat rose to T'Ash's neck. The very thought of the too-brief feel of her body against him made his own body harden. He shifted in his chair.

Holm grinned. "I thought so. How long have you been in this state?"

"Since she walked into the shop."

Now Holm looked appalled. "Impossible. It would be impossible for a Holly—"

T'Ash sent him a dark glance. "Be glad I channeled most of the energy into the spells of Tinne's main gauche."

"Oh, I am. I most assuredly am." He clicked the eggs together again, the veined cream one with the deep carnelian. "An animal Healer." Holly's tones were hushed. "I believe there was an Earth Family or two on the starships that had that Flair. But their lines did not survive here on Celta. We have animal communicators and trainers, and Healers, but not the combination. She will be welcomed and valued. You have chosen extremely well."

T'Ash lifted his head in pride.

Holly smiled. "Not that you had much to do with it, HeartMates being foreordained, but she will be a worthy addition to the FirstFamilies."

"Keep this in confidence. This courtship is plenty rough without my every move being scrutinized."

Holm stood. "T'Ash, your every move has always been scrutinized. You've kept a discreet presence these last few years, but the FirstFamilies have been fascinated with you since you first went hunting for vengeance. You fuel the interest since you only attend the compulsory rituals. Even then, you only provide a modest amount of strength and energy to the circle."

"I provide what is requested, my share."

"And no more." Holm's voice held an edge.

"How many others provide more?"

"My Father, and others active on the Council."

"Those who want power."

"T'Holly believes in service! So do I."

"The FirstFamilies never did anything for me to dedicate my life to service." But his life would change with his marriage. With a Family he would have more interest in extending his duties. "I fully expect my HeartMate to take her place at my side, including the Great Rituals. We will consider increasing our participation in the affairs of the First-Families' circles."

"Humph."

T'Ash softened. "You, Holm, were the only one who helped me when I needed it."

Holly smiled bleakly. "And now I demand repayment."

"As is your right. You also asked something of me as a friend, and I render it as a friend."

"I can see the cost to you. You've lost weight, energy, and stamina. From what I judge of your HeartMate, you will definitely need energy and stamina." He winked. "I've witnessed a Testing, which was a duty and a pleasure. I will file the certificate of results with the NobleCouncil Clerk."

"I'll put down Zanth witnessed, too." T'Ash smiled. From a drawer he removed a piece of the finest papyrus. Placing both hands on the sheet, he visualized the artistry he wanted on the certificate. Words formed in his mind. Uttering the spell, he held his vision. Light flashed from the document. When he raised his hands, the papyrus had turned a pale blue. Just under the gilt edging, another border marched, a detailed rendition of every T'Ash Testing egg. Danith's name and the outcome of her Testing was embossed in fancy scrollwork, along with larger holo images of the two stones that encompassed her Flair.

Holm picked up the paper by its edges. He whistled. "Very impressive." He put the thing back down and added his holo Heirmark as witness. "Decorative and informative, but the pictures of the Testing tools are some of the best advertising I've seen in many a day." He grinned. "I'll teleport this from T'Holly ResidenceDen. It will cause a stir."

"Thank you."

Holm bowed with his usual theatrical flourish. "My thanks to you for the weapon. Tinne says it will be ready tomorrow morning?"

T'Ash thought of the final adjustments he wanted to make, the sleep he needed. His own Passage. "Perhaps Tinne should pick it up tomorrow evening. I would like to give it one more check after resting."

Holm nodded. "A good idea. I'm glad he will have it for his Passage. Though, I tell you, I envy him it. Merry meet."

"And merry part."

"And merry meet again. Until later, T'Ash."

"Until later, Holm."

*D*anith plodded home, vaguely aware that Zanthoxyl followed her. She was in no mood to accommodate him in any of his cat wishes, so she ignored the Fam.

The Testing had so agitated her emotions, it felt good to be weary and know that her body would demand sleep. She would slip into someplace where she didn't have to struggle with all the brand-new multitude of problems that came as a consequence of her Testing.

She had Flair! Great Flair, even. HollyHeir Holm had witnessed. Happiness gave her a brief surge of energy, and Danith executed a few of Mitchella's joyful dance steps. Oh, yes. Yes, indeed. No one would ever sneer at poor, little Danith Mallow from the Saille House of Orphans ever again.

She may have lost her parents. She may have grown up in an institution. She may have been rejected many times on many levels, but now she was the equal of any other woman she knew.

She danced through her door. And was greeted by an exotic Pansy, still draped in as much jewelry as possible. Danith had been in too much of a hurry to gather every one of T'Ash's gifts.

Pansy wore a heavy redgold chain that dragged behind her, a long string of winding ruby beads, a small glisten chain suspending what looked like a breathtaking Skycrystal, and had even managed to insinuate a clustered diamond clip on one feathery-furred ear.

T'Ash's jewelry carried his strong emanations. Danith's heart thudded. What was she going to do with the man? Without giving herself time to think, she picked up her new deck of divination cards.

She drew two.

The Lord of Blasers.

The Lovers.

No! She set the two cards and the pack on the table, determined to ignore them. She knew what she wanted. Though the last septhours had given her more options than she'd ever had, though her fondest wish had come true, though her future looked shining, bright, and all together different, she would continue on the path she had planned. She would marry Claif.

T'Ash gave her flowers.

T'Ash gave her jewels.

T'Ash gave her a wonderful future.

T'Ash gave her passion.

But he gave nothing of himself.

Claif didn't give a great deal, either. But she would never expect more than what Claif wanted to give. What he was was what she wanted—a cheerful, simple man. And he came with many related Clovers that would meet her huge need for Family.

Still set on her own way, Danith went to her bedroom, slipped off her weaves, and fell onto her bedsponge, asleep a moment later.

A soft, murmuring voice woke her. "GentleLady. GentleLady Mallow . . ."

The words insinuated into her sleep, persistently drawing her from slumber. She opened her eyes, blinked.

"GentleLady Mallow."

She jerked around.

A stranger in her bedroom.

She gasped. Inhaled.

He raised both hands. "Please, don't scream."

She licked her lips. her scrybowl was in the kitchen.

His smile was too charming to be true, matching falsely innocent brown eyes. He took a step or two back, hands still raised, into a patch of early afternoon sunlight. "I mean you no harm. I merely wish to return an—item—to you."

He made no sense. And he smelled funny, too. Not unpleasant, but wrong somehow. She inched back to the headboard.

"Allow me to present myself. Ruis Elder, at your service."

Seven

❦

"I don't know you," Danith said to the man calling himself Ruis Elder.

"Entirely my fault, GentleLady."

"Miz."

He inclined his head. "Miz, then. I assure you, I am completely harmless."

He wasn't. He had the same smooth and charming manner as Holly, but while she sensed it was innate to Holm, she
suspected this man used the manner as a mask. He had a
hard edge underneath. He was also bigger and stronger than
she. "What do you want?"

"Only to return something and have a few words with you."

"I've lost nothing."

Another quick, supposedly reassuring smile. "It's for a
friend of yours."

The Clovers? Young Trif was a little wild, and always losing things. Danith had a soft spot for the girl. "Then you
won't mind waiting in the grassyard. There's a café table
and chairs there."

His brown gaze sharpened. She met it steadily. For all the
controlled power he radiated, he was not nearly as dangerous as T'Ash.

He dipped his mahogany-colored head again. Holding his arms out from his sides, he slowly glided from the room. Danith bolted to the scrybowl, visualizing the guard station nearest her. Nothing happened. She touched the water of the bowl. It was cold, not warm with the hint of magic. Cold and dead.

Damn!

She should run. She should scream. She should do anything but stand and dither.

But she had sensed no threat from him. And she was curious.

She put on her weaves and straightened her clothing.

The back door to the grassyard was open. She stood on the threshold, ready to slam the door and retreat if necessary.

He appeared to lounge in one of her black café chairs set in a close-clipped circle of grass, but tension emanated from his body. He had his gaze fixed on the corner of her fence.

Zanthoxyl perched there. His lip lifted in a nearly soundless snarl. Danith's headache returned.

Elder's far hand clenched into a fist. His face showed nothing of the charming smile he had used earlier. In a flash of insight, Danith recognized the man's power. Rage drove him.

She knew it from the echo of old anger it roused in her. Rage at being trapped. She had been trapped in the Saille House of Orphans, at once angry at being forced to obey institutional rules at all times, and fearful of the outside world.

Timkin, her old playmate and first love, had once contained such rage, greater and more destructive than her own. It had faded when he made a life for himself outside the orphanage.

Destructive anger. This Ruis Elder was a destroyer. His fury would allow him no other outlet. And Danith was as sure as if she saw words of fire circling his head, that in the end, he would destroy himself.

She caught her breath. He turned, and when he looked at her, his face was once more slightly amused—but deeper than that, Danith saw self-mockery.

"GreatSir Elder."

She hit a nerve. She knew it. He was of the nobility.

"I don't care to be called GreatSir any more than you like GentleLady."

Heat rose to her cheeks. Perhaps she could defuse the tension a little. "What time is it?"

He looked startled, then glanced at his old-fashioned watch. Danith peered at the piece, fascinated. She had never seen one before, had only used timers herself.

"One septhour past midday."

"Thank you. Now, your business?"

From a concealed pocket in his shirt he took a long, thin flat box, a jeweler's box.

He placed it on the café table in front of him and snapped it open.

The seduction spell necklace.

Before she even saw the gems, the power struck her, dizzying in its force, its sexuality. T'Ash. She thought of his hard body against hers and the scent he carried of man and hot metal. She felt the virility of the man, and something more, an essence of the man who compelled her. And she wanted the necklace. Wanted his touch. Wanted more.

She made a mewling sound and retreated to the threshold of the back door.

Ruis Elder snapped the jewelry box lid shut and placed long, fine fingers atop it. Somehow that eased the frightening lure of the thing. But now she knew it was here, in the box.

She pressed a hand to her breast, found her heart thumping, and her breath came raggedly. A residual sexual heat flushed her body. She trembled.

The man sighed as he studied her. He smiled crookedly. Now his self-mockery was open. "Yes, I see. I made quite a mistake. All this time with me and it still has that effect on you. That's truly powerful Flair." He shook his head. "A bad mistake."

Danith wet her dry lips. "How?"

His smile turned more amused. A pity he had such rage in him; his humor could have saved him. "I took it."

"You stole the necklace from T'Ash?" Inconceivable.

His brows lifted. "It wasn't protected by spellshield. That wouldn't have mattered, of course. But to see such an extraordinary piece displayed without even the hint of protection . . ." His shoulders lifted and fell. "Simply irresistible."

He opened the lid, and liquid desire surged through her,

settling in her loins. She gripped the doorjamb with all her strength to keep from moving toward the radiant temptation of the necklace.

He shoved the box away, to the far edge of the table, but the tiny distance didn't help. The virile, carnal power of the necklace poured off it in waves.

Elder looked at the thing, ran his forefinger down the beads, redgold links, and gems to touch the roseamber heart. "The magnificence of the piece. Obviously an early work, but the sheer skill it displays! And this, a great roseamber heart with a flaw in the shape of licking flames." He shrugged again. "Positively too tempting."

His smile was once more ironic. "I said skill, not Flair. I am blind to that, but not to pure creative artistry. And my blindness ambushed me, as always." He sent her a slanting glance. "How was I to know it was a HeartGift?"

The last word penetrated the sensual fog enclosing her. Shattered her plans. They fragmented before her.

"No," she said. That morning she had been able to deny that she'd lost her desired future with Claif. She couldn't now. But even with the potency of T'Ash's necklace—she would not even think "HeartGift"—swirling around her, making her knees so weak she slid down to the floor, she still would not accept that her only future lay with T'Ash. Not T'Ash.

"No," she repeated.

"Danith," T'Ash said.

She turned her head. He stood just inside her back grassyard gate. Zanthoxyl sat straight and proud by his side. "Lord and Lady," Danith prayed. Passion matching the necklace burned in his eyes. He looked large, dark, strong. And very hard. The muscles of his shoulders tensed, his hands clenched, his thighs strained the fabric of his trous. All of him was hard.

She gripped the doorjamb tighter, closed her eyes, and turned her head away.

"Thief." T'Ash flung the word like a knife.

"I returned it," Ruis Elder said.

"To the wrong person. She did not know it was a Heart-Gift. Now you'll pay."

"Damnation! Just my luck."

The table crashed. Danith's eyes flew open, she jerked to her feet to see two men fighting on the ground. T'Ash was the larger, the broader, but he fought a man whose checked fury lay beneath a shallow surface.

They rolled. They punched. They grunted and swore.

Danith could almost see the raging emotions pouring into the summer afternoon sky, heating the grassyard. Emotions that were magnified by the necklace.

Zanthoxyl circled around the two, eyes narrowed, as if waiting to pounce on Ruis Elder. Now and again a fast paw would strike out at the thief's leg or back. It only made the man fight harder.

"Zanthoxyl, the necklace! Get it and put it away!"

The Fam spared her a feral look and growled.

"Do it!" Danith ordered, wondering if he'd obey.

His growl rolled louder. They matched gazes.

Danith narrowed her eyes and set her mouth.

With a final snarl, he picked up the necklace with his teeth, the box fell off the table. His muzzle pulled back from the thing.

He shot past Danith and into her house. She ran after him. He knocked over two chairs as he raced to her bedroom. He jarred the bedside table with his shoulder before depositing the necklace square in the middle of her bedsponge.

Then he roared a sound of utmost glee, and shot by her, back to the still fighting males.

Danith slammed the door to her bedroom. One glance in the Mainspace showed Pansy cowering on top of a bookcase, with only the ruby beads and two chains on, peering at the action.

Danith stomped back to the grassyard. "Stop this at once. T'Ash, I will not have you fighting in my yard. The necklace was stolen. Now it's back. You've pounded the man. That's enough! You, Ruis Elder, take your anger away. You pollute my home with it. Stop!"

They paid no attention. She thought of the waterhose. The idea didn't satisfy, not physical enough. She ran over and crouched near. She grabbed a handful of T'Ash's hair, he was on the bottom. He clenched his jaw, but stilled. Elder reared up, and she interposed her body between the men, absorbed a breathtaking blow on her shoulder, and collapsed on T'Ash's chest. Pain threatened darkness.

Zanthoxyl yowled.

"Danith!" T'Ash cried, clutching her close.

She forced her eyes open, sputtered words around the pain as she met Ruis's eyes. "Go. Now. Fast."

To her amazement, fury drained from his gaze, replaced by regret. He bowed quickly, respectfully. He ran into the house before Zanthoxyl reached him and slammed the door on the Fam. Zanth darted around the house and out to the front. Danith heard her front door slam, and Ruis's running footsteps down the stone sidewalk.

"Danith, dear one," T'Ash murmured, then lapsed into wordless crooning, cradling her awkwardly.

She turned a moan of pain into a sigh. And though some weak part of her wanted to remain in such strong, tender arms, the changes in her life were too new to be readily accepted. "Please. Release me."

His jaw hardened, his eyes glinted ice blue. He stood with her, made sure she was steady, and stepped back.

He met her angry gaze with equal intensity. "Now you know. Not an illegal seduction spell. The necklace is a HeartGift, made during my last Passage."

"No."

"You always deny it. 'No.' But it's 'yes.' A HeartGift. We will be bound together forever, HeartMate."

She shuddered. "No. I don't want that."

"Too bad." His smile looked more than a little like Zanthoxyl's feral one. "I am making another HeartGift, to reflect more of the man I am now. You may be able to resist the necklace, and my Testing Stones, but not the new HeartGift. We've kissed. I've felt your response. Kissed only this morning, yet I've thought of it all day. You'll think of it, too, won't you? I'm making marriage armbands, also."

She ran to the stoop, jerked the door open, and slammed it behind her.

Her blood thundered in her ears, more from the fear he was right than the minor exertion. She stared, but didn't see anything but an image of both of them as entwined lovers.

"Do you always run from challenges?" His voice easily penetrated her door, making her jerk with surprise.

Ire flared in her. "Always from danger," she said, raising her voice.

"I can help you get over that."

She didn't see it as a fault.

She spun to the door and opened it again. He stood in the grassyard, a wicked smile on his face, hands on his hips.

She simmered, gestured to herself. "Look at me. I'm smaller than average, of common birth, an orphan with no Family name and no relatives. I'm insignificant in this world. Nothing. Avoiding danger not only makes sense, it works!"

Though his face softened, a molten, caressing look entered his eyes. "You're not nothing to me. I couldn't admit it before, but you are my HeartMate."

She scowled and crossed her arms. "I don't want to be a Noble. Your life includes too much obligation, and is too public. All I want is a simple life, surrounded by an easy man and a large Family."

The fire of desire in his gaze transformed to flickering anger. Instinctively she stepped back and took hold of the doorknob.

"We're HeartMates." Now it was he who flicked a hand down his large body. "I will suit you."

"You . . . don't appear to be an easy man."

His eyes narrowed. "Sorry. But we have much in common. I, too, am an orphan, without Family—"

"That's not what I want—"

"I've been even less than middle class, I grew up Downwind." He prowled forward. "I want a large Family. A new Family. With you."

She whirled and stepped back inside, then shut the door again, refusing to hear any more.

Once more she stopped just over the threshold. She stood for several moments, but did not hear him leave. His knock jolted her.

"Danith, Miz Mallow. I would like to get to know you."

"No."

His sigh was audible. "No, again. Unfortunate that you

know we are HeartMates, but I didn't tell you myself. That will be taken into consideration when brought before the Councils. Common Council, NobleCouncil, perhaps even the FirstFamilies Council."

Danith gnawed her lip.

"Holm Holly has registered your Testing as a Noble. That will generate some publicity. I will send a Healer to tend you, causing more talk. With my claims before the Councils, everyone will talk."

He tapped on the door again. "Let me in. Let us get to know each other on an *informal* basis."

Danith muttered under her breath. "You will leave when I request it?"

"Of course. I am an honorable GreatLord."

She opened the door, but wrapped her arms around herself and kept a wary distance from him.

He strolled in, once again reminding her of Zanthoxyl. His hands were in the pockets of his black trous. He glanced around her home, slanted a look at her, and closed his eyes, tilting his head back. His nostrils flared as he inhaled deeply.

Danith froze. Danger swirled around her. Sensual danger.

A flush came to his cheeks. His hands fisted in his pockets. When his eyes opened, they were heavy-lidded. "Nice. Not ugly like my Residence. Warm. Welcoming. You."

Her heart picked up beat.

Now he looked around with a lingering gaze. He smiled. Once more it was a genuine, engaging smile. Deep inside, Danith felt an attraction to him on more than a physical basis and squelched it.

"Where is the HeartGift?"

Danith gestured to the closed bedroom door. He walked to it. With a deep breath that expanded his large chest, he opened the door.

"Take it with you," Danith said, averting her eyes from the tangle of jewels pulsing with sexuality on the bedsponge.

"I don't think so." He snapped the door shut. "I touch that bedsponge and you'll be under me."

Danith trembled. She compressed her lips at an image of them as lovers. "I don't have anywhere else to sleep."

He went into the mainspace and saw the too-short divan.
"I see." He looked at her, desire in his eyes. "Come with me."

"No."

"You're going to fight me on this."

"Yes."

His lips curved. "A 'yes' at last. This time I would have
preferred a 'no.' As you wish." He rolled his great shoulders.

Danith lifted her chin, knowing he took his winning for
granted.

He moved around the room casually, but she sensed he
was noting every texture, every objet d'art, every book, every
hologram.

He went into the kitchen and she heard a hissed breath.
"Your scrybowl is disabled."

"GreatSir Elder."

There was muttering, a small clap of air. "Come here,
please."

She walked to the open threshold of the kitchen. A large
flowered cloisonné bowl with a soft yellow background that
exactly matched her walls sat on her counter.

He looked at her, a satisfied expression on his face. "A
bowl from my Residence." Gently he traced his finger
around the rim, then dipped fingertips in the bowl and sent
the water swirling. "Not mallow blossoms, but Ash. Come
anoint it with your own energy and dedicate the scry image."

She gestured him out of the kitchen. It was only big
enough for one to comfortably work in.

His brows lowered, then he passed her as she stepped
aside.

She concentrated on setting the image and initiating the
spell. The metal didn't make it easy, like the porcelain did.

"I can help," T'Ash said.

"No."

This time he smiled. "No. You must encourage your Flair,
nurture it, starting with minor tasks. The bowl will accept
your spells. You have the power to work with it. And it is,
after all, my bowl."

"Crafted by you?"

His smile broadened. "Indeed."

"Another gift."

He matched her irritated gaze, gestured briefly. "You need a scrybowl. There it is. Will your pride make you refuse it?"

She felt more than irritation flare between them, but wanted nothing of it. "I have little pride. It is not a luxury an unwanted orphan can afford. You, I think, have more than you should."

She saw he didn't like that and couldn't refute it. He turned abruptly to prowl her mainspace.

Focusing once more, she worked with the air and the water, the image and energy. Knowing she had the Flair to bespell the bowl made all the difference. For the first time in her life, she didn't use a programmed spell on a magical object, she created her own. And it felt wonderful.

When she left the kitchen, she saw him hesitate by the table where the two cards she'd drawn earlier lay in all their glory. She hurried to stop him, too late.

His mouth quirked again as he tapped the Lord of Blasers and the Lovers. "Good." He hesitated, then touched his finger to the deck of cards. His breath hissed out, a shock rippled through his arm and down his body. The cords of his neck stood out.

He turned to look at her, pure passion glinting in his narrow gaze. When he spoke his voice was thick. "HeartMates. We two. Loving. Ecstasy. Forever."

She sidled to the front door and watched him. He turned his head away, and silence enveloped them for a few moments, a quiet that seemed to spin a strand between them.

"You might have noticed that I revert to short Downwind speech when—emotionally charged."

She didn't say anything.

Pansy mewed.

He looked up, a quick laugh broke from him.

Pansy was sitting, regal as a queen, on top of the bookcase. Once again she was draped in every glittering piece of jewelry she could insinuate on herself. The diamond earclip was back.

T'Ash walked over to her and held his hand up before her nose. She was easily within his reach. Danith would have had to use a stool to pick her cat up.

Pansy sniffed at his hand, then rubbed it, her loud purring filled the quiet between the people.

"Pansy, who would prefer to be called Princess, I presume."

The statement jolted Danith from her complacency. "Princess?" She looked at her cat. "Surely not."

"She is very beautiful. I thought so." He shot Danith a glance. "Like her Lady."

"Princess?"

"So Zanth says. She would prefer to be called Princess." Danith muttered.

"I've designed a collar of citrines for her, and later an EarthSun pendant."

"No."

"Rrrow!" The wail for attention came from outside the front door.

T'Ash crossed to it and opened it.

Zanthoxyl strolled in, the bag of jewels that Danith had returned to T'Ash clamped in his teeth.

Danith saw the open door and took advantage of it, ignoring the gentle clink of the gifts as the Fam lowered his burden carefully to the floor. "It's time for you to go."

T'Ash's jaw tightened and he looked mutinous before stepping out onto the front sidewalk. "You won't come with me? Stay at my Residence?"

"No."

He nodded shortly, and reached in a hand to grab her broken antique scry table.

"Don't—" Danith started.

He smiled coolly. "My mistake, my redress."

The table looked delicate in his large hands. Despite the scry table, he managed a creditable bow. "I will send you a bedroll that will fit in here. Also expect a Healer to tend your shoulder; you've been favoring it. Merry meet."

Danith glared at him.

"Merry meet!"

She said nothing.

He put down the scry table and crossed his arms, leaning against the doorjamb. "Merry meet."

She met his gaze. He looked fully as stubborn as she was. And she wanted him gone. "Merry part," she muttered.

His attractive smile flashed over his face. "And merry meet again." He lifted the table with one hand and inclined his head. "Soon."

T'Ash strode along, then slowed. The many things he had to do and the lack of time pressed upon him. He couldn't afford to expend any extra energy, even energy given by the anger flowing through his veins.

He wasn't nearly as nonchalant as he'd acted. And he'd concealed the deep hurt and banked ire that had speared through him at her words.

Sucking in a breath of fresh sun-warmed afternoon air, he practiced calming exercises. Exercises he hadn't had to employ in years.

She wanted a fight. He wouldn't have expected that she'd be one to fight. But she was strong, and determined, and her Flair was powerful. He smiled grimly. It would be a good fight.

A testing of wills. He usually won fights.

He concentrated on using his muscles as he walked. And though he'd lost a few individual fights, he had won several personal wars; vengeance, acceptance by the twenty-four other FirstFamilies, reestablishing his GreatHouse, building his shop and reputation, honing his Flair.

He wondered if she had fought as much as he, but doubted it. She looked as if she still thought there were rules to fighting.

She'd probably faced a few battles, what with being a female only as high as his shoulder and an orphan without Family. But she wasn't in his class.

Class. The word hurt as much as being called a Downwind scruff. And he knew class would be an element in this conflict with Danith—his rank and wealth. She'd made that clear.

Being elevated as a new Noble would be rough for her. Jumping from middle class past GraceHouse class and up to GrandHouse class was rare. GrandHouses were usually at least three centuries old, except for the twelve highest GrandHouses that were included in the FirstFamilies, descendants of the founding colonists.

GrandHouse and FirstFamily society would expect her to act in a certain manner. When she married him, his rank as a FirstFamily GreatLord would bring her to the highest station of the Noble class. If she lacked the proper attitude, being accepted as a HeartMate by the Nobles would be a problem. Ah, well, he would stand with her.

But she was right. After she married him, she would never have the anonymity or the simple life she said she wanted.

He had obligations to his heritage, to his descendants, the twenty-five FirstFamilies, and to civilizing Celta itself. All Heads of households and their spouses were expected to participate in the Great Rituals, and Danith would be no exception. T'Ash frowned. Noble responsibilities would be one aspect of this tough battle with her.

The FirstFamilies interest in Danith as his wife would go beyond attention into greed. T'Ash lengthened his stride. Energy and power were always needed by the ruling class to shape the events of Celta. As his wife, titled GreatLady D'Ash, Danith's simple celebrations would be a thing of the past. With her strong Flair and affinity to animals, she would be ordered to the Rituals and expected at the Council meetings. She wouldn't like that.

Another facet of the fight to win her would be the nature of his own character. He knew he was nothing like the easy-going gallant who squired her now. She knew it, too. T'Ash had an introverted personality, tending toward brooding darkness. It was nothing he could completely reshape.

He could try to lighten his soul, and since Danith had entered his life, he'd felt nearly giddy with hopeful delight. He could work with that. Just being near her made him less gloomy, if no less complex. But she was a complex creature herself.

He frowned. The yearning for Family radiated from her— his greatest challenge in this rough courtship. He felt a touch of foreboding down his spine and hoped that this would not be his downfall. He would give her Zanth and promise her children. He could provide a few close friends with the

Holly Family, but, in general, the FirstFamilies rarely were friends—more often allies or enemies.

He had some advantages. She was soft and generous. She would not fight with the ruthlessness that he would.

And he'd planted the seeds of passionate desire in her imagination of them together as lovers. A woman as creative as she would return to that idea again and again. It would work on her. As the necklace ensconced in her house would work on her.

He had destiny on his side. He even had the law. His mood cheered. He would win, as always.

*D*anith sat on the sofa, warily watching Zanthoxyl. His head bobbed in and out of the cloth bag of gifts that he'd fetched back from the T'Ash estate, all the gifts she'd returned to T'Ash.

Zanthoxyl would look around the mainspace, or jog into the kitchen, and spot an acceptable place for an offering. Then he'd push his head in the bag and delicately pull a piece of jewelry out with his teeth. He'd position the item exactly, stand back to check it in its new home, grin at her, and repeat the whole procedure.

She sighed. Chains and beads draped over tables and around the few figurines she owned. Glittering necklaces, collars, and a bracelet or two were arranged in complicated patterns pleasing to the Fam. The whole place looked like a museum displaying exquisite, priceless jewelry. Further, a faint but palpable ripple of Flair from T'Ash permeated her house, powerful and inherently elegant. Only Pansy appeared tacky. She still wore her own portion of the jewels, including earclip.

The other earclip Zanthoxyl had managed to attach to his collar.

Danith reached over with her finger and petted the three-centimeter square of undecorated Pansy. Pansy purred.

Danith scratched Pansy under her chin and stared deeply into dark yellow eyes. "You really would prefer to be called 'Princess?' "

Her cat chirruped loudly and gave her a sweet smile.

Danith shook her head in disbelief. "Princess. That is so—trite. It has no charm. You're really sure?"

Pansy dropped her head and emitted a small mew.

Danith sighed and rubbed her cat's head. "Very well, Princess it will be." She grimaced. "But it might take me some time to get accustomed to it."

Pansy's—Princess's—purr increased. With a soft clinking, she rolled on her back and curled her paws, so Danith could pet her soft light gray stomach fur crisscrossed by beads.

DONE!

Danith heard the word, with a rush and a clap around it. She looked up to see Zanthoxyl sitting proudly with his tail curled around his paws.

"Very nice, Zanthoxyl," she said politely.

ZANTH. ZANTH. ZANTH! NOT ZANTHOXYL.

She pressed her hands against the stabbing pain in her head. "Zanth. I hear you. I think." Beyond her new, fearsome headache, she didn't want to explore the consequences of this development.

HARD TO TALK.

"Yes." She clamped her hands to her head and rocked back and forth in pain.

WILL GET BETTER WHEN YOU MATE WITH MY FAMMAN.

Danith moaned.

She felt a rough tongue between her ankle and her weaves. Opening her eyes, she saw Zanthoxyl—Zanth—trying to copy Princess's sweet smile, and it bordered on frightening.

She rose and went to the bathroom for a feverfew hurtease. As she pulled out a small soluble vial and swallowed it, she noticed a line of little precious stones carved in the shape of animals. There was a whimsical pink-quartz pig, a graceful purplebird with wings out-stretched ready to fly, even a green malachite cricket. She wanted to stroke them.

Instead she mumbled a swear word. Master and Fam, they were determined to get her.

*T'*Ash once again yanked on the T'Ivy Residence bellpull. He had hoped to avoid this last-ditch effort, hoped that Danith

would come to him on her own. Now he would have to tacitly
admit that his HeartMate had once more rejected him.

Hurt and anger resurged. The anger he could acknowledge. His HeartMate continually ran away. How could she
not know that he would be the best thing in her life? He
mumbled curses under his breath.

When the haughty T'Ivy butler appeared by the gates with
raised eyebrows, T'Ash scowled at him. The man backed up
a couple of steps and T'Ash entered, pleased that he could
still intimidate someone. He smiled at the notion. The butler
backed up farther and cleared his throat. "GreatLord?"

"T'Ash to see D'Ivy. She is expecting me."

"Ahem. I believe so, but not for a few days—"

"Now. My request is for now. If she cannot provide the
required service, I will be glad to inform the FirstFamilies
Council clerk of the debt."

The man blanched, drew himself to his full height,
straightened his cuffs, which showed him a distant relative
of the GreatHouse Ivy. "We have never had a black mark in
our History Ledgers. Come. I will show you her sunroom.
You may wait for her there."

T'Ash marched after the man, down the glider path to the
estate, and around to a glassed-in side entrance. In the sunroom he glanced around. He admired it, but not as much as
he would have if he'd not seen Danith's home. This room
was done in cool blues, not the warm colors Danith preferred, that he, himself, now knew he favored.

Short moments later a young woman swept into the room.
She was dressed in a long golden gown shot with silver and
had a many-braided hairstyle that must have taken hours.

"You are D'Ivy?" T'Ash asked.

She looked down her nose at his rudeness. "I am."

He stared at her, examining her up and down. Another
piece of discourtesy, he was aware, but something in her
very presence irritated him. "HeartMate, T'Ivy said."

She smiled a small, smug smile. "True," she said it with
the tiniest hint of scorn. And T'Ash knew she'd heard all
about his Downwind upbringing, his vengeance stalk, his
current quest, and she didn't think he deserved the honor of
a potion from her lily-white hands.

He had run into this opinion before. And she was stupid to think that a son of a FirstFamily, a GreatLord, would not sense her disdain. His Danith would not have made that mistake.

"I do not believe I have seen you at the FirstFamilies Rituals," he said softly, reminding her of his status.

She paled, now looked at him as if she really saw him for the first time, and not some image she had built in her mind. She bowed her head. T'Ash thought it hid a scheming face. She would not be a pleasant companion, this one. Not for him. He pitied T'Ivy and wondered at the match. He'd liked T'Ivy.

"I do not often attend," she said.

Now T'Ash smiled. Her power must be sufficient for the D'Ivy duties but not strong enough to hold her own during those Great Rituals that demanded it.

"What birth House?"

She raised her head. "Is this necessary?"

"You've had the ring I wore since a child for a day and a half, ample time to study me. You should know my power. Do you wish to provide me with an object for telemetry so I can judge your skills? That second-rate jade pendant you wear should be acceptable." He held out his hand, palm up.

Her very white skin flushed. "GraceHouse Aloe."

A solid Healing House, they also used their Flair with plants. He inclined his head. "Good. Let us proceed. You understand that T'Ivy swore to keep the matter confidential." He didn't doubt T'Ivy's honor, but he was not sure of hers.

"I understand." The contempt was back in her voice, along with anger. "I was not expecting you so soon. Further, you do not look as though you could sustain a long, difficult Passage. I would be derelict in my duty if I provided you with the herbs to induce Passage." She smiled, too, meanly.

T'Ash narrowed his eyes. "Then you refuse service and concede a debt from the House of T'Ivy to the House of T'Ash."

"No."

"Then what do you propose?"

She stood simmering a moment. "An infusion for a short Passage."

T'Ash considered how long it would take him to create the earrings. He knew the pattern, knew his lady, had only to release his emotions. "How long?"

"Two hours."

It would be long enough to shape them, but not to infuse them with everything he wanted, needed. "Too short."

Her mouth set mulishly. "Very well, half a night."

"Done. But since your service is less, so is mine. My only service will be to choose and obtain a sky-crystal as a Testing Tool for the T'Ivy GreatHouse. My trip expenses to Gael City will be paid by T'Ivy. You will provide a Family member to accompany me to witness my honorable and best service, his or her trip expenses to be paid by T'Ivy. That is my entire recompense for your Passage herbs. If T'Ivy wishes shaping of the current sky-crystal into pieces, or his Testing Tools realigned, have him make an appointment with me to negotiate further. Agreed?"

She blinked, as if she had never bargained a transaction before. He wondered how pampered she had been, was. He shrugged. It was a fair deal.

She looked around.

He set his hands on his hips. "I wait."

"Agreed."

He nodded. "Done. When will the herbs be ready?"

Again she blinked. "Four septhours."

"Done. I will send Holm Holly, Heir of the Hollys, as witness to your honorable and best service. He will bring the vial to me, along with my ring. Four septhours."

He strode from the room, then down the path away from the Residence. He took a deep breath once outside the gates. The air seemed purer, less stifling.

As soon as he got home, he called a Healer to go to Danith. Then T'Ash vized Holm Holly.

"Here. T'Ash!" Holm scowled. "You've been fighting, and didn't let me in on the fun?"

T'Ash lifted a shoulder. "A mere scuffle, is all. With Null Elder."

Holly's frown deepened. "You took care of him."

T'Ash looked at his slightly scraped knuckles. "Yes. The man returned the HeartGift, but also informed Danith she was my HeartMate. That makes it difficult."

Holly whistled through his teeth. "I'd say so, but if you didn't tell her yourself . . . I'd guess your rights would be upheld."

T'Ash grinned. "So I thought. I've called Winterberry and told him of the situation. He'll substantiate my word. Danith isn't pleased."

"You push too hard sometimes, T'Ash."

T'Ash flexed his hands. "Not hard enough at the Null."

"Does that mean I have permission to beat on him a little?"

"He didn't look as if he learned his lesson. Danith cut the fight short."

Holly sighed deeply. "Females."

"Yes. Speaking of which, D'Ivy has promised herbs to stimulate another Passage in four septhours. Would you act as my witness-agent in this?"

"I'm not sure this is wise—"

"Please. Tinne's main gauche will have finished steeping in Flair by then. I have left space for a Family blessing at the end of the spell. Would you care to say it?"

"You have a way with bribes, as usual. I'll collect the potion from D'Ivy and come there." Holly ended the call.

T'Ash went upstairs to his bedroom to clean up. He compared it to the brief glance he had of Danith's bedroom. Though his wasn't nearly as homey, it was somewhat more comfortable and had a bit more character than the rest of the rooms in the Residence. Layered Chinju rugs provided texture and color. A gleaming framed bedsponge sported a boldly patterned cover. The outer wall curved around the length of the room, bowing outward. T'Ash liked the sensual curves, and knew they'd please Danith. The wall contained a large round window with two long lozenge-shaped windows on each side of it. The round window was stained and sectioned forceglass delineating the World Tree, ancient symbol of the GreatHouse T'Ash. And in the center of the window, where the tree trunk split into boughs, was a huge rough-cut and polished rose quartz crystal the size of his head.

T'Ash used the crystal as a scry for his grounds and his shop. He smiled with pleasure now. Danith would approve.

When he went to shower, he stared at himself in the mirror and winced. No wonder D'Ivy was so contemptuous, and Holm a trifle envious. T'Ash's hair was tangled, his chest bare, and the dusky hue of his jaw showed the beginning purpling of a bruise. But Danith had not said a word.

DINNERTIME! Zanth's word projected over the sound of the waterfall. T'Ash turned the shower off and stepped from the small room into the steamy bathroom.

Zanth sat on the far side of the open door, as far from water droplets as he could get. *It's Midweekend. Me get furra on Midweekend. With bones.*

"That's right." He'd started the tradition as an inducement to keep Zanth from prowling all night when T'Ash had first finished his Residence. The reward had only worked for a few months.

Crunch. Crunch. Yum.

"How are Danith and Princess?"

FamWoman ag-gra-vated. Me made many beau-ti-ful designs with jewelry. Still not calm. Princess happy.

"I see."

FamWoman feeds Cats in morning. Me here now.

"So you're eating at two places, hmmm? Are you sure you aren't getting a nip or two at the T'Spindle Residence where you have a queen?"

Zanth's gaze slid away from T'Ash's. He laughed.

Furra best. Life is good.

"Very well. Let's go eat."

After dinner T'Ash finished work on the main gauche and its scabbard and set it in his ResidenceDen. Power glowed from it, a piece that looked both beautiful and deadly. He nodded with satisfaction. For once, the item had come close to his perfectly imagined design.

T'Ash descended to the HouseHeart to prepare it for his Passage later. He stood outside the door and braced himself. The inner sanctuary always affected him—as it was meant to. Sometimes it excited, sometimes it soothed, sometimes he even felt an awful greatness hovered near.

It was the only place in all of Celta where he actually felt connected with his ancestors, those who had lived and fought for GreatHouse T'Ash before him. And it was where he was most aware of his duties and responsibilities to T'Ash traditions and his own descendants.

He shivered and placed both palms against the rough wood facing of the meter-thick stone door.

Here were the strongest spellshields, ancient and intricate, with a final layer cast by himself over the years. The spells had protected the chamber during the explosion and the fire. T'Ash had rebuilt around it, slightly changing the alignment of his new Residence to hide it even further.

Though T'Ash had suffered his last Passage at his then-new forge, for this out-of-cycle and critical Passage, he wanted to be surrounded by the essence of his GreatHouse—the HouseHeart.

Taking a deep breath, he spoke the low incantation that would reveal it to him.

The door inched open and a dim red glow brightened into soft yellow flames in the firepit. T'Ash entered.

He'd last been here a few months before, celebrating the annual founding ritual, alone as always. He smiled as he thought that this was the last time he would have to celebrate something alone.

He murmured a Word and the door swung closed behind him.

The chamber was six meters square, and most of the floor was covered with a painted World Tree. As a dedication to his murdered Family, he had laid a mosaic of semiprecious stones over the primitive Rainbow Serpent portion and grouted it with gold.

The Rainbow Serpent snaked up the trunk of the World Tree, imbued with Flair powerlines. On one side of the World Tree was the firepit, never extinguished, on the other, the ritual pool, wide enough and deep enough for T'Ash to bathe in. And in the farthest reaches of the World Tree's twigs stood the altar to the Lord and Lady.

The power of the room enveloped him, pulsing around and through him, a warm balm on his nerves. He closed his eyes and gave himself to the comfort. He did not know how long he stood, but when he opened his lashes once more, he felt renewed. The HouseHeart had given him precious strength and energy. His heart beat in the same rhythm as the small fire crackled, in the same tempo as the pool swirled.

He prepared for the coming night and his Passage, summoning a bedsponge pallet of permamoss and an old workbench that had once been his first altar. He teleported his best, most consecrated tools to the room, as well as the redgold he would use for his new HeartGift of earrings and marriage armbands.

Just as he left the room, he heard the deep reverberating gong of the GreatHouse, with an added note telling of a delivery.

When he reached the ResidenceDen, Zanth was already reclining on Danith's new bedroll, rumbling a deep purr.

Me like. Mine.

"No. It is Danith's bedroll for her mainspace. If you recall, *someone* left the HeartGift necklace in the middle of her bedsponge. Danith won't touch it, and I don't dare. If *someone* wants to remove the HeartGift from her bedsponge, you could have that bedroll, as well as a furra hide post higher than the desk."

Zanth raised his muzzle. *No. Me not like necklace.*

"Your choice. But that bedroll goes. Now."

Zanth sniffed, stood and leisurely stretched, sending his claws and scent into the pad, and stepped off the thing. He lifted his small nose in the air and pranced over to the leg of the desk to use it as a scratching post. *Bed not soft enough.*

T'Ash narrowed his eyes. "True." He closed his eyes to locate his cloak made of the softest llamawoolweave. He smiled. Another gift for Danith containing his emanations. The woman would have to surrender. He whisked the cloak from a closet and onto the pallet, then gently arranged it.

The gong rang again, this time at the entrance gate. T'Ash activated the viz holo. "Greetyou, Heir of the Hollys."

"Greetyou. Merry meet."

"Indeed. You have the vial and the ring?"

Holm nodded. "You the spellblade?"

T'Ash stepped back, and widened the view of the image so Holm could see the forest green enameled scabbard behind him, with the gold design of holly leaves carried onto the hilt of the weapon, and the smooth spiral-incised smoky quartz set in the pommel.

Holm grinned. "Can I 'port there?"

"Come."

With a whoosh of displaced air, Holly joined T'Ash in the ResidenceDen. Holm strode to the main gauche. His hand hesitated over the hilt and he glanced at T'Ash.

T'Ash nodded. "It is attuned to your brother, but you can add a Family blessing and I will engage the circuitry of the spell."

In one swift move Holm pulled the blade from the scabbard, flinching at the Flair. "Very powerful. I can feel the discipline and the protection. Good," he said between gritted teeth. He inhaled deeply and chanted lowly. With a final word, energy snapped through the room and to the weapon.

Gingerly, T'Ash took the main gauche from the sweating Holm. He raised the long dagger straight overhead, tracing a pattern and speaking the last Word. Power coalesced from the air around him, through the blade, down his arm, and into the ground. Unheard vibrations resonated.

He sheathed the thing, placed it on the desk, then turned to Holm.

Holm pushed T'Ash off balance. Slammed him against the wall. Holly's brawny arm pressed against his windpipe, a sharp dagger pricked beneath his jaw.

Holm grinned ferally over the naked blade. Sparks of blue showed in his gray eyes. "Got you."

Eight

❦

T'Ash *struggled and bruised his throat against Holm's arm.*

Holm grinned wider. "You can't beat me. Not now." His voice rasped unnaturally. "I am linked with T'Holly and T'Ivy. We are concerned about your mad venture to experience Passage once more, particularly since you are at the last reserves of your strength."

T'Ash would have sworn Holm's bared-teeth smile swallowed up the whole room, until the man captured his glance. Everything began to slowly spin, somehow matching the strange, whirling flecks in Holm's eyes.

"That I could subdue you so easily shows how sapped your energy and reflexes are. So you will sleep. For a full sun-cycle, twenty-eight septhours. Sleep. Good thing you have a pallet in here."

"Danith—" T'Ash whispered, but only that, he could not think past those odd lights in Holm's eyes.

Zanth yowled. *Me guard My FamMan. Now!*

Darkness engulfed T'Ash.

D*anith spent a rotten night trying to sleep on her too-short divan in her underwear. She awoke late the following* morning. Attempting to grab some clothes from her bedroom, she slammed the door shut mere seconds after opening it. The sensuality in the room had built to explosive levels. A wave of pure lust had instantly rushed through her.

She grumbled to herself. Then she grumbled to Pansy—Princess. And the name change was one more thing to add to her list of all the irritating items caused by T'Ash.

It was Ioho, the last day of the weekend, but tomorrow, Mor, was Discovery Day and she didn't have to work. Four days off in a row—the three weekend days and a paid holiday, quite nice.

Discovery Day was a major holiday because the colonial starships had gone astray after leaving Earth. The three starships of colonists had been desperate to find another habitable planet, and then they'd discovered Celta.

For Danith, getting such a long weekend off work was worth a murmured prayer of thanks.

She bathed, then pulled a few clothes from the cleanser, glad she hadn't transferred them to her closet. Still, she had worn the turquoise onesuit last week and would have preferred something different. Another item to add to T'Ash's account.

Something tinkled and fell on her foot. It was the string of beads and crystal that Zanth had delivered yesterday morning. She closed her eyes and leaned against the tiled bathroom wall, thinking about T'Ash's account. How in the names of the Lady and the Lord was she going to balance T'Ash's account?

He gave her a fortune in jewels and spoke of HeartMates, yet had the most minimal tender words for her. He'd given of his Flair, of his skill at Testing, of his influence with Holly to witness her Testing. He spoke also of desire and HeartGifts, yet revealed nothing of himself save he thought his Residence was ugly. She knew nothing of him except a few details of his past and that he accepted the outrageous idea that they were HeartMates without question. Incredible.

Nothing of him attracted her except the physical—and his craft. Surely that wasn't enough to build any sort of relationship? Let alone jumping immediately into being bonded as a HeartMate to him.

She shook her head. Impossible.

She knew everything about Claif, could anticipate nearly his every action, almost every thought he might consider. That was stability. That was security. Linking herself forever to a enigmatic, intense man who surprised her at every turn would be disturbing.

And just as she had been originally disappointed when she'd believed a seduction spell had imbued the necklace, now she felt equally depressed that T'Ash had not provided a bedroll for her. Of all things, she would have expected T'Ash to be a man of his word.

He had sent a Healer, a supercilious man in apprentice green, who had looked down a hooked nose at her address and efficiently but compassionlessly Healed her bruised muscle and skin. She had no trace of soreness in her shoulder. And the man hadn't mentioned payment, just whisked in, Healed her, and left as fast as his scrawny legs could take him.

The scrybowl pinged in the kitchen. She pushed back her hair and went to answer it. "Here."

"GrandLady Danith D'Mallow?" a middle-aged, professional woman asked in a friendly tone.

"Miz," Danith replied, as she had so often lately.

"I'm afraid not." The woman smiled sympathetically. "Let me introduce myself. I'm Melissa of GrandHouse Balm, clerk of the NobleCouncil for the initiation of new nobles." She glanced down at several papyrus. "Congratulations, you have been elevated to GrandHouse status. Do you wish to keep your Family name? We do have several other GrandHouse names that are available, perhaps Nepeta would suit—"

"It's the weekend—Ioho," Danith said blankly.

GrandMistrys Balm laughed. "Some of us love our jobs. I must admit, it isn't as often as I'd like that we have someone move from common to GrandHouse nobility. I get excited."

Danith couldn't prevent herself from smiling in return. She blinked, trying to process the information. "Ah, yes. I would like to keep my own Family name." She lifted her chin. "It is quite common, but—"

"Very pleasant. Mallow." Balm made a notation with her writestick. "GrandHouse Mallow. Hmmm. Yes."

GrandHouse Mallow! It echoed in Danith's head, started her heart beating faster. A Noble, she! Because of her Flair. She caught her breath, felt tears back up behind her eyes, and glanced around for a softleaf. How proud her parents would have been.

"Mallow. Now. You are designated as Head of your household?"

"I have no other Family."

"D'Mallow then, head of the Mallow GrandHouse." Balm's brown head bent, showing an even part as she ticked off several items and wrote a few words. She shuffled a papyrus or two. "The base NobleGilt for a GrandLady is 80,000 a year."

Danith choked. It was four times what she made. Dizziness struck her. "Excuse me. I . . . I need some tea." With shaking hands she poured water into a mug and placed it on the instanthot. A few seconds later she sank a basklette with her best tea in the cup. She watched as amber streamers spread throughout the hot water and the leaves steeped.

GrandMistrys Balm continued. "I will deposit the first quarter earnings in your bank account immediately come TwinMoonsday morning. Where do you bank?"

"Pennyroyal."

"Hmmm. Very good. I've studied your Testing and agree with T'Ash's conclusion." Her voice held an odd note and Danith looked up at the vized image once more. The woman stared at a fancy certificate with something bordering on awe. "Amazingly detailed Testing. His stones must be calibrated to an extent that I didn't know was possible. . . ." She shot a quizzical look at Danith.

"He is very good with stones, gems, jewels. . . ." Danith flopped a hand in what should have been a smooth gesture but didn't quite make it, she felt so overwhelmed. She pulled the basklette from her mug, added sweet, and gulped.

GrandMistrys Balm's gaze had sharpened, but she merely nodded. "I shall keep that in mind when we have questionable Testing." She tapped the end of her writestick on the desk. "Though it would not do to bother T'Ash for anything less than the most important cases." She made additional notes on a pad. "Now. Animal Healer." She positively beamed at Danith. "I'm delighted. Truly. That such a Flair has resurfaced."

"Animal Healer?" Danith squeaked, looking around desperately for a chair that her tiny kitchen had never held.

"No room for error," Balm said with satisfaction. "I'll set up a double-apprenticeship for you with GrandHouse Heather for Healing and GreatHouse Willow in their animal training branch. With sponsorship by T'Ash, HollyHeir, and Fam Zanthoxyl, only the best will do, of course. The fees will be steep, but under the circumstances, I believe the NobleClass tithe should pay three-quarters. We do want to promote new skills." She smiled encouragement.

Danith could only nod.

"Your apprenticeship should start soon, shall we say next Midweek?"

Danith nodded.

"Very good. Now." GentleLady Balm whisked through some checklists. She peered past Danith and clucked. "We also have several available properties on the GrandHouse level that will be given to you as part of your advancement. Do you want holo information or would you prefer a personal tour?"

Too much. Too fast. Shock quaked her familiar world, and when it finished, her life would be arranged down new and foreign paths.

"I prefer to decide that later," Danith managed.

Balm gave her a questioning look, but nodded, squaring the papyrus sheets together. "That's all for the moment, then. A good morning's work. Congratulations once again, GrandLady D'Mallow. Blessed be." Her image blinked out.

Danith clunked her cup on the counter just before the tea slopped over the rim. She stumbled into her mainspace and onto her much-maligned sofa. She was an Animal Healer. Her apprenticeships would begin Midweek. She was Grand-Lady D'Mallow, to be gifted with an estate and 80,000 gilt a year!

She didn't know how long she huddled in a daze, Princess purring against her, until a cheerful whistling from outside roused her just before some quick raps on the front door. Danith got up, shook the wrinkles from the full sleeves and legs of her onesuit, adjusted wrist and ankle cuffs, and went to the door.

Peeping through the spy-hole she saw Holm Holly grinning at her. She shut her eyes. She didn't know how much more nobility she could take.

He knocked again. "I know you're in there, D'Mallow." His voice lilted and she shut her eyes, feeling a load of responsibility drop onto her shoulders with the title, and she was a GrandHouse of one!

"I come to make T'Ash's apologies." Holly still sounded too cheerful; what would make a man that lighthearted? She didn't know, not a man like Holly, but she had the odd feeling that T'Ash would know, and the gloomier feeling that now she was a noble, she would be finding out.

"T'Ash is indisposed," Holly said.

Unbelievable. She jerked the door open.

"I knew that would make you open the door." His look was long, lingering, and approving. "Just the right woman for my friend." He beamed. "He needs someone of a more optimistic nature. And an uncommon lady of common background elevated to the nobility will understand his own downfall and victory."

She didn't think so, and knew she'd have to find out more about T'Ash in self-defense. "Indisposed?"

Holly brushed past her and strolled into her small rooms. "Be at ease. Zanth and the T'Ash Residence are guarding him. T'Ash was on the receiving end of a strong arm last evening. He's out for a sun-cycle."

"Two fights in a day?" She was incredulous.

Holly frowned. "I missed the fight. This last was a matter of—ah—forceful persuasion. Not a bit of struggle. And once upon a time two fights a day would have been an easy day for T'Ash."

When Holly turned, his gray gaze was straight and serious. "He traced his Family's murderers, you know. Vengeance isn't a light thing for a man, especially not a man like T'Ash." Holly slid back into his more cheerful mood. "But he has become positively staid of late. No fighting at all. Until you."

She flinched.

His eyes went back to studying her home. "Very nice. I like this. You obviously will do well by T'Ash Residence. In fact, I like this place better than my own, and I'm stuck with T'Holly Residence. Can hardly change the angle of a chair."

He noted the many coils of jewelry and grinned. "T'Ash being a little pushy, eh?" Holly walked to a table where the various necklaces lay and touched a ruby pendant, a string of twisted glisten interspersed with amber beads. "But you must admit, he does fabulous work. You'll have to forgive him for his inept courting. He hasn't had a real Family since he was six. And the Ashes ran to males even then. He had a father and two brothers, but only one female—his mother. I've tried—" Holly shrugged. "But he hasn't been interested, until you."

Danith felt more and more entangled in a silken steel web.

Holly stood, hands on hips, dominating the room, just like every noble male she had ever met. A sudden smile lit his face. He clapped his hands and it echoed like thunder. "Allow me."

An instant later a tall, intricately carved, and striking redwood chest with several drawers stood in the place of her missing scry table. The piece was antique and valuable.

Holly looked vastly pleased. "My gift to you, D'Mallow, upon your ascension to the nobility. A jewelry chest, large enough to house all the baubles T'Ash has presented you so far."

Danith snapped her open mouth shut, then struggled for words. "I cannot accept—"

"Of course you can. The chest was in storage. It's too damn delicate and attractive to mix with the furniture of T'Holly Residence. Besides," he added with a winning smile, "it is customary to give gifts to the head of a new noble House, to pave the way for alliance, if nothing else."

"How did you know I've been named D-D'Mallow," she stumbled over her new title.

"The noble Houses get notification of these things. Be

glad no one from journalism, BindWeed House, or Grace-House Daisy, is here yet. A commoner jumping two classes is news."

Danith shuddered. She certainly hadn't considered all of the ramifications of her sudden change of fortune. She needed to viz her friends, soon.

Holly sifted some bloodstone worry beads through his elegant fingers. "Actually, I'm fulfilling a few errands on behalf of my friend T'Ash. Is there any outstanding commission?"

She frowned. "He promised me a small bedsponge."

"Ah, that's why he had the pallet in his ResidenceDen. Well, he is occupying it himself, I'm afraid. What's wrong with your bedsponge?"

She gestured to the closed bedroom door a few feet away.

Curiosity passed over his face and he went to it, resting his hand on the knob. "May I?"

"Yes, of course."

He opened the door. Danith felt a shock of intense sexuality from where she stood and her body reacted. She backed to the farthest corner of the mainspace, considered going into the front grassyard.

Holly turned to her with raised eyebrows. "So?"

"In the middle of the bed. The necklace. Supposedly a HeartGift."

He disappeared into her bedroom. "Hmmm. I think I see it. It has a roseamber heart? With a flaw in the shape of crossed swords? It's difficult to see. . . ."

Danith raised her voice. "Do you think you could take charge of it?" A tendril of hope curled through her. Maybe she could get her bedroom back. Having her innermost sanctuary off limits added to her stress.

Holly popped his head through the open door. "I don't think I'd better touch it. T'Ash is sure to be unhappy with me as it is. If I retrieve his HeartGift from his lady's bedroom—" He shrugged. "There could be a real fight. And as much as I enjoy fighting, not with T'Ash. He has a tendency to take things too seriously, not to mention the odd time or two he went berser—" He snapped his mouth shut.

Danith chewed her lip, wondering how she could get her

bedroom back. She sighed at Holly's refusal. "Very well. Could you bring me some clothes please, HollyHeir?"

"Call me Holm. My pleasure," he said, back in the bedroom. A few short minutes later he had a nice selection of her clothes neatly stacked on her settee.

"Underwear?" he asked.

Heat flushed her face. "Third drawer of the bureau."

Holly patted her on her shoulder. "Consider me a brother. T'Ash does—did." He brought back half the contents of her drawer. "I like the bold colors but think you should invest in something a little more sexy than commoncloth cotton for T'Ash."

Danith choked.

"I've always found merchandise from the shop Queen of the East extremely fetching."

She stared at him in disbelief.

A rustle and clink.

Holly spun, whipping his blaser from its holster. Princess ambled in the open front door, bedecked, as was usual now, in one set of ruby beads, three silver chains, a heavier golden one with an amber pendant, and her diamond earclip.

He stared at her in apparent awe. "Now, that is one beautiful cat."

Danith rolled her eyes.

"I'll bet Zanth is positively eaten up with jealousy."

Holly stooped down and trilled his tongue in a mock purr. Princess jingled to him and allowed him to pet her.

He glanced up at Danith. "We Hollys breed hunting cats, you know. Once you have established yourself, give me a call. We'd like to put you on a retainer as our Animal Healer. Also, I believe you could be of great help in determining the best genetic strains to breed for. A Healer has access to so much information at a DNA level, that your insight would be very useful."

Danith managed a nod.

With one last pat to Princess's head, he stood. "I'll arrange for delivery of a small bedroll. T'Ash had his covered with llamawoolweave, so it will include that. It has been a pleasure, D'Mallow." He held out his hand.

She put her own in his, and he raised it to his lips and kissed the back. It was the first time that had ever happened to her, and Danith suppressed a disappointment that it hadn't been T'Ash who had made the gesture.

"Merry meet," Holly said.

"And merry part."

"And merry meet again. Until later, D'Mallow." He bowed and left, closing the front door behind him.

Danith stared around her. Her home, even her cat, had changed in three days. It staggered her. After a while she went to a tiny closet and unfolded a pretty pale green and shot-silver scarf, placing it over the top of the jewelry chest.

Princess had sniffed the curving, carved legs and wound herself through them. Now she sat looking up at the top.

"No," Danith said firmly. "You can't jump on top of it. You will never make it with the weight of all your jewelry."

Princess mewed a little pleadingly.

"No. You will land on the scarf and go skidding off the cabinet. Then you will be embarrassed and have to pretend you didn't do something foolish. Besides, I'm going to put the scrybowl on top of it. You know how you hate the scrybowl." Princess—when she was Pansy—had dumped the bowl over on herself no less than four times.

Danith hurried to the kitchen, returning to the mainspace with her scrybowl. It was much larger and heavier than the small china bowl it replaced, but it also felt incredibly comforting since it contained her first use of Flair.

Her fingers automatically traced the cloisonne lines. When she set it up and stood back, she found the pale leaves on the bowl matched the scarf. As the creamy yellow background matched her walls. A scarf she had purchased matched a bowl T'Ash had made. It was frightening.

Again and again she ran her hands over the pattern of the bowl, imbuing it with her own lifeforce, hopefully banishing T'Ash's. Hoping they didn't meld instead.

She should call her friends but didn't know what to say. Despite everything, she wasn't sure of her status. What would happen to all her common friends if she became noble? The Clovers were very important to her. She must keep them in her life. She would need the support of friends. She shivered. Her old life was looking better all the time.

A rumbling came against his chest. *T'Ash knew it was* Zanth's heavy purr. He opened his eyes.

You awake. Me guarded. All fine. Feel good?

T'Ash stretched. He felt great. His energy levels had mostly replenished, no doubt helped on a little by Holm, T'Holly and T'Ivy, damn their hides. He moved carefully, but no hint of hangover, stiffness, or weariness bothered him. He took stock, inside and out. There was a delicate touch that smoothed the way for his healing and strength— D'Holly. She had a light hand with Flair, as light as Danith's would be.

Danith. T'Ash smiled and stretched more, testing his strength. Not complete, but sufficient enough for the Passage. He pushed dread from his mind, and concentrated on the unfamiliar mellowness of his mood. With the dregs of his weariness, his depression had eased, and he almost recaptured the sense of triumph he'd experienced when he'd first realized he'd meet his HeartMate. Hope fizzed through his veins.

Hungry! Skipped breakfast.

"Both of them? Here and at Danith's?"

No lunch, either. No snack. Even sewer rat sounds tasty.

T'Ash shuddered. He sat up and the llamawoolweave cloak slid onto the floor. When he picked it up, his fingers caressed its soft texture, as soft as Princess's fur.

Danith. He'd slept on the bedroll he'd purchased for her. He had broken a promise to her, inadvertently, but she didn't trust him in the first place. To break a promise, no matter how small, would only deepen her distrust. Damn!

"Holly!" he roared.

A full-sized holo blinked on. "Merry meet, T'Ash. I hope you feel well. No need to worry about anything—"

"Stop."

The prerecorded holospell froze. T'Ash narrowed his eyes. Despite Holm's usual lilting tones, the image looked a little strained around the mouth, Holly's expression a trifle tense.

Zanth sniffed. It was barely a sound. *Listen to Holly. Good man.*

T'Ash turned and glared at his Fam.

Zanth lifted a paw and began to lick it.

T'Ash turned back to the holo. "Go."

"—I set major temporary spellshields to reinforce the regular ones on your Residence. It can't be breached. I also dropped by D'Mallow's—"

"D'Mallow's? Cave of the Dark Goddess. D'Mallow."

"—and told her you were indisposed."

"Meddler. Strolled over to make time with my woman while I was asleep."

"—and ordered a bedroll for her. I *didn't* retrieve the HeartGift from her bedroom. Nice piece, though, what I could see of it. She looks a little frazzled. Try not to push, T'Ash."

Holm's gray eyes seemed to focus on T'Ash. "I don't think a Passage will bring what you want, but also don't think you'll heed me, either." The holo man shrugged. "Take care. The vial is on your desk. I left your old ring with D'Mallow. Slipped it in a bowl of stones. Her place is beginning to feel a bit like you—"

"Good."

"—If she finds the ring, and focuses on it, she'll learn a lot, won't she?"

"Oh, Lord and Lady, too much."

"But every little bit helps. My brother, Tinne, is restless—"

T'Ash snorted.

"—and Mamá won't be able to keep him here longer than a septhour or two after dinner. He'll be by then for his main gauche. T'Holly sends his regards. Merry meet again." The holo vanished.

Time for food. Zanth didn't wait for T'Ash, rudely opening the door with a FamWord and loping to the small room they used for dining.

When T'Ash entered the room, Zanth was licking his whiskers, then pressing a lever for a second helping.

T'Ash extended his senses—his cook had not been in that

day, Ioho, but had left several meals, both warm and cold, in the no-time pantry. T'Ash reviewed their images and chose a thick bifuth steak, potatoes, a selection of green vegetables, and a large carafe of willem juice. It would prime him for the Passage.

Dessert. I deserve dessert.

"What do you want?"

Mousse. Cocoa mousse. Cook made lots. Too much for just you.

T'Ash frowned. There was no such thing as too much cocoa. He stockpiled it like jewels. It was a luxury that both he and Zanth shared.

Know something.

Zanth's sly tone alerted T'Ash. He raised his brows.

Want big portion of mousse. Bigger than My head.

"You shouldn't ever eat things bigger than your head."

Mousse fluff.

"True."

Know FamWoman has lots of cocoa.

"Does she now?"

Zanth nodded and licked his chops. *Bars and drops and covered nuts and fruit, cocoadrink.*

T'Ash snapped his fingers, and a large plate of soft cocoa mousse appeared. Zanth plowed into it.

T'Ash sat and summoned his own dinner, then worked his way through it without tasting, planning for the Passage and muttering spells to brace and protect himself.

As he slipped the last spoonful of cocoa mousse into his mouth and let the delicious treat melt on his tongue, Zanth jumped on the table.

T'Ash eyed him.

Me not on table when you eating. You done.

"It's a rule."

Me know rule. You done. When you do Passage?

"In about a septhour."

Me go hunt. Be back by then. You swing wild when Passage.

"Thank you for returning."

Zanth lashed his tail. *Don't like. You leave more mousse for Me.*

"I will."

Good. Life is good. You re-mem-ber.
"I won't die."
Promise?
"If I die, the T'Ash Residence is yours."
Don't want by Self. Too big. FamWoman will be nice here.
"I agree."
Even Princess.
"Yes."
Cat has no taste. Smug in his superiority, Zanth left.

*B*reathing deeply, T'Ash lay naked on his back, fitting into the trunk pattern of the Rainbow Serpent and World Tree in the HouseHeart. The mosaic floor beneath him was as warm as his body, the room was lit by a faint yellow glow. He had cast the greatest of circles, purified himself, honored the Lord and Lady. Now it was time.

He sucked the mixture from the vial. It tasted both bitter and sweet. A tang sank into his tongue that he knew was his own taste. A flavor of ripe apples—Danith's flavor—lingered.

Power whipped through him, stripping all the control he had built over years away in atoms, scattering it to the four directions, filling him with emotions, memories, and hot desire. His body roused.

He rested on the cool earth, felt the softest breath of air, the tiniest droplet from the fountain, the most minute flicker of heat of the fire.

Fire! Fire and fire and fire. Engulfed, enveloped by fire. Fire that seared the screams from him before he could voice them. Fire that exploded through him. Fire that ate his Residence. And his Family.

He jerked into a protective curl, all muscles tense. How could he have forgotten? Even the smallest detail? He remembered all, all. He cried and screamed.

His memories imploded inside him. His power and Flair spiraled wide.

A rough, wet tongue against his equally wet cheeks. Zanth.

A cold, snow-laden swirling breeze in a gray day. The Residence, his ancestors.

A small, gentle hand stroking his face. Danith.

Danith.

His years in Downwind flew at him in stunning, dreadful images. Death, decay, filth. His second passage—gleeful, wild fighting beside Holly. Plunging his aroused body in willing, wanton women. Scents of blood and fear and victory.

The vengeance stalk flashed, more fighting. Rage unleashed until he berserked. The cold FirstFamilies Guildhall. Judging eyes. Pride. Anger. Triumph.

His last Passage—the sexual hunger, his Flair firmly fixed, chained to bedrock, channeled. Ah, Lord, the desire. He'd seen his HeartMate in one sparkling instant, felt her generosity and strength and Flair. And with trembling fingers had fashioned a HeartGift Necklace.

Danith. Danith. Danith.

His body writhed with passion. He needed her. He *reached* for her with all his might.

*S*omething called to her. The Necklace. Slowly her wits dissolved under the pressure of molten sensuality battering at her mental shields.

She rose as if sleepwalking and glided to the bedroom door. She flung it open. A wall of sexuality struck her, penetrated her, so real that it felt like large, strong hands drew her to the bedsponge.

She fell to her bed, her fingers claiming the necklace, clutching it between her breasts. Her vision misted until she could barely see. He was in shadow, but she knew his powerful body, his intense gaze. T'Ash.

Not Claif. Never Claif. Now she knew she could never go to Claif Clover. Only T'Ash. For an instant she wailed, then the hot desire poured through her again, banishing all thought, all feeling except passion. All desire except for learning his body, letting him learn hers.

T'Ash lowered himself to lie beside her, and the air in the room heated with his presence and his scent—hot steel and hard man. She had trouble breathing. Her throat dried with the searing desire pulsing through her blood. Her breasts swelled, their crests tightening in aching passion. Damp heat flooded her womanflesh, and she waited for his touch, her hips tilting, waited for her man, the one and only for her for the rest of her existence.

His fingertips feathered over her body and she whimpered. They weren't the calloused hands as she remembered, but they were T'Ash. He teased her with the lightness of his touch, until she hungered for his hands on her body, firm and demanding.

He pulled her atop him, and his big body encompassed her. His torso supported her body and arms, his legs, slightly spread, were solid and muscular under hers. He was everything.

Her blood beat in her ears like a hammer on an anvil, and she wanted him more than she had wanted anything in her life. She slithered down his slightly haired body until his sex touched that most needy part of her.

Now big hands curved around her hips, and with a powerful surge, he joined them. She thought she screamed with pleasure she'd never felt before, pleasure built of emotion as well as passion, but the sound never reached her ears.

She trembled, too shaken at all the tumultuous feelings inside her to move. She wanted only this man. She needed the touch of only his body. She craved the all-encompassing climax that only he could give her.

Waves of intense, pulsing sensation flowed through her until they built to unbearable heights, and whirled her tumbling into an undertow of ecstasy that went on and on and on.

He plunged into her and his power swept her away once more. She felt the throbbing of his shaft, and it was the most exquisite sensation she'd ever had.

His body arched in explosive release.

Before his breathing could even, before he lost himself once more in resurging desire, he jerked to his feet and dashed the sweat from his eyes, stumbled over to the fountain and plunged into the water, then staggered out of the pool.

With a whisk of a Word he dried himself and walked unsteadily to his old workbench. Passion filled him once more, burning his blood, pounding through him. And he mastered it, as he had once mastered Flair, and used them both, now.

Jaw clenched, he designed and cut. Shaped and hammered. Sculpted and engraved. Now and again he had to pause, to concentrate on cooling his blood, ignoring his erect flesh, conquering his lust. Then he continued.

As he worked, he chanted.

He was T'Ash. T'Ash. T'ASH!

Of the GreatHouse T'Ash. Of the Thirteen GreatHouses. Of the twenty-five FirstFamilies. Of T'Ash's Phoenix. A noble son of a noble house. Honorable. Strong. Flaired. Determined on his course. He *would* have his HeartMate.

Everything he ever was and everything he hoped he could be, he sent into the earrings and the marriage armbands.

He *reached* once more for Danith. And found her. Her soft body clung to his own, her full, round breasts against his chest, the width of her curved hips cradled his manhood.

With control he didn't know he had, he ignored both his throbbing passion and hers. He demanded her essence, and he found it. Love. Generosity. Flair. Strength.

Keeping her close, eyes barely seeing, fingers working by instinct, he melded their vibrations together into redgold knotted earrings and four redgold marriage armbands.

And when he finished, he yelled in triumph, holding the earrings and her marriage bands in his hands, his own arm bracelets around his wrists. He raised his arms and power, the power of the room, the power of his ancestors, the power of the Lord and Lady flowed through him and into the jewelry.

He staggered to the soft permamoss pallet and collapsed. Too exhausted to fight the continuing relentless psychic winds of Passage, he was sucked down. Buffeted by winds of destiny, he saw two different fates unroll before him.

Nine

☙

His Passage opened two futures before him. In one prospect Danith laughed with him, surrounded by children and animals. Four children, the largest Family ever for the Ash, two girls and two boys. They romped in the PlayRoom, which now looked both comfortable and gracious. The children's auras were strong and healthy, the continuation of the GreatHouse Ash assured.

Danith had matured into a confident, joyful woman, all the qualities he prized about her in full bloom. Love encompassed him, and when he met Danith's eyes, he knew they shared a HeartMate marriage that could never be equaled. She looked at him with love and passion. And he knew, if he wished, she would open her innermost soul to him, as well as her lovely body.

He strove to grasp that future. But it came no closer.

He tried to ignore the other destiny. In it his Residence towered gray and secluded in the sleet of a winter day, only one small light flickering in a massive window, all the others black with darkness. His body ached with old and new wounds, barren solitude leached all contentment from his being, and he brooded on the future, knowing he'd lost his HeartMate forever.

With all his might he hurled himself at the warmth, but fell, finally, onto a lonely, stone road, bruising his body and soul.

The earrings rolled out of his hand.

"*Danith! Lady and Lord, help. Danith, answer me.* What's wrong?"

The words stabbed her head, dragged her sweating and weak from a sluggish doze.

Her fingers hurt. Slowly she disentangled them from the chain and stones of a necklace. Her heart lurched. The Necklace.

She shuddered. Had she stroked her body with the piece? How decadent, too decadent. She couldn't face that. She shoved the thing into Mitchella's hands.

"Here," Danith croaked.

Mitchella fumbled at it. "Thank the Lady and Lord you're all right. What is it?"

Danith struggled to sit up, and saw the soft evening rays of Bel painting her bedroom. "Necklace."

"By Avalon, it's huge. And beautiful." Mitchella squinted. "How unusual. A roseamber heart with a flaw that looks like a mother and child."

Danith had seen entwined lovers in the flaw. She pushed her hair away from her face. It was as damp as her perspiring hands. Ugh.

"Put it away," she said.

"In that new jewelry cabinet you have? Where did that come from? Danith, I saw in the evening newsheet that you're a noble now. What is going on?"

Danith sank her head in her hands. "There's a box on the table in the back grassyard. Can you put the necklace in there please, and in your pursenal, and take it away?"

Mitchella started. "Me? A necklace like this, you must be—"

"Please, Mitchella? It's magic. Powerful magic. And it—affects—me. You don't feel anything, do you?" Danith finally looked at her friend.

Concern glowed in Mitchella's eyes. "No. I have trouble

seeing it, which is beyond odd, but it doesn't seem bespelled to me."

Danith laughed, a rusty, unamused sound. "Please, put it away."

Mitchella nodded and left the room. Danith rose from her bedsponge and gasped as aches that she shouldn't have twinged. She hobbled into the bathroom and took a short, scalding shower.

After wrapping herself in a commoncloth robe, she found Mitchella in the mainspace, pulling out drawers and gaping at the multitude of jewelry in them.

"It's so good to have you here."

Mitchella flushed an unbecoming red and took a couple of quick steps back. "I was just curious—"

Danith blinked at her friend's behavior. "Of course you were. Anyone would be. Did you see everything?"

Mitchella's smile flashed and faded. "I think so. Except the jewelry on Pansy."

"Princess," Danith corrected.

Mitchella stared at her. "Princess? You've changed the name of your cat, too?"

"*I* didn't." The last few days rolled over her like an inexorable Wheel of Fortune. She crossed to her divan and sat. Her head started pounding. She dropped it into her hands.

"Danith?"

"Lord and Lady," Danith said softly.

Mitchella came over and put an arm around her. "What's wrong?"

"Everything. You can't believe it!" She started talking slowly at first, then the words came faster and faster, tumbling from her. Mitchella couldn't even get a word in edgewise and sat staring at her with her mouth in a round *O*.

Danith had just finished telling of her visit to T'Ash and the Testing, when her scrybowl pinged.

She stared at it. She didn't want to answer.

It pinged again.

"Are you going to take the call?"

Danith looked at her friend. "Everything has happened too rapidly. It's all too much."

Mitchella raised her red eyebrows and went to the scry-bowl. "Here."

"Mitchella, there you are. Thank the Lord and Lady! You must come at once—"

"Aunt Pratty, I can't. Danith needs—"

"But you must! It's Trif—"

"Trif?"

"Trif?" Danith asked. "Is there anything I can do to help?" She walked over to the bowl.

"Danith. Oh. I didn't mean to bother you."

"Not at all." Danith forced a smile beyond her headache.

Pratty Clover's smile was as strained as Danith's. "I just need to borrow Mitchella. Trif decided to roam the streets tonight, and everyone knows gangs will be out—Downwind and Noble. I told her she can't, but she doesn't listen to me anymore, does she? But maybe she'll listen to Mitchella. . . ."

"Are you sure you don't want—wouldn't like me to come, also?" Danith asked, her heart sinking. Pratty had always welcomed her.

"No. No. I'm sure you have plans. Ah, plans that don't include us. But, Mitchella—"

"She'll be right there," Danith said, and ended the scryspell.

"I can stay," Mitchella said.

Danith shook her head. "It isn't necessary. And I'm getting a headache; I think I'll try to nap."

Mitchella looked worried. "All right. But you are coming to our Discovery Day party tonight, aren't you?"

"Of course."

"And the Ritual and picnic tomorrow at Uncle Pink's?"

"Yes."

Mitchella took both Danith's hands and kissed her on the cheek. "Good. Do you feel all right?"

"I'll be fine."

"Fare well."

"And you."

"Till tonight." Waving a graceful hand, Mitchella left.

Danith refused to feel. Too many emotions battered at her.

After feeding Princess, Danith stood on the threshold of the shadowy bedroom. Dusk had claimed it. She went to the two small, high windows and, standing tiptoe, opened them. Then she smoothed out the cover, plumped up her pillows, settled herself, and opened the gates to all that threatened.

Rejection. Always rejection. Pratty Clover was distancing herself, and Trif, from Danith. Since Danith had been welcomed by the Family, it hurt all the more.

Tears trickled down her cheeks. Her heart ached, as if she had been scoured hollow by the passion forced on her by T'Ash.

A lick of anger ignited. T'Ash—she'd felt his touch, his mental seduction. Why had she expected more of him than initiating a tawdry affair with telepathic passion? Why had she started to believe him when he nattered of HeartMates and HeartGifts, instead of following her common sense and knowing that she would never be his match, that he simply played games with her?

Anger at his loathsome act, at all the changes in her life that had been initiated by him, mixed with the hurt of rejection. She couldn't fight for what she wanted when she was in the Saille House of Orphans; she had to bow her head and accept that couples preferred other children to her. She couldn't fight Timkin, who, glowing with happiness, told her of his new life and new love.

But she could fight for this new life, a life shaped by her. And she could fight to keep her good friends.

Mental seduction, intrusion on a person's thoughts. Now that was a violation of the most basic laws of privacy, of individuality. It was forbidden, particularly to the powerful FirstFamilies. T'Ash had crossed the line this time, and she would nail him.

The air around her heated with her anger. A little, high-pitched steaming whistle escaped her clenched teeth at the thought of such betrayal. Timkin's dismissal of her was nothing next to this looming hurt of being deliberately overpowered and mentally seduced by T'Ash.

A great bubble trapped inside her burst. She found herself flung, whirling through space in an instant.

She landed in T'Ash's ResidenceDen.

One moment she was on her bedsponge, the next she was in the Den of T'Ash Residence, trembling with rage.

T'Ash jumped back. The black silkeen robe draped around him flapped. The drink in his brandy snifter sloshed, releasing potent fumes.

"You!" she screamed. "You *beast!* Getting in my head, having mental sex. That is everything despicable."

He paled. He looked exhausted. It infuriated her more. They had certainly spent themselves. In sex. "I hate you. Don't you ever, ever, come near me again. Physically or mentally. And you will hear about this, you GreatSlime, I'll call the guards myself!"

He grabbed her threatening fist. "Danith, Tinne Holly is on his way to this room."

She jerked from him, slanted his open robe a glance of contempt. "You like boys, too?"

"Danith—" His mouth thinned into a white line. He found her hand again, held it.

"Keep your hands off me!"

He dropped her hand.

There was a polite knock on the door.

"I go. But you will pay, I promise you."

"Go, how? Do you plan to 'port out?"

For the first time rage receded enough for a little logic. She looked wildly around the room.

"This is a ResidenceDen. There is only one door to the room," he said steadily, tying his robe around him, and fingercombing his hair. "You are overwrought—"

She hissed hatred at him.

He flinched. "We must talk. But not now. Look at yourself. You're not presentable." His eyes flickered even more intensely than usual. She ignored it, but glanced down at herself. She wore a thin commoncloth robe. She suspected he knew she was naked beneath it.

"How could you?" Angry tears started down her face, infuriating her further. She loathed the apparent weakness and lifted her chin. She wasn't weak, and if he took her tears for frailty, he'd learn better soon enough.

"GreatLord T'Ash?" A young man called from outside the door.

T'Ash held out a hand to her. "Let me 'port—"

"No. You keep your filthy mental fingers off me."

"Wait, Tinne." T'Ash raised his voice. Then he frowned and a couple of claps echoed.

Danith jumped back as a softfleece trous and shirt crumpled onto her bare feet from thin air.

T'Ash walked carefully past her. When she heard a scraping noise, she turned. He was unfolding an ugly, ornate screen and putting it around a chair in the farthest corner of the octagonal room. "Please?" He inclined his head.

More rapping at the door, sounds of impatient pacing.

With dignity, Danith scooped up the clothes and marched behind the screen. She muffled a curse when she found they were her size.

T'Ash opened the door.

"Merry meet!" The young man sounded thrilled to be here.

Danith flung her robe off and pulled the clothes on.

T'Ash's voice rumbled. "I have your main gauche. There, on the desk, please take it and go."

"GreatLord? Is something amiss?"

Danith shoved the screen aside and strode to the door.

T'Ash blocked it.

She tossed her head. "You get away from that door. Now."

"We need to talk."

"No and no and no. No more talk. No more scrying. No more visits. No more jewels! You get out of my life and keep out. I don't want you anywhere near me."

"Danith—"

"Get away from that door. You are in deep trouble as it is. Forced telepathy carries heavy punishment. Even a common woman like I am knows that."

"I called you and you came. My lady—"

She stomped her foot. It made no noise on the thick Chinju rugs. "You seduced me. I had no choice. *No choice.* Open the door."

"I had no choice, either—"

She whirled to the white-faced boy watching. She pointed to T'Ash. "I cry harm. Extreme harm done to me by this GreatLord. Witness this—"

T'Ash stepped from the door. A muscle in his jaw

worked. "You are too crazed to talk rationally. Go, then. But know this." He bent a heated look on her, but it didn't faze her. He turned the cold blue gaze on the young Holly. "I broke no law. Implied or written. Violated no Laws of Conduct for FirstFamilies. I—"

Danith wordlessly screeched her fury and grabbed the doorknob, jerking open the heavy door and stalking out. She hardly noticed the cool oak flooring under her bare feet. "Never again!" she shouted. "Do you hear me? Never contact me again."

T'Ash felt the blood drain from him as he heard her angry words and the quick pattering of her feet down the corridor. He could trap her inside the Residence, but it would solve nothing.

The bang of the main door came a minute later.

"Oh, Lord and Lady!"

T'Ash turned at Tinne's epithet, to see the young man quickly slipping the main gauche on his sword belt, settling the belt on his hips and buckling it. Tinne looked at him. "GreatLord, I was followed from my home by rivals of the Hollys. There are more than six young men my age, all armed, and they wait for me outside your gates."

T'Ash slammed his palm on the holo crystal. It showed the front gate swinging open, then shut behind Danith. A swarm of youths engulfed her.

A cry wrenched from his lips. How could he have forgotten?

She was a woman surrounded by blasers.

T'Ash pulled on leather trous and vest. His finest sword and blaser flew to his hands.

He said a Word and a grid appeared on the hologram, delineating the exact square where he wanted to teleport. He 'ported to outside his gate, dragging Tinne Holly with him. The street was empty, but raucous cries came from a few blocks away, in the direction of Downwind. At that moment T'Ash knew this would be one of those years where clashes between the gangs of Downwind and Noble youths would mar Discovery Day. He swore under his breath; FirstFamilies Rituals should have addressed this issue more.

Tinne ran toward the young voices, his aura flashing bril-

liant white as his second Passage threatened to overcome
him. Deathduels, T'Ash remembered. He shuddered. He had
to get Danith away.

T'Ash overtook Tinne and ran past him. A wild shriek
came from his right. Zanth.

We go. We fight. Downwind ferals. Noble stups.

"The gang has Danith."

WHO?

"Who, Holly?" called T'Ash over his shoulder.

The young man grimaced. "Whitey Hawthorn. He can't
ever keep up with me, and T'Hawthorn is envious of
T'Holly's influence—"

T'Ash cut him off with a wave. "Purple and white, Zanth.
Look for purple and white. Find her. Give me an image, and
I'll 'port."

The Fam sprang forward, lengthening his stride, stretching out his body in full as he ran. His muscular hindquarters
bunched with effort. He disappeared in seconds.

T'Ash ran, aware of Tinne behind him, also aware of his
fading strength. He had undergone Passage this night, and
used most of his reserves of Flair in fashioning a new Heart-
Gift and marriage armbands.

Instead of being able to weld a golden net of protection
and send it to cover her, he could only mutter prayers with
each pounding stride.

As the minutes stretched out, he fought fear that would
spark his berserker nature.

Zanth's triumphant cry!

Sounds of human pain.

A distorted image from Zanth's point of view.

T'Ash stopped, sucked in air, 'ported.

Into the middle of a crowd of young men.

He pulled his blaser, thumbed it on stun and whirled in a
circle. The youths screamed and toppled into heaps.

Silkeen gleamed in the nightpole light. Zanth jumped on
the teenagers, prodding them.

Scuffling noises from about a block away.

A cry of pain. Swearing.

A slap.

A whimper, female.

"Danith!" Finally able to see the shadowy figures, T'Ash pursued a pack of raggedly dressed young men who threaded through the streets, then took to alleys.

He knew this area, it bordered on Downwind. He knew it all too well. He 'ported to behind the young men, caught them in an alley with a low wall at the end.

When they faced him, his swordblade rippled silver.

"Lord and Lady," one breathed.

T'Ash's teeth bared in a fighting grin. His sword point made small circles in the air, challenging them.

"Come to me," he crooned. "Who wants to fight T'Ash?"

"T'Ash!" A large boy let go of a squirming bundle. Then fell as one delicate, bare foot swept his legs from under him.

Another youth jumped to the two.

T'Ash and Zanth snarled together.

"Touch her and you die."

The teenagers froze. One stepped back and held up his hands. He jerked his gaze to his other two cohorts. "Is T'Ash, recognize voice. Downwinders know Zanth."

The boy on the ground crawled away from Danith.

The ringleader licked his lips. "Ah, T'Ash. A pretty lady. Took from stupid nobles. Ransom?"

"Don't pay for my lady. Kill for her."

"I go," the leader said, hands still high. He glanced at the end of the alley and saw Zanth crouched on the wall. The boy sidled carefully past T'Ash.

"Me, too."

"Me, too."

Some boys vaulted the wall, escaping the swipe of Zanth's claws, but the Fam chased after them. Others slid along the walls, trying to blend with the dark shadows, slipping past the shining steel sword. T'Ash pivoted to keep them in sight, then watched as they took to their heels and ran back to their Downwind holes.

Sounds of explosions peppered the night air. Fireworks, both mechanical and magical. Discovery Day celebrations had begun. T'Ash flinched as he saw red flare in the direction they came. The holiday was instants old, and the first fire ate at the city.

Danith sat in the cobblestoned alley, rubbing her bruised

feet, wondering what to say to her savior. She should have felt gratitude. Perhaps it was there, under the great relief and the festering resentment. She shivered with cold and reaction, all too aware that she only wore the softfleece trous and shirt, both of which had torn in places. There was a rip in her left sleeve above her elbow, and one near her right knee.

T'Ash sheathed his wicked blade with a rasp and walked over to her. She didn't like him towering over her. Before his hand reached her arm to help her up, she scrambled to her feet.

"My lady."

She sighed. Hiccuped. Hoped that he wouldn't see the tracks of tears from her fear and anger on her face. "Just Miz," she reminded in a quiet voice.

"No. My lady. My Danith. You all right?" He reached out as if to run his hands down her body to assure she was unharmed.

She stepped back. The last thing in the world she wanted was his hands on her body. She feared what feelings they would stir in her. Now time had passed, she admitted to herself that she had responded wildly to his mental touch. Lady and Lord knew what would happen if the mental became physical.

And he still wasn't what her sensible mind wanted. She tried to smile and managed to quirk a corner of her mouth. "I'm a bit bruised but otherwise fine. I got caught between two rowdy bunches of boys, is all." She shivered. "They were surprised to see me. They weren't ready to quit roaming the streets, and I don't think any of them exactly knew what they were going to do with me."

His eyes narrowed as he examined her slowly up and down. "Sure you don't need a Healer?"

Danith thought of the supercilious man who had treated her before and didn't want a repeat of the experience. "No, thank you."

"I follow your wish." His voice was just tender enough to make her weak, make her want to walk into arms she was sure would close strong and hard around her. She glanced at his face, but it didn't seem as if he expected the words of gratitude that she couldn't give him. She adjusted the clothes twisted around her.

"My fault," he said with self-directed anger. "My fault you're bruised. I will—"

"No." It was her turn to deny his words. She straightened her spine. "I was the one who 'ported to your home on a wave of anger. I left your Residence without thought of the consequences, again in anger. My mistakes, not yours. I thank you for your help." There, she'd gotten her tongue around the words.

He met her gaze steadily. "I'll protect you. You trust me for that? To get us home safely?"

Evading the intensity in his eyes and his Downwind short-speech was impossible for Danith. And she literally felt the emotional waves of his sincerity. He'd said he'd kill for her, and abruptly she knew it was the simple truth. She shivered, then jerked her head in a nod.

He glanced up the alley. The night was alive with noise. Strident yells of roving men—nobles and Downwind bands—small explosions of personal fireworks, the clash of blades in a fight or two, even the sizzle of blasers. Danith shivered again. She'd rarely been in this area during the day, never at night.

She took a deep breath and lifted her chin. "I'm lost."

He gave her a dark, brooding gaze. "I'm not." Once more he looked over her head. This time she turned around, only to see red reflected off of low gray clouds. A line of fire.

He stiffened, and for the first time she noted that he wore form-fitting leather trous and a vest that did not cover his muscular chest. She pushed away the attraction.

"I must ask you to teleport us back." She hated doing that, being dependant on him. But though she'd teleported instinctively in anger, she didn't *know* the real spell to do it cool-headed.

Now his jaw clenched. "I can't. I've used too much power and Flair this evening. I have no reserves."

"I see." She did—the white line around his lips, the underlying pallor of his olive complexion, how he moved with conscious grace instead of the easy predatory suppleness innate to him.

He looked at her again, then the fire again. His mouth compressed. "Don't like fire."

Danith licked her lips, wanting to comfort him as much as she wanted to hit him for all the emotional ups and downs he'd put her through in the last few days. But he'd also let her realize her innermost desire, she now knew she had Flair. And he saved her from an unknown fate.

Again she thought of account ledgers, and though he was still in the red, his unthreatening manner soothed her. "If you know a way back to my house, we can go the long way around, not near the fire."

"Yes," he said softly, and held out one large hand.

She hesitated. She didn't want to take it, but his expression told her that he expected her to reject him, and she couldn't refuse. She placed her hand in his.

His large, calloused fingers closed over hers, gently. With the lightest of pressures he guided her down the alley. She hurried by his side. He shortened his stride and slowed his pace.

"Thank you," she said stiffly.

They walked a few moments.

"Where are all the men and women?" Danith asked.

T'Ash studied her. She saw phantoms in his gaze. "The men are at the bonfires between Downwind and uptown, drinking and taking sex. Or lighting other fires. The women and girls are drinking or taking sex behind locked doors and barred windows. This night, at least, only the boys roam."

He shifted his shoulders as if to rid himself of memories and cleared his throat. "Do you know of HeartMates?"

She flinched.

His hand tightened a little over hers.

"Only what I've heard, or read in tales," she said.

"My parents were HeartMates."

That explained why he accepted the whole matter so easily. But she didn't accept it. Perhaps she never would. She tried to bolster some indifference to him. Why did her anger always fade at the slightest show of tenderness from him?

"You believe in HeartMates, then." She glanced up to see his jaw flex.

"Yes. And you do not. You don't believe in much, do you?"

"Wrong. I believe in what life has taught me, and much of that is good, but you must remember I am simply a commoner. HeartMates and HeartGifts and Flair are all too new to accept unthinkingly. I may hold different beliefs than you, but I'm willing to bet that my outlook is far less cynical than yours."

His fingers tightened a bit around her hand. "I grew up Downwind." His chest rose and fell as he took a deep breath. He slanted her a look. "The HeartBond brings intimate knowledge. Not only joining the bodies, but the minds and souls. Each knows dreams and hopes—and fears and regrets."

Wariness crept up her spine. She didn't want this conversation. She was tired of dealing with new concepts that changed her life in a moment. "So?"

"Tonight. Passage," he reverted again to Downwind speech.

Danith sighed. "I don't know what you're talking about."

"Tonight. . . ."

He ducked into a door alcove, and with one smooth pull of his arm, had her against his strong body. She pressed her palms against his chest.

Slowly he lifted his hand and touched her hair, then smoothed it lingeringly back from her face, his fingers tangling in it and following it down to the ends, causing delightful sensations in her scalp.

She watched his eyes darken, but he made no move to kiss her.

"Earlier. I—ah—was caught in a dreamquest."

She blinked. A dreamquest? Something no one of her acquaintance had experienced.

"I . . . reached. You came. We . . . met. Not done on purpose, not." He stopped, and when he spoke again, his tone sounded more cultured, as if he mastered his Downwind tongue. "I did not willfully mentally seduce you. We came together because we belong together."

"I don't want to think of it."

He laughed shortly. "You never want to think of what I tell you."

She tapped his chest lightly with a fist, scowling. "Do you realize my entire life has changed in the last few days? Do you know how hard that is—"

"I know." He pulled her body closer, and she sensed that it was not desire that motivated him, but fear. He didn't want her passion, but her comfort. She looked up. His expression was stark.

"I know. Nobody better. At six my Residence was destroyed in a firebombspell. My Family perished. I escaped, survived, in Downwind. It is difficult when life changes so rapidly, but one survives. I did. You will."

"Six!" How terrible. Her hands went to his large shoulders and began stroking them in compassion.

Both his arms wrapped around her, and she placed her head against his chest. His heartbeat was fast but steady.

"One survives," he repeated, whispering. "Downwind, time to adjust and think things through is a deadly luxury. You have to act, and act fast and right. I'm used to that. Holm Holly says I push, but it is difficult for me not to do so."

They stood there for a moment, silent.

"Why are you telling me this?" she asked.

"Because you know I have Downwind roots. You need to know why. I was born noble, and have reclaimed my status, but I grew up Downwind."

T'Ash looked down at her lovely face, felt the heat and desire building once again between them, but he needed to focus on her mind, not her body. The night's events and the conversations between him and his lady had been a balancing act. How much to reveal and still hide his deficiencies.

In the short time of contemplation in the HouseHeart after the wringing Passage, he'd understood that to have his magnificent future with his HeartMate, he'd have to share some of his emotions. This wasn't a comfortable notion, and now he tried to limit the disclosures. He wanted to tell her enough to make her sympathetic, to touch that generous heart of hers, but nothing that would make her retreat.

She still didn't trust him. He did not dare tell her the

dreadfulness of living in Downwind, how he'd fought and schemed to get out. And he hoped never to tell her of the man he'd become when hunting vengeance. Though he would use the skills that time had taught him, he would never be that man again.

He could divulge his hopes, his dreams, perhaps even a small fault or two, but nothing major on the downside. That would not attract her.

He thought of the earrings he had left in his Residence and how they would win her for him. He could depend upon them. Then, when he and Danith had joined in the Heart-Bond, and his self was revealed in all his flaws, she would still be his. She would love him despite everything he had done. He hoped. He was sure it worked that way. No need to try and make her love him before the HeartBond.

He shied away from the idea that no one could love him now. After all, even when he was six, he was constantly in trouble, and not quite sure how deeply his Family had loved him. Certainly his mother had not loved him enough to live instead of die with his father. But that was because they were HeartMates, of course. She would only have had a year more of life. But in that year of life, she might have provided for him, and everything would have been different. . . . He pushed the hurtful conclusion aside, as he always did. Soon he would have his own HeartMate, who would love him despite everything.

Me here. Zanth announced, swaggering up. He burped.

"What's that smell?" asked Danith.

"Zanth."

"Zanth?" She left his arms to stare down at the Fam.

Sewer rats fast hunt tonight. Caught a skirrl, too. Fat. Yum.

T'Ash winced. "Do you hear him?"

"Hear Zanth?" she said, with just enough uneasiness that let T'Ash know she just might hear the cat.

"That's right. It isn't unusual for a HeartMate to receive telepathic thoughts from the House Familiar. Not to mention that you're an Animal Healer. I've heard that Animal Trainers are telepathic with quite a few animals, so you should be, too."

"Ah." She shifted from foot to foot.

She hears me when I shout.

"Zanth says you hear him when he shouts."

She looked up and down the cobblestone alley. "Yes. I do. And he understands my words." Now she stared down at the Fam, whose white-furred areas seemed a little slimy. "But if he shouts, he gives me an awful headache."

Zanth plopped down and lifted a hind leg.

T'Ash cringed at the crudeness. A view of Zanth's large male attributes was unavoidable. Danith glanced away.

"Let's go," T'Ash said.

We walk? Zanth stopped his grooming, stood and stretched.

"No power to 'port."

Zanth narrowed his eyes at T'Ash. *You do too much tonight.*

"Yes, I did too much tonight," T'Ash repeated the Fam's comment for Danith, a habit he'd have to cultivate until her Flair bloomed in full.

Me lead. You not here in long time. You not know best ways, good holes. Zanth sauntered down the alley, tail waving.

"True, I haven't been here in a long time. I've learned to use my Flair and skill instead of having to run and hide." He slanted a look at Danith.

She understood his implication and lifted her chin. "You think I'm cowardly. Perhaps you're right, but I've never had any sort of power before, not even to choose my own job." She shrugged. "By the way, I had a viz from the clerk of the NobleCouncil. I start an apprenticeship with GreatHouse Willow—"

"That would be with the Sallow branch of the Family, animal training," T'Ash nodded. "They are exceptional with animals. You could have no better tutors."

Zanth stopped a moment, scouting the area ahead of them. *Sallows good. Caprea likes Me. Good beast-trainer. Talks with horses.*

"Zanth says Caprea Sallow feeds him. And that the man is outstanding with horses."

NOT say he feeds Me. Zanth looked over his shoulder with slitted eyes.

Danith rubbed her temples.

"Don't shout. You made Danith's head ache."

Zanth stalked ahead of them, tail waving haughtily. *Not talking more. You don't say My thoughts right.*

"Merely a twinge," Danith said, but she felt it every time T'Ash and his Fam mentally conversed. "What did he say?"

"He actually said that Caprea Sallow liked him. It's obvious now that Zanth has a food round."

Danith made a face. "He's nibbled a bit of food that I leave out for the feral cats."

"Zanth also apologizes for hurting your head." He stopped her with a hand on her arm. "As I apologize to you for this afternoon. I never meant to touch you. I lost control. I wanted you, and found you." As her expression remained doubtful, his own temper began to slip. He couldn't lose her. "I didn't seduce you. I reached and we came together. Because we both wanted to. Didn't seduce you. Not deliberate. Not."

Danith looked toward Zanth. He was carefully choosing a side street. "I don't expect an apology from him, not any more than I expect one from you."

Her words hurt. Would this woman always hurt him with her words? He drew a deep breath and pushed the pain aside. He curved a hand around her face. "I am no suave nobleman, but can you credit me with being strong enough to admit an error?"

She smiled crookedly. "I think you're strong enough to do anything you please." Her voice softened. "And that's a problem. You are so strong, and I am no match for you."

"Wrong. You are my match in every way. My HeartMate."

"Speaking of credit, I'm an accounting clerk, and I can tell you that the credit side of your ledger far outstrips the debit side."

He liked the idea, but she said it with a lightness that he sensed was false. She was being generous. That notion also pleased him, but she'd once again avoided the issue of Heart-Mates. She had a habit of refusing him, of not believing what he said, of running. Faults of hers he'd already discovered, and though they hurt, he knew they were far less than any faults of his she would eventually know. The ones he hid for now. And he could teach her to master her own faults.

Perhaps he could offer one flaw to her. "I've been aggressive."

Her lips twitched up.

The three of them turned down a wider street lined with empty, decaying warehouses. Again he stopped her. "Tell me the truth. How does my account stand with you?" Gently he touched her chin, hoping she'd raise her eyes. She did, and the honesty and kindness in her gaze weakened him.

"You gave me my fondest dream."

"If you have the courage to go after it."

Now a spark lit her eyes. "You may think I am a coward, and perhaps I am, but I will follow this dream."

He nodded. She had the strength to do anything she wished, she just had to realize it. He'd help. It would be much better to have her concentrate that strength on ordering her new life instead of having it directed at fighting him.

He slid his hand down her fine-boned arm and took her hand in his again. "I—"

Shouts bounced off the building walls.

Battered and bloody, Tinne Holly cannoned around a corner. An unruly band of young men wearing purple and white followed.

T'Ash pushed Danith behind him, whipped out his broadsword. These scruffs had taken Danith. Now they would pay.

He smiled.

Ten

❦

*S*eeing *them, Tinne tried to stop. He skidded on muck* and flailed past them. Danith watched as he windmilled and finally found his feet.

Zanth yowled. One young man stumbled over him. It activated his collar.

"You!" shouted the fierce hologram of T'Ash.

The boys lurched back, away from the apparition. T'Ash took advantage of their confusion and joined his image. Danith shivered at the eerie sight of twin T'Ashes.

"Know you that this is my Fam, Zanthoxyl. Harm him and you answer to me!"

The teenagers faced both the holo and real T'Ash. Equally intimidating. The solid one didn't bother with words. Only a growl issued from his lips as he began stalking the group, unaware or uncaring that they outnumbered him nine to one.

The Holly flew by Danith to join T'Ash. He was laughing. Nine to two.

Steady light from the twinmoons and flickering light from fire gleamed down their naked blades. Both T'Ash's broadsword and the long dagger-sword Holly held were nothing like Danith had ever seen before and they both cut nasty patterns in the air.

Holly danced small steps, ready for fighting. Danith could see a trickle of blood from the corner of his mouth. He licked it away with relish.

T'Ash crouched in a predatory stance. Measuring his bulk, particularly next to Tinne Holly, Danith saw he would have made three of the youth. She glanced at the band of young nobles, now warily treading backward. None of them was much more substantial than Tinne. They were wild boys, in their first flush of youth.

T'Ash was a man grown, solid with muscle built by work at the forge, with strong, well-defined arms, shoulders, thighs.

Four to nine?

Danith wanted to run. The atmosphere pulsed with raging male hormones, primed for violence.

She couldn't.

She was barefoot.

There wasn't even any good place to hide.

Unless she wanted to crawl on her belly in filth to a hole in the south wall.

She wondered if a fight could be averted. The thought made her blood freeze, because she knew if she had the thought, she would have to follow up with action.

She stepped from the shadows, trying to attract the attention of the young men. But she wore black and their wide-eyed gazes were fixed in horrified fascination on T'Ash.

She eyed the Holly. Despite the ripped sleeve and tunic, he looked like a gentleman, much like his brother, Holm Holly. She didn't think he'd let her stand beside him. And it was impossible to outmaneuver T'Ash.

She made a wide circle around Holly, who was humming to himself. He didn't see her until too late.

Danith licked her lips. "Let me introduce you young gentlemen. This is T'Ash."

One gulped. The others seemed to go even more motionless.

"Danith!" A whiplash order from T'Ash.

"This is Zanth," she continued.

The Fam prowled to her side and sat, then grinned with all his teeth showing.

"This is Tinne Holly, of the fighting Hollys." Danith knew that much.

"And I am . . ." She sucked in a deep breath, ready to use her clout as a noble for the first time. "D'Mallow, head of GrandHouse Mallow."

Tension built in the youths, they started shifting, shuffling, ever backward.

"Now, what would your Families and the NobleCouncil say to fighting on Discovery Day eve, a time of thanksgiving and jubilation?"

One boy faded next to the dark wall of a building and vanished with a slight *pop!*—teleporting himself from trouble.

"They took you!" T'Ash snarled.

Danith swallowed. "They didn't hurt me." Much. And they hadn't had the time to decide what to do with her before being attacked by the Downwind gang.

Another teenager slunk out of sight; from farther away there was a clap of displaced air as he teleported, too.

"Took my woman. Jostled her. Lost her to Downwind scruffs. Failed to protect her." T'Ash's voice gained volume as he listed their crimes.

Two more deserted, vanishing noisily, not bothering to go undetected.

"Now, T'Ash," Danith breathed much easier. "Evidently they didn't realize they were outside your estate, or recognize your Residence, distinctive though it is. They'll know better in the future. I'm sure they rue their actions."

Tinne squawked. Zanth hit her in the ankle with a claw-sheathed paw. Hard. The teenagers themselves trembled and none drew breath.

For the first time T'Ash took his eyes off the youths.

They bolted.

When she met T'Ash's gaze she saw such icy fury, she jumped back, landing on something sharp. She ignored it. Not only fury but deep pain lived in his eyes.

"You said?" he whispered hoarsely.

She didn't know what she said that caused such a reaction in everyone, but she wasn't going to repeat her words. She scrambled to find different ones. "I said the youngsters must not have understood—"

"After." He prompted with a hand.

She frowned.

"She said those scruffs are damned sorry they crossed you, GreatLord," Tinne said loudly.

T'Ash seemed to relax, muscle by muscle.

"Women," Tinne snorted. "Always interfering. Mixing up in men's business." He thrust out his narrow chest. "Stopping fights."

T'Ash looked less grim. "You sound very like your brother." His gaze sharpened as he scanned the boy. "How do you fare?"

Tinne sighed a little mournfully, shook his head. "Only three fights. Hard to believe, almost like something's holding me back. Humph."

With one smoothly efficient motion, T'Ash's sword disappeared into his sheath. He clapped the young Holly on the shoulder. "Well done." T'Ash looked down the alley where the band of teenagers dressed in purple and white had disappeared. "I think that's as much excitement as you'll get this holiday eve. 'Port home."

Tinne's mouth set in mulish lines. "I want—"

" 'Port home, GreatSir Holly." T'Ash's voice contained as much steel as his sword.

Muttering under his breath, Holly sheathed his sword and his long dagger. Still unhappy, he made a short bow to T'Ash. "My thanks for the main gauche."

"A gift from your brother. You are welcome. Use it sparingly, but when you use it, use it well."

Holly snorted once more and winked out of sight.

Zanth loped to the end of the street and took a less lit off-shoot to the left, deeper into Downwind.

"Zanth says we must hurry," T'Ash said, holding a hand out to her.

For some reason she felt relieved that he was still speaking to her, that she hadn't offended him. Why? Didn't she want him out of her life?

She darted a glance at him. He obviously wasn't going to explain himself. It had cost him, she knew, to reveal all that he had earlier. She suspected that there was an incredible amount more to know about the complex man, and not just that which was publicly available. Did she truly want to get so deeply involved?

She didn't, but began to feel her own heart would give her no choice.

A whistling blaze of light burst into the sky, a stream of magic fireballs to celebrate Discovery Day. She hastily put her hand in his, and it was instantly warmed by his large, strong fingers.

The Fam's flat and tattered ears seemed to curl inward as the pops and bangs of homemade fireworks and magical displays increased in volume and brilliance.

"Zanth doesn't like the noise. It sets his already belligerent nerves on end. I've no doubt that once we two are safe tonight, many sewer rats will lose their lives." A smile hovered on T'Ash's lips.

"How long will it take to get home?" Danith asked. It was getting harder for her not to give into the ache in her foot and limp.

Her head throbbed, as it did whenever Zanth and T'Ash spoke telepathically. T'Ash frowned. He pulled Danith down a narrow, crooked passageway to a dead end. An abandoned Zanth complained behind them.

To Danith's amazement, T'Ash pulled off his vest and reached high above her head to swipe with the soft leather at a protruding stone. It appeared part of the wall, until T'Ash scrubbed some of the grime away.

He looked at Danith, hesitating. "It's an old public scrystone. Though it doesn't look it, it still has a little power left. I can feel it. Zanth says the bonfires have gotten out of hand and have drawn drunks and the gangs—Downwind and noble alike. It would be rough getting through without injury. The streets tonight are no place for a lady like you."

"And?"

"If I can clean the scrystone, I'll be able to see if Zanth is right. Get an overview of things instead of merely a cat's-eye view."

Zanth hissed at the perceived insult.

Danith nodded.

Holding his besmirched vest in his hand like a rag, T'Ash shifted a little.

"You need to clean the scrystone," Danith prompted.

"Yes."

"So?"

"I need to spit on the vest."

"Yes?" she said, failing to see the problem.

"My mother told me that spitting is foul. You might not want to watch."

Danith stared at him. "You think I am too delicate to see you spit?" If the light weren't so bad, she would have sworn his cheeks darkened. "You need to clean the scrystone. Spit. You want me to spit on your vest, too?"

Now he stared at her, then a smile cracked his face as his gaze lingered on her lips. "I doubt you have much spit in you."

She crossed her arms and lifted her chin. "I probably have enough."

Zanth harrumphed.

T'Ash looked down at him. "Zanth probably has more spit than both of us."

"You could hold him up to the stone and have him lick it."

NO!

This time the pain was such she clapped her hands to her head and closed her eyes. "Just joking, Zanth."

Zanth grumbled near her feet. When she opened her eyes, T'Ash was swabbing at the scrystone, obviously having taken advantage of her momentary lapse to do the dreadful deed and spit on the vest.

He turned back to them and eyed the scarred gray opaque crystal. Then held the vest under her chin. His eyes dared her, as if he really thought she was too good to spit.

She rubbed her tongue around her teeth, gathering saliva, then spit. They both looked down at the small wet spot on the leather.

"I'd better hurry and use this or it will disappear."

Zanth gave a rusty chuckle.

T'Ash spit himself, then turned and applied the vest to the scrystone again.

"I'm a common woman, T'Ash. I eat. I drink. I spit. I— relieve myself."

T'Ash didn't turn around to answer. "You're small and

delicately made. You move with grace. You have a refined taste in jewelry, furnishings, and flowers. Your Flair is strong but subtle. Your mind, when I touched it earlier, has a cultured tone. And I wouldn't have said 'relieve myself.' "

Danith felt heat rise to her face. He thought that of her? That she embodied such characteristics? That she was something special, perhaps unique?

"There." T'Ash tapped on the glass. It glowed a little, surprising Danith. As far as she knew, none of the old city scrystones worked and were long forgotten. By everyone except T'Ash. He truly had an affinity for stones.

"Damn. Zanth is right. There's nowhere it wouldn't be risky to pass to get back to your part of Druida. I can mentally contact Holm and ask that he send a glider for us. But I'm angry with him, and he knows it; he'd charge us for the trip. And I'd never hear the end of it. We'll have to hole up for the night."

Vindicated, Zanth made a superior cat noise.

Danith moistened her lips. A night with T'Ash. She didn't know whether to dread or anticipate it. She was becoming much too accustomed to being in the company of the man. "Where?"

"Only one place." T'Ash looked grim again.

Zanth murmured approval.

"And that is?"

T'Ash threw his erstwhile vest in a corner. His large shoulders set. "T'Blackthorn Residence."

"Ah—"

He caught her hand and started swiftly down the passage. "Don't believe what they say. It's not really haunted. Much. More like cursed."

*T'*Ash watched Danith curl on a cushion in a corner of the gardenshed on the T'Blackthorn estate. She looked comfortable, and homey, and the sensual way she sipped the tea from his stash of supplies made something deep inside him twist with longing. She belonged wherever he was, adding warmth and civilization to his life.

The "shed," an outbuilding of a GrandHouse estate, was

as large as his ResidenceDen. And though it might once
have housed landscaping machines, T'Ash had visited the
place a few times over the years and made it a bolt hole of
his own. Only a thin coat of dust had lain over the shelves,
and had disappeared with a simple cleaning Word. A large
permamoss bed was rolled in the corner, ready for sleeping.
He had a box of supplies he'd gathered and food in a small
no-time unit. He'd activated the waterspell in the sinks.

Danith shifted and pain crossed her face. He scowled.
She'd been hurt more than she'd said, and he hadn't noticed
until then. Why hadn't she said anything?

He crossed to her where she rested against some old
loungechair cushions and knelt beside her. He took the tea
mug from her hands and set it aside. Then he slipped his
hands through her hair and examined her scalp. Nothing.

Her face showed no bruises, and the dainty nape of her
neck, while tempting to him, was free of cuts and scrapes.
He smoothed his hands down her neck to her shoulders,
checking the muscles, she didn't flinch, but pulled away
from him.

"What are you doing?"

"You're hurt. Since you didn't tell me, I'll find the injury
myself."

She frowned at him, huffed a breath, and touched her
instep against his calf. "My foot. I'm not used to going barefoot, and I stepped on something sharp."

He matched her frown, tapped her small chin with his finger. "You do not hide such things from me. It is my responsibility to protect you, to care for you. I will not fail in my
duty."

Her eyes narrowed in what he thought was a direct mimicry of his own expression. It didn't amuse him. She lifted
her chin. "I am an independent, common—"

"D'Mallow," he said silkily.

Her breath caught, confusion dimmed her eyes. She
blinked several times. Then she breathed in and out, deeply,
and met his gaze again, and when her chin lifted even more,
it was an elegant gesture of a noblewoman.

"I can take care of myself."

"No need, when I am here for you."

Now her gaze flashed anger. "I had to live with plenty of rules, T'Ash. Now I can make some of my own, and I intend to. Don't push."

He opened his mouth to speak but was interrupted by the scrape of the small door he'd made for Zanth years ago.

Come! said Zanth.

"I'm busy."

Too busy to see lam-ben-thyst? Glows in twinmoons light. Cymru moon re-flect-ed. Beau-ti-ful.

Zanth being poetic was something T'Ash couldn't ignore. Not to mention the small vein of acquisitiveness for a unique stone that was never buried very deep.

He turned to Danith, who watched him warily and rubbed a temple.

"Zanth wants us to see the lambenthyst in the fountain of the Dark Goddess. He says it is a sight to behold tonight. The stone is the largest and least flawed lambenthyst I've ever seen."

He glanced at her foot, scraped and with a puncture. Touching a finger to the wound, he murmured a cleansing spell.

Danith yelped.

T'Ash stood, then bent and scooped up Danith. "We will care for your foot further, shortly."

Unlatching the door with his elbow, he kicked it open and followed a stately treading Zanth down a crushed-stone path that had once been white and well-tended. T'Ash concentrated on his steps rather than the woman in his arms. The thread of his restraint was thin, and he couldn't have her.

The fountain of the Dark Goddess was on the far side of the grounds, down a twisting footpath and situated in a grove of towering trees.

As he walked, he cast a glance at the palatial T'Black-thorn Residence. Unlike many first colony Family mansions, it didn't resemble a fortress. Once thought the most beautiful of all the Residences, its tall windows looked blind and dark, and the fluted columns of the back terrace were streaked with unsightly blotches of gray leechmoss that had claimed one side of the house.

Danith made a shocked noise. "How terrible that something so gracious is so neglected."

"Yes."

T'Ash remembered the first night he'd spent in the shed, a few days after the destruction of his Family. The Blackthorn estate had been deserted, the Residence shut up for the winter, with the Blackthorns situated in their winter "cottage" in the south.

Even then there had been rumors of the Residence being haunted by more ghosts than acceptable for a FirstFamily, and the curse of the stone. The Residence had brought a dreadful fascination, awe, and grief with the air of a dark fate lingering around the beautiful place.

Every month or two, when he was desperate, he would return to the shed. It was never locked or spellshielded. He didn't know if that was due to oversight or the generosity of the Blackthorns. He didn't know if they had been aware that a small, lost, once-noble-but-now-Downwind boy had taken shelter there.

T'Ash had been too afraid to ask them for sanctuary. He didn't know whom he could trust.

Only in extreme times would he come to the shed. After all, GrandHouse Rue neighbored the Blackthorn estate, and GraceHouse Flametree was too close, also.

He remembered one time, a year or so later, that he returned, after being completely integrated into Downwind life. The T'Blackthorn Residence had seemed like a thing out of legend, nothing to do with him. The Blackthorns had been entertaining and the Residence had echoed with cultured music and the delighted laughter of ladies.

It had been a very long time, since before he'd ended his vengeance stalk, that he'd been here.

"Isn't there still a Blackthorn alive?" asked Danith, as if prodding her memory of the history of the FirstFamilies.

"Straif. Once Heir, he's now T'Blackthorn. He's not often in Druida."

The Blackthorn Family, too, had died, all but Straif. Disease had claimed them. Wildfire whispers stated the curse had struck again. Every few generations, the Blackthorn Family was reduced to just one. The last time T'Ash had encountered Straif in a tavern, the man had spoken of a genetic flaw that made the Blackthorns susceptible to one of the common ailments of humans on Celta. He'd vowed to try and find a cure, and wandered Celta in search of it.

T'Ash moved his shoulders uneasily. He didn't know if Straif looked for a special Healer, Scholar, or herb, but the circumstances of their lives were too alike for him to often think of T'Blackthorn.

You slow!

T'Ash increased his pace, and at his jog Danith tightened her arms around his neck and her scent wafted up to him. He nearly closed his eyes in pleasure at the feel of her body against his.

Finally he was holding his HeartMate, not just touching her hair, face, arm, not taking a gentle kiss. And not experiencing mental lovemaking that only simulated the physical, without even twining their minds together. How frustrating that had been.

She lay quiescent in his arms, weighing less than a block of celtastone, less than he'd expected. His body wanted her, his sex pulsed with every step, but his heart yearned for her even more.

His mother and his father had shown their love for each other in frequent glances, and less common touches. The Ash Family had never been very demonstrative. T'Ash had noted how Danith often touched her cat, his Fam, or a textured surface or two.

He wanted her hands on him. Their marriage would heal all the emotional wounds he'd taken in his life, without him ever having to tell her of them.

He could barely wait. But he had to. He didn't have the new HeartGift with him.

Once they reached the grove with the fountain of the Dark Goddess, he placed her gently on her feet and kept an arm around her so she could stand only on one foot and lean against him.

The sight of the towering fountain took Danith's breath. The grove had been planted and maintained so that the moonlight only touched the fountain. Even the grassyard around it was in deep shadow. Consisting of five descending tiered white marble bowls, the fountain only held leaves, twigs, and grit in its ever-larger, cascading basins. The statue of the Goddess herself gleamed of black marble. And in the round bowl at her feet a fabulous labenthyst reflected Cymru twinmoon.

Danith looked up at T'Ash. His eyes glinted.

He pointed to the deep gouges in the mortar surrounding the stone. "Zanth has been working on freeing the stone. He wants it."

She stared at him. "Isn't that theft?"

"Cats don't think in that manner. He wants it, no one else is here to appreciate it or defend it, so he will take it." His brow furrowed. "But the curse of the T'Blackthorns' is supposedly linked to the stone. It's said it screamed when removed from its living place in one of the T'Blackthorn mines."

Danith looked at him with a measuring gaze. Ever since she had fallen in with nobles, the sense of being surrounded with the great Flair and magic they wielded escalated. Few of her friends could speak at all, let alone seriously, about teleporting, dreamquests, curses, or screaming stones.

But looking at the purple stone, appearing to glow from the inside, she couldn't prevent a shiver.

He smiled down at her, and she wondered how he could be so carefree, given the circumstances. "And Zanth has some notion that if anyone can placate an angry stone, and break a curse, I can."

She squeezed his hand. "He's right."

His eyes lingered on the Dark Goddess. "You know, the Dark Goddess watches over blacksmiths." He flexed his fingers. "And that is part of my calling. Perhaps She will not mind if a Fam to a blacksmith takes the stone from Her fountain. If I can break the curse, I will probably claim the stone as my fee."

Danith sucked in a breath. "You said this curse has lasted generations?"

His eyebrows dipped. "Seven, maybe eight."

"Then the price would be worth it, but what if—" She stopped, feeling embarrassed at her thoughts.

"Yes?"

She cleared her throat, thinking she was going to sound

foolish, or like a noble who was steeped in tradition and Flair, or—

"Yes?"

"What if the stone wants to—ah—go back?" She waved a hand.

"Go back?"

"Be returned to its"—what had he called it?—"living place?"

He shrugged. "Then I'll take it back."

"A stone has feelings, too?" She wanted it to sound mocking, but it came out in too much of a questioning whisper.

"Perhaps." His gaze shuttered, and she knew then that whatever his true thoughts on stones were, she wouldn't hear them now.

She looked at the fountain, the small grassyard surrounding it and the looming trees of the grove that protected it. It should have been gloomy and threatening, but to her it brought a mystical peace with an undertone of excitement. The Dark Goddess emphasized that change and rebirth were always inherent in the present moment.

She had forgotten that. That all life was change. Perhaps she never connected with deeper truths unless she relaxed and was still. Her life had galloped out of control, and perhaps she was trying too hard to think about it, force it into patterns she knew, instead of learning new patterns.

She sighed and leaned a little more against T'Ash. She liked the feel of his strong body next to her. And his scent drifted to her on the night air—deep earth, hot-metal, T'Ash—and at this instant it didn't rouse desire, but contentment.

"Mmmm, I like this place. Do you think any of the Blackthorns ever held their rituals here?"

"They are of the FirstFamilies, duty bound to contribute to the Great Rituals in the GreatCircle Temple."

Danith made a disgusted noise. "Too bad. There is nothing like celebrating holidays outdoors, with stones and trees and streams marking the directions." She shivered. "I could not give that up." She laughed a little. "I join the Clovers, now, for Sabbaths and Albans, as long as they perform their services outside. It's wonderful, being a part of the huge whole of their

Family. Why, the Family alone can make a large circle, not just standing at the points of the directions. It is very comforting."

"Cold outdoors in the winter."

"Yes. But there is a sheltered place I go—it is rarely too deep in ice or snow to welcome me. And I must admit, I usually observe only full twinmoons in winter."

"You're getting cool. We need to look at your foot. It's time to return to the shed."

"The shed? That's what they call that little stone house?"

"That's what I call it. Zanth, we're going back."

Zanth, who had been amusing himself by jumping up to the topmost tier and walking around the bowl rim, gave them an aloof stare and continued with his rounds.

T'Ash swept her up into his arms. She ignored the speeding up of her blood as her body made contact with his. She looked past his large biceps at Zanth. "Do you think he's practicing his own ritual?" She liked the whimsical notion.

Zanth glanced up at her and narrowed his eyes. Her head throbbed a moment.

"Zanth says cats remember the generation starships that set out from Earth. The cats hated being in timesuspension crystals, and the ships themselves were too small. They are glad our ancestors detoured to this star system and settled on Celta after the spaceships got lost. Trying to find the original destination would have been difficult, and taken light-years longer."

Zanth yowled.

T'Ash chuckled. She liked the sound, she rubbed her cheek against his lightly haired chest.

"Zanth is complaining again that I'm not translating his thoughts accurately. He says you need to hurry and learn your Flair so you can talk to him."

Danith smiled. "He is as impatient as you."

His arms tightened around her, and he set off down the path at a lope, as if in a hurry to return to the gardenshed. "Not possible."

After tending her foot and sharing a meal, *T'Ash* renewed the heatspell one last time and glanced over to where Danith lay on her side, nearly dozing, on the soft per-mamoss. Her injured foot was tucked under her.

T'Ash had been relieved at the smallness of the wound, but wary of a puncture covered with dried Downwind slime. He'd used the most powerful cleansing bandage in his supply. She'd laughed at the strength, then gasped at the sting, but he was satisfied that the wound was clean. He'd followed the directions on the little healing spell included in the bandage. The spell demanded the most minimal of Flair, the easiest of the small Healing Words. Her foot should be fine by the morning.

He'd also used a little of his accumulating Flair to show her how to mend the tears in her clothes, though the cloth looked melded together rather than seamlessly woven.

A small surge of power, a few Words of a welding spell—he didn't know a weaving spell—and it was done. He liked teaching her. She was an eager but focused student. He thought that time they'd spent together would definitely qualify as the "quality personal contact" written of in D'Rose's book. He was doing better at this courtship business.

Her fine, shoulder-length chestnut hair tumbled about the pallet, some wisping over her pale complexion. White and soft and delicate, everything opposite him.

She'd revealed some of herself earlier. Too bad it was something that caused tension to wind tight inside him. She liked having a large Family around her, a Family he could never offer her. Even were his vision true, there would only be six of them at Family rituals, a child to stand at each direction, himself and Danith by the altar as embodiments of the Lord and the Lady.

His mouth set.

Then there was all that female talk about preferring the outdoors for ceremonies instead of something like the HouseHeart or the GreatCircle Temple. That gave him a few uneasy moments, too. As his HeartMate, a HeartMate with powerful Flair, she would be expected, even ordered to attend and participate in the FirstFamilies Rituals that shaped the world. It was written in the laws of Celta.

He examined her narrowly. He would be able to get

around the issue of celebrating outdoors, somehow. He didn't know how. He couldn't conceive of how. He sighed. He was afraid that this issue would have to be addressed by consulting others, again. Costly, again. Time consuming and not guaranteed to work, again.

Then he cheered, he'd conquer that matter after she had accepted his new HeartGift and they were HeartBound. That would make everything simpler.

She snuffled and sank deeper into the warm, green moss.

"Danith?" he asked softly.

Her eyelids opened slightly, the glinting color made more green and less brown by the permamoss bed.

She was soft, and generous, and on the border of sleep. He could tell her something of his wishes, his desires, maybe a fault or two. This could strengthen the chains he was slowly forging between them. And if his goals clashed with hers, she would be too drowsy to object. She would just listen and the knowledge would sink into her thoughts, and her dreams.

He slid onto the pallet next to her. The summer night was warm enough to sleep well without covers. And should it cool too much, he would keep her warm.

T'Ash reached out to touch her hair, and as he saw his own hand hover near her head, another memory flashed to his mind. Of his father, gently soothing his mother with strokes down her head and her long, midnight hair. For a moment his throat closed; the image was too strong and sweet for him to handle without shattering in grief at all the past times lost.

"Danith, dear one." He pushed her hair back. Her ear looked pink and slightly pointed.

Her eyelids lifted slowly, as if bearing a great weight.

"I am T'Ash," he said, having trouble with words, as usual, fumbling in following his strategy. Why was the execution never as smooth as the plan?

She smiled.

"I am the last of my line."

Her lips lost their curve, she put a hand on his chest, over his heart. Progress.

"I have . . . My fondest dream"—he winced at the sissy

words, but they were ones he recalled that she had used—"is to continue my line."

"You will," she breathed, her eyes closing again.

"I want a Family."

"Family is very important." These words were even softer than before, slurred.

He lowered his voice to match hers. "I want a wife, a HeartMate. To love me. To live with me. To be the mother of my children. To make my Residence a home."

"Umm-hmm." It was more like a sigh.

"To follow old traditions and found new."

"Umm."

"I want you," he said, putting all the yearning he felt into his tone. She didn't answer and he could only hope she heard him.

He watched her breathing, and with every movement of her luscious breasts he felt desire build and his loins tighten. He hadn't been able to admit one further fault, to be even a little vulnerable.

He dared not overwhelm her with his passion or his dark spirit. But his control with her was always questionable, and tonight it could so easily slip his grasp.

He knew now he could not introduce one more disturbing element into her life at this time, one more new concept. Let her ponder being a HeartMate without pressure from him.

He didn't want it that way, hated the idea. He wanted to claim her and bond with her and make her forever his own. But if he did that, if he overwhelmed her and took her choice away, despite that they were HeartMates, he would lay the foundations of ruin in their marriage. He could not grab. He would have to coax.

He brooded. He had never had to coax or lure anyone before, and it made him seethe with frustration. He was used to grabbing and explaining later. Grabbing would not work with Danith. He'd be left with only her haunting ripe-apple scent.

Lord and Lady but he ached for her. And his body, primed for days, was less painful than his heart.

The cat door scraped open and shut. Zanth entered.

Eleven

❦

"*S*hhh!" T'Ash hissed as Zanth paused by the cat-door of the gardenshed.

Zanth burped loudly. *Many slow, fat skirrls.*

"Haven't you had enough to eat, today?"

Zanth walked over to the permamoss pallet, deliberately clicking his claws noisily on the stone floor. *Snack. Missed many meals today. Went some Passage with you. Did much magic. Deserve skirrls.* He yawned, then his pink tongue came out and swiped at his mouth.

"How are the fires?"

Firemages control. Burn some deserted buildings in Downwind. He sniffed. *One of My favorite holes.*

"Too bad."

Zanth jumped up to a bench where an old pillow, retrieved from T'Ash's cache, sat. He trod around on it, kneading it until it took his scent. He smiled, a sickeningly sweet smile, as sweet as a cat-smile got.

Life is good.

*D*anith awoke groggily, but her eyes widened at the view of water droplets catching the morning sunlight as they trickled down a muscular back.

Lord and Lady, what had she done! Then she forced herself to calm. She'd been good. She winced. She'd reverted to the earliest childhood concept, "good." Be "good" for your father when he gets home, her mother would say. Be "good" and follow the rules, Maiden Brigit at the orphanage would admonish. And she always had been. Good.

But as she caught a glimpse of T'Ash's hard profile, she knew it was no time to think of being "bad." Too dangerous. Too damn dangerous. She couldn't afford the further complications in her life.

She scrambled to her feet.

He turned.

She'd hoped he'd smile at her, but he didn't. His gaze was as intense as ever, as challenging, as passionate. She didn't dare drop her glance to below his waist. He efficiently dried himself with a ragged towel.

"How's your foot?"

She glanced down at the bandage that swaddled her foot, then sat and peeled it off. She rotated her ankle, arched her foot, wiggled her toes.

"Great!" Her smile died at his smoldering expression. "I'm ready to go home." She walked to the window and looked outside. "A bright and beautiful Discovery Day. A good omen."

"Happy Discovery Day."

"And to you." She gazed at the green verdancy of the Blackthorn estate, noted the mixture of Celtan trees and Earth trees and hybrids. Danith lifted her gaze to the sky and rubbed her arms up and down. "Imagine leaving your home planet because you were persecuted for Flair." She shivered. "All those long generations on the starships, being born and living and dying on the way to a new home. Or being locked in a timesuspension cube, flying to a new planet and a new future for your people and the culture you wanted to establish." The sun, Bel, was a small blue-white speck radiant in the deep blue sky. Danith shook her head. "Such courage and hope."

T'Ash crossed to stand next to her. She could feel his breath disturb her hair. "You have courage and Flair. But do you have hope of a beautiful new future?"

Danith tensed.

Before she could reply, he asked, "I gave you a bracelet with a charm of the ship, *Lugh's Spear*?"

Though she was gland he turned the subject, she bit her lip, trying to remember it amongst all the other jewelry he'd gifted her with. When she did, her heart softened. "Yes, it is very beautiful. You made the tiny spaceship?"

"My design, sculpted, then cast in silver."

"Yes. Thank you."

He watched her with wary hope in his eyes. "You didn't return it again?"

She cleared her throat, considered telling him of the antique jewelry chest Holm Holly had provided, and decided against it. "No."

He smiled. "It is not too much as a Discovery Day gift."

Perhaps not for the nobility, but it would have set Claif back a pretty penny, too much for a holiday token.

Danith smiled brightly and opened the door. "You look ready to go, too. Where is Zanth?"

He grinned and Danith's heart flip-flopped.

"Zanth has a standing breakfast appointment with my chef."

Danith frowned. "It's Discovery Day. You make your chef work on Discovery Day?"

T'Ash blinked. "No. I have no live-in help; most of my Residence is cared for by permanent spells. My chef comes in on weekdays. For a moment I forgot it was Discovery Day. I wonder if Zanth remembered that the chef is gone."

"So your chef is Zanth's first station in his daily food round?"

"Yes. The cat must have a food round. He's familiar with more GreatHouse Families than I." He tossed the towel aside and held out his hand. "My strength and Flair are much restored. I can 'port us home."

She looked at him in silence. Why could she never ignore that strong hand held out to her? She bit her lip again and took the few steps to place her hand in his.

"My house," she said firmly, thinking it would be safer.

"Front or back?"

"Back."

"All right. I'll visualize it and 'port us there. Try not to think of it yourself. We don't want contradictory images."

"Fine."

His brow furrowed.

His power built.

A flash of colors.

They arrived. She stumbled headlong.

With a smooth, effortless tug he steadied her.

Her mind stopped spinning. She blinked in the morning sunlight.

"Hello, Danith," Claif said.

He lounged on one of the café chairs, studying Zanth, who sat near the food bowl on the stoop. Zanth watched him back.

Claif raised his eyes and smiled. His cheerful, guileless smile that always made her heart warm to him.

T'Ash pulled her behind his back, his grip changing to her wrist.

"Let me go!" she cried.

"You have an intruder," T'Ash said emotionlessly.

"It's Claif." She struggled to get free, but T'Ash wasn't letting go. With a frustrated noise she stepped to one side to see.

Claif rose slowly to his feet.

"Who?" asked T'Ash.

"Claif Clover," Claif introduced himself. He looked T'Ash up and down, expression mild but a hint of anger in his eyes. "New friend, Dani, m'love?"

T'Ash pushed her behind him again. "Mine."

Danith closed her eyes and ground her teeth. "Let me go. Now."

T'Ash released her wrist, but kept his arms out, blocking her way to Claif.

"Interesting," Claif said, staring at T'Ash's wide, bare chest and leather trous. He met her gaze and raised an eyebrow. "Sporting out of your league, Dani?"

"It's T'Ash," Danith said.

"T'Ash," Claif repeated in a meditative tone. He cocked his head. "Downwind background, noble status. Mitchella mentioned him. Downwind or Noble, he's still out of your league."

Danith sighed. Claif was right. She rubbed her wrist.

T'Ash took a step forward. She got the impression that he was still primarily focused on her, and she'd have no chance to get around him.

"We two are a league of our own," T'Ash said.

"You missed the party last night, Dani. The Family worried."

How appalling, that she should cause good people anxiety. "I'm so sorry, there wasn't any place to scry from—"

"She was safe with me," T'Ash said.

Again Claif scanned T'Ash up and down. Claif smoothed back his thick blond hair, cut short as this year's fashion demanded.

Danith caught herself looking at T'Ash's long, tangled black locks. He cared no more for current hairstyles than he did fashion. She wasn't sure why, or what it meant to her, and didn't have time to figure it out.

Just days ago Danith had thought Claif a fine figure of a man. Now she saw him in comparison to T'Ash. Claif was not as tall or as muscular. His blond hair and fair skin also made him appear less substantial than T'Ash. Claif's eyes were also blue, a darker shade than T'Ash's intense sky-crystal blue, but they still appeared washed-out next to T'Ash's.

Admitting to herself that she no longer wanted Claif, and admitting it to the men—and the Fam—were two different matters.

"I have a Discovery Day gift." Claif patted his jacket pocket.

She smiled. "And I have one for you, too."

He returned her smile. She wondered at his ability to completely ignore the large, scowling man between them.

"You are coming to the Family Discovery Day Ritual, aren't you? In Pink's big grassyard? After the ceremony there'll be quite a feast." Claif's smile widened.

T'Ash spoke. "No. She's D'Mallow. She attends the First-Families Ritual in GreatCircle Temple with me."

"I'll make my own decisions," Danith said between gritted teeth. "Let me by."

When T'Ash shifted to block her every step, a surge of pure fire blazed through her veins.

Pop!

She 'ported to right before Claif.

She staggered and would have fallen if Claif hadn't reached out, caught her upper arms, and placed her on her feet.

T'Ash and Zanth snarled.

The little jump left her breathing hard, trembling with sudden exhaustion.

Claif brushed her face with the lightest of touches. His fingers carried no hard callouses like T'Ash's.

Zanth appeared at her feet, hissing.

"Zanth!" Danith said.

The Fam subsided into a continuing subvocal growl.

Claif's new smile was lopsided, echoing a trace of sadness in his eyes. "D'Mallow. A noble name. A noble lady. Perhaps you are, indeed, finally in your league."

He took a step back and bowed formally, elegantly.

"Merry meet—"

"Claif—"

"Go away," T'Ash said.

Zanth raised the note of his yowl.

"Merry part, and merry meet again," Claif ended. "If it pleases you, come to the Ritual this afternoon. It starts Belhigh. Noon."

"She attends the FirstFamilies Ritual at GreatCircle temple with me."

Claif smiled again, the same half-smile. "This is a jeweler?" He looked at them both, then took a small gray velvet box from his pocket and placed it on the café table. "My gift cannot compete with his, but know this, it is given with all my love." He turned and, spine straightening, walked away from them, around the corner of the house to the front path.

Danith reached for the box.

"Don't touch!" T'Ash ordered.

She flung him a simmering glance. All her nerves felt afire, as if a web of flame lived and grew within her. Before she could close her hand on Claif's gift, Zanth jumped on the table and carried it away in strong jaws, hissing all the while. He disappeared.

Danith stomped her foot. She opened her mouth to shout

at T'Ash and nothing came out. He matched her glare. Finally she found and controlled her voice. "No! I will not attend the Discovery Day Ritual at GreatCircle Temple with you!"

T'Ash rocked back on his heels. He stared at her from narrowed eyes but clasped his hands behind him. "You will come with me."

"I run my life, GreatLord. Me, Danith Mallow. I make my decisions, and I don't take orders from anyone anymore. I had enough of that in my old life. The Maidens at the orphanage, my boss." She sent him a searing look. "You wouldn't know of that, of how petty a boss can be."

He jerked a thumb at his chest. "Apprenticed four years to a mean glistensmith bordering Downwind. I know. We match, D'Mallow and T'Ash. You will be expected at First-Families Ritual."

Her vision began to fade behind a red haze. "I doubt that. I don't even start training until next Midweek. Or do you nobles insist on subservience of the newest at the very instant they're made noble? You allow no time—" Her words dried. She stumbled past him on the way to the door.

"Danith—"

Hot tears poured from her eyes. An emotional storm gripped her too hard for her to care about the sight she made.

A shouted Word and her door opened.

"Danith!"

"Leave me be. By all that lives in this universe, leave me be."

"I'll be by to take you to Ritual one septhour before Belhigh."

She barely heard him. Slammed the door in his face.

She staggered to the bedroom and shoved that door open. A faint, lingering sexual wave from the necklace washed over her. Her entire body torched into burning fire. Pain too dreadful to voice swallowed her.

She fell facedown for the bedsponge, turning her head at the last moment.

Shudders took her.

A strong wind whirled through her, drying the film of

sweat on her body from the inside out. She shivered and soon ice encased her.

Her shudders increased.

Weird, surreal images came to her, followed by hollow, echoing sounds. Elongated figures of her father and mother towered over her. Mother pleaded at her. Father shouted, as usual.

More flashes of color, bright enough to sear the inner lids of her eyes.

She burrowed into the bedsponge and the scent of heady earth, with its solidity and slow rhythms, soothed her for a long moment.

But only a moment.

Pansy came to her side and gave a fearful mew.

Using the last of her strength, Danith blindly reached out and tangled her fingers in Pansy's fur wrapped with T'Ash's jewels.

With only the small cat as her anchor, Danith tumbled, shrieking, into an all engulfing darkness. An emptiness that was not a true void, but pulsing with tearing emotions, hurtful flares of light, raucous noises.

Fury and fear gnawed on T'Ash. He banished them. Staring at Danith's closed back door, his jaw tightened. He would let her go now, but only for now.

With a little concentration he visualized his HouseHeart. He needed to be there, instantly. So he was.

The place welcomed him, the fire crackling with renewed vigor at his presence, the pool gently lapping its rim in greeting.

He sat on a bench and pulled his boots off. It took several tugs to strip the trous from his body, and he sent them directly to the cleanser.

Nude, he took a short dip in the warm pool. He dried off quickly, then bowed to the altar and in each direction, welcoming the Lord and Lady and the Guardians. Then he fit his body once more into the pattern of the Rainbow Serpent and the World Tree. Immediately he felt a connection, and the renewal of his strength and power.

The ancient cadence of the Residence pulsed through him, and he relaxed. Until the first little shock. A ripple of agitation came with each wave. And it grew.

He searched for it. Nothing could be allowed to harm his Residence, nothing so disturbing that it affected the very HouseHeart.

And he found it.

Danith!

His mind jumbled. His stomach clenched in fear.

Danith!

He reached for her and was caught in the great undertow of her first Passage.

Lord and Lady. Lord and Lady. He whispered desperate prayers as he grabbed a robe.

He teleported to his ResidenceDen.

Zanth was amusing himself by half-heartedly chewing on the furniture and batting the gallant's stupid little box around. T'Ash ran his finger around his scrybowl.

"Here," the Holly butler answered.

"Holm."

The butler inclined his head. "Of course, GreatLord."

"Urgent."

The man's features tightened. "Yes."

Seconds later Holm's concerned face projected larger than life over T'Ash's desk. "T'Ash?"

"Not at Ritual today."

Holm's nostrils flared. "You—"

"Can't. Emergency. Danith. Passage."

Holm's eyes widened. He jerked his head in a nod. "Right. I'll inform the others. T'Hazel will modify the Ritual to function without you. Go to your lady."

T'Ash cut the air and the spell.

Wait! Zanth called.

He didn't.

On the next breath he materialized at the back of Danith's house. He ran to the door. It opened under his hand. She had closed the door, but not spellshielded her home. Awful fear rose to squeeze his heart. He entered, then uttered a Word to protect the house.

He followed short, fretful mews to the bedroom. Princess whined, licked Danith's face, and kneaded her.

Danith barely breathed, and moaned in pain. Lord and Lady, he had brought her to this, raised her emotional levels, particularly the powerfully inciting emotion of anger. He'd thrust her time and again into conflict—and into close contact with Tinne Holly, who was on the flashpoint of his own Passage. T'Ash had taught her a few small spells that tapped, then unlocked her Flair, a great Flair that had slept for years instead of being released bit by bit. Now she would pay the price.

Yes. He had brought her to this, then stomped off in a temper without recognizing the signs of imminent Passage.

He wanted to slip off his robe but dared not. The energy buzzing around him both aroused him and irritated his nerves. He lay on the bed beside her and slowly turned her to her side. Her skin held a clammy grayness and fear rose into his throat. Did she even know what she was experiencing? None of her friends had great Flair.

She wouldn't know how to fight it, how to endure it, how, finally, to control it.

He slipped one of her hands to his neck, and it curled naturally around his throat, her thumb over his carotid artery so she felt his pulse. The sweet scent of spicy apples floated to him and he groaned. He could not possibly lose her! He cut the thought off. They could not afford a whisper of a negative thought.

Her other hand he placed inside his robe on his heart. She would learn he was here, and soon the beat of their hearts would match.

He positioned his own hands the same way on her. Her pulse fluttered lightly under his thumb.

He drew in a deep breath and prepared to sink deep inside himself, then to reach out for her, always for her, and find her.

It would be rough, but with a sliver of luck and his help, she would survive it.

And when it came down to the basics, she fought. He admired nothing more.

He shut his eyes.

*H*er mind echoed with her own lost cries in the timeless dark. She screamed until she could scream no more. Then, exhausted, she let the great whirlwind whisk her away. Soon she realized that huge waves of emotions overwhelmed her at odd intervals, shocking her with their intensity and detail. They tormented her with memories, and she couldn't do anything but suffer. And endure.

First came humiliation. Every embarrassing childhood mishap, every stupid word she'd ever said, every ill-advised action she'd ever made, beat on her until she writhed, feeling hot with mortification.

The cyclone spun her away. She tried to breathe. Guilt slammed into her with sins of commission, and the more afflicting sins of omission. What she should have done, could have done, to save someone pain. What she ignored. She swirled in an agony of self-flagellation.

Endless moments lapsed before despair descended. How could she ever think she was worthy of her Flair? She was nothing, deserved nothing, common and unfit to hold and craft a shining dream. She'd failed at many things, too many, large and small. Each failure an obstacle to climb. How could she go on?

"HERE!"

"Who?" she asked. Before the flash of words faded from her mind, she knew. She always thought of his strength first, and a strongly muscled arm wrapped around her, pulling her against a hard body.

"T'ASH!" his mind shouted to hers. Other words whipped away from her.

"What?"

"PASSAGE!"

Passage? Passage! The dreadful cost of great Flair.

Passage. She shuddered, and cold, icy fear plucked at her soul. The whirlwind transmogrified into a whirlpool. T'Ash held her tightly, but they both half-drowned in the spinning water.

Fear.

The first fear of pain as a child.

Fear of being alone when her parents died.

Fear of the House for Orphans.

Fear of being the smallest child in a new place.

Fear of the rules.

Fear of leaving the House for Orphans.

Fear of living on her own.

And new fears battered her.

Fear of punishment.

Fear of fire.

T'Ash's fears.

And the fire was one of the worst. It shadowed all his others. The strong body beside her in the turbulent waters trembled at the shadow of fire. She turned in his arms and held him tight.

Fear of being alone.

"I know that fear," she said, and hugged him close. The fear disappeared.

Fear of bigger children, tougher children, adults. His in Downwind, hers the first days at the House of Orphans.

"I know that fear," she said, and they faced down the line of images marching toward them.

Fear of fire.

"Water surrounds us. Fire cannot touch us." The maelstrom cast them away from memories of fear.

Each circuit increased in speed.

Rage.

Rage at her Father and Mother leaving her in death.

"I KNOW THAT RAGE!" T'Ash shouted. Visions of their lost families wrung tears from Danith to mix with the white waters around her.

Rage at the murderers of the Ashes.

"I KNOW THAT RAGE. I PROWLED THE VENGEANCE STALK AND IT IS DONE." T'Ash dismissed it.

Rage at the inability to pursue a dream.

"I KNOW THAT RAGE. MY DREAMS NOW COME TRUE. YOUR DREAMS BECKON TO BE FULFILLED."

"I know that rage. Let it go," she echoed.

A touch of a brighter emotion swept by.

Triumph.

Danith's joy at her first paycheck, her purchase of Pansy, her healing of Pansy.

"Yes!"

Vast exultation at fighting, at bodies spurting blood and falling into the rictus of death.

Danith gagged and choked, water entered her mouth, darkness threatened.

"NO! AND NO! AND NO! OVER AND DONE."

Triumph vanished.

Danith panted.

The pace increased. Pain. Joy. Grief. Confidence.

Rejection.

Five couples, faces she'd thought she'd forgotten, who'd preferred other children over herself.

Two respectable smiths who sneered at apprenticing a Downwind boy.

Timkin.

A disgusted GraceMistrys raising her eyebrows at T'Ash.

The pool whirled faster and faster. Instead of emotions wrenching through her, memories flashed by, incidents she barely recalled, T'Ash's memories she couldn't understand.

Finally the last few days rushed by—showing flickers of Mitchella, the Hollys, more.

She grabbed at the episodes T'Ash experienced, felt his pleasure in finding a HeartMate, his anger when the Heart-Gift was stolen, his hurt when she rejected him. The explosive memory of his last Passage shattered hers.

She heard herself moan and smelled the odor of her cold-sweated body before she could open her eyes.

T'Ash's hands rested on her body, one over her heart, the other encircling her throat. Pansy—Princess—snuggled against the small of her back.

She took her hands from him to rub the gluey substance from her eyes. She almost heard the creak of her lashes when they lifted.

T'Ash's startling light blue eyes stared into her own. His olive skin held a sheen of perspiration, like her own. His long black hair had tangled, once more like her own.

Her lips felt dry. She wet them with her tongue.

T'Ash groaned. He jerked his hands to himself and rolled over, his back to her. She saw the harshness of his breathing beneath his ash brown silkeen robe.

She didn't quite dare to reach out and touch him. Now he knew all her secrets, and despite the fact he was a dozen centimeters away, she didn't know if she could face him.

"T'Ash, are you hurt?"

"Not 'xactly."

"T'Ash?" She stopped, fingertips hovering close to the muscled indentation of his spine.

"No desire in Passage this time. Or Passion. Or happened too swiftly to impinge consciously. But the HeartGift's vibrations still linger. Don't you feel them?"

A sudden rush of pure carnal lust hit her. Her nostrils widened at his now-familiar scent of searing steel and man. Yet her mind, sluggishly, began to work.

Lust. It was there, but not overpowering. And suddenly she knew with absolute truth that he was using that as an excuse to draw away from her emotionally, just as afraid as she was to have his secrets probed by the other.

It piqued her, stirred a little remaining anger that had sparked the whole Passage, but she let it go, only noting in her accountant's brain that though they had just experienced Passage together, now he had once again withdrawn.

So, he fought desire. She scrambled to her feet. Princess rose with her.

Zanth stalked into the room. He raised his lip at her in disapproval. She glared back at him. Her head started to ache. "He's your Fam, deal with him." She headed to the bathroom.

T'Ash heard the flow of water start and stiffly uncurled himself. He rubbed his hands over his face and wondered what the odds were of Danith letting him use her shower. She probably expected him to teleport home while she bathed.

His blood pounded hotly, his muscles were stiff with sexual tension and his body was hard and ready to mate. He ached.

He wanted Danith. But more than he wanted her body, he wanted her company, now. He had to be sure she was well.

He should leave. He knew he should. He was in a weakened emotional state—a weakened emotional state? Where had he ever come up with that idea? That damned book of D'Rose's, the gushy, flowery one. The more he thought about it, the more he was sure a woman wrote *The Manual of Manners for the Gentleman of Noble Background,* and what, by the Cave of the Dark Goddess, would a woman know of a man's emotions? Stupid. But women probably made up this whole manners stuff, anyway.

My travel hard when FamMan and FamWoman in trance Passage. You not wait for Me.

"I was in a hurry."

Zanth tried a sniff, barely audible. T'Ash suppressed a smile; just being with Danith was curing Zanth's sinus condition. Soon it would be completely gone and Zanth would lose his sniff as punctuation.

Zanth growled.

We Family. Together. My help priceless. He jumped over T'Ash, and hit him hard with a paw to the jaw. *Remember.*

Zanth's stench billowed over T'Ash as he rubbed at his jaw. He choked. "Lord and Lady, you are ripe."

Zanth sat down, smugly. *Took long way. Two good kills.*

"That bedsponge cover is never going to be the same. I hope it isn't Danith's favorite."

"It's Danith's only cover," she said from the doorway. She narrowed her eyes and lifted her chin, actions T'Ash was beginning to dread.

"You, Fam. Leave or smell better."

Came to help. Un-grate-ful woman. Zanth huffed.

T'Ash slowly smiled. "How about the de-stench spell?"

Zanth shot a nasty look at Danith and hunkered down.

"What's this on your collar?" T'Ash plucked a piece of jewelry from the emerald collar. "A diamond earclip? Why would you want to ruin the appearance of your elegant collar with a diamond earclip?"

Zanth turned his head and stared out the window. His tail lashed. *Cat wears earclip. Other Mine.*

"Cat? What cat wears a diamond earclip?"

"Pansy, ah, Princess." Danith sighed. She waved to a shelf in the corner where her cat preened. Princess turned her head, and the diamond clip on her ear caught in the sunlight from the windows.

T'Ash grinned. Not only did her furred ears sport the clip, but chains bedecked her, a thick gold one, a spiral glisten one with an antique pearl pendant, and some matched ruby beads.

"There sits an absolutely beautiful cat with no need for any adornment but her own fur, loaded down with jewelry and here . . ." He snapped his mouth shut before he made any disparaging remarks about his Fam, tempting though they were. "Zanth, stick with just the collar. You look quite—"

"Debonair," Danith ended. "He's beautiful."

T'Ash stared at her. She really meant it.

He looked at Zanth.

Zanth smirked.

A soft smile on her face, Danith crossed to touch Zanth but stepped hurriedly back when she got another whiff of him.

"You're going to have to submit to the de-stench spell if you want to keep your admiring female audience, Zanth," T'Ash said.

Zanth hunched down again and curled the tips of his ears inward, preparing for the spell, but his gaze showed something close to adoration for Danith. *FamWoman has good taste.*

"He says you have good taste, Danith."

She winced and touched her temple. "Thank you, Zanth."

T'Ash clapped his hands together, and the sound reverberated with Flair. Danith decided she didn't want to watch and went into her mainspace.

Colors swirled on the ceiling over the scrybowl. She had message holos. Going over to the new bowl, she flicked a fingernail against the rim. The soft ping got lost in an outraged yowl coming from the next room.

"Play," she said.

GrandMistrys Balm, the clerk of the NobleCouncil, beamed from the message holo. "Happy Discovery Day, GrandLady D'Mallow." She smiled with self-deprecation. "I've assembled a display of the currently available Grand-House estates."

Danith watched in stunned fascination as holos of Grand-House Residences and their properties were projected. Views inside and out of the Residences and grounds were shown, including aerial scans and walk-thrus.

"And"—a note of excitement entered the GrandMistrys's voice—"I've heard rumors that GrandLady D'SilverFir, the renowned telepath, is placing the D'SilverFir properties on the market. What a plum!" A shadow briefly crossed Balm's face. "A FirstFamily estate, founded by one of the Earth colonists herself. It's so rare for those to be sold. A pity for GrandLady D'SilverFir, of course, but luck for you—"

Danith stopped listening and staggered over to collapse on her settee. It struck her that every aspect of her life had changed. The Flair she'd always felt within herself had been freed, she had been named Noble, jumped two classes, had her yearly salary quadrupled, and was offered a choice of prime property. Nobles constantly intruded on her life. And a cat talked to her!

Pansy meowed from the other room. Even Pansy. Pansy was no longer Pansy, but a walking advertisement for T'Ash's Phoenix called Princess.

Her scrystand was gone, an antique jewelry chest in its place. Her whole house reeked of powerful Flair and the persistent sexuality of the HeartGift necklace.

T'Ash had made himself felt.

Her friends deserted her.

Her entire life rocketed out of control.

She caught a misshapen reflection of herself in the little glisten vase holding T'Ash's rose, his first gift to her, just a couple of days before. Only her appearance hadn't changed, but everything else, every single thing in her life had shifted in the earthquake called T'Ash, and in moments.

She sank her head on her hands. She wanted to cry but felt beyond that, close to simple shrieking horror.

Large arms scooped her up, shifted her, cradled her as he sat on the settee and placed her on his lap.

"Stop holo," T'Ash commanded. The holo abruptly ceased. "You will live with me. From this house to T'Ash Residence. Nowhere else."

The earthquake T'Ash had spoken and expected everything to be conducted as he wished.

She giggled, a high, hysterical giggle.

A hand soothed her, stroking her head. "You're reacting from the Passage. Calm. It will pass."

"You're sure you don't want me to color my hair, my eyes, my skin?" she asked.

His muscles tensed a little under her cheek. "You are perfect as you are."

How trite. The man had no delicacy with words that pleased. She looked up at him and saw an unyielding jaw. "I want my Discovery Day gift from Claif."

His narrowed blue eyes blasered at her. "No."

"Then let me go, and leave yourself. And take the cat. Your cat. I haven't had much say in anything lately, and I want my gift."

She lifted her chin.

Zanth hissed. From the angry throbbing in her head, he and T'Ash were exchanging snarls.

A tattered, little velvet box appeared on her lap. She sat up straighter, but T'Ash's arm around her waist didn't waver.

She opened it and gasped at the lovely white-blue diamond. Tears for all she'd once wanted, all she'd lost, dampened her eyes.

T'Ash picked up the ring box. "CeltaDiamond, not of the first wat—"

Danith placed her fingers over his mouth. "I don't want to hear what it isn't. What it is, is an engagement ring."

He put his own hand over hers, nibbled at her fingertips. An arrow of pure desire speared through her.

He took her hand from his lips. "I have crafted marriage armbands, from redgold, during my last Passage. You've seen the old HeartGift I created during my third Passage, when I was a young man of twenty. A new HeartGift awaits you at my Residence." He lifted a hand.

She stopped it. "Don't summon it."

He looked at her slyly and snapped the box closed, tossing it to a nearby table. "And you don't like diamonds. You like colored stones."

She sighed, inwardly. She'd almost forgotten that teasing, intricate game he'd played with her over the months. She'd been half-aware of it. Majo would hustle to a corner of the shop when she'd enter, bringing out a new item that wasn't displayed in the cases, pitching its quality and uniqueness.

She tilted her head up. T'Ash's face looked hard, all angles, his skin swarthy, his light blue eyes intense. He'd always carry some part of Downwind about him. She wondered, secretly, if that was part of his attraction. The toughness he would always have, the strength of mind and body she could lean on.

She sighed.

"I didn't think of engagement rings, or of an engagement. I thought of marriage," he said.

Without a word Danith slid from his lap.

T'Ash stood to tower over her, his eyes fierce. He gestured to Claif's jeweler's box. "He doesn't want you. Not like I do. He isn't fighting for you."

Danith spun to face him. "He bought me an engagement ring!"

"He left you. He didn't stay to fight, to claim you or deny me."

Danith stomped her foot, crossed her arms. "You left, too."

T'Ash made a sweeping gesture. "That is irrelevant to this argument. That is between you and me and has no bearing."

Zanth hopped onto the settee, turning his head back and forth to watch T'Ash, then her. The Fam appeared amused.

Danith whirled around, afraid T'Ash's words were right. The tears returned. Rejected by Claif, too. She blinked the wetness from her eyes, looked at the timer. Gasped. "It's four septhours after Bel-high." Unsteadiness swept her, she tottered over to put her hand on the wall.

"Correct. Ritual time has come and gone. The Clover Family knows you are mine, not theirs."

First she'd missed their party, now their Ritual. Pratty would be spreading word that Danith was a noble and too good for them. Tears started rolling down her cheeks. She stared blindly at T'Ash.

"They were going to be my Family. I have gifts for Mitchella, and Trif, and Claif, and Pratty. I have a house gift for Pink. I have a token for the Ritual. I have food to contribute to the feast. It's over. They think I abandoned them."

"I am here. We are two, matched. We need no one else."

"I do."

"We have Zanth and Princess."

"I need more. I need a Family."

He set himself squarely before her. A gleam lit his eyes. "I can give you Family."

"You can't—" Her voice broke. "You can't give me aunts and uncles or sisters and cousins."

The air around him deadened.

She looked at T'Ash and Zanth, uncompromising in their maleness. "I need females, too."

"Zanth." He opened his arms and the huge cat leaped into them. "We go." Without the merest hint of sound, they vanished.

Danith didn't know what to do. She'd hurt him again, and now she felt guilty again. But why couldn't he compromise, for once?

There was no chance now she'd marry Claif, and she desperately fought to hold off her deep attraction to T'Ash, an attraction she knew he reciprocated, but with no idea whether he felt more than lust.

"Play," she said to the scrybowl.

GrandMistrys Balm faded away to be replaced by a worried Mitchella who paced in and out of scry range. "Danith. You've missed both the party and the Ritual. That's not like you. Are you all right? Everyone asked about you, and Claif sniped his way through the Ritual. He heard from Pink about that, let me tell you. I've never seen Claif's temper so ruffled. Viz me as soon as you can—that is, as soon as you get home. Blessed be."

Twelve

🍃

Danith found herself bone exhausted, and quietly weeping. Passage, she thought. She wasn't accustomed to using Flair, but it would now be integral to her life—to spend energy and need to renew it. She went into the kitchen for some redberries and swallowed a quick handful before she returned to her scrybowl. The antique jewelry stand kept it too high; she'd have to rearrange her mainspace to accommodate the larger bowl and the new piece of furniture.

Her bedroom held both the telepathic and sexual scents of T'Ash. The little glass shelf in the bathroom still housed his carved gemstone animals. The mainspace displayed gifts from T'Ash, Zanth, and Holly. Now only her kitchen was free of any hint of her new life, and she couldn't hide in her tiny kitchen!

"Mitchella," Danith said. The water in the scrybowl spun, then the image formed.

"Here. Danith, thank the Lady and Lord. Are you all right? Where were you last night?"

"Downwind."

"Downwind. I'm coming right over. Don't move. You look awful. Have you been crying?"

Danith nodded.

"I'll be right there."

"Thank you."

Gloom, Gloom, Gloom. Zanth grumbled.
T'Ash lay in the center of the Rainbow Serpent mosaic, encompassed by the painted World Tree in his HouseHeart. He tried not to think, but to let the ancestral pulse of his land and his Residence calm him and imbue him with revitalizing energy.

He heard the swishings of Zanth rolling in the dirt. The smell of scorched whiskers tinged the air. T'Ash opened his eyes but only saw the gently rounded dome of the chamber overhead. When he heard the tiny slap of a paw in water and a cat hiss, he smiled. Zanth was conducting his own ritual.

Though the Fam made no more noises, T'Ash knew the cat had padded over and jumped into a niche, holding his paw out to the draft of fresh air that swirled in the duct. Then the Fam would jump down and go over and sit before the black Egyptian cat-goddess statue that graced one of the dim corners of the room. The statue was smaller than Zanth.

Zanth didn't often use the HouseHeart. T'Ash wondered if his Fam sought answers to the same questions that plagued himself.

At least they were both replete with cocoa mousse. T'Ash shifted a little. They'd finished the large batch for evening meal. T'Ash would have to order at least two batches from his chef to tide them over during the next holiday—Summer Solstice, six weeks from now.

The chef would be back tomorrow. The holiday was over. Most people would return to work, including T'Ash's shop manager, Majo.

T'Ash had just fulfilled a demanding commission and could rest. On the other hand, he'd given most of his backlog for women's jewelry to Danith.

Danith. His thoughts circled round to her. They always would, his HeartMate. Again, he wondered what to do. How he could win her. All she had to do was accept the earrings, his new HeartGift, and he could draw her into the Heart-

Bond Ritual, a mental and physical consummation that would bind them to each other forever.

Zanth traipsed over and flopped himself on T'Ash's ankle, then wriggled around, finding his personal painted space in the roots of the World Tree.

T'Ash grunted. The Fam felt considerably heavier on T'Ash's ankle, and his stomach rounder than the last time they'd been like this.

T'Ash stopped thought and let his mind drift once more.

The scent of jasmine rose around him. Jasmine. Both his mother's name and the perfume she crafted. She hadn't been a great Flair, but an adoring wife and a fine mother. Mother. His father loved Mother. The younger Nuin, the Heir and his brother, loved Mother. Gwidion loved Mother. Rand, who became T'Ash, loved Mother, too.

And then he knew his mind would wind back to the fire or to Danith and HeartMates. He chose Danith.

He wanted the same sort of marriage his parents had. For once in his life, he wanted someone to put him first. Danith had to accept the HeartGift.

He didn't want to think that she'd reject the HeartGift, or him, again. That it wouldn't be so easy as just giving her the HeartGift to win her.

Nor did he want to think of what he could offer her as a HeartMate. A week ago he could have offered her wealth, rank, and an end to the drudgery of her job.

Now rank and wealth had been conferred upon her, along with a future of Flair and fulfillment. It was only a matter of time before she gained a prominent reputation.

He couldn't give her wealth or rank or freedom from a struggling life.

She had to accept the HeartGift.

All he could give her was himself.

Too frightening to contemplate.

She had to accept the HeartGift.

His meditative state destroyed, T'Ash rose.

Zanth grunted. *You woke me!*

So much for a Fam's heavy thoughts.

T'Ash went to the altar and blew out the candles. The room dimmed to the flickering fire that never died.

T'Ash dismissed the Guardians of the Watchtowers and opened the circle.

"Coming?"

You SURE no more cocoa mousse?

"No more."

Zanth's tongue flicked out and swiped around his mouth. *Mice in GrandHouse Wheat Res-i-dence. Fat, tasty mouse. Yum. Yes.*

"You're thinking about your belly again? Let me tell you, Fam, if we don't win Danith, we won't care about anything as simple as our bellies."

Zanth stretched luxuriously. *FamWoman your Mate. Dice say so. Her cards say so. Done.*

T'Ash gritted his teeth. "Then you believe everything is destined, every single paw-step is preordained."

Me do what Me want and everything follows.

"That's contradictory."

Zanth shrugged. *Me want mouse. One, two.*

"You're getting fat."

Zanth narrowed his eyes and hissed. *You not only one in Passage with FamWoman. Me there sometimes too. Hungry.*

T'Ash put his hands on his hips. "You remember that lean, gray alley cat that hung around our hovel? I bet you couldn't beat him in a race to a sewer rat now."

Zanth lifted his head haughtily. *Cat dead. Ferals not live long. Two years.*

T'Ash narrowed his own eyes. "I think I've seen a youngster or two around that looks a lot like him, maybe even one in Danith's neighborhood, that eats from her outside bowl. To beat a rival, you have to be tough."

Me tough.

"You're fat."

Muscle.

T'Ash snorted. "Ask Princess. Race other, younger toms. See if what I say isn't true."

Zanth lashed his tail, stalked to the door, and waited for T'Ash to open it. T'Ash did.

Nice night. Good to hunt celtaroons.

"You can't eat celtaroons, they're poisonous."

Big celtaroon nest near Druida East Gate. Long hunt. Much running. Much fighting. Me kill. Me hero.

"Be careful." T'Ash closed and locked the door with the tortuous twenty spell Word.

Me not fat. Me Tough Noble Fam. Celtaroons fast, sly furry-snakes, but Me get them ALL.

"Good idea."

Will bring skins home.

"Not necessary."

You must count. Know.

"You can donate them to the East Gate GuardHouse. They like to use the blue and orange furry-snakeskins to line their boots."

Take to FamWoman. Show.

"No. Recall how she feels about sewer rat smell. If you bring her celtaroons . . ."

Big stink. Zanth chuckled. *Take to guards. You viz. Tell them Me come. Tell them Count.*

"I'll do that."

The entrance gong by the front gate rang.

Me go.

"I'll see you later. Use the air scourbath before you jump on my bedsponge."

Good hol-i-day deed, kill celtaroons. Hero. Hero. Hero. Rumbling under his breath, Zanth trotted for the nearest Famdoor.

T'Ash strode to his ResidenceDen, pulling on a robe. He tapped his imaging crystal to activate the estate scrystone. When he saw the woman striding back and forth before his greeniron gate, he enlarged the holo. She was a voluptuous redhead that just a week before would have made his blood burn. Her complexion rivaled true cream, her eyebrows delicately arched over nicely lashed eyes of emerald. A straight nose and winsome mouth. A face a man could fall for, if he could tear his eyes off her body.

T'Ash narrowed his gaze. She looked all wrong at that gate. Not Downwind enough for a licensed tavern wench, not Noble, unless she was a daughter of one of the many GraceHouses he didn't know.

"Here," he said, not engaging the spell that would show himself.

Her smile should have taken his breath, but to him, it couldn't hold a candle to the slightest curve of Danith's lips.

She struck a pose, hip cocked with a hand on it, eyelids lowered. "Can I interest you in a little female companionship?"

"Thank you, no."

She looked surprised, and white teeth showed in a genuine smile.

"You don't look as if you need food or gilt," T'Ash said.

Her smile broadened and the beastfur-edged coat slipped a little off shoulders as magnificent as her breasts and hips.

A woman outside his estate, offering pleasure, was so unusual as to be unlikely. "You are?"

Her eyebrows lifted again. The dancing flicker in her green eyes faded, the sultry pose dropped, as she drew herself to an impressive height. "Mitchella Clover."

Not a name he cared to hear. "What relation to Claif?"

"Sister—and," she added deliberately, "best friend to Danith Mallow."

Zanth strolled out of his small gate at the estate entrance and walked around her, examining her. *Smells ac-cept-able. Some smell of FamWoman.* Intentionally encroaching on her space, he sat in front of her toes.

She looked down at him. "You look familiar. Haven't I seen you around?" She pursed her lips. "One of those strays that hang around Danith's place." She shook her head. "Look at those ears, completely flat. You're the most disreputable cat I've ever seen."

Zanth growled.

"He is familiar. T'Ash's Familiar, Zanthoxyl," T'Ash said.

She made a moue. "Oh, dear."

Something about her reminded him of Danith. "A friend of my lady?"

She looked at him straightly. "Yes, O Lord of Blasers, I am."

The Lord of Blasers, the card Danith thought represented him. The card that had lain with the Lovers on Danith's table.

She tapped her foot, and T'Ash wondered which of the women had picked up the mannerism from the other. "Come in. Zanth will show you the way. Zanth, give the GentleLady some room."

Grrrr. No nice talk.

"Zanth wants an apology."

She looked down at the cat. And sniffed.

T'Ash suppressed a smile. Zanth's sniff was gone. He'd lost one of his major ways to comment. The fact that an insulting female could use it instead would ruffle his fur.

Zanth arched his thick neck so the nightpole lights caught his emerald collar.

Mitchella gasped in admiration.

With a preening grace, Zanth stood and turned to the massive gates, tail arrogantly upright and waving.

"Pray excuse me, Sir Familiar," Mitchella said, her tone light.

T'Ash didn't know whether she was being sarcastic, or just amused. He shrugged. Zanth could handle himself. If worse came to worse, the woman would find a messily killed celtaroon on her doorstep.

T'Ash hummed the spell that lowered the protection of the front gate and the grounds. She'd still feel the spell-shields as an irritant to the fine hair on her skin, but T'Ash was in no mood to grant quarter to any Clover.

With a slow force the left gate opened. Mitchella stepped aside, then through when it came to a solemn halt. She followed Zanth down the wide, dark-graveled glider path and stopped at the beginning of the meadow and grassyard. T'Ash saw awe and appreciation in her gaze as she studied his Residence. "Quite extraordinary. I'd heard it was one of the architect Ebony's last projects, quite controversial—"

"Designed as I wanted it."

She pressed her lips together. "And you got it. The question I have is, what do you want with Danith?"

"Come, I'm waiting." He flicked off the sound and watched her march down the path behind Zanth, muttering.

Female knows good swears. Zanth sounded once more in charity with the woman.

Though she strolled into the ResidenceDen with an essentially female arrogance, her expression appeared stunned. "Your Residence is—extraordinary, GreatLord, but have you—ah—considered a decorator?"

"Danith will do that."

She set a hand over her heart in a gesture that reminded him of D'Rose. He stared at her. In person she had an allure that teased a man's senses. It might have charmed him had he not been immune to her. He only wanted his HeartMate.

She made T'Ash uneasy. She didn't fit here as Danith did. Obviously Zanth felt the same since he led her to one of the chairs that Danith hadn't graced.

Mitchella sat and crossed her legs gracefully. Zanth jumped to the corner of the desk closest to her, keeping a watchful eye out.

She glanced around, then met T'Ash's eyes. "Perhaps Danith can't—" she started.

"Danith can do anything she tries. I like her home. She will do well by T'Ash GreatHouse Residence."

"GreatLord, the furnishing of a Residence is a massive undertaking. From what I understand, Danith is on the verge of building a new and exciting career—"

He smiled. "She will master that, as well. She will be very content, with her career, with this Residence. With me." He dared her to contradict him.

"But will you be content with her?"

The mellow mood he'd received from his HouseHeart was quickly being eroded. He leaned intimidatingly over his desk. "She is my HeartMate. Found during Passage. We will bond together."

"I've just been speaking with Danith. She has great doubts." Mitchella made an elegant gesture. "And if the Residence reflects the man, I would say she has cause to doubt. You display very little comfort here. The atmosphere begs for warmth—"

"Danith's very presence will provide warmth. You think I don't know that?"

"And you, will you remain cold?"

"She will teach me—"

"While she is decorating your Residence, pursuing her career, catering to your needs, befriending your Fam, fulfilling the responsibilities demanded by the FirstFamilies Council for people of your rank. Just what do you plan on doing for her?"

He hissed in a breath. Then slowly circled the desk. She shrank in her chair and he was pleased. He smiled, showing all his teeth.

She clasped her hands tightly.

"Perhaps you should consider who you offend."

Her spine straightened. "That's just it. Look at you. A GreatLord. Your lifestyle and Danith's are too different. She is right to worry. You would demand and order and badger her until she had no will of her own." Mitchella tossed her red head. "Well, consider this, GreatLord. Danith is barren. She contracted Macha's disease as a child. It left her sterile."

The blow was so quick and devastating, he didn't feel the pain at first. Then a great agony built within him, setting him afire from the inside out.

The scream tore from him, the power of it flinging his head back.

Thunder.

Lightning.

The Residence trembled around them.

Zanth teleported.

Mitchella ran.

T'Ash grabbed her. His vision dimmed as always before he went berserk.

"Stop!" she cried. "Let me go. I lied. I lied. It's me who's barren. Me. Not Danith. Let me go!"

With his last rational thought, he visualized Danith's house and mentally flung the deceitful bitch there.

*T*he sound of the timer striking the hour woke him. His whole body ached. He stretched, but didn't attempt to rise from his sprawl on the floor. His mouth itched. He brushed his hand against it, rubbing away dried froth.

Damn.

His eyes started to feel a little wet. He bit his lip, hard. He'd thought he'd never be so out-of-control again, thought the feral savagery was now beyond him. His steady life had lulled him. He'd hoped he wouldn't have to reveal this one, awful, fault—this unforgivable defect—to Danith. It had been years, and surely was long past. Newly triggered, the bestial berserker incident would be in his immediate memory, easily reached by the mental touch of a HeartMate.

He had wondered if she would accept the earrings, pledge to him, before he had to completely bare his soul. With fatalistic calm, he knew she would never simply accept his new HeartGift, and him. That, somehow, he would have to win her.

But first things first.

"ResidenceLibrary, present Analytical Spell: Truthfulness."

A small, warm draft bearing words whistled around his ears. He managed to get his tongue around the complex chant. Then he ordered, "Review the events of the last septhour. Interview with Mitchella Clover. Two statements before her teleportation. First Statement: 'Danith is barren.' "

The chamber hummed around him. His mother's voice answered. "Subject's blood pressure rose, perspiration increased, heart beat increased. Analysis: first statement is untrue."

The dreadful shadow on his heart began to recede. "Now examine the Second Statement: 'I lied.' "

"Analysis difficult. Subject in a state of hysteria. All bodily signals are agitated." There was a moment of silence. "Recommend a Level Four Analysis Spell."

T'Ash sighed. He stretched again, shifted until he felt more comfortable. "ResidenceLibrary, present Level Four Analysis Spell: Truthfulness."

This time a murmur of a distant waterfall came to him, and he found the proper Words in the sound. And this time he chanted the spell more easily. "Review the last hour, analyze all bodily signals of Mitchella Clover, at every level, tabulate results on the truth of her last statement."

A long silence resulted. Long enough for T'Ash to rise and shake his stiff limbs out. He looked around. The desk was kindling, a heap of unrecognizable wood. A pile of indestructible papyrus and info crystals were tumbled in one corner. Shreds of cloth and more wood indicated the remains of three chairs.

Two chairs and the ugly screen appeared untouched by his mad rage, an unbelievable fact. T'Ash ran his fingers over them, felt faint emanations of Danith. His jaw relaxed. He hadn't destroyed anything his HeartMate had used. The bedroll and llamawoolweave cover were also intact. He picked up the soft cover and wrapped it around himself. His robe, too, had been ripped from his body and shredded beyond redemption.

"Conclusion available," the spell said.

"Play."

"Last statement of Mitchella Clover, in a hysterical state: 'Stop!' is truth. 'Let me go.' Truth. 'I lied.' Truth. 'I lied.' Emphatic truth. This emphasis is key to the analysis. 'It's me who's barren.' Additional truth. The addition of information in a frantic condition leads to the conclusion the statements were completely honest at the time. 'Me.' Truth. 'Not Danith.' Truth. 'Let me go!' Truth."

"Cease spell."

T'Ash glanced at the timer. Though it felt like an eternity since Mitchella Clover uttered the fateful word *barren,* it was less than a septhour. Another thing to be grateful for, that his primal berserker seizure burned out with uncommon rapidity.

After one more glance at the timer, he figured that Zanth must be chasing celtaroons by now, burning fat. T'Ash smiled.

He walked from the ResidenceDen to the master bathroom, summoning the D'Rose courtship book on the way. He glanced at it as he adjusted the waterfall temperature in his shower room. As he suspected, the book had both holo and sound capabilities.

"Read to me at highest volume," he instructed as he stepped into the cleansing downpour. A new strategy to be forged. Time to do it right.

"*D*anith, I'm scared."

Mitchella didn't have to tell Danith. Her friend's wide

emerald eyes and pasty skin gave her away. So did the trembling of her body.

Danith pressed another cup of hot and soothing hybrid chamomile tea upon Mitchella.

"The man is wild. His eyes went all blaserhot blue. I thought he'd erupt." She shivered again.

Danith tugged the llamawoolweave throw around Mitchella, who sat on the settee, and took her own chair across from her friend.

"He has a Downwind background," Danith said.

"It's more than that. What, I'm not sure. But more."

"He's a member of the thirteen GreatHouses and of the twenty-five FirstFamilies. They all had great Flair when they left Earth centuries ago to find a place to develop their Flair. They bred for it in the generation starships, and ever since we landed. I've felt T'Ash's huge power. And those Families all have secrets of their own. They aren't like us."

Mitchella swallowed the last of her herb tea and set her mug down on the table beside the settee. "You're right. They aren't like us. You'd be mad to get involved with them. Let them run the world, but don't let one in your life." Her restless fingers plucked at the fringe of the blanket.

Danith only partially agreed, and pondered how she'd changed. She once would have completely agreed, yet now a doubt or two niggled at her opinions. But she didn't want to upset Mitchella any further, and she still didn't know what to do about T'Ash.

She slid her eyes to the deck of cards that Mitchella had given her for Discovery Day.

"Have you read them lately?" asked Mitchella.

"No."

"Let's. A three-card divination—"

"Family. Career. Love."

Mitchella frowned. "I was going to suggest 'Future,' 'Environment,' 'Helps or Hinders.' "

Danith nibbled on her lip. "Family. Helps or Hinders. Love." Wondering whether the cards would indicate T'Ash once more in "Love," kept prodding at her. But she didn't want to face it alone.

"All right," Mitchella said.

Danith crossed to the table and picked up the cards. She'd only used them a couple of times, yet they felt strong and familiar in her hands. And they also contained an underlying energy that she now recognized as the vibration of her own personal Flair. She smiled and shuffled the cards.

Mitchella drew a table in front of the settee. Danith hooked a foot around a chair leg and dragged it to the table, still imbuing the cards with her question and her power.

She sat, cut the cards three times to the left.

"Family," she said, plucking the top card from the far left stack and turning it over. Two of Stars, a binary star system of two stars revolving around each other; it signified a situation that could remain in balance or go out of control. Danith shivered, not what she wanted to see.

"Helps and Hindrances." She flipped over the top card from the second stack. The Fool. Was being impulsive, going blindly, following her intuition, helpful or not? Another equivocal card.

"Love." She turned over the last one. Lord of Blasers.

"T'ASH ARRIVES!" a stentorian voice announced just before the clap of teleportation.

Mitchella flinched and kicked the table over. Cards flew everywhere.

Danith jumped to her feet.

T'Ash arrived.

He looked awesome. Dressed all in black furra leather, blaser on one hip, broadsword on another, his eyes were as blue and intense as ever against his olive complexion. His long hair looked straight and blackly wet.

He stared at Mitchella, and a midnight blue aura crackled sparks around him. "She's here," he hissed.

Mitchella huddled in the corner of the settee.

"She lies," T'Ash said, turning his hard glare to Danith. His eyes might have softened, but she saw the pulse in his temple beat rapidly.

Mitchella flinched.

Danith blinked, looked from one to the other.

"She told me you were barren."

A hand seemed to squeeze all Danith's insides together. She didn't know what to say, who to defend.

T'Ash's gaze burned. She saw torment, a deep torment that looked as though it had lasted years, in his eyes.

"I thought it would be a measure of his love, to know if he'd still want you if you were barren," Mitchella whispered.

Danith ached for her. The fact Mitchella was barren was like a great hole she covered up and tried to forget. The Clovers had been very supportive, but everyone knew Mitchella would not add her children to the Family.

T'Ash spoke. "Whatever mate I wanted, T'Ash can't marry a sterile woman. My line, ancestors, demand children. That female lied. Not honorable. Not kind. Not right. Not deserving of friends. Payment due." He stared once more at Mitchella. She rose and edged toward the front door, looking white as salt.

Danith squared her shoulders. "She's my friend. She made a mistake."

Mitchella bolted, slamming the door behind her.

Danith closed her eyes for an instant to regain her strength. When she opened them once more, T'Ash was picking up the spilled cards. She bent down to help.

They worked quietly. When she'd gathered the ones near her, she evened the deck. "Is that all of them?"

"One's over here." He took a couple of steps, and reached down for the last, but halted, mid-crouch.

"Is something wrong?"

"No." The very tone of his voice, leeched of all expression, lied.

"What card is it?" She started toward him.

"Nothing to be concerned about." He stood and slipped the card in the middle of his stack before she could see the image.

She raised her eyebrows. "You know as well as I that a card falling away from the pack is an omen."

"Some omens mean nothing."

He protested too much.

"It wasn't the Cave of the Dark Goddess, was it?"

"No." Now he squared his bunch and handed them to her. "They feel good. Like you." His hand closed over her own.

Instant awareness of him as a man flooded her, with the usual sizzle of power pulsing between them.

Danith narrowed her eyes. She could have sworn he'd been furious a few moments before. "You aren't angry anymore," she said.

His fingers caressed her own until she withdrew, busying her hands with straightening the entire deck.

"Because of your touch. It calms me. Because I now know you aren't sterile. Having you here, in this pleasant home, alone with me, is very nice—comfortable."

"Where's Zanth?"

"Chasing celtaroons."

"Celtaroons?"

"He's getting fat. He needs the exercise."

"They're so poisonous, isn't that dangerous?"

A half-smile curved T'Ash's lips. "Zanth is a match for a nest of 'roons. Besides, Celta now has an Animal Healer."

Heat climbed to her cheeks. "I'm not trained yet."

He shrugged. "A fine-tuning of your Flair, only. You need to learn spells and skills." He lowered his eyelids a little and Danith caught her breath at the intimacy of his gaze. "Zanth would be pleased that you care for his welfare."

"I—like him."

T'Ash's smile broadened, his lashes swept up to reveal sparkling eyes. "Not an easy thing to do, often, to like Zanth. He has a unique personality."

"But he's your Family," she said softly.

T'Ash's face stilled, the expression in his eyes turned wary. Pounding came on the door.

T'Ash pivoted, reaching for his blaser.

"Stop that." She glared at him as she passed to answer the door.

"Don't!" he ordered.

"My house, GreatLord." She threw the door open.

Pink Clover and his brother, Mel, the two largest men of that Family, both wide rather than tall, stood with Mitchella and Trif Clover on the front stoop.

"There he is!" Mitchella pointed to T'Ash.

Pink gulped but gathered his bulk and walked in, followed by Mel and Mitchella. Remaining on the porch, Trif looked fascinated, but also stood poised to run for help at the slightest hint of danger.

T'Ash bared his teeth at them, keeping his hand on his blaser hilt. No one else was armed.

The air in the room roiled with tumultuous emotions.

Pink eyed T'Ash, slid a hand over his balding head, and spoke to Danith. "Mitchella's concerned about you and the GreatLord. She—"

"Danith is always safe in my presence," T'Ash said.

Pink stiffened and faced T'Ash squarely. Though sweat beaded his face, he answered the challenge. "Danith is like a daughter to me. I won't have her bullied or intimidated. There are laws that the FirstFamilies must follow, GreatLord."

With a long, strong arm T'Ash swept Danith behind him. She grabbed at his shirt to keep her balance. "Wait just one minute—"

"Danith is mine. She needs no other Family."

Mitchella spoke. "She needs us and we need her."

"You only care that she is Noble now."

"Stop this, T'Ash." Danith tried circling around his other side. He kept her behind him with his other hand.

"You can't have her. Not anymore. Tell that puppy, Claif. She's mine now, and I'll take care of her."

"Stop!" Danith cried.

"Danith?" Pink craned his neck to see her. "Are you all right? Does Trif need to go for the Guards?"

T'Ash made a low, anticipatory sound in his throat.

"No." Danith said, holding on to the shreds of her temper. A temper that had been tested all too often lately. "Please leave, Pink and Mel. I appreciate your thoughtfulness, but let me handle it."

"I'm not going until he does," Mitchella announced, jerking her chin at T'Ash.

Danith wrenched herself away from T'Ash. "I think that's a good idea. The last few days have been very wearing, and I haven't been composed enough to conduct my Discovery Day Ritual. I'd like some peace and quiet. Please, all of you, go."

Mitchella glanced at Trif, who lingered on the porch, then Mitchella crossed her arms and adopted a solid stance. Pink sighed and copied her, as did his brother.

T'Ash also adjusted his stance, shifting on his feet just as he had when he faced the Downwind gang. He kept his hands loose and near his weapons.

He had to leave first. But the man had an abundance of pride.

Danith sidled to his side. "Please leave, T'Ash," she whispered for his ears only.

"No."

She knew she reddened from tension and anger and embarrassment. She put a hand on his near elbow. His glance darted to her, then back to the others. Again she made her voice so low that only he could hear. "Are you going to deny me, T'Ash? Deny my request in front of my friends? Is that how you care for me?"

His eyes narrowed and his jaw tightened. "They are not your Family."

She didn't retort that neither was he. "We have spoken of this before, and will do so again. Right this minute the issue is my request of you and whether you will honor it."

Thirteen

T'Ash glowered at her. "You are always asking me to leave. I don't like it. You are choosing them instead of me. Not right." Now his mutter was too low to carry to straining ears.

"Why must we decide this issue this very moment?" Danith asked.

"Because this very moment is when it's happening," T'Ash replied.

"I'm not ready."

"You're a coward."

Too much. Once again the whole thing was too much. She lurched away from him before he could grab her. "Trif," Danith called to the girl on the porch, horrified at the sound of tears clogging her own voice. T'Ash couldn't care for her, not if he humiliated her in her own home this way. He didn't have the least bit of sensitivity.

"Here, Danith," the girl replied.

"I go," T'Ash's voice overrode everyone else. "The rest of you, leave within two minutes. I will know."

Pink nodded, eyes wide. Mitchella glared at T'Ash. Trif hopped from foot to foot in excitement.

T'Ash teleported out with a clap of thunder that expressed

his feelings and must have rid him of some of his seething anger.

"Danith, you all right?" Pink repeated.

She managed a smile, shook her head. "My life is a mess. But, all in all, I'm fine."

"You come to us, girl, if you need to." He squared his wide shoulders in an action that made his big belly jiggle. "We'll stand by you. GreatLord or no." With a short nod he left. Mel copied the nod and followed.

"Thank you," Danith said, her tears from anger turning to tears of gratitude. "Blessed be."

"That man, that T'Ash, doesn't like me." Mitchella tossed her head. "And he won't for some time to come. I hope you don't get too involved with him. I thought Claif was bad for you, but T'Ash . . . he's beyond me." She patted Danith on the shoulder, even as she stared suspiciously at the space T'Ash had occupied. Then she hugged Danith tightly and kissed both her cheeks. "You take care of yourself. You deserve to."

Danith smiled. "I get to saunter into Cinque and Poppy tomorrow and quit."

Mitchella grinned. "Now, that's something to savor, isn't it? Keep your spirits up. If you need anything, just viz." Glancing at her wrist timer, she plunged from the room.

Trif still stood on the front porch, eyes large and round and an excited expression on her face. "You think that Great-Lord can sense me from here?"

Danith shrugged.

Trif peered around the door frame. "I think it's been two minutes. I think I'm safe," she said in satisfaction, obviously pleased with an exciting experience. "He's terribly gwr, Danith. Really virile. Possessive and rich and Noble. I think you should keep him."

Danith laughed.

"Yeah. And if he has any young friends—young and gwr and handsome and rich and noble, you let me know." Trif winked.

"I'll do that," Danith said, thinking of Tinne Holly, then discarding the notion. Trif and Tinne—what an explosive mixture for trouble.

"But I suppose this means I'll have to fill that *wretched*

job for the family firm that everyone thought you'd take after you married Claif. That's like stinkweed." With a wave, Trif skipped away.

"Merry meet!" Danith shouted.

Trif stopped. "Merry part."

"And merry meet again."

Trif waved once more and disappeared into the night.

Danith sighed and sank down onto her settee. Absent-mindedly, she picked up the cards and occupied her hands by sifting them in a slow shuffle. With each touch, they resonated more of her. She smiled.

Closing her eyes, she traced other vibrations—a paw or two of Princess and of Zanth, Mitchella's dynamic energy, and the intensity of T'Ash. Concentrating on her fingertips, she went through the deck, card by card, until she felt one that hummed of T'Ash's emotions more than the others. Undoubtedly the one he'd found fallen away from the rest.

She opened her eyes and looked at the image.

A woman surrounded by blasers.

A woman in danger.

T'Ash paced. Everything had splintered again, like poorly cast glisten. He mumbled under his breath. This Family stuff was going to be a major thing with Danith. He knew it. Hadn't she told him so twice?

Damn. What should he do? What would a smooth Holly do? For an instant he contemplated vizing Holm, but still felt irritated at the Holly heir for his interference. And if T'Ash actually asked Holm to further interfere . . . He shuddered. Too many people were being mixed up in this whole affair. Hard to keep quiet, hard to control.

Rumors would be rife about Danith and himself. He wondered if that would help or hinder his courtship.

He couldn't think. When he thought, he got bogged down in all the confusion of what to do with a female, trying to judge her and anticipate her.

Though when he acted he didn't seem to do any better. What to do next? Perhaps a small, a very small, strategic retreat.

Danith would be coping with her new status tomorrow. Perhaps in the evening she would be grateful for a helping hand. He must become as important to her as those damned Clovers. And they couldn't do much in the circles she'd now be traveling in.

Yes, he could and he would help her and earn more of her gratitude. He might even carry the earrings in his pocket, maybe even show her them—not that he'd offer them to her, of course, because that could lead to one more rejection. But if he showed them to her, he could gauge her reaction, at least.

He didn't like the Clovers, and wondered how he could remove Danith from their bothersome influence.

He walked up to his suite and carefully set the blaser on his bedtable, and the broadsword by the edge of the bed-sponge. He peeled out of his clothes.

He was just sinking into the welcome blackness of sleep when he heard Zanth's gleeful shout. *Fourteen celtaroons. ME Hero. Hero. Hero. Life is good.*

The persistent chiming of an urgent First Family viz woke T'Ash the next morning. "Here," he said, not bothering to rise from his bedsponge or turn on the holo from his end.

"T'Ash?" The deep rumble of T'Holly addressed him. T'Holly looked like an older version of Holm—silverwhite hair, elegant visage, dark-gray eyes. Though T'Ash respected him, he was wary of the GreatLord.

"Here," T'Ash repeated.

"I request a personal favor, both on my behalf, and on my Heir's."

T'Ash jerked up to sit. "I'm listening."

T'Holly's well-shaped lips thinned. The holo showed a man with a pallor to his skin. "Tinne has not returned. We have been unable to locate him, his vibrations fluctuate too wildly to get a fix upon him. Apparently he has—mis-placed—his HouseRing. His Mother worries that his finger could be gone, his hand, even his arm. We cannot determine his health."

"Holm?"

"My Heir searches in Downwind. We believe Tinne's still in that area, nothing could hide him from us anywhere else. Is it possible that you can locate the main gauche you made?"

"Probable." T'Ash pulled on clean clothes and strapped on his weapons. "I'll send my Fam out to hunt for Tinne immediately, and will follow as soon as I grab a meatroll."

T'Holly closed his eyes an instant. "My thanks. Smoke covers Downwind, it's hard to tell whether the smoke is completely natural or not. Several guards are missing, and there are reports of gangs, fighting, fires"—he gestured—"general turmoil."

"Downwind matters should have garnered more attention from the Councils this last year," T'Ash said evenly.

T'Holly nodded. "So you said. I regret we did not follow your advice."

"Downwind must be renovated or else we will be faced with some of the problems our ancestors left Earth to escape. They didn't come here only to use their Flair freely, you know. There were numerous difficulties on old Earth. One of them was the gap between rich and poor, powerful and helpless. We cannot allow a great discrepancy to develop between Downwind and the rest of society."

"I hear you. Your concern is so noted in the FirstFamilies Council records and will be given the deepest consideration."

T'Ash thought of the fighting Downwind. Of smoke and fire. Of danger. Of a woman surrounded by blasers. "I have an unclaimed HeartMate. Should anything happen to me—"

"She will be cared for by the Hollys, now and in the future, no matter what occurs."

"Protect her at all costs."

"I promise."

"Good. Fare well." T'Ash disconnected the scryspell.

He went to the round window and placed his hand upon the large rose quartz crystal. Aligning himself with the House-Heart rhythms and matching them to the angles of the crystal, he sought Tinne's main gauche. He stretched all his senses to penetrate the distance between his estate and Downwind. For an instant he touched the main gauche, felt the wetness of new blood on its blade, the exhaustion of the hand that held it, a young Holly hand. Then his vision disappeared.

"Scry T'Holly," T'Ash ordered.

"Here." The older man snapped.

T'Ash engaged the holo on his end.

"T'Ash!"

"The main gauche remains with Tinne. I felt fatigue and unconsciousness, but no great wounds. Tell your wife he lives."

"My deepest thanks."

"I go."

"T'Holly allies for three generations with T'Ash."

T'Ash felt heat rise to his face at the honor. "Agreed. A distinction I appreciate."

"You deserve it. Tinne—"

"I like the boy. I am glad to be of assistance. Blessed be."

"Blessed be." The scry holo went dark.

"Zanth!" T'Ash yelled.

Me here. Zanth burped. *Eggs with cheddar.*

"Did you hear T'Holly?"

Some. What we get?

T'Ash frowned. "I did not set a price."

Zanth extended a hind leg, separated his toes, and began to groom long curved claws. A faint but distinct odor of celtaroon permeated the air. *Stupid. What we do?*

"You will recall Tinne Holly?"

Very nice-smelling boy.

"He's lost Downwind."

Zanth flicked his claws in and out. *Me find.*

"I'll follow."

You need food.

"Meatrolls."

Get four. Now send Me.

"The alley where we last saw him." T'Ash constructed a detailed picture in his mind, adding morning sunlight and shadows.

Me go. Me set price with Hollys.

"We'll decide that later. Find the boy."

"Grrrr." Zanth lashed his tail, and disappeared, propelled Downwind by T'Ash.

"HouseHeart, all systems to be keyed to Danith Mallow, all systems to be operated by Danith Mallow at her command."

The Residence breathed a sigh of acceptance.

"Scry Danith." He limited the holo to his head and shoulders. No need to display his weapons.

Her line buzzed but with no reply.

"Mallow holo cache," T'Ash ordered.

"Mallow cache," Danith's scrybowl echoed.

"Danith. This is T'Ash. I'll see you this evening. Merry meet."

One last call. "Scry Woodlands Florist."

"Woodlands Florist here," a fussy voice answered.

"Charge T'Ash's account for a dozen blush roses to be sent to D'Mallow."

"As you wish, GreatLord."

"Later."

He 'ported down to the kitchen, listened to the chef's complaints about Zanth, downed two meatrolls and put five more in his beltpouch, then walked out to his greeniron gate. He took one last look at his estate, again visualized the alley where he'd seen Tinne, and teleported himself there.

He tensed. Heavy smoke shrouded the tops of the buildings. It closed about him like an ominous, smothering fog. He tested it. Not magical, but awesome evidence of a fire gone amok. He made himself ignore the smoke and hoped he wouldn't have to deal with the fire.

"Zanth!" he called.

A faint response came, a denial that Zanth had found anything.

T'Ash unholstered his blaser and set his back into the corner of the alley. He shut his eyes. *Holm!* he called mentally.

Here. Holm's mental voice echoed over a kilometer or two.

Where? T'Ash asked.

The Blue Griffin.

T'Ash sighed. Holm wouldn't find his brother in the nearly respectable taverns of Downwind. T'Ash remembered the sleazy places he and Holm had frequented during their Passage. Most of those bars had vanished, only to be replaced by equally repellent saloons.

Meet at the Putrid 'Roon, T'Ash said. The inn's sign said "The Pewter Celtaroon," but it wasn't called that.

Holly gagged but agreed.

Zanth hunts, too. T'Ash said, taking off at a hustle for the inn. He murmured a deverminizing spell as he went.

Before he'd gone a hundred meters, he was propositioned by two wenches; before he'd gone five hundred, he'd been in three scuffles, using blaser and broadsword, winning. It focused his concentration, and when he moved again, it was with the step and predatory grace of a Downwind tough, a man to fear.

Then word must have gotten out that T'Ash prowled the streets, looking for trouble, because when people saw him in the distance, they melted away. Even when he turned onto a busy street, an aisle was formed for his anticipated path. T'Ash kept smiling and the corridor widened.

T'Ash arrived at The Putrid 'Roon first. Stepping inside, he glanced around the dimly lit room and found no sign of Tinne. T'Ash formed an image of the main gauche, recalled the smoky quartz in the pommel, how it felt, its facets, and its resonance. With a short spell, he sent a high-pitched tone zinging through the building. A woman screeched, but no response came from the stone he had shaped and set in Tinne's weapon.

Zanth squawked, too. *Not a nice sound.*

"Sound of the smoky quartz in the main gauche."

Holm arrived. "Is that what it is?" His usual cheerful grin lopsided. Worry looked as if it lived under his skin.

Want meatroll.

T'Ash glared down at his Fam. "Haven't you had enough to eat this morning?"

Missed crunchies at FamWoman's.

T'Ash unbuckled his pouch and tossed a meatroll to Zanth before turning to Holm.

T'Ash gazed at his friend. "Did T'Holly tell you? I sensed Tinne. He's exhausted but unharmed."

Relief relaxed the lines around Holm's mouth. "Thank you." He reached out and gripped T'Ash's arm, hand to elbow. T'Ash returned the clasp.

Boy drugged.

"What?"

Slurping down the last shreds of furra meat, Zanth

repeated, *Warehouse fire. FogLeaf burned. Boy close. Found hole. Two others dead. Boy overdose FogLeaf.*

T'Ash related the information to Holm. They both squatted down in front of the cat. Zanth licked his whiskers.

"Where is he?"

Hole too small for you. Can't get boy without much effort—one big machine or three great Flairs. Boy sleeps. His Passage delayed.

T'Ash parroted the words to Holly.

"Damn," Holm said.

"How long do you think he'll sleep?" asked T'Ash.

Don't know, ask Healer.

"Zanth says you need to consult a Healer on this."

Will guard. For price.

"Zanth says he'll guard Tinne, for a fee."

Sparks of anger lit Holm's eyes. He stared at the cat.

Zanth lifted a forepaw and licked it.

"You show me where he is and I'll set my own wards."

Stupid. Not Downwind. Boy safe as is. Hole too small except for other boys. FogLeaf too strong for animals.

Holm continued to grumble when T'Ash told him what Zanth had said. Both men wanted to see Tinne's hole, and a slinking Zanth led them. The men kept their weapons loose.

"By the Lady and Lord, what a stench!" Holm exclaimed.

T'Ash shrugged. Holm hadn't been spending much time near Zanth lately. The FogLeaf smelled potent and musky, but nothing like the dreadful stench of sewer rat or celtaroon.

They came to a deserted, ruined building that might once have been a warehouse. At the base was a small darkness indicating a hole.

"There's no way you can fit in that hole to look, T'Ash," Holm said, handing his weapons to T'Ash and trying to squirm under the collapsed beam only to get stuck around his shoulders.

T'Ash kept a wary eye out for Downwinders, but the area remained deserted. "Can you see him?"

Holm grunted. "Barely. He appears to be pale, with a minor wound or two, but healthy. His breathing is that of true sleep. Zanth is right, it's not restless Passage dreams.

Damn. I don't like to think of his Passage stretching over another night or two."

"Can we bring him out of there?"

"I don't see how. I'm not sure enough of his health or the exact coordinates to 'port him out, and the building seems shaky—"

T'Ash studied it with an outreach of Flair. "I can shore the thing up, but if I do, the wreckage will be welded into solid lattice, and the only way Tinne will be able to get out is by himself."

Holm hesitated only an instant. "Do it." He took his weapons back.

Trusting Holm to defend them, T'Ash shut his eyes and studied the angles of stone, timber, foamsteel, concrete until he knew the thing as a whole. With a short spell he molded all the pieces into a single structural unit. "Done." He opened his eyes. "By the way, T'Holly said Tinne's House-Ring couldn't be sensed."

Holm grunted again, brushing white plaster dust from his elegant clothing. Finally he looked up at T'Ash. "The stone is shattered and the metal broken. Only the Two know what happened. Tinne might have taken a blow on the ring, a blaser hilt could have done the damage."

Holm grinned at T'Ash. "We have a rule in our Family. Whoever ruins his ring must pay for a replacement, both for the crafting and the spell. I wager my brother will be coming to you in a few days for a new HouseRing, spending the last of his allowance."

"Allowance? He doesn't have an annual NobleGilt yet? He hasn't been confirmed as a noble? His Flair hasn't revealed itself?"

"Three potentials—fighting, of course."

"Of course."

"The second is cleansing and banishment of evil vibrations."

"Interesting."

"And animal training. He could be apprenticing with the Sallows at the same time as your Danith."

"Then I am glad he is still a boy and not a suave Holly."

Holm chuckled, then pinned his gaze on the small black

entrance to Tinne's sanctuary. "I'd like to place a protection spell on this. You'd know how to camouflage it so it will go unnoticed amongst Downwinders. Will you help?"

"T'Holly pledged himself allies to T'Ash for three generations."

Holm's eyes widened, then he bowed formally. "As the second generation of the promise, I affirm that I honor it."

"Thank you. You provide the energy and strength for the spell, I'll weave it into a protection that no one will notice, and add an insinuation that the place should be avoided."

They clasped arms and each touched the outside edge of the building, completing a circuit of magic. They had used their Flair together before, outside rituals, and knew that their energies didn't mesh well. They layered the spell, first Holm, then T'Ash. With a final Word the hole seemed to disappear.

Zanth sniffed. *Smells bad.*

"Zanth says it smells bad."

Holly nodded. "And there's something about it . . . a touch of dread that the whole thing would collapse if someone got too close." He clapped T'Ash on the shoulder. "We did very well. I also left a message for Tinne."

Time to go. Men come.

"Zanth hears men coming."

Holm grimaced. "Far be it for me to contradict Zanth and his excellent hearing. I'd stay and fight, but I don't want to call attention to this area and Tinne's refuge. Shall I 'port us out of here?"

Zanth stepped away from them. *Me go. Me have Plans.*

"You have plans?" T'Ash asked.

"Plans?" echoed Holm.

Zanth lifted his nose in the air, twitched his tail insolently, then darted down the alley and out of sight.

The slurring words of loud, drunken men rose from a street away.

"Where to?" asked Holm.

T'Ash wanted to go to Danith's, but he didn't want Holly near her. He glanced at Bel. The sun brightened the early afternoon sky. He'd told her that he wouldn't return until the evening, and Danith needed to learn he would keep his promises, especially when it came to her and giving her a little time to understand her new circumstances.

"I feel like a swim," T'Ash said. "My pool or yours?"

Holly grimaced. "Yours is blue and beautiful, attached to your spacious conservatory at the back of your Residence. Mine is gray and dank in the T'Holly dungeon. What do you think? Yours. By the way, before we swim, we should make a report of Downwind conditions to the guardsmen and the NobleCouncil." With that, he whisked them away.

*D*anith stretched luxuriously, waking to *Pansy's*—Princess's—softly rumbling purr. She glanced at the clock. Mid-morning. She grinned. Last night she'd sent her resignation to the Cinque and Poppy collection box.

Welcome contentment filled her for the first time in days. She never had to work again! At least, not as an accounting clerk. She knew her Flair avocation could be just as demanding, more so in pulling strength and energy from her body and mind, but it would also be so rewarding. An Animal Healer.

The Animal Healer, she smugly thought. The only Animal Healer. Oh, yes. She was going to enjoy this.

She looked at the calendar. It was TwinMoonsday, tomorrow she would report to her apprentice appointments. Except for tidying her house and checking on the now-fat status of her bank account, she had nothing to do. She stretched, rolled to her stomach, repeated the motion and rolled back.

Ping!

Whir.

Urga, urga, urga, arrgh, ka-CHUNK.

Well, she did need to have her collection box chime fixed. Something tasteful and with a discreetly pleasant tone.

She walked into the mainspace and pulled the box from the wall. A stack of papyrus at least fifteen centimeters thick sat there. She pulled them out in bundles, and found them to be forms: "Biography for the NobleCouncil," "Verification of Life Papyrus," "Application for Noble Name, Coat-of-Arms, Motto, Heraldry." Finally there was a red-bound

book, *Responsibilities of a Head of a GrandHouse, Laws,
Rules, and Regulations Pertaining to the Nobility (Examination Upon Completion).* Ugh.

The collection box whined again, and Danith hastily
closed it. A moment later the potent smell of roses spread
throughout the room. She opened the box and retrieved the
beautiful flowers. The gilt card simply stated "T'Ash," as
always.

She smiled, then went humming to shower and change
into a soft maroon tunic trous casual suit.

Two hours later her head began to ache as she tried to fill
out the documents in detail. She wasn't sure of her ancestors
for the last five generations. Her mother and father had both
been only children of dead parents, one of the reasons
Danith had ended up at Saille House of Orphans. Children,
except those Downwind, were prized. She should have been
adopted. Adoptions weren't as socially acceptable as having
blood children, but fully as legal.

Danith shrugged and tested herself for any residual disappointment at not being adopted, and sighed in relief.
With the validation of her Flair, that disappointment had
finally vanished.

Fifteen minutes before the end of the workday, Danith's
scrybowl chimed.

"Here," she said, looking up from the dining room table
covered with papyrus. Soon she would have a place with an
office, perhaps a little house of her own. . . .

"Monkshood, Chief Clerk of All Councils," an arrogant
voice said.

"D'Mallow," Danith replied, glad her new scrybowl
didn't make her move from the table to look into it for a viz.
She'd figured out how to project a holo. Molecules of magically magnetized water surrounded her, showing through the
scrybowl to the caller.

"We must schedule a mental, telepathic psychological
test to place you in relation to others in GrandHouse Rituals.
We need to understand how your *obscure* Flair will interweave with other members of the *established* GrandHouses.
No doubt you will not be close to the *real* GrandHouse
nobles, those twelve that belong to the FirstFamilies." His

long nose wiggled as he made a note with a writestick. "Humph, yes, testing. Let me check on an appropriate time for an appointment."

Danith raised her eyebrows. "GrandMistrys Balm didn't inform me of this."

The puce-jowled man in the holo frowned. "She has contacted you? She oversteps her authority. Again."

"She said she was the clerk of the NobleCouncil. That sounds as if she is the one in charge—"

"Humph." The man waved Danith's words away as if they were bitemites. He looked down at a sheet of papyrus and his long nose wiggled. "Half into ThirdBell, tomorrow. Be at the gardengate of Acacia GrandHouse."

Danith stared at him.

The air shivered around her. With a snap T'Ash appeared. He looked at her, then directed his gaze to the holo. "Little Mister Monkshood."

"ThirdSon of the former T'Ash," Monkshood sneered back.

Danith sighed. Another person T'Ash disliked and who returned his dislike. She wondered exactly who T'Ash did like, and felt a sinking feeling that she was included in a tiny minority.

"What's he want?" T'Ash asked her.

"Something about psychological testing."

"Is that so?" He turned to the holo man with a fierce smile. "Don't you have my confirmation of D'Mallow's Test in front of you, Monkshood? How negligent." T'Ash sounded smoother than she'd ever heard him. Was this his Noble GreatLord side, something she'd missed?

Monkshood's eyes narrowed and a small hiss came from his thin lips. He jerked a papyrus in front of him.

"That's it." T'Ash smiled again. Danith wouldn't ever like that smile directed at her. "Nice certificate, isn't it?" He drew out his broadsword.

Danith gaped at the length of steel unsheathed in her mainspace.

T'Ash whisked a cloth from his belt and began rubbing the sword to a bright shine, applying Flair Danith felt straight to her bones. He glanced up at the functionary. "You don't have any questions with my certificate or the Heir to the Holly's now, do you? Nothing like those questions of me before I was confirmed as T'Ash, do you?"

The uncommon melodious note in T'Ash voice made Danith shiver.

"No," Monkshood said. He hesitated a moment, then his mean little eyes seemed to light with an inner, obsessive fire. He glared at Danith. "Half ThirdBell, tomorrow—"

"Now, before you go—" T'Ash interrupted smoothly in turn. "Read me the rule where it says D'Mallow must subject herself to some sort of psychological test."

Monkshood smiled a smile as nasty as T'Ash's own, but his color heightened. He pulled over a book, a well-thumbed rule book that appeared to be always near at hand.

"The new noble may be asked to allow his/herself to be tested by a certified Healer and Psychologist."

"Why don't you read the entire paragraph for us, Monkshood, all the way from the section number," T'Ash advised.

More narrowed eyes and bared teeth. Monkshood's gnarled finger moved up the page.

"Just a moment." With a thud a large dark blue leather-bound book appeared in T'Ash's hands. The sword balanced point down on the cloth, gleaming. The smell of hot metal and graphite cleaner wafted to her nose. Danith stared at the weapon. Did T'Ash just do three simultaneous magical actions?

She narrowed her own eyes to match the men's. Three simultaneous actions made him great in Flair indeed. He was showing off. To Monkshood? Or to her? Probably both.

T'Ash flipped the heavy pages of his book. "The section number, Monkshood?"

"Section four, Paragraph two: 'If the test results of a nominee are equivocal, upon request of two Nobles, one of Head of GrandHouse or greater status, the new Noble may be asked to allow his/herself to be tested by a certified Healer and Psychologist.' "

"Hmmm," T'Ash said. "Very creative reading, as always. My testing of D'Mallow placed her in the 98th percentile of a GrandHouse, did it not? That is hardly equivocal. And perhaps you will tell me the names of the two Nobles who requested further testing?" Now T'Ash leaned on his sword. Somehow the weapon didn't sink into Danith's floor.

Monkshood stared at them flatly. "I seemed to have misplaced the request. I'll viz back—"

"No. Council Record Verifier on."

From the background of the clerk's office a metallic voice wheezed, "Verifier."

"T'Ash, FirstFamily GreatLord, requesting immediate notification of questioners of D'Mallow's Testing. As the testor, do I have this right?"

"You have the right," the magical-machine stated.

"Can I also request the entire matter of further Testing be dropped if the names are not provided?"

A whir. "Correct."

"Well, Monkshood?"

The functionary slammed his book closed. "The matter is closed."

"Good." T'Ash said. "Just as well. Though I would have liked to hear whom you would have scraped up to go against my Testing Stones. Gliding very close to a rollover, Monkshood. Barely escaped with your skin, don't forget that. And Danith doesn't succumb to intimidation, I've tried. You remember that, too. Call over."

The droplets forming her holo evaporated in a rush of warm air. She could only think of one thing to say. "You called me 'Danith,' before him. The gossip will fly."

"I teleported here. Monkshood will think I'm a close friend or you have poor security. Which do you want a petty man like him to believe? He can make your life a misery. He was a thorn in my side a few years ago."

He sheathed his sword and paced up and down her mainspace. It didn't provide much room for his energy. "The evening newsheets shout of your new Noble status. We're mentioned in the Society column." He shrugged his shoulders. "There could be rumors that you have a fortune in jewels here."

Danith shivered.

"You have lousy security. I don't like you staying here alone."

She lifted her chin. "I have Princess."

T'Ash looked at the small, furry, jewel-bedecked cat lounging on the settee and snorted. He crossed to Danith and cupped her chin in his hand. "Come with me. The T'Apples are having a party. They have great food. I suspect Zanth haunts the underside of their tables even now."

Danith smiled at the thought. "No."

"Then dine at T'Ash Residence. We have a variety of wonderful food in the no-time. You haven't seen the MistrysSuite—"

"No."

His jaw tightened and bleakness came to his eyes. He looked at Princess and said lowly, "I am tired of being alone."

So had Danith been, a few days ago. Now so many people, and cats, came and went in her life, she needed more time to try and put her life back in order. She sighed once more. "Not tonight, and not at night."

One side of his mouth quirked upward. "Not at night. You don't want to see my MasterSuite? My bedroom is large and pleasant. I have a GreatLord-size bedsponge, nice windows. My view of the HardRock Mountains is good."

The view was probably fabulous. The man, and everything about him, had brought riches into her life. Nothing was in a scale she understood anymore. Not small houses as a living space, not a mediocre accounting job, not Common status.

She crossed her arms.

His eyes glinted at her from half-lowered lids, his lips curved a bit more. He dipped a hand in his trous pocket. "You might want to look at these."

When he unfolded his fingers, two exquisite redgold earrings sat glowing fire on his palm. They were made from layers of fine wire, intricately twisted and knotted. She'd never seen anything so complex and beautiful so small. They pulsed with a dark, intense power that pulled at her marrow, stirring her deepest urges.

"Another gift?" She couldn't seem to manage more than a whisper. She couldn't tear her gaze from them. Somehow she tried to follow the twists and turns of the wires and even as she traced them, hidden pathways within her opened.

"You may have whatever I can give you," he replied, as softly as she, but with a husky note. He seemed to be holding his breath.

Her hand hovered over the earrings glittering on his palm. The tips of her fingers dropped.

A shattering scream plunged knifelike into her head.

Rage. And pain.

T'Ash's head jerked back. His hand fisted. "Zanth!"

Fourteen

❦

T'Ash shoved the earrings in his pocket and grabbed her. Cold and blackness shocked her as they teleported away. When she opened her eyes they stood at the fountain of the Dark Goddess on the Blackthorn estate.

T'Ash climbed up to the fourth basin of the towering fountain and balanced on the rounded rim, looking into the top bowl. Danith scrambled after him. Inside Zanth lay crumpled, a black and white heap dark against the shimmering white marble of the fountain. Beside him lay the great purple lambenthyst. The hole where it had been freed from the marble by his claws gaped black as death.

The odor of singed cat-hair hung in the air.

T'Ash reached for his Fam.

"Don't touch him!" Danith cried.

He looked at her, torment in his eyes. Then his expression relaxed a bit. "You're Animal Healer. Heal." His gaze swept to the stone. "I'm Stonemaster. The Stone is mine."

His hands shaped the air around the stone. He sucked in a sharp breath. He closed his eyes and the stone rose slowly.

A low keening hurt her head. Danith tore her stare from the stone and T'Ash, and she reached for Zanth.

She hesitated, her hands a few centimeters from him. His fur lifted to touch her fingers. Shock. Shock. Shock.

Electricity pulsed to her from him. Somehow Danith pushed it through her and into the marble, felt it rippling down the fountain instead of water, then grounding in the earth.

After a minute she laid her hands on Zanth. His heart beat rapidly and irregularly. She knew the rhythm of a cat's heart from Princess. His delicate nervous system, as developed as a human's, had frazzled, and needed mending. Danith recalled the lesson T'Ash had taught her. Welding wasn't what was needed here, but perhaps she could do some binding and then interweaving, like making a flower chain.

She tried a simple chant she used while her fingers worked stems and flowers in the spring ritual, adapting some of the words to Healing phrases. She felt her heart pick up beat to match Zanth's, then her own even rate steadied the cat's.

She transformed the electricity still crackling in him and between them into the power, the Flair to Heal. She closed her eyes. And in her mind, she saw frayed nerves bind and meld into a solid system once more.

ME HURT! BAD STONE HURT ME. TOO STRONG. Zanth's eyes opened.

Danith shuddered. His eyes had once been the color of light green jade. Now they matched his emerald collar.

Very slowly she withdrew mentally from his body, like cautiously pulling invisible hands from him until the energy fit once more into her own fingers and palms.

She toppled sideways, off the fountain.

A hard, strong arm caught her before she fell.

She looked up to T'Ash. The lambenthyst floated over the open palm of his other hand. His body felt sturdy and safe against hers. He smelled of great Flair and man. A glimmer of sweat touched his brow.

Her eyes locked with his. Something deeper, but just as shocking, passed between them.

Great Flair that he was, he had deferred to her, trusted her with his most precious friend. She had used a spell he'd taught her, something he'd given her to achieve a feat of Flair of her own.

They had worked together.

Nothing would be the same.

T'Ash looked at Danith. He could look at her forever. Her stunned gaze snared his. His gaze. His heart. His soul. He fell into the depths of her greeny-gold eyes and beyond, into the rich fruitfulness of her generosity—to heal his Fam when she had no training, only instinct to guide her.

He'd known, with his mind, even with his body, that she was his HeartMate. Now he knew with his heart, to the depths of his being. His heart forever lay in her hands, to do with what she would. He was irrevocably hers.

His mouth dried. He spoke anyway. "I—" He couldn't say "love," though he thought it was what he felt. He couldn't. He couldn't be so vulnerable. "I want you more than I can say."

The pupils of her eyes widened until the irises were only a rim of brown-green. The beat of her heart, beneath the sweet breasts, pressed close to him, grew stronger. His own body reacted.

He pulled her flush against him. He liked the feel of her softness against him, of her pliant belly against his rapidly hardening sex. He closed his eyes at the powerful pleasure bordering on pain.

Now his heart, his mind, his body were all one in knowledge. She was his HeartMate. Everything in him resonated to her vibrations.

He drew her hand down, into his trous pocket, where his HeartGift lay, waiting for her touch. And with her acceptance, he could take her. Take her deep. With his mind. With his body.

HeartBond.

Her fingers ignored the earrings. She pulled her hand from his pocket to slide sideways, caress his erect flesh.

He fell.

They fell.

He 'ported them a few feet, standing again where they'd originally landed.

She squeaked. Her heart thundered. "I almost killed us."

Unimportant.

The fact she'd withdrawn her hand to clutch his arms was important.

"My Danith," he whispered, bending his head.

She stepped away from him. "Where's the lambenthyst?"

He couldn't care less.

He took a step to her, but she backed away.

"You 'ported. You 'ported us—not only yourself, but me, in a life-threatening situation. That's not supposed to be possible. I read newsheets. Even great Flairs aren't supposed to have the concentration to do that. Not instantaneously."

For the first time since they'd met, she looked at him with fear.

His heart still pounded, from her touch and from the fall. He let his legs fold under him, till he sat, knees up and open, feet crossed at the ankles. He rested his arms on his knees and dropped his head, taking deep breaths to steady himself.

"I 'ported us only three meters, to a locale we'd previously teleported to only moments before." His voice sounded husky with irritation, but he couldn't retreat on this, not before her fear. "Unlike your work with Zanth, my spell with the lambenthyst was standard, something I've often done." The lambenthyst and its near sentience had shaken him a bit, but moving stones around, carrying them, was second nature. "The 'port location pattern must have still been in the back of my mind."

He dropped his head again and his teeth clenched as memory pummeled him. Downwind speech came easier. "My mother—in the fire. She had time to 'port. Barely. She looked out the window. At me. Then went to Father."

He leveled his breathing even more, hoping his heartbeat would follow, not race through his chest raggedly. Now he was afraid, letting Danith know this deepest part of him.

"Mother wasn't large Flair. Didn't teleport often by herself. She could have. If she concentrated. Maybe. But she went to Father. Don't know what happened to Father." And the unknown tormented him.

In his imagination, in his nightmares, he'd seen his father die many times and many different ways, quickly, before his mother touched him to comfort him. Long and lingering—or as lingering as the quick explosion and collapse allowed, but always eons in his dreams. His mother would race to his father, and his father, already burning with the inextinguishable flames, would ignite his mother, too. They died together.

"They died together." It came out loud. "I think." T'Ash shrugged, trying not to remember what young Rand felt. "Father wouldn't have left Nuin, Gwidion, me. Fire was too fast. The disintegration of the Residence too total and rapid to survive. The fire—" Now he shuddered in the cool night breeze, his skin clammy with fearful, drying sweat as it had been so many years ago. "Flametree insured once the fire bit you, it ate you up." T'Ash lifted his head, wanting to see his HeartMate instead of the old, awful memories.

She met his eyes, her own gaze soft and lustrous. And she came to him, sat next to him and put her arms around him. She held him. Not sexually, but it felt equally wonderful, and it was the first time since he was a child that anyone had held him to comfort him. Prickles of wetness behind his eyes threatened. He fought them back. He was a man, and tough. Since six he was a man. And since seven, he was tough.

She cuddled close, something no woman had ever done with him as a man, and he felt some great thing inside him break free. He smelled her scent and his muscles tightened with desire. He draped an arm over her shoulders, then slid it down to her hip.

ME. ME. ME! YOU LEFT ME UP HERE.

Danith flinched.

T'Ash looked up. He should have been able to see a standing or sitting cat of Zanth's bulk over the lip of the top marble fountain bowl. He couldn't.

Danith rubbed her temples.

T'Ash cradled her face in his palms. "You hear him. Does it still hurt when he shouts? Don't shout. We're coming up."

She save me. We Fams. My FamWoman. Mine. Mine. Mine. Mine. Mine. Mine. You got My gem for her gift?

Danith's head jerked up. "I heard that. All those mines." She projected her voice. "I can hear you, Zanth." She touched her head again. "It only hurts a little if you don't shout."

My FamWoman, Zanth repeated smugly.

"Mine. Is that all you two think about? Possession?" she muttered.

"I haven't possessed you, yet." How he needed to. Possession and passion ran like a hot river through him. He stood, curved his hand around her wrist and brought her to her feet. "And Zanth says six 'mines' to confirm that he's serious."

"I heard him the first time."

"And you've heard me several times, too. But ignored me." They walked to the fountain and climbed. Though it was easy, he watched her every step, every placement of her fingers.

They peered into the highest, smallest bowl together. Zanth lay on his side, not even a whisker moving. The bulge of his stomach looked less than it had before he'd killed the celtaroons, T'Ash noted absently.

Me blown. Can barely talk.

"Too bad," T'Ash said.

A hind foot quivered.

Me want strength. Energy. From big, strong FamMan.

Zanth only referred to T'Ash's overwhelming size in flattering terms when he wanted something.

T'Ash stared down on his rough-looking friend and felt the awful prickle in his eyes again. If he left Zanth, the Fam would be dead by morning, and Zanth still didn't ask for help. He demanded.

T'Ash turned to Danith. "Is it safe for me to funnel him energy?"

Danith shifted on the rim of the fountain bowl beneath her feet. T'Ash placed his hand on the small of her back, and reviewed the 'port locale, ready to save her again, if necessary. The upper bowl caught her much higher than it did him.

Her hands went out and felt Zanth, stroking him with not only a Healing touch but in a near caress T'Ash envied.

Her eyes took on a distant look of concentration. T'Ash sensed she checked Zanth's strength, pulse, heart rate, and other bodily functions. T'Ash kept his stance solid.

"Yes, slowly and in increments. You'll know when to stop."

He would. He'd done this before. Not often. The damn cat had saved T'Ash more than he'd returned the favor.

Foot by foot, Danith crept around the fountain until T'Ash could stand directly over Zanth. T'Ash slid his hand under the Fam's head, hearing the small chink of emeralds against marble. The stone bowl of the fountain was cold on his knuckles, but soothing nonetheless. Except it sapped heat from the cat.

T'Ash curved his other hand around Zanth's rib cage. The cat's heart beat slowly and hesitated once, and again. Fear caught at T'Ash's throat.

"Easy," Danith said, crab-walked back to him, and placed her near hand in the crook of his elbow.

T'Ash drew in a deep breath and closed his eyes to the brilliant stars in the night sky and the two watching moons. He measured his energy, regulated it, sent it in a small stream to Zanth. He started draining himself.

Done! Zanth leaped to his feet, shaking off T'Ash's hands. *Life is good.*

T'Ash wanted to grab Zanth and hold him tightly. "Your hair's sticking out. And you look fat."

"Grrr." *Me full of zing. FamMan zing. Feels good. Where My gem for FamWoman gift?*

"What's he talking about?" Danith asked.

"The lambenthyst. He wants me to make a pendant of a pink diamond, to match your aura, as a gift. The lambenthyst was the price."

Her eyes rounded. "You charge your Fam for your work?"

T'Ash snorted. "He charges me for his. He started it. He's a cat, they don't think of service without strings."

"He's giving me a gift."

"Because you love him. You've already given him one. And now you saved his life." He smiled. "What are you going to pay her, Zanth?"

Zanth grinned. *Kittens. All My kittens. Forever.* The Fam bounded easily and gracefully down the fountain, showing off for the humans.

Where My gem?

T'Ash helped Danith down the fountain. He lifted her off the last basin and kept her close. "HeartMate."

"You say that because you think it in your head, not because you really feel it in your heart."

"I feel it, all right." He let her slide down his body. His increasingly hard body. He wanted to feel her soft gentleness against him, and more, he wanted her to feel his need for her.

He looked down at her oval face, her pretty lips, her large eyes. He bent his head.

WHERE MY GEM?

Danith whimpered.

T'Ash glared at Zanth. "You're shouting, you ungrateful cat. You're hurting a woman who just saved your worthless hide."

Zanth's muzzle dipped, then he turned his head to gaze beyond them, examining the fountain. *Sorry.*

T'Ash's mouth fell open. He would have sworn Zanth didn't know that word, maybe not even the feeling. T'Ash had certainly never heard the cat use the word before.

Zanth stood up and walked to Danith. He looked at her feet. A long, red tongue swiped his whiskers.

Danith jumped at T'Ash. "Not the toes. I hate the toes."

Too late, T'Ash figured out what she meant.

Zanth licked her toes through her weaves.

Danith whimpered again. This time it sounded like disgust.

"Well," T'Ash said. "I'm glad I know you don't like your toes licked."

Her head whipped up, her eyes wide. Even in the dark T'Ash could see her blush.

My Gem?

T'Ash waved a hand. The lambenthyst was suspended, touching another purple stone in the bottom bowl. It glowed, and T'Ash knew it was from pain. The gem had been split when the fountain was built and its other piece had been embedded in the lowest portion of the fountain.

"What's wrong?" Danith asked.

"We'll have to take the other out, too. They were from one piece of raw crystal."

"It looks intelligent," she whispered, seeing both the stones pulse in time.

"Not quite. But I think what you said the other night, about replacing the stone in its old mine, is good. I'll buy the property." He shrugged again. "I own several mines, buying another won't cause any comment."

A streaking, incandescent fireball slashed the sky. They all ducked reflexively.

"Damn. Downwinders rioting, spreading uptown. I was afraid of this. I warned the Council."

Danith heard wild shrieks of exultation and victory nearing. A gang of youths poured down the path and into the dark grove. They stopped when they saw T'Ash, Danith, and Zanth, almost tumbling over each other.

Three boys moved forward, spaced like an arrow point. They looked infinitely more threatening than the Downwind gang that had captured her before. Glisten chain bracelets gleamed on the trio's left wrists. When they lifted their lips in sneers, Danith saw that all three had their incisor teeth filed to points and gilded with the same metal. She shuddered in horror. Something about the triad threatened primally. An atmosphere of darkest black seemed to coalesce around the three. They moved in a triangle of seething malevolence.

They whipped out knives.

T'Ash pushed Danith behind him.

The point boy, the oldest and tallest, grinned wider than the other two. "Can't go back. They,"—he gestured with his knife to T'Ash's group—"know we violate Blackthorn estate."

"They know we steal. Destroy," said the second.

"They see us. They die," ended the third.

"It's T'Ash." A boy behind them edged away from the others.

"They two. We nine," said the leader.

"We win," the triad said together.

T'Ash measured the distance between himself and the nearest youth. If the boy was fast, he could nail T'Ash's blaser hand before T'Ash got the weapon free. He slipped his hand down his hip to the smooth handle of his blaser.

"Three of them," another boy from the back said. "One's Zanth. Mean cat. Took twelve 'roons last night."

"Two. T'Ash. Zanth," the first boy said. The three boys' teeth flashed in the twinmoonslight.

"We save pretty fem. Looks soft," said the second.

"Much fun," said the third.

"She's Noble!" the protester cried.

"Shut up." Again the words issued from three mouths.

The triad started prowling forward, light on their feet. "Sport with fem," the first boy said.

"Then slay," the second boy said.

"Two pleasures," finished the third.

Anger bubbled up in T'Ash. He held his control hard, clamping down on the mindless berserker savagery. He could not go berserk before Danith. It would destroy the ever-strengthening connection between them.

He matched the young scruffs' feral smiles. Matched the Downwind words, cadence, arrogant tone. "T'Ash. Baby boys. Run while legs work."

The leader hesitated, then trod forward. "Time for T'Ash's rep to die like T'Ash."

Jealousy. Resentment. Fury of the poor for the rich. Delight in destruction. Viciousness. Sadism. All poured from the triad and the band behind them.

T'Ash grabbed his blaser. A small fireball clipped it from his fingers. T'Ash ignored the pain and pulled his broadsword, sending fire down the blade to make it as bright as any fireball. "Come to me, Danith, Zanth." He'd teleport them from this place in instants.

A flash of white-and-black-fur streaked past him. Jumped.

Long, high screaming from the third boy.

T'Ash had no time to damn his Fam, but whirled in a deadly dance. Broadsword to knife, but two to eight, and a woman who mattered more than his life to protect.

"Teleport, Danith."

"I can't. I don't know how."

"Call Holly."

"I don't know how."

"Run!" He strode three paces ahead of her. The two left

standing of the triad parted before him. A twist and a leap. His sword screamed and flashed. Three boys of the gang fell in their blood.

Pivoting to escape a knife slash. Ducking to avoid pelleting fireballs from the second boy.

No Danith.

"Danith!"

"I'm looking for the blaser."

"Run."

Cat yowls, boys' yells.

Only the triad and the bodies stayed.

A cold line of pain across his biceps, slicing down his chest, turned fiery. He wished for a main gauche instead of a sword. The leader was within his reach. The sword was useless. He dropped it. It flared, the youth gasped and jumped back. T'Ash crouched, went in low, wrested the blade from the boy and buried it in him.

His breath gurgled out, his eyes went blank. He died.

The other two screamed, staggered. Both had cat scratches on their faces. They threw back their heads at the twinmoons and keened. They sent evil glances of retribution at T'Ash.

They vanished.

T'Ash let one geyser of pain and rage erupt through him, cleansing his shallow wounds. He thrust the anger that would spark the berserker into the ground.

"Danith!"

"What?"

"Whole?"

"What?"

"All right?"

"I guess so. These boys need help."

"They're dead."

She sounded shocky. Blood and death. She probably hadn't seen anything like this before. He hoped he hadn't ruined their courtship.

"Stay away. Don't look. Three dead. Rest gone. Them or us, Danith. Them or us. Zanth?"

Here. Me hurt two boys. Good fight.

T'Ash heard rustling around him. He pressed his arm to

his side, slowing the welling of blood. He turned carefully. Danith dug in the bushes, face white.

"Danith?"

"I'm looking for your blaser."

From her fumbling efforts, he could tell she didn't see anything.

"Blaser." He held out his hand and the weapon smacked into it. He holstered it.

"Broadsword." It flew to his palm. He sheathed it.

FamMan hurt.

Danith's dilated eyes turned in his direction. She blinked, rushed to him. Stopped before she touched him.

"Where?" Her eyes scanned him.

He touched his arm and chest with his other hand. His fingers came away bloody.

"Oh, Lady, oh, Lady, oh, Lady," she chanted.

"Small slices."

She insinuated herself under his good arm. "Lean on me." Hopeless. She staggered from shock even without his weight.

"Zanth, show me the way to the gardenshed," she ordered, straightening her shoulders. T'Ash felt reason returning to her as her movements became more coordinated, felt the feminine energy coursing through her to help and protect. He set his arm around her shoulders. She sighed.

He should 'port them out of there, to his estate. But Danith had been adamant about not staying at his Residence, as if it were the first step to perdition. She would leave. And he would spend a night in his big bedsponge that felt increasingly empty.

If he teleported them to her home, he would be invading her space again, giving her no place to be alone with her thoughts.

It suddenly became important that she choose him, not only because of the HeartGift or fate, or even because of attraction and emotion, but because she rationally decided she wanted to be with him.

And he knew, now, too, that being alone with her thoughts matched him. He, too, occasionally needed time alone. Plenty of years had passed with only Zanth as company, but when he thought of the many Clovers, even the gregarious Hollys, he wondered if he could live with them.

Living with Danith would be no problem. He'd spoken of the MistrysSuite. She could keep an office, a sitting room, an entertainment room in the suite, but not a bedroom. She'd sleep with him.

If he took them to her little house, he'd be tempted to take her to bed. She'd insist that one of them sleep on the bedroll. He was getting tired of sleeping on bedrolls, even though that awaited him in the gardenshed. A large bedroll with her.

"Zanth?" T'Ash asked.

Me here. The cat's tail quirked before T'Ash.

"Check the perimeter of the estate. That gang got in. We don't want them or others coming back. Tell me how big the security breach is."

Me go. Shed ahead. Me rhyme. Nice.

"Nice," T'Ash said.

"Nice," Danith repeated.

They looked at each other. He rolled his eyes. She bit her smiling lip.

Good, a light moment. He brooded too much. She'd help him with that, too. He needed her. He leaned a little more on her.

She caught him closer, and he shut his eyes as sweet revelation burst upon him. She needed to be needed. One of the reasons she must want a large Family, and why she made herself integral to the Clovers. She needed to be needed. And no one could ever need her as much as he.

No one.

He took a deep breath, and another. He dreaded needing anyone so much, but he also gained some odd pleasure from it.

And he could use this in his courtship.

They entered the dark gardenshed together, and she kicked the door shut behind them. The atmosphere spoke of sanctuary and intimacy. He relaxed. The spellshields he placed on this building would hold off an army or four GreatLords, and could be engaged with a Word.

"Word Safe," T'Ash said.

She lifted puzzled eyes to him.

He drew her hand to his mouth and kissed her fingers. "The Word for my spellshields on this place is *Safe*."

She frowned. "That's all? I thought you great Flairs used long chants."

"It depends. Something simple and often used can be activated with a single Word or phrase. Now only you, I, and Zanth can use this place tonight."

"Oh. Can you stand while I unroll the permamoss bed?"

T'Ash leaned his good shoulder against the wall and watched as she hurried off to unroll the soft evergreen pallet, pull food and a water pitcher from the no-time, and prepare bandages. He missed the warmth and softness of her against his side.

She dusted off crumbles from the surface of the permamoss bed and smoothed it with her hands. T'Ash stared. It never would have occurred to him to do that.

While he was thinking, she ran back to him and placed herself beneath his arm, once again next to his heart. He put his arm around her shoulders and squeezed. She walked them to the bed, and tried to lower him.

He fell back with a wince.

"Sit up. We need to see how much damage there is."

We. He liked that.

He grimaced. "Not much, some slashed skin that's painful but not debilitating. If there'd been poison on his blade, I'd be dead already."

She squeaked, pressed herself against him, then rose and got the water and the medical supply box.

She looked around. "Light," she commanded, as if the ordinary spell would work.

T'Ash had disabled it long ago.

"Dark windows," he said. Black-tinted steel shades rolled down over the inside of the windows with little metallic clinks. T'Ash had made and installed them in the shed himself.

"Fireball near right arm," he commanded.

A bright, steady, white fireball flashed into light next to him.

Danith watched everything with great concentration. "Hmmm."

"You'll get the hang of it soon. By the end of the month, you'll be using and creating simple spells so often, you won't even think about it."

She shook her head and knelt beside him. "Is there a Word to make your shirt vanish without hurting you? Or do you want me to dampen it around your wounds, then take it off? Yes, that would be better, the shirt is such fine silkeen."

T'Ash contemplated having her hands on his body. He wouldn't have said the word to disintegrate the shirt for thirteen EarthSuns.

She soaked a pad in the water and placed it against his arm to loosen the shirt pasted by blood against his skin. He hissed at the sting.

She patted his cheek. "There, there." He watched her bent head as she concentrated on his cuff tabgroove. She carefully pulled it open. The sleeve was wide, and he'd have no trouble getting his arm out of it.

Then she tugged the shirt from his trous, pushing it up his chest until it reached the area of the wound. Again she wet the whole area and cautiously peeled the shirt upward. She gasped.

"Have you never seen a knife wound before?" he asked.

She shook her head, dabbing the slice with an antiseptic pad and cleanheal. From what he felt it seemed a long but shallow injury.

"How does it look?"

She pressed her lips together. "Like it needs closuretape." She rooted through the large box of medical supplies. T'Ash knew she'd find a roll. He'd stocked the box with everything he could think of a few years ago. While she found the closuretape roll, opened it, and measured it, he took off his shirt.

She ran a thumbnail across the tape, and it parted from the roll.

T'Ash lay down on his right side, so she could work better, see better, and use her hands more, on his skin and not his shirt.

"Ready?" she asked.

"Yes. The arm will need flexiclosure tape over the muscle."

"Oh. I should have done that first."

He smiled at her. "You'll learn."

"Does it hurt much?"

"Yes."

She bit her lip. "There's all sorts of medicines to drink from restwell and acheaway to comatose healer."

"I know."

She flushed a little. "What would you recommend?"

"We'll see, later. Having you in my arms will be as soothing and healing as most."

She flushed and he congratulated himself at finally giving her a smooth compliment, and the truth. After shooting him a wary glance, she adjusted his hurt arm, then started pinching the skin on his chest and applying the tape so it bound the edges of the wound together. The slowness and thoroughness of her care increased the pain, and any sensual feelings at having her hands on his body died under the fierce need not to cry out or pass out. He wanted her to finish, fast. She didn't.

Finally it was over. He panted in relief, closing his eyes and unclenching his hands.

She used a soft, cool cloth to wipe his chest around the tape, down to his waist, his back, and around his neck under his hair.

He heard a small dribble of water and a fine silkeen handkerchief blotted the sweat from his face. "Thank you."

She released a heavy breath. "The arm is next, and it's worse. Let me give you some painease."

"Not maximum."

She sighed.

"I need to be alert."

"Can't Zanth—"

"We don't know the status of the estate. This building is secure, but I owe an obligation to the Blackthorns for the use of this gardenshed throughout the years. I'd hate if the Residence burned."

He couldn't watch another Residence burn, torching lovely landscaped grounds, not ever again.

T'Ash heard her rise to mix medicines.

"You can use a Healing spell on my arm, too."

"I only know the basic one, for little cuts and scrapes."

"That will be enough. I know several, though they will work better for you, as a natural Healer, than for me. I can give you energy and instruction. We'll work together." When he opened his eyes, she was holding a tumbler full of lavender medicine and frowning.

He smiled. "We can do it."

Fifteen

❦

*H*er gaze had fastened on the wound in his arm. "Drink this. I'll get flexiclosure tape."

T'Ash took the tumbler, watched as she chose a wide band, and inwardly winced; it would be hell going on and ripping off. Maybe he'd get a Healer to dissolve it tomorrow. He drank the medicine down. It tasted of sweet, pleasant herbs. He stared at the glass. It must be a natural outshoot of her Flair, to make medicine good-tasting. Everything he'd put in the medicine box had been bitter and astringent.

The painease took the edge off his torment. Now he would be able to enjoy her hands touching him.

When she sat on the permamoss bed again, he took the tape from her and tossed it next to him. Then, he put the tumbler aside and closed his hands over hers, placing her palms on his wound. Together they recited the simple Healing couplet that every child knew. T'Ash boosted her natural Flair for Healing and felt the heat of the injury closing and knitting together.

They were both panting at the end. She pulled away and picked up the flexiclosure tape. Firmly, efficiently, rapidly, she wrapped the bandage around his biceps. Again they chanted the spell. He sighed. Over all too soon.

FAMily, Zanth called.

"Here," said T'Ash.

"Here," said Danith.

Small person-door in corner wall broken. Good thicket for hiding. Alley to Downwind.

"Damn," T'Ash said. "Can you guard it?"

Not by Self. Other Fam roams this night. Hunting Cat, Fam of Tinne Holly. Some Downwind ferals will fight for food.

"How much food?"

Quarter furra beast and innards.

T'Ash sent his mind to his Residence and scanned the large no-time larder. "We don't have that. We have half a hog."

Done!

"Do you need anything else?" T'Ash asked.

No. We sit. Wait. Where's My gem?

"It's still by the fountain."

Gem very expensive.

"I've seen to its security. It can't be stolen."

You best with stones. But you using lots Flair.

"I'm fine."

Zanth gave a mental snort. *Holly Cat comes.*

Danith looked worried again. "How is your energy level?"

"I'm fine."

She scowled at him, then shook a finger.

He smiled, liking her fussing. Professional Healers had never fussed over him. "I've enough to do what needs to be done, tonight. It would be easier on us all if we stayed here. Scruffs still roam the streets, and strong shieldspells guard the gardenshed. I want to ensure that T'Blackthorn Residence stands in the morning."

Danith nodded. "All right."

He suppressed a jubilant grin. Danith, sleeping in his arms all night, would be both a delight and a torment for him.

The draught, the emotion of the day, and the energy he'd spent made his eyelids heavy. Finally he dozed off.

Danith watched T'Ash sleep. Her heart tightened at seeing him hurt. She must admit it to herself. She was falling in love with him, with his strength she could always count on.

Even his intensity didn't matter very much anymore.

She'd been utterly useless in the fight, unable to help

T'Ash or Zanth, unable to run. That she couldn't run scared her more than anything else, showed her more than anything else that she was changing. Who knew what other new developments lay ahead?

She considered T'Ash's previous offer to take her to T'Ash Residence. And show her the MistrysSuite. Obviously he was envisioning her staying there, with him. That was impossible. Living with T'Ash would be wrong. He, and his friends, the FirstFamilies Council, would have expectations about her responsibilities and duties. Much of her life would be taken up with a reflection of his, and if she became a GreatLady, would she even know Danith Mallow? Would she ever know what D'Mallow, Head of a GrandHouse could have ever been?

Her past in the Saille House for Orphans had forced rules and regulations upon her. A future as a GreatLady would do the same. These few years she'd been on her own, able to make decisions based only upon herself, would vanish in her memory as if a dream.

T'Ash moaned and she placed her hands over his wounds. They felt no warmer than the rest of the man, and beneath his bandages, she sensed they healed.

T'Ash opened his eyes. His fingertips came up to stroke her cheek. A thumb swept an errant tear from under her eye. "You worry."

She smiled crookedly. "I was useless back there."

"You should not be subjected to fighting. It's not decent. And you weren't useless." His hand dropped to her ankle, his voice sounded slurred from the medicine, his eyelids closed. "You were there. For me to protect. If you hadn't been there, I would have . . ."

Curiosity stirred. He was sincere, but what was he talking about? "You would have what?"

His lashes lifted and Danith saw sharp awareness, then concentration as if he were thinking back to what he'd said. "If you hadn't been here, Zanth and I probably would have killed them all, instead of three. That's not good, they were just boys. Must do something. . . ." His fingers relaxed around her ankle, and his breathing took on the cadence of deep sleep.

His words shook her to the core. Twice tonight the man had revealed portions of himself. And while she welcomed the fact that he was opening up to her about his past, it made her wonder all the more who he was, and who he'd been.

A wariness had surrounded him at times tonight, as if he was afraid that she'd run from him if he were honest with her about his past. No doubt he'd wish those words about killing unsaid when he woke.

She nibbled at her bottom lip and glanced at him again. Scars showed on his torso, scars that other men she'd seen shirtless didn't have. Not Claif, Pink or Mel Clover, or even Timkin. Timkin's scars had been internal. Danith grimaced. She sensed T'Ash's inner scars might even be more formidable than the ones marking his body.

At least she could figure out which painful topic she'd poked at a few nights ago, and not do it again. She might even learn a little more about this man who claimed her as his own from his equally scarred Fam.

"Zanth?" Danith kept her voice low but called loudly with her mind.

Me hear.

Danith cleared her throat, as if it would do any good in mind-to-mind communication. Her first telepathic conversation. How easy would it be? How draining would it be? How much could Zanth actually hear, just her words or emotions, too? Would he perceive her physical sensations?

"Zanth, a couple of nights ago, when we faced that gang, I said something that made the situation worse. What was it?"

She heard the humming of his cat mind, it seemed to dart here and there, then click.

Rue, Zanth said.

Only a little hurt in her head came with the word. She'd need to learn how to converse with Fams without any hurt at all.

Never say rue.

Danith nodded, then realized she needed to answer with her mind. "I won't."

You hear Me.

"Yes."

T'Ash not hear. Only You. He sounded satisfied that he'd been able to selectively aim his thoughts.

"T'Ash is sleeping."

Me can talk to only you anyway. Me know how.

"Why can't I say rue?"

Zanth's mind hummed again. *Rue killed Family.*

The Fam went silent and Danith knew he was finished talking. His thoughts became cat-sensings of movement and sound. Now was not the time to find more out about T'Ash.

So, she'd made a dreadful mistake, but plant and herbal sayings were commonplace and loved.

She curled within the curve of T'Ash's large, muscular body. His arm settled around her and drew her close. She closed her eyes, and ignoring the multicolored flashes of the day's memories on her eyelids, she fell asleep.

T'Ash jerked himself from the nightmare. A new, unu-sual horror, not the old one of the fire. His telling Danith about that awful time seemed to have made it less hurtful. Now he wasn't the only one to know his lingering hurt at his mother's choice.

Scenes of the fire and the aftermath had flashed during the Passage they experienced together. She'd have seen them, felt them, and would remember them. And if not now, someday. He knew that from when he and Holm experienced Passage together. The two boys hadn't been as close as Danith and he, physically or mentally, but their memories still bled over from one to another. Holm, too, knew of the fire. And Zanth. And none of them had betrayed him. It was past.

He was delaying thinking about the new nightmare. He shuddered, needing water. The painease and fear had dried his mouth and dampened his body with sweat.

He slipped from the bed, pulled the cover up over Danith and stood looking at her for a while. He could think of Danith instead of the nightmare. She haunted his thoughts. Thoughts of her were more wonderful than anything else in his life, past or present.

T'Ash went over to the sink and gulped the cool water in

the pitcher, letting droplets splash in his face and trail down his neck and chest.

The slices on his arm and chest stung, both from movement and from the cold water. And that brought him back to the dreadful dream.

In the nightmare he stood, knife in hand, filled with feral rage, staring at an Uptown man who shielded a pretty woman. When T'Ash looked at the woman, his body hardened with fierce, vicious lust.

He'd been a Downwind scruff, not his lady's protector. He'd been the one who wanted to thrust into her, with his body and then with his knife. He had no morals, no qualms, no compassion, no shred of decency.

Hot, destructive fury had blazed through his veins, and he wanted to hurt, hurt, hurt. And he knew he could win. He had the Flair and the skill, and the Downwind streetsmarts to kill the man and take the woman to play with.

He strutted before his gang, men that would obey his slightest wish, because he was meaner and tougher and bigger than any of the rest.

T'Ash shuddered and shuddered again. He could have been that boy, all too easily. If he hadn't clung to the memories of his Family, the teachings of his FatherSire, Father, and Mother, precepts set out in the history book he'd saved. If he hadn't been determined to avenge the deaths of his loved ones. If he hadn't dedicated himself to reclaiming his heritage and carrying on the T'Ash name.

Even so, a kernel of Downwind still lurked inside him. He went berserk when he fought, became wild and uncivilized, and was no better than the young scruffs who'd faced him that night. At least he hadn't become a member of a triad, brothers and more to two others as wild as he, joined mentally and emotionally into an entity that embodied and magnified the worst characteristics of all three. Perhaps he had managed to hang on to some scrap of honor.

He had a minimum of manners, no courtship knowledge, no optimism or ideals. Nothing to offer Danith, the lady he wanted so desperately—the woman who embodied his future and the future of his line.

The sweat and droplets of water chilled on his skin, as cold as the fear that he'd never be able to win her, and that she would escape his grasp. He'd face the lonely, gray future he'd seen during his Passage alone.

Danith brought color and vividness to his life. She brought hope and delight. She brought innocence, a freshness that made him feel renewed, as if he could finally shuck the dreadful tendrils of the past and learn to live as a normal man.

Except the dream haunted him, reminding him he was nothing in his childhood. Except he berserked when he fought. How would he get beyond both? How could he hide them until he could bring a good man to her?

He would bury his doubts and flaws so deep, she would not find them until they HeartBonded. Surely he could play the Noble GreatLord until then. He would only reveal himself to her after they were wed.

FAMILY! Zanth's shriek rattled the glass in the windows.

T'Ash whirled to the door. Danith jackknifed up on the bed. He darted a glance to her; she looked mussed and confused.

"We hear," he said.

COME! Tinne Holly here. Came for Fam. Passage. Death duels. Scruffs followed. Gang of young toms here. Two Glisten Teeth come.

Foreboding chilled T'Ash's spine. He envisioned the whole horrific scenario. The young man, calling for his Fam, leading the Downwind toughs that fought with him to the T'Blackthorn estate. Being joined by the still hurting and enraged two remaining boys of the triad. By now they must have rested, also.

Tinne would be fighting in the exaltation of Passage, but slowing. Other youths would be circling around him, waiting for the kill.

T'Ash felt a surge of emotion from Tinne. Only combat occupied the boy's mind, the next thrust, parry. Kills—the boy had seven kills this evening—Downwinders who'd attacked what they saw as an easy mark.

"Stay here!" T'Ash ordered Danith, and plunged from the

gardenshed. He ran to the gate, faster than he'd run in years, too upset to 'port.

The scene looked both better and worse than he imagined. Tinne held off the Downwinders, a mixture of men and boys, his emptied blaser cast aside. He fought with broadsword and main gauche. There were too many Downwinders. Tinne's death was merely a matter of time.

Zanth and the hunting cat attacked an opponent together. Brought him down. Claws slashed. A man died.

Tinne's blades flashed in the twinmoons' light. A detached portion of T'Ash noted the bespelled aura around the main gauche, giving extra protection, more skill to the boy. Good.

T'Ash grabbed his blaser and fired. Nothing. A tingle in his hand told him that the second boy of the triad, the Flaired one, lurked in the shadows and chanted a spell to negate blasers.

T'Ash drew his broadsword and waded in. Through slashes and cuts, clangs of sword against sword, he saw the difference between Tinne and the Downwinders. The Downwinders, some men, some boys, all held a bitter, destructive expression in their eyes. Their clothing was as tattered as their decency. They smelled with layers of dirt. Scruffs. Just like him.

Tinne flashed T'Ash a grin, a clean, honorable, well-dressed fighting GreatSir grin. A grin inspired by Passage.

A dying cat howled. Not Zanth.

The Holly hunting cat.

Tinne shuddered, his defense faltered. Then his face hardened in fury at the thought of his dying Fam. The additional anger fed his Passage. His hands blurred, too fast for T'Ash's eyes to follow.

A ululation of agony tore from the boy's throat, a denial of the truth, an emotional demand that his Fam be whole, even though he knew better. Then vengeance for the loved and lost friend rushed through him.

T'Ash fought with efficient precision.

They were winning.

Until Danith screamed.

T'Ash spun. Damn! Of course she'd respond to a dying animal. His worst fears crashed through him.

She stood in a circle of fire flaming higher than her. Blazing streamers arced above her, caging her, surrounding her. Flames from fireballs catapulted to the dry summer grass around her.

The second Flaired triad youth did this, tried to kill his HeartMate with firespells. T'Ash shouted with rage.

A sheet of flame obscured her from view, then subsided.

She stooped, threw rocks. Boys grunted. She held her hands palms out, chanting some small, useless self-defense spell.

Terror burst inside him. His opponent fell under his blade. T'Ash ran toward her.

Black fear and red fury darkened his vision. He fought them with every gram of strength. He could not go berserk now. He could not. Too dangerous for Danith.

He sent a knife winging to the young, Flaired boy with cat wounds on his face and pointed, glistened teeth at the rim of the circle. The youth fell, but the flames he'd set remained.

T'Ash screamed a battle cry.

He jumped through the fire, smelling the searing of his hair and flesh. He ignored the pain to sweep a circle with his sword, catching a man. The Downwinder crumpled.

Torrents of desperation, determination, anger merged into a blazing union. His past, present, and future clanged together in a whole.

They were outnumbered.

He must protect Danith.

T'Ash reached past his instincts honed by a Downwind boyhood. As his arm swung the sword automatically, he fought the inner battle—through his feral nature to face the deep-seated agony and despair he harbored from the murder of his Family, destruction of his House, and his own abandonment.

Sweat rolled down his body. He conquered the old emotions, the pain, the desperation, the frenzied wrath. With the mastery of the childhood fury, his wild berserker madness dissipated.

He backed a step and Danith's body glanced against his. Hot anger faded, replaced with cold calculation and an icy, pure will to triumph.

T'Ash said a Word. The flames vanished, leaving a black ring of grass and earth.

Boys ran from him toward Tinne. The last three men pressed their attack.

T'Ash fought.

A final, mental groan of the dying Holly Fam pierced T'Ash's mind.

Danith echoed the sound. She ran. To the Holly hunting cat. To Tinne. To the fight.

T'Ash swore and picked up his pace. Two men bolted, wounded. One fell.

T'Ash ran. The two glisten-braceletted boys hunched together, the healthy one supporting the wounded Flaired one. As he passed them the unhurt one jumped; only T'Ash's instincts kept him from being gutted. He kicked the knife from the boy's hand.

"Go, Nettle!" cried the fallen youth.

"Shade! No!" said the other, crouching, circling T'Ash.

"Go, Nettle. We kill later. Slower. By selves. Better."

"Better," repeated Nettle, baring his teeth at T'Ash, then bolted into the trees.

T'Ash joined Tinne. Five against one. Danith curled over a huddled shape, her hands spurting the green Flair of Healing in sheets of raw power. Zanth guarded, growling.

A man toppled at Tinne's feet.

Tinne grinned, pivoted, slashed at a new opponent.

T'Ash fought.

Two ran.

Two hit the ground with bleeding wounds.

Danith moaned.

T'Ash spun. She lay still over the cat. Blood trickled down her cheek from some cut she'd gotten before and he hadn't noticed.

Fury claimed him. T'Ash strode to the fallen boy with glisten teeth, Shade. The boy faded, trying to teleport, but his wounds made him too slow. T'Ash grabbed him, pressed one large hand on his thin chest, raised his blade.

"No!" Danith cried.

She struggled to sit and looked at him, pale from the loss of the energy she'd used Healing the cat, eyes huge and smudged in her face.

He lowered the blade to gently rest against the boy's throat. The Downwind youth glared with hate-filled eyes.

"No," Danith repeated, her voice slurred. "The fight is won. Now it's time for Healing."

Tinne straightened, his face as white as Danith's. He shook himself, looked around the scene of destruction. He swallowed. He staggered over to where Danith and the cat lay. Then his knees buckled. He reached out a hand and caressed the cat. "Ilexa?" His voice shook as he touched her side. "She took a blade, here."

A tremor shook Danith. T'Ash wanted to go to her, but some subtle connection between the young Holly, her, and the cat held him in place, an outsider.

Danith smiled, a wondering, lovely smile T'Ash had never seen. It radiated joy. "I think she'll be fine. I think I Healed her."

With a shaking hand, Tinne picked up Danith's limp one. He kissed her fingers. "My Fam. Anything you ask in my power is yours, D'Mallow."

D'Mallow. Danith deserved the title. She was the epitome of a true Noble—mannered, honorable, generous, kind, responsible.

T'Ash only wore a noble's title. He'd been mean in his life, destructive, obsessed, and murderous in his vengeance against his Family's killers. He'd been dishonest with Danith, and manipulative.

She'd seen his feral nature. She'd seen him fight and kill.

Me hurt, Zanth said.

T'Ash whipped around to see his Fam limping over to Danith. The cat collapsed beside her, the fat bulge of his side evident. He waved a paw in the air, a little too enthusiastically to be hurt much.

My paw cut. My ribs bruised. My ear gone, he whined.

T'Ash looked at Zanth's ears. They were the same tattered folds as always. He wondered which ear Zanth thought was gone.

The boy beneath T'Ash's blade expelled his breath on a hissing moan.

"Send him to a Healer, T'Ash," Danith said, looking at Zanth's paw. "Send all the wounded. You can afford it, and there's no reason to repeat the vicious cycle of killing."

"No," T'Ash said. She was right. The seed of an idea germinated in his mind. Downwind had to be improved, he'd said so for years. But he hadn't done anything further than attend some FirstFamilies Rituals that only superficially addressed the problems. Now he'd take action.

He studied the boy beneath his sword, one of a triad. Three bound together, nearly one mind, giving up individuality for the power of three. He wondered if the boy's mind could be healed as well as his physical hurts, if the youth's Flair could be developed and channeled for good.

T'Ash glanced at the others lying on the grassyard. Perhaps it was too late to turn the men into decent, productive people, but the remaining boys . . .

"No! What do you mean, no?" Danith scowled.

T'Ash put a foot on the boy's chest to keep him from trying to escape, and sheathed his broadsword. "No. There's no reason to repeat the vicious cycle of killing."

Danith smiled once more, and T'Ash felt her approval, in his heart and lower, a reflexive response to his HeartMate. It felt good.

Tinne moaned, then toppled slowly sideways. T'Ash glanced from the Noble to the glisten-toothed Downwinder. T'Ash shuddered again at the obvious differences.

He cupped his hands in front of him, crafting a message to the AllClass HealingHall, telling them to care for the wounded and bill T'Ash. Then he attached the spun-light message globe to the youth's chest and teleported him away.

T'Ash strode over to Tinne. The boy breathed deeply, exhaustion showed on his features. His death-dueling Passage was over. Whatever Flair had been freed this night, the young Holly would use worthily and honorably. Envy stabbed T'Ash at Tinne's pleasant past and fine future.

"Holm!" T'Ash called with his mind.

"Here." A misty viz of Holm Holly stood before him, looking worried.

"I have Tinne and his hunting cat. Tinne is tired but free of Passage. The cat had wounds, Healed by D'Mallow, but you should probably have a vet check them." He cocked an eyebrow at Danith to see if she approved. She nodded.

"Thank the Lady and Lord! Mamá has been frantic. He just 'ported out and we couldn't locate him without his House Ring." Holm expelled a breath.

"Focus on my position, and teleport them both." T'Ash shooed Danith away, moved Tinne to lay beside his Fam, and curved the young man's arms around the hunting cat. "Ready," T'Ash said.

Tinne and the cat disappeared.

The viz of Holm remained. His eyes narrowed and he craned his head as if to see through the night. "What do you have there? Bodies? There was a fight, and I wasn't invited? How many?"

T'Ash flicked his fingers. "Call ended."

Silence and the night shrouded the T'Blackthorn estate.

Slowly T'Ash turned, drinking deep of the night air, summoning his strength to look at the other shapes on the ground, to discover whether they lived. He used some of the adrenalin energy racing through him to teleport the wounded to AllClass HealingHall.

Moments passed as he completed his task. Zanth hummed mentally in satisfaction at Danith's Healing and fussing. By the time T'Ash returned to them, Zanth sat upright with a smug cat-smile on his round face, and one folded ear now straight up.

T'Ash stared. "You Healed his ear."

"Yes."

"But only one."

"The other wasn't hurt."

"He looks odd."

Zanth glared at him. *Food for feral cats. They wait in shadows.*

T'Ash closed his eyes and heaved the half-hog from his Residence no-time to small moving shapes near the garden door.

Danith looked at Zanth, proudly sitting with one ear straight up. He swished his tail. *Life is good.*

She sighed. "Sooner or later the other will be hurt again. Maybe then I can fix it." Her gaze went beyond T'Ash to the still forms on the ground.

"Dead," he said. "I can teleport them to the Downwind DeathGrove." And one by one he teleported them away.

Her lips pressed together.

He crouched down. When he looked in her eyes, they appeared large with tears. Her expression was of a woman totally lost. His heart clenched.

Then she fell into his arms.

Darkness filled his vision. His knees gave out.

Passage took Danith.

He swore. Passage. Now. Her Flair was breaking completely free at last. She'd suffer both her second and third Passages together, and over a matter of hours, not days.

He grabbed her. Her skin felt chill against his palms, a very bad sign. She moaned. The convulsions began.

They were alone in a breached GrandHouse estate. The strength of the Passage would be deadly. Would they survive? Would only one survive? Terror ripped through him.

Blackness swept him away.

A million fingers of intense emotion plucked at her soul, each one laced with the powerful Flair swirling through her, tinting memories with different aspects she'd never felt before.

She hadn't really remembered the sound of the speeding airship that had plunged into her little home, killing her parents and miraculously sparing her. She hadn't remembered the blistering heat or the shattering of brick. She'd suppressed it. She remembered now. In every detail.

She hadn't really remembered the dread of the towering, formidable strangers dressed in eye-hurting bright robes muttering things she didn't understand—her first contact with the Maidens of Saille. She remembered now.

She had forgotten the rough, urgent hands and body of a sweaty Timkin as he took her maidenhead. She had coated the memory with the love she'd felt. She experienced each harsh touch now.

All her memories battered at her, flashing through her too quickly for her to grab and master, as the Flair roared through her like an enormous fire. No wonder T'Ash feared fire.

The thought was swept away, all thought seared by the blaze within. She could not protect herself from the emotions, she could not grasp control of the Flair. She could only exist and suffer, and only for a short while.

A shield came. Strong and dark. Buffering her from the emotions. Holding her. T'Ash.

Some awful pain smashed both of them—when she was told she had no Flair. T'Ash grunted, her Flair resurged in flames around them, carried them away.

But they survived, together.

She closed her eyes. She felt safe.

Then she felt safe and separate from T'Ash.

She shivered with cold and emptiness.

She became capable of thought, the battering emotions limited enough to sort out into surprise and fear. She found herself walking down dim stone corridors of an ancient Residence, and knew it had been the ancestral Residence of Ash GreatHouse. Light streamed from a square doorway on the left.

An image formed of three boys, a young woman and man, and an older man. The oldest boy already held himself with a noble bearing, the second child displayed a reckless, winning grin. The third son—T'Ash, she realized—stood tall under the hand of the young man, his mother watched with tender, loving eyes, the older man with stern acceptance. "I'm proud of you, Rand," his father said.

Danith's heart trembled at the loving scene. She reached out a flat palm and felt the warmth of emotion, stepped nearer. Something restrained her. T'Ash. She couldn't see him, but could feel him around her.

"He said he was proud of me," T'Ash whispered. "I was always in trouble, but he said he was proud of me. Once."

Danith managed a smile and continued walking down the hallway, gathering her strength and energy for the storm she sensed still raged outside these walls. The walls T'Ash had built to contain and master his great Flair, the memories he had ordered and controlled. A lesson for her to do the same, with his help.

Another door beckoned, the jamb around the cracked-open wooden door was splintered. She walked to it, peered in.

Winter. A small, tattered, dirty boy running with stolen items he could sell for food—dodging a sleek looking man who dealt in boy-flesh—finding his hole and hiding. He shivered himself to sleep next to a cat nearly as large as he.

Danith touched the door, whether to open it or close it, she wasn't sure. It whipped from her hands and slammed.

She walked to a door further down the hallway, this door with copper inlay and a fancy knob. It was locked and did not turn under her hand.

A pointed arch. Green contours of the Ash grassyard hosted a party.

"My Nameday. My Flair began to show. Everyone was pleased," T'Ash's voice reverberated in her mind, yet his tone held a hollow note.

She hesitated by the arch, then continued. The corridor became smooth, like the armourcrete over stone of his new Residence. There were mere indications of doors, thin square outlines against the walls. She touched one.

"You don't need to go in there."

His words hurt, then pain gathered like a stone and sank into her. He would not let her in to his memories. He'd mastered his Flair and constructed this wonderful sanctuary for her during her Passage, but he would not share any further personal experiences with her.

She hurried down the hall to the door leading outside. She stopped.

He instructed her. "Build a place—brick, stone, armour-crete—materials don't matter, but build a place that will shield you. Where you can stand and take the Flair and forge it to your needs."

She knew it wouldn't work like that for her. She considered his words. Perhaps she had the strength and knowledge to form a thin layer of glisten hardglass between herself and the emotions, a tube encasing her. With an opening for her to gather Flair and shape it into workable streams.

She closed her eyes and began fabricating the capsule around her. T'Ash helped—not doing it himself, or giving her energy—but showing her images of how she could create it.

When she thought she was safe, she sucked in a deep breath and opened the door.

And fell, again, into a void whistling with emotions. The same! She shrieked until her voice was raw; fear whipped through her again and again until she understood that she was more afraid of what had happened and what could happen, than what was actually happening. The thin tube around her held.

And the revelations began.

Her homelife as a child. A moody, temperamental father who struck and bruised her mother, raised a hand to Danith now and again. If she looked, she could see what her life would have been if the airship hadn't killed her parents. She shuddered. She didn't want to see. Hard to believe the airship had been a blessing. She grabbed a handful of burning Flair and splintered the vision.

The love that Maiden Brigit of the Saille Home for Orphans had for Danith. Not a wholesome love, not a love of a mother/sister for a daughter/sister. Danith whimpered, then caught herself. Maiden Brigit had restrained that wrong sort of love, had controlled her sexual impulses, had never hurt any of the children. Danith grabbed a fiery spear of Flair and shattered the image.

Timkin's lust. His affection and words of love that were merely a joint past and a young man's raging hormones. He'd said the words and Danith had believed them, but they had been empty.

Her own love for Timkin. More than his, but not true love, not HeartMate love.

Tears streamed down her face as she used Flair to banish the knowledge.

Mitchella. Love for a sister. Love returned. Respect. Affection.

Claif. Affection, but no love, no passion, no HeartMate. His love for her a matter of desire and possessiveness and a knowledge that she would always make life easy for him, that she pleased and was loved by his Family.

It hurt. Why did confirmation of what she knew to be true hurt?

She despised herself. She'd used the Clovers, feeling that being a part of the big Family would mean she'd never lack for love.

She let Claif use her affection for him to avoid the effort of finding his true HeartMate, whom she sensed beyond the reaches of her Flair. Finding and winning HeartMates was rarely simple, but full of pitfalls and agonizing emotion.

Love lost. Love found. The losing shredding pieces of the soul, carving deep hollows and filling it to the brim with love. Claif wanted it easy.

As she had.

She'd used the Clovers. A crack appeared in her hard-glass tube. She watched in horror as it quickly arrowed tiny fissures.

No! She accepted the disgust at her failure, but she grabbed at good emotions, too. She had used the Clovers, but she had given of herself, too.

A branching crack disappeared.

She had spent time with the Family, helping them in errands, with tasks. She had added her energy to Rituals to Heal MotherDam. She had listened and counseled Trif, reaching her as a friend and an outsider when the rest of the Family had despaired.

It was not a matter of use, of debits and credits. It was a matter of Family and the love streaming between each member.

Her tube mended seamlessly.

Once again she rolled through sweeping waves of emotions, battered in her tube, but surviving. She endured the landslide of memories, the whirlwind of alternative futures.

With her, surrounding her, was T'Ash. He held distant from her, how she didn't know, but she knew it was so that she would control her Passage. That she would master her Flair.

She sensed he would hurl himself into the turmoil at any

moment if the Flair took her, because he'd convinced himself that she was integral to the continuation of his line.

She pushed the thought away. She, and she alone, could control her Flair. And before the Passage was done, she would have it harnessed. Harnessed like a powerful, senseless animal. An animal she could Heal. Her Flair, Healing animals. A unique, powerful, welcomed Flair.

Yes. Pride. Triumph. She used those emotions and those tools to garner more and more Flair, to shape it. To subdue it. To create her future.

One overwhelming maelstrom, earthquake, tornado, conflagration rolled over her, pierced her tube and her heart.

She loved T'Ash. With HeartMate love. Love that was fated never to belong to any other, past, present, or future.

And she feared that love.

Too soon. Too soon. Once again too soon for her to grasp and understand and control as she had finally controlled her Flair.

What would happen to her if she fell into T'Ash's arms? Would she be overwhelmed, Danith D'Ash before she ever learned who Danith D'Mallow could ever be?

Now she celebrated many rituals by herself, in a special place outside the city she'd found and treasured. A wild, natural place. Her heart swelled with love as she thought of the peace it gave her.

As D'Ash, she would be chivied into the GreatCircle Temple of the FirstFamilies, part of the heavy and burdensome future-shaping rituals, integral to the potent spells, sharing in the obligations and responsibilities of building and civilizing Celta. Personal wishes and goals would have to be subjugated to the wishes and goals of the many.

She would always be in the public eye, always held to the rules of conduct of a GreatLady, always expected to be a flawless example of nobility. A life of common, private, casualness would be exchanged for a life of noble formality and manners.

The Clovers would forever be lost to her. A large, laughing Family that would always provide Danith with affection and love and support would be gone.

She loved T'Ash, but could she live the life his wealth

and power and Flair and position demanded? Would it smother her?

She had ignored the outside memory-emotions tossing her tube around as she'd considered her future, and now she found herself standing within a deep forest. The trail behind her had vanished.

Several paths opened before her, and she froze. One road glowed with shining brightness. Death? Love? Flair?

One looked rocky and cold and barren.

Smoke roiled and boiled over another, giving glimpses of eerie landscapes.

One appeared solid and well-marked, passing through uninteresting scenery.

She plunged down the bright path. She turned a corner and heard T'Ash cry out.

Everything stilled.

She saw T'Ash. The man, the GreatLord, she loved. And she could look deep inside him.

Sixteen

❦

*S*he stared at *T'Ash*. *At first his powerful Flair nearly*
blinded her, then she learned to look beyond that. She
observed the loneliness of the man, to see a kernel of some
lingering darkness in his heart. Could she separate the man
from the GreatLord? Would that help her decide?

The young Rand had been third and last of the Ash sons.
His Father had "once" said he was proud of him. His Mother
had chosen to perish with the rest of her Family rather than
to stay and care for Rand.

Rand, who still grieved, who hid within GreatLord
T'Ash, not allowing anyone close, any other loved one to abandon
him.

Her love for him grew.

But did he love her? He used the word *HeartMate,* but
never mentioned love. Could he love her?

She looked deep into him and knew the dark seed could
grow once more, consuming him as the fire had devoured his
Family.

She knew she could demolish that black kernel with her
love for him, if she dared to love him with all her heart, if
she gave herself to him body, mind, and soul. If she joined
with him in a HeartBond.

And if she failed him, it would destroy her.

She could fight for him and win. She only had to prod him until he opened his whole self to her. When she knew all of him, and only then, she would HeartBond with him, and then love would come to them both. She would fight to know all his demons.

But not now, Lady and Lord, not now. She could not engage in that battle after so many recently fought. Not when it was so extremely important. Not when failing would destroy them both.

She'd run away—just for the moment, just until she found the courage to run back. Just until she knew she could win.

And for the first time she felt him draw near, as if he knew she'd confronted her worst demons, harnessed her Flair, and survived.

She let the tube dissolve.

Chaos no longer swirled around her, instead, bands of rainbow light pulsed in prismatic order, with silver and gold and iridescent glisten sparkles looking like stars and a swath of glittering gold veiling. T'Ash might have reconstructed his ancient Residence during his Passages as a bulwark against the chaos, but that was not her style. Instead, she had this pulsating rainbow, and each star—like each door of T'Ash's Residence—would mark a memory. And the gold was her Flair, to be drawn upon and used to Heal.

She smiled.

With deep delight she tapped the pulsing thing to Heal her cut cheek and other scrapes, and to mend T'Ash's blistered skin and knife slashes. She dissolved his bandages. Then she gathered and showered them both with glittering energy.

Slowly she withdrew from the rainbow. Slowly she began to feel sensations of the physical world around her. She felt the heaviness of her body, the superficial coolness of her skin in the night air. She heard the rustlings and peepings of night creatures. She smelled the fragrance of crushed grass, and something more primal, a tang of blood.

Danith shuddered. She opened her eyes to see T'Ash lying on his side in front of her. The twinmoonslight brushed the angles of his face with silver. His eyes appeared stark, until she met his gaze, then she saw a flame of passion.

She loved him. She wanted him.

Between them tension built, the last vestiges of all the emotions of Passage melted into a craving for him, a desire she had no will to deny.

She needed his arms around her. She hungered for the taste of him on her tongue. Most of all, she wanted his sex stroking within her, giving her the ultimate climax she would only find with him.

T'Ash looked into Danith's eyes, deep pools of green, melting with desire that threatened to whirl him away into a passion he'd never experienced. Within him lust mixed with tenderness, possessiveness, protectiveness—an exciting, new sensation.

She wanted him. She wanted him. Now.

He remembered how it had been between them during his own recent Passage. His body hardened beyond refusal. His breath rasped. His heart raced.

His heart. He should think of his heart, of his HeartMate. He should resist the temptation. Her life had changed too fast, and once he claimed her body, he didn't know if he'd ever be able to let her go, let her have even the space of a septhour from him. And if he took her, his heart would be affected as much as his body. If she later rejected him, it would rip him to pieces smaller than Zanth with a lizard. And he had to hide his flaws.

Me guard. Zanth trotted away, humming cat-satisfied sounds, one ear and his tail sticking up.

Danith pulled T'Ash's head down to her own. When her lips touched his and her taste blossomed on his tongue, he was lost.

Blood heated and streaked through his veins like molten fire, and the fire felt good. He embraced it, liked how it caused his body to tremble.

She was soft beneath him, her hands urgent on his back, kneading his flexing muscles.

He groaned and rolled aside tearing his lips from her eager ones, capturing her wrists.

Her lovely face showed passion's flush even in the twin-moonslight. Her eyes were wide with desire, her lips parted, and her expression squeezed his heart—a deep yearning, as if he were necessary to the fabric of her life.

When he looked at her, time stopped. All the energies and emotions that forged through him, leading him to this point, eased. He had to take this slow. He had to make this perfect.

Her hands would incite his lust beyond control.

The scent of the sweet earth rose to him, comprised of grass and night flowers.

He slipped a finger in the shoulder tabs of her tunic and peeled the cloth back, spreading it open and exposing her breasts. The twinmoonslight caressed them, shimmering over them, painting them silver with dark, berry tips. Her fragrance insinuated itself along his nerve endings.

His mouth dried. He grabbed at spinning wits, shards of reason, the control that rarely deserted him, and never for sex.

She tossed her head back and forth, whimpering with desire.

"Easy, dear one." He didn't know where the words came from, or the tenderness. He only knew the passion building within him was stronger than anything before, and that he wanted to stoke it and savor it, until the shattering explosion flung him beyond all sense.

She wriggled her trous off.

He gasped and could not speak.

She was more beautiful than anything he'd ever seen, finer than the richest stone. She lay like alabaster, waiting for him, wanting him.

Blood pounded in his temples, banishing reason, but not caution. His fingers trembled as they curved around her face, dropped a kiss on her pale pink lips.

He had to touch her, know her through touch, shape her as he had so often shaped his creations. He had to learn all the textures of her body. He wished he was a sculptor.

He laid his hands on her shoulders, thumbs tracing her collarbone, and absorbed the contrast between them.

His hands were large, the bones solidly made. Her bones were delicate, refined. His skin was olive dark against her fairness. His palms were calloused against her silkeen softness.

Would she like being touched by calloused hands? He slid them down over her breasts. She arched upward. Gently he molded her flesh, feeling the softness of the mounds, the pointed nipples in the palms of his hands.

He wanted to speak some sort of love words but his brain froze and his throat felt too thick. So he lowered his head to press a kiss on her lips. Her tongue darted out, tempting him, but he wanted to taste more than her lips.

Still caressing her breasts, he brushed kisses across her collarbone, down between his enveloping hands, further down over her stomach, until he came to the delta of her thighs.

Her scent was everything he'd ever wanted. Ripe apples. Passionate lover. Sweet, generous, woman.

He kissed the curls at the top of her thighs, but went no further. Her womanflesh would tempt him into raging madness, and he wanted to give her gentleness. He wanted to show her all she meant to him—the lover to fulfill him, the woman to walk by his side, the mother of his line. His HeartMate.

He stroked the satin columns of her thighs, curved his hands around the firm flesh of her calves, cradled and flexed her feet in his hands. And all the while a pretty glaze of passion bedewed her body, telling him of her desire. Her fragrance grew stronger, luring him to his fate.

Slowly, more than his hands trembling, he unclasped his sword and placed it on the ground. More quickly he shoved his clothing off.

She gasped when she saw his great need for her. Then she licked her lips.

His body pulsed under her gaze. He felt himself thicken, ready for the possession of his mate.

He closed his eyes and stood before her, letting her know of the strength of his body that would take her. And its scars.

He felt vulnerable but powerful. This was right. This was destiny. Mating with her on the rich earth beneath two shining moons, taking her to the summit of sensation amidst the calls of birds and the scent of flowers.

He opened his eyes. She lifted her arms.

He went to her, thrust into her, and she moaned with pleasure.

Passion ripped through him, desire that couldn't be denied. He needed her. Needed her to cradle him, to sheath him tightly, to encompass him. To hold him.

But now he craved her passion as a drug, heard her little cries and shuddered with delight. He set the rhythm of the age-old mating, thrusting, rocking, feeling her tight and wet and caressing his shaft until he could only strive for release.

She cried out, clenched around him, and he surged once more and gave her his seed and his heart.

When he could move, he rolled so she lay atop him. He needed her close. Her body was limp and supple in his arms. She breathed evenly, in the depths of sleep.

After her Passage, she had hungered to mate, firing his own desire that he could no longer contain. He joined with her.

Slightly worried, he touched the edges of her mind. She was slowly descending into dreams, dreams he sensed would be pleasant and comforting.

Not wanting to break the contact with her, even for an instant, he kept a bare foot under her hip as he stood. "Robe, on," he softly called. The ash brown robe from his Residence garbed him. He took the earrings from his trous pocket and put them in a secured pocket inside his robe.

He wanted to take Danith to his Residence but did not dare. Nothing must upset her upon waking. Nor could he chance teleporting them to her bed. A gentleman did not sleep in a lady's bed without being asked. He'd learned that much from the courtship book, though it had danced around the issue in mealy-mouthed language. And though Danith had wanted his loving in the moments after Passage, he didn't think sex, even sex mixed with caring, constituted a real invitation to sleep with someone.

He stared at her in wonder, his woman, his HeartMate. Fire had ringed Danith, and he had walked through it for her, braving the flames, letting his clothes steam around him. He shuddered now. He had faced his deepest physical fear and mastered it. As he had mastered his deepest emotional fear, his berserker nature.

Danith was very good for him. If only he knew he would be equally good for her. And he hadn't been able to tell her of his old hurts, or let her open those doors to his past when he'd sheltered her in her own Passage. Her Passage had been clean, leaving no demons unfaced and no doors locked. He grimaced, then fell to his knees to stroke her hair and soothe himself.

Desire curled in him. He kissed her temple and the taste of her made his body harden. Sweet temptation. But something even more sweet tempted him.

Now, as she slept, he could meld with her. Insinuate himself into her very dreams until she accepted him, and initiate the HeartBond. He wanted it more than he wanted anything in his life. His heart throbbed with aching pain at their separation.

But he knew her now. Knew she was more than a beautiful smile and green-gold eyes.

He clenched his fists. He could not do it.

She must ask it.

And for the first time, perhaps the only time, he understood the ancient rules for HeartGifts and HeartMates.

She must accept him of her own free will.

Somehow he had to win her outside of the HeartBond, while still hiding his flaws and wretched past.

His fists tightened. Somehow he, T'Ash, a man without grace or manners, a man with little knowledge of women, would win this fight, too. On his own terms.

A battle-shriek ripped the air. T'Ash rolled to cover Danith, scrambled in grass to find his sword.

Weight slammed into his back. An arm appeared, knife flashing, in front of his eyes, darted to his throat.

T'Ash lunged up and back. Before they hit the ground again, his enemy twisted. They rolled together on the ground.

The boy, Nettle, was young, slighter, and less muscular than T'Ash. But his lips pulled back in a feral smile, his eyes rolled with the madness of grief of having one triad-brother slain, the other captured. From his strength, T'Ash knew both surviving teenagers, Nettle and Shade, were linked, with Shade feeding power to Nettle.

They tangled, wrestling, hitting, kicking, jabbing.

Danith stood, her body white and perfect in the moon-light. She ran, grabbed a knife from the ground. It looked old and nicked and bloody. Now she ran toward them.

"No!" cried T'Ash.

"Yes." She bared her teeth, hovered near them. "I won't run. We're a pair. I'll fight, too."

"No, not you!" Anguish flooded T'Ash. She should never be tarnished with the stain of violence. She Healed, she could never kill.

"Yes!" She danced around, her eyes intent on the fight, holding the knife all wrong. "We're together."

T'Ash rolled on Nettle, pinned him. He let his body hold the youth as he visualized Danith's back grassyard. He flung her there, her anger and objections echoing in his mind.

The boy flipped him, jumped up, withdrew step by step. "Not this time. You wait and suffer. We get you, Shade and me." He stabbed the air viciously with the knife. "Then we get her and play." He ran, breath gasping and obviously near the end of his strength, until he once more disappeared into the dark shadows.

T'Ash mentally tracked Nettle across the estate and out to the streets, then to Downwind.

Putting his swordbelt on around his robe, T'Ash let the quiet of the night wrap around him and fill him. He and the youth had fought and he'd felt fear for Danith, but no berserker fit, no descent into bestiality had threatened. And now he knew he'd placed it firmly in the past and it would never rise in him again.

"Zanth!" he bellowed.

Me here. Bad scruff. He odd Flair. Made Me sleep. Bad. Bad. Bad. The Fam paced, tail lashing.

T'Ash sighed. The two survivors had joined to bespell Zanth, then the free one had attacked.

T'Ash stretched, his muscles working smoothly and easily. No other men, boys or cats remained on the Blackthorn estate.

Zanth followed, grumbling. *Me tired. Do much today. Me want food. Me want cocoa. Me want My pillow. Me want . . .*

T'Ash stopped listening. When they reached the small door

in the wall he stood, hands on hips, and examined it. The only way to keep the estate safe, now and in the future, would be to strengthen the wall forceshields. T'Ash leaned his sword against a nearby tree and slipped off his robe. It would be a long and sweaty business, to imbue power in the wall surrounding the estate brick by brick. Then he could go home to Danith.

He got to work.

*D*anith fumed. *First she paced her mainspace, mutter-*ing swearwords. It had been only moments after T'Ash teleported her that she sensed the danger was gone and he was well. Still, he didn't come, and she had a lot to say to him.

She'd whiled away the time by taking a shower and washing the grime of the night from herself, wondering what T'Ash had done with her favorite tunic trous casual suit. That he, and it, hadn't appeared by the time she'd cleaned up continued to be a thorn.

Since she felt so irritated anyway, she decided to finish filling out the multitude of forms that needed to be submitted to the NobleCouncil.

How dare he just fling her away. They were a couple, a pair, friends—even lovers. She felt the heat of a flush, but continued in her angry thoughts.

He wanted her to be his HeartMate. He'd taunted her with being a coward, yet when she'd stood to fight by his side, he'd taken the decision from her hands and used his great power to send her home, like she was a child. As if she had no say in the matter.

The forms went surprisingly quickly as she made instant decisions that would form her future.

Yet when she heard the announcement "T'ASH COMES" resound in the thin air of her mainspace, she prepared to argue.

With a small clap the man stood before her. She lifted her chin, narrowed her eyes, and tapped her foot. The fact that his face was set in weary lines, that his olive skin had a pale cast, that he looked as if he'd lost a few more kilos, and that he held a drooping Zanth, made no difference to her.

She sensed his thoughts—she should not be touched by violence. She should never experience it again. She was special, and precious, and something to be protected at all costs.

This softened her heart a little, until she realized that he wanted to place her under glass, like one of his expensive and exquisite creations.

She crossed her arms and stamped her foot. "No. We are lovers now, and we have begun to share things, things like Passage."

He flinched, dropped Zanth.

The Fam stared at each of them haughtily, then stalked out of the mainspace to the bedroom.

"You want us to be HeartMates," she accused.

He nodded.

She threw up her hands. "I've tried to fight you, but now you're too close. I have to admit that I can't go back to my old life, I can only go on into a new one."

The hint of a smile curved his lips. It didn't placate her. She stabbed a finger at him. "And you want to be part of this new life."

The smile disappeared. He slitted his own eyes. "I am part of your life. You are all of mine. We will be all in all to each other."

"No. We won't." She bit her lip, flicked her tongue over it, felt heat ebb up her neck and cheeks. "We will try being lovers."

"We are more," he rasped.

"Are we? You first mock me and say I'm a coward, then when I decide to fight with you, you push me away. You've been pushing me away from many things, from your emotions and your past, for instance. Until you let me closer, we will stay lovers only, not HeartMates HeartBonded."

He reached out and whirled her into his hard body. Her own instantly appreciated his virility, and her blood started pounding again.

"We are much more than lovers. I've made a HeartGift, two. Mitchella returned the necklace. It waits for you. Soon we will wed. You will be Danith, GreatLady D'Ash."

She tried to free herself and glared up at him. He wouldn't

even admit he was keeping his essential self from her. Hurt stabbed her. She'd known this new life would be painful, and had struggled against it, and now was caught in the riptide. "We are only lovers. We have sex, that's all."

He tilted her chin up with one hand. "We desire each other. Let's come together in passion. I like it."

She liked it, too.

T'Ash held her tightly all through the night. When she awoke in the morning, fear of the incredible future mixed with excitement. Today she started her apprenticeships. What if she should fail in her new life?

"You won't fail," T'Ash murmured. "You will impress the Sallows and Heathers with your Flair, its strength and the innate power."

His eyes opened and the contrast of the sky-crystal blue and his dark complexion aroused her.

"Besides," T'Ash continued, his mouth setting in arrogant lines. "I verified your Testing. I do not make mistakes with Testing Stones."

Danith smiled and leaned down to kiss him on the lips. She shut her eyes to hide incipient tears. The sex had been marvelous, beyond anything she'd ever imagined, but not quite enough. She yearned for words of love, but would not say her own first. She would not yield to be overwhelmed by him.

And she knew that deep inside him the small seed of darkness still lurked.

She let the kiss spin her mind away, felt the delicious caress of their bodies gently brushing. His warm, full soft lips became demanding, moist ones.

She moaned.

Princess mewed.

T'Ash rolled over and released Danith.

He smiled. "I'll feed the cat." He glanced at the timer. "You get ready for your appointments."

She went and showered. When he returned, she was pulling on some new, body-hugging but comfortable troustights under her knee-length matching brown tunic.

T'Ash scowled, his stare blaser-intense again. "You'll probably be working with Caprea Sallow. He's unwed. Don't let him get any ideas."

Danith raised her brows. "No?"

"No. Perhaps I should make it clear to him—"

"You don't have to." She sighed, looking around her increasingly cramped home. Gifts from various Great and GrandHouses—each one more elaborate than the next as if it were a matter of competition—had started materializing in her back grassyard. For some reason, probably because of T'Ash's lack, the offerings were mostly antique furniture. She wondered if she'd given the Nobles a chance to clean out their attics, or whatever they called the top floors of their castles. "Everyone knows the new D'Mallow is sleeping with GreatLord T'Ash."

He stepped toward her, hands fisted at his sides. "Don't say that."

"It's true."

"It's more than sex. I've made a HeartGift, two." He fulminated for a moment, looking as if he searched for words. Danith sighed again. Three little words shouldn't be difficult to find.

"I'll 'port with you to the Sallows."

So he would be seen with her. "We could take the public carrier, or your private glider."

"'Port."

A few moments later Danith and T'Ash stood before the brick-walled Sallow property. He kissed her slowly, lingeringly, possessively—for the scrystone she was sure someone was watching. But that didn't stop her from enjoying the sensation of his mouth on hers, the heat building deep in her core.

When he lifted his head, he smiled and curved a hand around her face. "You'll be fine. Your Flair is now just under the surface to be tapped. An Animal Healer will be prized. With you the FirstFamilies might be able to increase the size of the delicate horse herds. We might save some Terran breeds that are threatened with extinction, ensure our heritage and our future."

Always heritage and line with T'Ash. She returned his

smile, easing herself away from him. Her timer beeped. Five minutes until she was due. She pulled the bellrope. "I'll be fine," she said.

And she was. The morning at Sallow was spent sitting in the courtyard and practicing simple Flair exercises. Now and again she'd open her eyes to find herself surrounded by animals. Zanth, another cat or two, a rare puppy, housefluffs, even an old horse.

In the afternoon the Heather Healers took her around to the slightly ill and wounded of the Primary HealingHall. The hospital itself was more elegant and richly furnished than any other building Danith had ever been in.

The Healers were gentle but strict, teaching lessons of proper flow of Flair for the illness; when and how to remain distant from the pain, thoughts, and feelings of her patients.

Danith felt her Flair, guided it, and mastered it. It throbbed through her body as necessary now as her blood. As pervasive as life itself. She loved the current of it, reveled in it as she had so long wanted to do. She learned the basics quickly.

Mentally weary and with some of her strength drained in the use of Flair, she still skipped into her home and ate a large dinner. T'Ash showed up as evening was turning into night.

"I want you to come to a FirstFamilies conference. You are expected."

"No."

He stomped a circuit through the kitchen, the tiny dining room attached to the mainspace, the mainspace itself, and back. "This is important to me. We deal with Downwind matters, what must be done, how to craft a ritual that will mitigate the tension and ill-feeling."

"I know it's important to you, and I thank you for inviting me, but I'm not comfortable with them—"

"You think I am?"

"I think you're one of them. You always were and always will be. And you know what must be done. The area of Downwind itself must be rehabilitated, so boys don't live in holes."

His face froze.

"T'Ash, can't you tell me of that time? Of the doors you keep shut on your memories?"

"No."

Danith wet her lips. His eyes sparked, but he made no move to her.

"Aren't we close enough?" she asked.

His jaw set and the blue blaze of his eyes intensified. "I want to be closer. I want the HeartBond—"

"I'm not even accustomed to you as a lover, let alone a HeartMate." She feared total surrender.

"How long do you need?" It was a challenge more than a sensitive question.

"I don't know."

He didn't say she was cowardly, but she only had to look in his eyes to see that he thought it.

He turned on his heel and went into the mainspace, where there was enough space to teleport in and out. "I'll be back late."

She didn't tell him not to come; her heart thudded hard at the thought that he might not come back to her. "Inform the Nobles they need to spend some gilt as well as craft spells," Danith called.

"You tell them. You tell GrandHouses. You will be summoned to their Council, soon enough." He left with a bang.

Zanth growled, startling Danith. He and Princess lay on opposite ends of her settee.

Downwind fine. Holes good places. Good hunting.

She stared at the cat, opened her mouth to argue, and knew she'd never be able to change his mind. "You're looking thinner."

Zanth preened. *Many 'roons dead. Many guards have new boots.* He narrowed his eyes. *Chef at Res-i-dence made cocoa mousse. In no-time place.*

"I don't know how to access the no-time."

Zanth subsided into fake sleep.

Danith shoved more gifts of furniture to line her walls and thought about storage, trying not to think about T'Ash, to no avail.

He was an ideal lover, his hands slow and gentle and caring, his lips firm and demanding, his body hard and delightful against hers. She shivered in remembrance.

During lovemaking, their needs had spurred the melding of thoughts. More and more their loving consisted of unspoken needs flowing from one to the other, being silently fulfilled by each, escalating into mind-numbing ecstasy. Every time they made love was better than the last. Again she shivered.

She still didn't know what to do. The man thought she could instantly adapt to her new life. No doubt he believed he'd acclimated to Downwind in the same amount of time. The poor boy. The poor boy, Rand, who still lived within T'Ash and would not let her near.

He'd shut that fragment of himself off, never to be exposed to anyone, never to be integrated into the GreatLord T'Ash. His Downwind years were to be ignored. His real life had started with his second Passage and the advent of Holm Holly.

Danith firmed her lips. At least she was trying to blend her old life with her new. She was trying to keep her closest friends and the Clovers in her life, trying to make new friends who wouldn't judge her just by her new rank.

The thought led her to action. She'd accept a dessert-party invitation with Mitchella over at Pink's. Despite the publicity of her nobility, she stubbornly refused to let the Clovers put any distance between themselves and her. Yet Danith felt the Clovers were only biding their time, waiting to see if she became D'Ash to completely sever the connection.

Her Flair already separated them enough. She set her shoulders. She was determined that she would not lose the Clovers.

T'Ash was another one who bided his time. He didn't like the Clovers. She'd returned Claif's ring, but T'Ash hadn't been satisfied. He stuck by his idea that she needed no one but him in her life.

She did need him. And she needed him to need her, sensed that his desire for her went beyond passion, but that, too, he never said. He had an idea that he could outwait her, wear her down, that eventually she would give in to all his demands.

Danith didn't think she could afford to.

T'Ash stood in the shadows near *Danith's* house. She should move into his Residence. Lower St. Johnswort Street was too unsafe.

She walked slowly, tired from her first day using and mastering her Flair, yet still with grace and a cheerfulness in her movements. His heart contracted. After every moment they spent apart, he realized his deep need for her.

A worry had begun to nag him, a feeling that she was progressing well into her new life, striding confidently down a road—and leaving him behind. She was managing to weld her past and her future together into a strong whole, while he was beginning to realize that he'd ignored his past. He'd put it far behind him, refusing to acknowledge any strengths his Downwind boyhood had given him, trying to forget that part of his life.

Did this make her stronger than he? He thought it might. It certainly added to the weight of the evidence that he did not deserve a woman like her.

T'Ash froze. He lifted his head, scenting the tang of twisted Flair. Another lurked in the shadows, glided after Danith. The stalker waited for her to leave the strong and protective light of the nightpoles and turn up her own path. It was the last teenager of the triad.

He was close and unshielded. T'Ash hit instantly and hard, spearing mental pain to the gangmember. The young man collapsed without a sound.

T'Ash scanned the golden web of protection he had once again spun around Danith and fed it power.

On her front porch Danith stopped and shivered. "T'Ash?" she called softly.

He gritted his teeth. He wanted her. He wanted to Heart-Bond with her. She smelled of the Clovers. "Here," he said.

He heard her sigh, then the soft opening Word for her door. Princess stepped out onto the porch and mewed. The cat looked in his direction and mewed again.

"We should talk, we have much to discuss and decide. But I'm too tired tonight. Come to bed, T'Ash," Danith said.

The fallen boy vanished from T'Ash's perception, teleported unsteadily away by his triad-twin who lay in the HealingHall.

T'Ash sighed, too. "I'm coming." His weariness matched her own. He'd fought long and hard at the Council meeting, this time with words and images and dire warnings. And he'd won.

If there would be no HeartBond with Danith tonight, at least she wouldn't ask him to reveal his past or his deepest self, not in words or in emotions. They would love. Then they would sleep.

*T*he next day, Danith's second day of apprenticeship, she Healed a dying housefluff, a genetic hybrid of an Earth rabbit and a Celtan mochyn.

She laid her hands on it and could feel the waning lifeforce, the rip deep in its body. With gentle fingers, she stroked its soft fur and visualized her Flair as hands, finding the ruptured organ and mending it. Even through her concentration, she smiled. This spell was close to the first welding one that T'Ash had taught her, but refined now, completely personal and Healing. The use of her Flair, especially for others, was her highest good and her greatest joy.

The housefluff jerked, trembled, opened its eyes, and rolled to its feet. After a pink-nosed snuffle to Danith's fingers, it hopped away to where a little girl anxiously sat on a bench.

She crowed delight and picked up the animal in her arms, dancing through the arch of the courtyard into a grassy meadow beyond.

A mid-aged GraceLady followed the scene with a teary gaze, then touched Danith on the arm. "We cannot thank you enough, GrandLady D'Mallow. The veterinarians, the Healers— They had no hope. And it's a precious life to the Family."

Danith thrilled. "My pleasure."

Her teacher, a Heather Healer, looked startled, then shook her gray head. "It is incredible how fast you learn." Her face folded into pensive lines. "As with all great Flairs, you must sense the correct way of using your power instinctively, and only need some practical knowledge. Good. Very good."

Exultation filled Danith. She'd freed her Flair and directed it as her inner self had always wanted. The whole process resonated with inherent rightness.

She had to tell someone, and the only one who would understand would be T'Ash. Her two-day-old great-Flaired friends were too new, and her old Flairless friends wouldn't understand. That left only T'Ash. And she'd encourage him to tell of his own experiences, try and lure the child Rand from the formidable GreatLord. She would learn all of him, soon.

She used some of her exuberance 'porting to T'Ash's Residence, where she found him deep in discussion with Holm Holly via scry holo.

He glanced up at her arrival, a brief smile touched his mouth, then disappeared as his gaze returned to the holo of Holm Holly. "I will scout locations and set up a fund for the buildings and staffing. I expect the other Noble Houses to participate, if not in my project, then in others. Wheat, Rye, and Silkeen should take care of the docks. Perhaps—"

"I understand, and I'll make sure they hear of your contribution. With effort, in a few years, there will be no Downwind," said Holly.

T'Ash laughed harshly. "There may be no Downwind in Druida, but other cities—"

"We will try our best!"

"There will always be outlaws, people who don't fit in." His gaze slid to her. Did he still feel like an outsider? Even transacting the highest level of business with HollyHeir? Incredible.

She blew him a kiss.

His eyes rounded as he stared at her.

Holm continued. "The misfits can explore the frontier, civilize it, carve out their own cities, disappear. I don't care. My concern is for the citizens of—"

"My Lady's here. I go. Merry meet."

Holm's holo looked around but didn't appear to see her. He sighed. "Merry part."

"And merry meet again," T'Ash replied.

"You're doing a fine thing—"

"Fare well." T'Ash cut the call and stood behind a new, polished reddwood desk that matched a large cat platform against the wall. The platform had areas of furra hide that showed signs of sharp claws.

"You're here," T'Ash said. He looked at her and all thoughts of the wonderful, hopeful things he had set in motion, all the flush of joy she'd had in her day, transformed into intense female awareness.

His eyes dilated so only a startling, dark rim of blue showed in his saturnine face. Her heart pounded as his glance stopped on her eyes, then moved to her breasts. The flush of desire she felt creeping up her was mirrored in the increased color over his cheekbones.

Without speaking a word, he readied her for his touch, for the possession of his body. She swayed forward without volition, giving way to temptation. A yearning ache started low and she could hear the raggedness of her breathing.

His chest rose and fell rapidly. Slowly he walked to her, so slowly the heat spiraling within her felt as if it would melt her very bones.

He touched her.

Seventeen

🍑

T'Ash's fingers brushed against her cheek.

She threw herself into his arms, then stood on tiptoes to nibble tiny kisses on his lips. The hot, smoky scent of him sparked her passion. "Mmmm." T'Ash lifted Danith against his body. His lips persuaded her mouth to open. He took it and drank like a man dying of thirst. Her mind reeled and she sank into blazing sensuality.

Their tongues mated and his hips began to rock against her. He sat her on the edge of his desk and stepped between her legs. Though she wore trous, she was open to him, and his thick, hard shaft drew moistness from her core as her passion rose. She twined her arms around his neck, tilting her bottom until the cloth separating them maddened her.

His large hands pushed down her trous and underwear, he freed himself.

He plunged his velvet, steely length into her.

Her neck couldn't support her head. It fell back. She whimpered with rising desire. "I need you," she panted.

"Yes." His reply was guttural. The skin on his face pulled taut. He buried a hand in her hair and supported her head so that their gazes matched. "Look at me."

Feelings trembled from him to her. His passion raged at

the edges of control, but the tightness of her was something he craved. He would not move until his control broke.

She moaned; she wanted his deep, hard stroking. She didn't think she could stand this waiting he demanded. She sent visions to him of her need for fast, intense mating. "Move," she pleaded.

His body shivered, but he didn't yield. He remained solid and quiet inside her, growing with every pulse. With every breath she issued a little moan, the spiraling tension was unbearable. "Move!"

His eyes blazed into hers, then narrowed. "Soon."

She felt the tsunami threaten, but not soon enough. She raised her legs and clamped them behind his waist, forcing him deeper into her than he'd ever been.

The pupils of his eyes widened until only a tiny bit of blue remained. They breathed unevenly together.

"You know how I feel," he said.

She managed a nod.

"You know how you feel around me."

She whimpered again.

"Want you. Crave you. Need you!" he cried out, then pounded into her.

She climaxed at his first thrust, screamed.

Waves rolled over her, each more forceful than before at his plunging body. And he saw it in her eyes, felt everything.

He lunged, his seed spurted deep inside her. And she felt his shattering pleasure, saw it in his unfocused gaze.

She fell backward to the desk. His big body covered hers.

It felt awkward, wonderful. She finally escaped his stare, but was too dazed to hide anything from him. Surely he could see love in her eyes, feel it in their bond, know that with him inside her she could refuse him nothing.

But moments passed and T'Ash did not take advantage of her weakness. Their breathing steadied. He inhaled deeply and Danith knew he was savoring her scent. She trembled.

"You are here, in T'Ash Residence." His voice held satisfaction.

She couldn't deny it.

"But our first time here should have been slowly, in my bed."

She cleared her throat. "This time was slow enough. I didn't think I could bear the tension."

He chuckled and nuzzled her neck, swiped his tongue across it, tasting her. She returned the favor. His taste went straight to her core, she tightened around him.

His hips arched into her, he groaned. "This is not sex. Since we aren't HeartBound, I don't know what it is. I've never felt it before."

She wanted to knock some sense into his head. Love. This was love, and he didn't recognize it.

He didn't recognize it. How long had it been since he'd felt any loving arms around him? She knew the answer— since he was six. Was Rand finally coming out from hiding, letting her love him? And how long was this going to take, to learn him, to love him, to let GreatLord T'Ash know she would never hurt Rand?

A timer struck the hour. The whispery Residence voice spoke. "You have an appointment at the AllClass Healing-Hall in twenty minutes."

Danith put her hands on his face, made him look at her. His eyes looked bluer than ever, and defenseless. "You're going to visit the HealingHall." She couldn't suppress a grin. She'd nagged at him to see the boys whose Healing he paid for, hoping that through them, he could accept the young Downwind man he had once been.

"Yes." Vulnerability sat oddly on his strong features. She kissed his eyelids, his cheeks, brushed her mouth against his, sent him the upsurge of tenderness that swelled her heart.

A tremor passed through him, and he gently eased himself away from her. "Cloth!" he said. An instant later a soft linen cloth appeared in his hands.

He closed his eyes, evened his breathing. When he opened them again, he fixed his gaze on her. "Water from the HouseHeart."

Danith blinked.

A small rattle came from beside her, and she saw a ritual iron cauldron full of water. The fragrance of deep earth, hot smoke, a trace of jasmine, rose from the water. She shivered as the scent made its way through her lungs into her blood and her very bones. It was the scent of the T'Ash Residence, and even comprised part of the scent of T'Ash himself.

T'Ash dipped the cloth in the water and washed himself, then straightened his clothes. They were ordinary trous and shirt in ash brown, nothing that would proclaim him a noble, neither his ankle or sleeve cuffs showed his status.

He swished the cloth in water again and pressed the cool, wet linen against her, stroking her gently to clean her.

Danith blinked, felt embarrassment tint her cheeks red. "We are using blessed water for washing? HouseHeart water?" Her mind boggled.

T'Ash met her eyes, his expression serious. "To wash T'Ash and his woman the first time they mated in the Residence. It is an event."

Danith blinked again. Before she could speak, he'd sent the cauldron and the cloth to the HouseHeart.

She pushed herself off the desk, taking some papyrus with her. When she picked them up off the Chinju rug, she saw they were architectural plans for several buildings, with a phoenix standard above the door.

"What's this? The project you were talking to HollyHeir about?"

T'Ash stepped close and efficiently smoothed her clothing down her. It didn't keep her from leaning into his touch. His mouth quirked and then the slight smile disappeared.

"The HollyHeir is named Holm. And he considers you a friend. He told me that he gave you leave to call him Holm; you should do it."

Danith bit her lip. "Tell me about your project."

T'Ash shrugged, turned, and walked to the door. "I'm funding several Downwind centers for boys, where they can come to be safe, be Tested for Flair, learn skills that will make them more than their fathers."

She couldn't see his face, and his voice was matter-of-fact, but his shoulders looked stiff. "That's wonderful!"

He spun to her, his hand on the doorknob, his expression tense. "You really think so."

She lifted her chin. "Yes. It's a wonderful idea, in keeping with your honorable character."

He looked startled, shook his head as if to clear it of some notion, and offered his arm. "Are you coming?"

She smiled a wicked little smile. "With you? I always do." She was pleased when a touch of red appeared under his skin.

*H*e hated the HealingHall. Hated the sights, and especially hated the smell—acrid herbs and incense to promote cleanliness and healing, wounded bodies, pain.

All the beds were small and narrow, made of cheap standardmetal, with thin white linens that showed various colored stains. Raw wood tables sat next to the beds with a minimum glowsphere and chipped china scrybowls.

The place had no charm, hardly any comfort. His Downwind centers would be comfortable, he suddenly decided, no matter what the cost. Downwind scruffs of boys should know the solace of a home.

He met a small woman with fine blue-black hair and delicate features. She sent him an icy smile. Larkspur was a formidable Healer, a GreatHouse Hawthorn daughter who had fallen in love with and married a Downwind man while her Family had been negotiating her marriage to another House. Her husband had died in a street fight between two noble Families, and Larkspur held a deep bitterness for her class.

When she turned to Danith, her smile became warm and generous, and was returned in kind. T'Ash knew Danith prized new friends who ignored her Nobility and valued her Flair. He wondered if she understood that this lady was so friendly because of some warped reverse snobbery. He narrowed his eyes and compressed his lips. If Larkspur hurt Danith, she would pay. If anyone hurt Danith, they would pay.

Only a few of the wounded remained. A couple of the teenagers had agreed to be placed in the Maidens of Saille House of Orphans, some had been released to vanish back into Downwind rubble. Or to try and vanish—T'Ash and the Healers had attached a small findspell to them, to ensure continued care.

Larkspur looked up at him and sent him a condescending

smile. "The boy you have finally decided to see is the third bed on the left. His name is Nightshade, Shade." Her expression became more genuine, she shook her head. "The wounds he suffered in the battle are all healed, except for the cat scratches from Zanthoxyl. I don't know what your Fam had beneath his claws, but I suspect something filthy. Those scratches will scar the boy for life."

T'Ash grimaced. "Zanth likes to hunt sewer rats and celtaroons."

"Well, no wonder the scratches became infected. If there was vestiges of celtaroon, it's amazing Shade survived."

"Indeed," T'Ash said.

"Please note that Shade has a DepressFlair bracelet that smothers anything but ordinary Flair. He doesn't like it, but he became violent and we had to leave it on."

"Not surprising."

Larkspur raised fine, arched brows at him. "What's not surprising?"

"That he doesn't like the DepressFlair cuff, who would? That he's violent, that should be expected, too."

Anger stirred in her eyes. "Just because he's Downwind—"

"The scru— the boy, Shade is one of a perverted triad. I'm sure you noticed the glisten-coated, filed teeth. He fought me and threatened Danith. Don't tell me about Downwind youths. I know. Some rise above their background."

"Like you?" Her tone was as cutting as her eyes.

"Larkspur!" Danith protested.

T'Ash reached out and squeezed her hand but kept his gaze on Larkspur. "Like your husband, Ethyn Collinson. He was a good man with a Flair for Healing. I knew him slightly Downwind. His loss is felt, especially in these times."

Danith lifted her chin. "Men bridging Downwind and Noble are sorely needed."

Larkspur looked away. She touched Danith on the shoulder. "I have a small problem for you." Her voice sounded thick. "Or, rather, it has been a small problem for the HealingHall. It seems Zanthoxyl smuggled a kitten into the building for one of our patients. The boy, Antenn Moss, is doing fine, but I'm not sure about the little cat. Antenn hides it from us, and I think you should look at the kitten."

Danith brightened. Her Flair nearly glowed around her. T'Ash saw her strong pink aura clearly. The sight banished all his irritation. He lifted her hand and kissed it with all the caring he was capable of, then released her fingers.

Danith smiled and stroked his cheek.

Larkspur looked astounded, then drew Danith away.

T'Ash felt a prickle on his neck and turned to face a hate-filled stare from the boy, Shade. T'Ash squared his shoulders and walked over to confront the teenager. He looked to be a year or two younger than the triad-leader of the gang, but resembled him closely. Trouble.

"You T'Ash." Shade's lip curled in contempt.

"Yes."

"You should be dead. My triad-brother, Slash, should have killed. I should have killed. Me or Nettle will kill." He narrowed his eyes. "You not fair. Not honorable GreatLord."

The words stabbed T'Ash. Right on target. He struggled against anger, forced himself not to reply in short Down-wind words.

"You outnumbered us, tracking and attacking a young noble friend of mine. You battled my Fam. You threatened my HeartMate."

The boy's eyes widened at that, and he glanced at Danith. T'Ash cursed his tongue and the mistake he'd made. He leaned over the bed and oozed intimidation. "Neither you nor your triad-brother will hurt what is mine."

Shade glared at him. His fist with the armband locking his Flair clutched the bedclothes. T'Ash was sure they were the only bedcoverings the boy had ever slept in.

"You think you good. Not me." Sneering, he jerked his chin up. "You stay Downwind, you nothing. You got out."

Shade continued. "You know Nobles, your friends." He made the word a blasphemy. "You kill my brother, so you die. I take your rep." His gaze shifted to Danith, stooping over another bed, muttering soft phrases, smiling at another boy.

"But first me and Nettle take pretty lady. You kill Slash, triad-brother, we kill her. After play."

His gaze fastened on Danith's breasts, outlined against her tunic as she held a kitten eye level, bathing it in healing light. Her face was soft with tenderness.

"You have pretty lady, but you no good." Shade smiled viciously, showing broken teeth and filed incisors. "We'll get pretty lady. Take her. Make ours."

Cold warning hit T'Ash's stomach. He grabbed the boy's DepressFlair manacle tightly. He melded the metal inside the soft covering together. With all his powerful Flair, he chanted a chaining spell, binding it to the cuff. The energy made Shade stiffen, arch off the bed. No one would be able to remove the cuff except T'Ash.

"You cannot take the cuff off. You cannot hurt my woman." He'd make sure Danith had additional protection that would keep her from any harm. "You dare, and I will make sure you die slowly, screaming."

Redoubled hatred mixed with defeat in Shade's glare. He bared his teeth again, rubbed the wrist around the cuff with his other hand. "You big. You use force. You just like me."

"T'Ash?" Danith touched his shoulder.

"This boy's not worth saving," T'Ash gritted out.

She looked shocked. The pleasurable glow surrounding her disappeared, raising T'Ash's anger. He blamed the change in her on Shade. "Let's go. I've summoned my glider and it waits outside the main entrance. I'll take you home." His home.

She stilled him, touched his cheek. He felt the residue of loving healing in the tips of her fingers and he warmed. When he looked into her eyes, he saw that she meant him to be soothed by the last effects of her power. She was growing very knowledgeable about the uses of her Flair.

Then she dropped her gaze and a nervous smile came and went on her lips. "I'm due in SweetGrass Grove. The Clovers are having a party in my honor to celebrate my ascent to the Nobility. It's a wonderful gesture for them. Please, come."

"No," T'Ash said.

They left the hospital with courteous farewells to Larkspur, then lapsed into silence.

T'Ash mulled over the boy's words that had wounded

him, making him doubt himself, as usual. The words had resonated with truth.

Once in his glider, Danith glanced at him. "T'Ash?"

"Yes?"

"You are invited, also." She laid a hand on his thigh. "Please come with me."

The offer pulled him from his brooding about Shade. He stiffened and frowned; he'd wanted her in his home, at last.

"That boy disturbed you. Is it because you think he reminds you of yourself when you were young?" she said softly.

T'Ash shivered at her insight. "I don't want to talk about—"

She stared at him with heated green eyes with golden specks. "Of course you don't. You never do. How are we to become closer if you never want to speak to me about yourself and your past?"

HeartBond! Then he would have her forever, and his old failings would not matter to her.

She sighed. "You were never like that boy, back there. You may have been tough, and ruthless sometimes, and—" She took a breath. "I sense in him a viciousness that never lived in you."

"Because I got out of Downwind."

"Really? I don't think so. Everyone knows the Nobility has bred for Flair, and certain qualities. Perhaps true cruelty and sadism is beyond you, bred from you," she mused.

He strangled on a disbelieving noise. The flesh-eating firespell Flametree had crafted, and the use Rue had put it to made a mockery of that theory.

"Tell me of your boyhood," she whispered, not looking at him.

He almost dared, but didn't. "No."

She sighed again. "Very well. She turned her head and glanced out the curving forceglass window of the glider.

He thought of something else. "You need to stop by your house for food for this picnic?" He was beginning to learn common customs as practiced by Danith and the Clovers. "Perhaps you would like to take something from the T'Ash chef, stored in no-time."

She smiled. "The Lady forfend that I raid your cocoa mousse. Zanth would never forgive me."

"He would just show up at the Clovers and eat it anyway. He will probably be there, won't he, for the free food?"

"Probably. Will you come with me?"

"Will you come with me to the FirstFamilies Council, tomorrow afternoon?"

"A NobleCouncil is not a picnic."

"They are both stressful, for each of us."

Danith worried her lip with her teeth.

"I'll stop at your house and you can get food, then I'll drop you off at the picnic." He kept his tone even.

She sent him a glance. "Please?"

"No."

Her shoulders curved and she angled herself away from him. T'Ash cursed inwardly but refused to budge on the issue.

She continued to run away from her responsibilities as his mate.

Despite the feelings between them, she refused to let him initiate the HeartBond.

She wouldn't marry him.

It was getting worse. At first, when he'd taken Danith as his lover, he'd thought that nothing would prevent them from becoming HeartMates. He thought that he'd be able to convince her to move to T'Ash Residence, slough off the Clovers, and become his bride. Hadn't he proven how much he cared for her by fighting for her—both physically and emotionally?

She'd been so lost and confused. She'd asked for time.

And he'd given her time.

And now she was growing away from him, not toward him. She was finding her feet in her new profession, mastering her Flair with admirable ease. She was combining her very different past life with her present and future in a way he had never been able to reconcile his own. He envied her that.

And the Clovers were still her Family, not he and Zanth.

He and Zanth were only outsiders in her life, just as they

had always been outsiders in everyone else's. He was only her gallant, her lover. Zanth was only another pet.

T'Ash didn't think he could bear it.

He waited in the glider while she hurried into her home to get her food offering. He glanced at the little house with yearning. His Residence seemed colder and emptier and darker every time he stepped inside it. Only Danith made it habitable.

If she wouldn't stay with him, she needed more protection. Closing his eyes, he searched his Residence vault for a protection stone he'd made for himself on the vengeance stalk. After his reinstatement, he'd drained the stone of any detrimental emotions. He found it, summoned it.

A tiger's-eye. He'd forgotten. How appropriate. He caressed the chain with a finger and uttered the brilliance spell.

Danith ran out of her door, a pan in her hands. She threw a powerful Guarding Word to surround and shield her house, a measure of her new skill with Flair.

She'd changed into an amber gown. She looked wonderful—curvaceous and generous, bright and optimistic and brimming with life. He stared at her, memorizing her appearance, knowing his black brooding made her withdraw from him.

When she came near, the glider door slid open and she slipped in. Now he saw that her cheer merely masked an underlying strain. He was doing this to her, making her sad, and nervous, and unsure of herself just when she should be experiencing the happiest moments of her life.

They didn't speak as he powered the vehicle to full townglide and guided it to the public park where the Clovers gathered for their picnic.

She looked at him once more, with pleading in her eyes.

"One last gift," he said, placing the chain and tiger's-eye over her head. It fell between her breasts, complementing the gown.

He wanted to kiss her, take her, keep her forever.

He tried a smile. She stared at him.

"Go." He waved. "Have fun."

"Please join us, T'Ash—"

He tried another smile; from her expression, it was no more successful. "I can't. They are not for me. They don't even like me."

She put a hand on his shoulder, and he shuddered at her touch, wanting it to sink into his very bones so he could remember it forever. "They don't know you yet. They're really very good people."

He didn't dare cover her hand with his own, didn't dare touch her. "I'm sure they are. Go, Danith."

She frowned at him. A chorus outside the glider called her name. She looked to the Clovers, then back to him. With a quick brush of her lips against his, she left. "Later," she said.

The glider door slid shut softly. T'Ash clenched his hands around the guide ball. "I'm not a good person," he muttered.

A laughing group immediately converged around Danith, petting her, joking with her, teasing her, and peering into her food dish. Acting like they loved her.

And she laughed in return.

She never laughed with him, not like that, though she made him laugh.

He looked at her, dancing an impromptu jig with Mitchella. If she bonded as HeartMate with him, he would be forcing her into high society and rituals, all the rules a GreatHouse demanded, all the laws a GreatLady must follow. And all she would get in return was him.

She would be much better off without him.

She deserved a true Noble, a man as sterling in character as she herself. If he let her go, she could marry a Nobleman when she was ready, a man who would not have any doubts about his background or his character or his honor.

A scream shattered the air.

A boy ran toward Danith, knife held high. The sun shone on both the raised dagger and his teeth bared by grimacing feral lips.

Danith and the Clovers stood, stunned.

T'Ash 'ported from the glider.

Nettle moved in jerky strides, then leaped at Danith.

T'Ash's blaser cut him down midstride.

They stared at him in shocked silence, at the dead Downwind scruff huddled at his feet. Horror radiated from them, the common Clovers.

The men frowned, as if knowing that they should do something, but at a loss.

T'Ash set his jaw and flung the boy to Downwind Death-Grove. A collective gasp came from the gaily clad Clovers.

He glanced down at himself, dressed in black and ash brown, as usual. Utilitarian trous and shirt, without even a hint of embroidery at his cuffs, scuffed boots.

He could not look like them. He could not act like them. He would never be naive and easy like them.

The children recovered quickly enough, rushing to Danith, high, piping voices full of questions. They surrounded her, plucking at her gown.

Staring at T'Ash, she tried to detach them. One who was hopping about in excitement fell and Danith's gaze was pulled from T'Ash as she bent down to straighten the toddler and brush him off.

Claif joined her and scooped up a child, pointedly ignoring T'Ash. With a few gestures and casual words, he turned the others' attention away from T'Ash and drew them back into the grove.

Danith could marry into the Clovers, marry Claif, the outgoing, easy sort of man she had said she wanted.

She had never said she wanted to marry T'Ash.

He only brought her trouble and pain, and nearly got her killed.

Danith had suffered life-threatening danger. She had been a woman surrounded by blasers. And all because of her association with him.

She deserved someone better. She was his HeartMate, but she could never love the real T'Ash. No one could love him now. Only the HeartBond would make her love him.

He had been balancing on the thin edge of restraint for two weeks and now knew he could not spend one more night with her without performing the HeartBond. And he was incapable of binding them together forever without her consent.

He had to let her go.

She would have a better life without him.

Blood drained from him. Pressure built at the back of his eyes. His heart lay like a cold, hard lump inside him. Now, after his decision to let her go, it was too painful to watch her and he set the glider in motion, not looking back.

He dared never look back.

A clammy sweat coated his body, and he wondered if he'd ever be warm again. His emotions numb from the blow he'd just given himself, he tried to concentrate on what to do next. Every thought struggled through his pain. What next?

T'Ash sucked in a breath, but it left him unsteadily on a low moan. He could barely breathe, let alone think. What next?

Automatically his hands sent the glider far from the park noisy with laughter and cheer, far into NobleCountry. What next?

Something to finish the whole thing. Everything was over. Nothing could be made right. All gone. Except a debt.

He had an outstanding debt, to T'Ivy. T'Ash would arrange a trip to Gael City to procure a sky-crystal as the T'Ivy Testing Stone. He would take a designated member of the Family as witness. He only hoped they could leave today. The sooner, the better.

Once more he faced T'Ivy in the Ivy ResidenceDen, across the ancient desk. The man stared at him under bee-tled brows, fingers steepled. "You're sure you want to travel to Gael City now?"

"Yes," T'Ash said, realizing he was lapsing into Down-wind shortspeech again and vowed to answer better, next time. T'Ivy didn't look as if he wished to drop the subject, and as a mighty GreatLord, T'Ivy was accustomed to doing what he wished.

"I understood that your request for a new Passage was based upon the necessity of crafting another HeartGift. What of your HeartMate?"

T'Ash bled inside, his wound too painful to touch, to think of, let alone speak of. He welcomed the annoyance that came from T'Ivy's probing.

He shrugged.

T'Ivy tapped his fingers together, one brow raised. "As a matter of the transaction between T'Ivy GreatHouse and T'Ash GreatHouse, the potion didn't fail you?"

"No." He struggled to add more. He'd thought he'd broken the habit of Downwind speech a long time ago, but he'd lapsed so often lately that he knew it was in just one more area that he'd failed. "T'Ivy GreatHouse honored its word; I've come to honor my own."

T'Ivy sighed. "You know, being HeartMates doesn't mean that you don't see the other's faults, or ignore them. It simply means that you love in spite of the faults."

T'Ash was the one with the overwhelming deficiencies, not Danith, but he had no intention of telling this to T'Ivy.

"During the time two souls cleave together, one can cleave the other," T'Ivy looked pleased at his turn of phrase. "Your soul, made just for hers, hers just for yours. The claiming of a HeartMate isn't easy very often."

T'Ash said nothing.

T'Ivy looked at him, then looked away. When his gaze rested on T'Ash once more, he had a hint of vulnerability in his eyes. "You know I met my HeartMate when I was midage. Before that, I'd had children by a wife and was widowed. I had a wife." He hesitated an instant. "T'Ash, it is not the same. Companionship, respect, affection, even sex, is not the same as when two souls entwine in the HeartBond."

T'Ash stood. He felt pale and his insides clenched with the still agonizing pain of what he'd lost. He could not take any more "words of wisdom." He formed his sentences deliberately. "I am here to fulfill my word. If you wish to waive my service, do so; otherwise let us discuss the bargain."

T'Ivy gestured to T'Ash's chair. "Please sit."

T'Ash sank back into the comfortable seat. For some moments more he endured T'Ivy's scrutiny, then a gleam came to the GreatLord's eyes, and a small smile graced his lips. He pressed a crystal, and the Ivy butler silently entered. T'Ivy nodded to him. "Eiddew, please locate Hedara and relieve her from her duties until further notice. Ask her to come here for her next project as soon as possible."

Eiddew bowed. "At once, my lord." He bowed to T'Ash also, before leaving.

"Now," T'Ivy said briskly. "The agreement you made with my HeartMate was that you would choose and obtain a sky-crystal as a Testing Tool for T'Ivy GreatHouse. Your 'trip expenses to Gael would be paid by us, and we would provide a Family member to accompany you and witness your honorable and best service. Her trip expenses would also be paid by us."

T'Ash just wanted to nod. "That is correct," he said instead.

"Hedara will accompany you. I think you will find her an excellent traveling companion." The door opened. "Ah, here she is now."

A woman slightly younger than Danith glided into the room, a long blue gown shot with gold swirled around her. She wore a many-braided hairstyle that would have taken hours to fix.

T'Ash reluctantly rose. She curtseyed to T'Ivy, then swept a deep curtsey to T'Ash, with a respectfully bowed head.

Danith had never curtseyed to him. He didn't even know until now that he'd missed the little courtesy. Then his heart stung at the thought that he had betrayed her with that complaint, a very minor thing.

When Hedara lifted her head, T'Ash saw she had the sky-crystal blue eyes of the Ivys, eyes that perfectly matched her gown.

T'Ivy came around the desk and took her hand to present her to T'Ash. "My niece, Hedara Ivy. Hedara, GreatLord T'Ash." She curtseyed again, exactly as deep as proper manners ordained.

T'Ash nodded shortly.

Her cheerful countenance dimmed a little.

He felt a brute but had no interest in any woman but Danith. He let Hedara find her own chair as T'Ivy explained the undertaking to her.

"Now for the trip." T'Ivy raised his voice slightly. "ResidenceLibrary present plan, time, and expenses for two nonrelated travelers to Gael City with a return to Druida."

"The Ambroz Pass through the HardRock Mountains is currently blocked from rockfall; thus glider transport is excluded. Air transport over the mountains is not cost-effective. Stridebeasts are recommended," ResidenceLibrary said.

T'Ash cursed.

Hedara looked taken aback, then tilted her head. "Do you ride?" she asked T'Ash.

"Yes." Damned if he was going to try and moderate his speech anymore.

She nodded, her blond-brown hair wisped around her face. "I do, too." She smiled, showing perfect teeth. "Very well. We should have no hardships there."

"For a moderate pace, the round trip itself will take a week, an eightday," said ResidenceLibrary.

"How long will it take you to conduct your business in Gael City?" asked Hedara.

He could pick the gem in under fifteen minutes, haggle with the merchant for another thirty. "A day in Gael City."

She made a little moue with her mouth, but her eyes were amused. "A lot of riding with little relief, but if that's what you wish, GreatLord—"

"It is."

Once again her head bent gracefully. "Then I concur. We can leave in two septhours, if that is agreeable?"

"Fine."

"Ivy GreatHouse keeps a stable. I'll have the stridebeasts waiting outside the gates for you, T'Ash," T'Ivy said smoothly. He studied T'Ash again. "I have a large HairyStrider that should carry your weight for the trip."

"Nothing too high-strung," T'Ash said.

"He's not a hybrid," T'Ivy replied.

"And my own mount, if you please, Uncle," Hedara said, smiling. She rose and crossed to T'Ash, holding out her hand.

He stood and shook it instead of kissing her fingers.

She raised her eyebrows again. "Until later."

"Yes."

She turned and exited, hips swaying with feminine grace and her innate poise, and with completely no allure for T'Ash.

"A man could do worse for a wife than my niece," T'Ivy murmured. "And an alliance between T'Ivy and T'Ash . . ."

T'Ash inclined his head. "Merry meet."

"And merry part."

"And merry meet again. I'll obtain your sky-crystal."

"Oh, T'Ash?"

"Yes?"

"I will want the old stone reshaped."

"We can discuss that later."

"Agreed. As long as you make it a priority. I hear you have many commissions."

"Agreed. You will have a priority."

"Then go with the Lady and Lord."

T'Ash strode out.

Once home, he prepared to travel, trying to put his love from his mind. He ached with the devastation of losing Danith, and would have preferred a male traveling companion.

The merits of a long trip slowly sunk in. The extended journey would make his break with Danith complete. She would be settled into a new routine by the time he came back. And the trip would give him time to become accustomed to the fact that she would never be his.

But he wanted her triply protected. He'd welded a strong golden net around her, one that should last while he was gone. Also, she now wore a powerful shielding stone. But this was not enough. He scried T'Holly and felt some relief when he was referred to the GreatLord's personal holo cache, and didn't have to actually speak with the perceptive man. "This is T'Ash. I'm journeying to Gael City. I remind you of your vow regarding the safety of my HeartMate. Blessed be."

Just as he'd packed his saddlebags, and was lifting them to his shoulder, Zanth entered his bedroom.

Eighteen

The Fam took in the situation with a glance and sat solidly before the bedroom door, hissing. *What you doing?*

T'Ash narrowed his eyes. This was no time for Zanth to get temperamental. T'Ash was holding on to the straining link of his temper as it was.

"I'm fulfilling my promise to T'Ivy in payment for the Passage potion. My last vow, and damned if I'm going to ever make another so important. Do you want to go to Gael City? An eight-day trip to go there and back."

You stay here. No time to go. You not Mate with Fam-Woman.

"And I won't. She doesn't deserve us, Zanth. We can never give her the Family she wants."

Zanth snorted. *She has Me as Fam, has Princess. Has many animals. You give her four children. Plenty Family.*

T'Ash wouldn't let Zanth tempt him to break his will in this. "No. We've forced our way into her life, but no more. And I must fulfill this promise, now. I've made plans with T'Ivy."

Zanth lashed his tail. His growl fed the heavy silence for a moment. He muttered cat-talk to himself then speared T'Ash with an intense emerald stare. *A week. Not flying?*

"No."

Not gliding?

"No."

Zanth snorted. *Then, how?*

"Stridebeast."

You take horses, Me go. Me like horses.

"Horses are rare and valuable. I doubt if T'Ivy has any. And I don't ride them as well as stridebeasts."

Sallows have horses. You rent. Me know those horses. Me and FamWoman play with them.

"No!" He settled the saddlebags on his shoulder and glanced at his timer. "I made a promise to T'Ivy, and I'm going to Gael City. By stridebeast. Come or not, as you please."

Me stay, Zanth huffed.

"Fine. Hedara Ivy waits for me. I'll teleport to the T'Ivy gates. I'll be back in nine days."

Hed-ar-a. Female?

T'Ash bared his teeth in a smile. "Yes."

Me come see.

Hedara awaited them with two grooms holding the stridebeasts. Native to Celta, the stridebeasts were one of the first animals the colonists domesticated four centuries ago, particularly since horses had a worse adaptation rate than most Earth animals.

One of the stridebeasts was hairy with a broad back and sturdy-looking long legs widening to fat padded feet. Its neck was straight with a well-formed broad head and intelligent brown eyes. T'Ash handed his saddlebags to the groom to place on the beast and took the reins. He rubbed the animal between the eyes. The gray hair was as long and as soft as Princess's.

The second mount danced a little until Hedara took its reins and patted it, dismissing the grooms. It was obviously an animal bred for generations for beauty and an even gait.

Hedara looked equally elegant, again clothed in blue that matched her eyes. Her trous suit was both fashionable and suitable for riding. Not a hair escaped from her blond-brown braid, a hairstyle that emphasized the fine bone-structure of her face due to ages of noble breeding.

Her loveliness, obvious self-confidence, self-worth, and Nobility left T'Ash unmoved. He wanted Danith. He banished the thought.

Female, Zanth said, sniffing her legs.

Hedara stared at the huge cat, then looked at T'Ash.

He shrugged. "My Fam."

"Nice cat," she said, stooping with a hand out.

Zanth snarled, and she snatched her hand away.

Zanth sprayed on her boots.

T'Ash closed his eyes. When he opened them, Hedara still appeared shocked and appalled.

"My boots," she choked, then panted as the warm, wet stench of cat urine enveloped them. "My best boots." She hopped from foot to foot. She stabbed Zanth with an awful look, sent a beseeching one to T'Ash. "I can't travel like this. Impossible." She winked out, teleporting away.

She not like Me. Zanth grinned with satisfaction.

"You cat!" T'Ash wanted to singe the Fam's fur with a Word.

Zanth raised his nose at the insult. *You man. You stupid. Go. Me stay with FamWoman.*

"No! I don't want you near her, speaking to her, or visiting her while I am gone."

Now Me say No. Me do as Me please.

"You will do as I say, or I will see that you no longer see the chef in the mornings and that he feeds you nothing but oily fish for the rest of your life."

They matched glares. Zanth's tail whipped back and forth.

"Do you hear me?"

Me hear.

"I mean what I say."

Zanth growled. He spat.

T'Ash didn't move.

Paws flashed, leaving deep scratches on T'Ash's boots, ruining them.

T'Ash stood still.

Zanth hissed and whipped himself through the dirt, a small, furious whirlwind.

Hedara appeared. She looked down her nose at Zanth.

"Now, that is a hissy fit." Her words were rewarded by clawed boots. She stared down at them with a pained expression on her face.

She would never like Zanth, T'Ash knew. Something inside him rejoiced.

"Zanthoxyl!" T'Ash commanded.

Zanth stopped, sat up straight with his solid back to T'Ash, and started grooming. *I not see FamWoman. But you stupid, stupid, stupid. Go away.* He ignored his person with more studied arrogance than he'd ever done before.

"You're nobody until you've been ignored by a cat," Hedara murmured, lifting an eyebrow at T'Ash as she easily mounted her beast and reined it in.

T'Ash gritted his teeth at the old saying. Something Danith might say. The black hole inside him expanded with every second. He mounted up. He refused to say farewell to Zanth and didn't even glance back as they rode away.

This trip would put his entire past behind him, and he could prepare himself for the bleak future.

*D*anith's spirits plummeted. *T'Ash didn't come to her* that night. She got chills and his big body wasn't there to warm her. She shivered all night long and told herself it was due to the cool summer night, not the insidiously creeping notion that T'Ash had given up on her.

She called his Residence but only reached the holo cache. She left a stilted message.

The next night passed without him. And the next.

He did not visit the AllClass HealingHall. The last living triad boy, Shade, needed constant care to keep him from dying.

Again and again Danith recalled how the other boy attempted to kill her, the appearance of T'Ash, the quick violence that ended the situation.

She remembered the emotionless stare T'Ash had left her with. She hurt more for him, for how that act had worked on his soul, than she grieved for the Downwind boy. T'Ash had handled the situation in the only way possible.

She missed him and didn't want to. She wanted a solid

life, to establish herself as D'Mallow, and to know herself before she surrendered to him. She had to believe she was his match, that he could not overcome her with his powerful Flair.

She studied for the test on the laws that governed Nobles, GrandLords and Ladies, GreatLords and Ladies. She sweated through the test and answered every question correctly. She threw herself into her work, rapidly building her career, until every minute of every septhour of every day were filled with activity.

But empty of T'Ash.

One morning during the next week, she was ordered to rest by all her instructors. Finally she faced the facts.

Her heart thumped hard. Her throat closed.

She was so tired and so hurt that tears seemed dammed inside her. She was beyond crying; it would bring no release.

She had waited too long. She hadn't summoned enough courage to tell the brooding man that she loved him. She hadn't tried to banish his darkness. She hadn't accepted his HeartGifts or the HeartBond.

She was glad her third and last Passage was over. If it hadn't been, the flagellation she inflicted upon herself for these regrets would have killed her.

Now she listened to her emotions. She'd lost him and she'd never live with him. That meant no more moments at the T'Ash Residence. That hurt, too. It was a beautiful house, with so much character and potential. She could make it into a comfortable home as well as a showplace.

No more Zanth. A fragment of her heart shattered. She missed the Fam dreadfully.

She shouldn't go to him if he didn't love her, didn't respect her enough to share himself with her. And was what she just thought true, or was it an excuse to be safe and not risk herself? She paced back and forth in her small house, following a pattern T'Ash had used.

It came down to trust and love and hope. Did she trust herself and him? Yes. She'd grown enough in the last few days to believe she could exorcize that seed of darkness within him. And she trusted his word when he said that he wanted them to be HeartMates, she trusted the emotions that flowed through the bond between them, feelings that were so much more than passion.

Danith went into the kitchen and made tea, keeping her hands busy as she sifted through recent events. He must love her. Even when he was infuriating, his actions told her she was special to him. He'd give her all his wealth, and his work he valued. He wanted her to live with him, involved in all aspects of his life. She should not be involved in fighting, so he teleported her away. He'd die protecting her.

He must respect her. He believed in her Flair when no one else had. He'd let her Heal his Fam. He had shown her how to master her Flair, but had not patronized her. He had given her time to come to terms with her new life.

Trust, respect, and hope. She didn't think he hoped. That she would have to do by herself. She would have to risk herself, as T'Ash had risked himself in offering the HeartGifts.

She sipped the tea standing up.

If he didn't come to her, she must go to him. That was the bottom line. If she didn't . . .

No more T'Ash. The thought nearly stopped her heart. She couldn't live without T'Ash!

No other man was so strong, so powerful, so intelligent. So honorable. So sexy. So loving.

He was her addiction. She craved him, the sight of him, the touch of his calloused fingers, his body plunging into hers as if she held the world for him.

She could not give that up. She *would not* give that up.

Her determination would have to substitute for courage.

Without further thought she teleported to outside the Ash estate.

She wiped her hands on the tunic of her raspberry-colored tunic-trous that she had donned that morning. "Danith D'Mallow to see T'Ash," she announced in her loudest voice. It still came out as a squeak. She wondered if he had shielded his home from her.

The greeniron gates swung slowly open.

Danith sighed in relief.

She'd just entered when Zanth appeared with a pop.

Shut! he said, and the gates did.

He bounded to her and circled her, sniffing the cuffs of her wide-legged trous. Then he sat and grinned at her.

Greetyou. Good to see you. You come. FamMan thought you stupid. That you don't want Me, or him, either. Told Me, ME, not to eat your crunchies. His rumbling purr was background to his happy thoughts. Danith had never heard him so talkative.

She stiffened her spine and lifted her chin.

"You are always welcome at my home."

Me know.

"I will tell T'Ash."

We FAMILY.

"Yes."

Before she could give in to her baser nature and turn and run away, she said, "Take me to him."

Zanth flopped his tail back and forth. *He gone.*

Danith's blood froze. "Gone?"

You Noble. He Downwind Scruff. You better without him, he says. Without him, maybe. Without Me, NO! And FamMan comes with me. We package deal.

Danith managed a smile. "When will he be back?" Perhaps she could wait. If worse came to worse, she could park herself in his bedroom and take a dreamtime to make her sleep until he arrived. That way she wouldn't have to nurse her wavering courage.

He go to Gael City for T'Ivy. T'Ivy sent female, too.

Danith's trepidation vanished in the blink of an eyelash, replaced by jealousy—a twining, furious emotion that squeezed around her heart and ignited anger. "A female? Well, T'Ash doesn't need any other female in his life. He has me, his HeartMate. And I want him."

Zanth smirked. *Good. Me piss on her boots.*

Danith choked with laughter.

FamMan back to-mor-row afternoon. You come then.

Firming her lips in determination, and muttering the affirmation that she wanted T'Ash, that he wanted her, and that they were destined HeartMates, Danith nodded.

Good. You right Family.

"Thank you."

Good hunting.

That caused her to smile again. The only hunting she was going to do was for one stubborn, self-denigrating Great-Lord. And, by the Lord and Lady, she was going to bag him!

Zanth teleported out of sight, and Danith 'ported home.

*W*ith relief T'Ash bid Hedara goodbye at the outskirts of Druida, where T'Ivy guards waited to escort her home. T'Ash was glad to see her gone. He suspected she was of the same opinion.

He'd been so lost in his thoughts, and so melded telepathically to his mount, that to quickly sever his mind from the stridebeast's and send the animal along with Hedara would harm the creature. The solid, sturdy mount, which had carried him without complaint and whose easy gait had even soothed T'Ash, deserved better from his temporary master than to be summarily abandoned.

And Danith would be very displeased with him if she learned he'd harmed an animal.

T'Ash began unwinding the tendrils of his mind from his stridebeast.

Uncaring of the time it took, he proceeded down an old, unused, twisting road that slowly made its way near his Residence. He welcomed the vacant route. Now he could really think.

His Residence meant nothing. His future was burdensome. He'd have to find and wed a woman he knew would never touch his heart. He must sire children for the sake of the line. Others in the FirstFamilies had done as much. He wouldn't be the only one to live a life of duty, to abjure his own needs to fulfill his obligations to his House.

With a start, he realized that though it was high summer, the road felt cold and empty, with a whipping wind biting the air as an omen of a dark, cold, dreary life. Just like his vision.

He shuddered and picked up the pace. In moments he dismounted wearily outside his greeniron gates and sent his stridebeast on to the T'Ivy stables.

His gates opened silently for him, issuing him into an

estate that would never ring with the laughter of his Heart-
Mate. He trudged up the path to the Residence itself.

Zanth met him at the door. Zanth lifted his nose and
curled his upper muzzle. *Me lonely, you not here. Me clean
out five roon nests and no one calls Me Hero. Cocoa mousse
all gone by third day. Me miss crunchies at FamWoman's—*

"Quiet!" T'Ash blinked rapidly and stared at his whiny
Fam. "She is not our FamWoman. She will not be my Heart-
Mate. That is over and done with. We will get some other
woman, maybe a daughter of a GreatHouse." Even a woman
of the highest lineage could not replace Danith in his heart.

*Not want another female. Only pink person, FamWoman,
matches you. You stupid. You not listen to Me. Me go to eating room. You get more cocoa mousse from no-time for Me.*
Zanth stood and stalked away, tail lashing.

T'Ash did as he was bid, teleporting an entire pan to
Zanth's placemat, enough so the Fam could get sick if he ate
it all.

Danith's loss hurt. Bad. Worse than anything he'd ever
felt before, any blaser ray, any knife or swordblade, any fist.
It was just as bad as that fire Flametree had concocted,
painfully eating away at him until nothing was left.

T'Ash wondered if his emotions would die soon and leave
him a walking husk of a man. That would be preferable to
spending every moment of the day in excruciating emotional
pain, missing Danith.

He peeled off his clothes and sent them to the cleanser
before checking his ResidenceDen. He had several message
holos and something in the collection box.

Opening the collection box, he flinched when he saw the
tea mug. The first thing he'd ever touched with Danith's resonance. Though overlaid by smudgy D'Ceylon vibrations,
T'Ash could still smell Danith's blossom-fresh scent. He
could still feel the generosity and daintiness of her spirit.

He closed his eyes and turned his head away. The report
caught his eye. It appeared to be several pages, but the top
papyrus said "Summary." He read the bold, black, calli-
graphic letters—Danith's fortune.

"You will be surprised by good fortune. Love—deep and
true, a HeartMate love—will come to you. You will receive

honors, accolades and gilt for your Flair. Beware of physical danger, but there is a protector who will always guard you and give you his strongest support."

T'Ash closed his eyes and banished the mug to the farthest reaches of his vault. "There is a protector who will always guard you and give you his strongest support." Lord and Lady, how he wanted to do that. How he wanted Danith. But he was protecting her, and guarding her, he reminded himself. Without him in her life, she would never be faced with the dark brooding that battered the emotions. She would also be spared the violence that seemed drawn to him.

He went upstairs to the showeroom, hoping some of his cares would be washed away by the waterfall, knowing that only the oblivion of sleep would ease his hurt. He'd try to sleep, perhaps he would be spared dreams of Danith. Or nightmares. By now he didn't know which was worse.

All Danith's doubts resurged, of course. She'd managed to hold them at bay during the rest of the day before, but they ambushed her sleep.

She hadn't rested the entire agonizing night but recalled each and every one of her experiences during her Passages. She rose and dressed carefully in a gown of green shot with silver. She had purchased the expensive robe for her initiation as a Noble but had postponed the ceremony. With her usual lack of courage, she realized she couldn't face the rite without T'Ash's support.

She looked around her small house, knowing that she could now leave her home without a pang. She had outgrown it, though she would always recall its comfort with fondness.

But now she had to confront T'Ash and confess her love for him, and her intention to never leave him.

She shivered at the life-altering decision.

She nervously shuffled the cards. Her fingers fumbled and one fell out. With no surprise, she picked up the Lord of Blasers.

When she inserted it in the deck, the corner of another poked out. The ten of cauldrons—a man and woman holding each other and facing a rainbow, with children dancing in the background. Tears of yearning trickled down her face. How she wanted the contentment and lasting happiness the card foretold. How she yearned for the perfection of human love, earned by overcoming the darkest fears.

And she only had one last, mountainous fear to confront. Going to T'Ash and giving herself to him. But the reward was worth it.

She put the cards down and gathered her courage, forged a core of steel determination within herself. She stirred the small bowl of polished stones that T'Ash had given her and found a ring. Gold and small, she turned it 'round and 'round in her fingers until she realized what it was—a Noble boy's HouseRing. Rand's HouseRing. She wondered if he ever thought of himself as Rand.

And she wondered what it would take for Rand to come to her and love her, an open, vulnerable man, and not the GreatLord T'Ash.

Panicking, knowing if she didn't go now, she might never have the bravery to ever do it, she slipped the ring on her little finger, teleported the jewelry chest to outside T'Ash's gates, and grabbed Princess.

With a deep breath, she closed her eyes and visualized T'Ash Residence. The place she would spend the rest of her life. An instant later she was there.

T'Ash rose from an uneasy rest and spent some time in the HouseHeart. It failed to comfort him. All he could think of was suffering Passage here, making mental love to Danith, creating his HeartGift and their marriage armbands, preparing the room for Danith.

He went upstairs to his bedroom and reached for the other source of solace in his life—the T'Ash Family History, the book he'd been reading when Rue and his cohorts had torched the original Ash Residence.

He read the first page:

*T*he Ash is the symbol of the link between inner and outer worlds. It is the Cosmic Ash, the World Tree. Its roots delve *deep into the circle of Abred—the past, or chaos. Its trunk is in the center circle of Gwynedd—the present, or balance. And its branches support the heavens, the final circle of Ceugent—the future, or pure creative force.*

All children of the Ash should meditate upon how all things are connected—lowest and highest, such as a person and their Fam; earthly and spiritual; will and action. Our actions form part of an endless chain of events, just as each individual forms the Family of the Ash.

Accept that each of us is part of a larger pattern, linked to the others and reflective of the Great Plan of the Universe. Just as each of us is connected with our Family members, with the FirstFamilies, with the GreatHouses, with the NobleCouncil. We each have our place and our responsibilities in the Rituals.

Awareness and acceptance of these concepts will remove all doubt, fear, and confusion.

Review the past, but let it not rule you. Always ACT in the present with thought of the future, but do not let fear of the future bind you. Welcome the destiny that awaits you!

*B*ut he had not integrated his past. He had not been able to merge the child Rand, the young Downwind scruff, and the GreatLord T'Ash. He had failed the basic tenets of his line.

He lapsed into introspection. Danith had helped, and he was struggling to overcome his lack, but he still feared telling her of the darkness of his past; feared letting her so close that if she ever abandoned him he would be truly lost.

It was that fear that made him leave her, made him rationalize that she would be better off without him.

HeartMates were never better off without each other.

And as for protecting her—living with him was her best protection. He'd had a stable, peaceful life for several years before the events of the last eightdays, and he'd make sure his life with Danith held no more violence.

He knew what he had to do, and he dreaded it. He set his jaw. He'd done many things in his life that he dreaded, and nothing, nothing, was as important as giving himself to

Danith. Only in giving all of himself to her, without regard of the consequences of rejection, could he receive the ultimate prize, Danith's love.

Muttering words of encouragement to himself, he dressed carefully, in his best garb that represented GreatLord T'Ash. He would give her everything.

He picked up the book, and went to the window to look over his estate, his lonely estate.

He spied a movement in the rose quartz crystal scrystone. Danith!

He could barely believe his eyes. He could not move. His heart started pounding. He could not take his gaze from her. His sex hardened at the sight of her small and rounded form. He remembered her body in his arms. Her Flair was now almost visible and he recalled the delicacy of her mind, particularly as it cleaved to his in passion. It had been too long since they had loved. It had been too long since they had simply been together.

T'Ash managed only to suck in a deep breath, his fingers tightened whitely on the book. He still felt stunned.

She had come to him.

She had faced her own fears and come to him. She ran away no longer.

Her pink aura was bright, the large, antique jewelry chest stood next to her, and she carried Princess in her arms.

His gut tightened at the coming discussion.

"Danith," he said softly, knowing the stone would speed his words to her.

She looked up to the linked scrystone set in the wall. She smiled, a blinding smile different than any he'd seen before.

It staggered him. He braced a hand against the window jamb. She'd come into her own, grown into her Flair and her new Noble status. Before him stood GrandLady D'Mallow.

And he'd missed it.

He hadn't been there to see the final transformation, something he would always regret. He wondered if she, too, regretted it.

"T'Ash. I'm here." She took a deep breath and cuddled Princess close. T'Ash wanted to be held that way, close and gently by his love.

He cleared his throat twice before he could speak. "Be sure, Danith. Once you enter, I cannot let you go."

She smiled again. Danith D'Mallow, GrandLady. "Open the gates, T'Ash."

He teleported the jewelry chest to the empty sitting room of the MistrysSuite. He said the Word to open the gates completely, as they had never been opened before.

Danith stepped back and let them swing wide. She nodded, a courteous, graceful acknowledgment of his welcome, then she walked through his gates, head high, shoulders back, stepping into her new home.

"I'll be in the ResidenceDen," T'Ash said, then ordered the gates closed behind her.

She carefully placed Princess down. The cat looked around her, gave a pitiful meow, and jumped back into Danith's arms. Exactly where T'Ash wanted to be. Exactly what he wanted to do.

Danith stroked her cat and murmured reassuring words.

T'Ash teleported to his ResidenceDen.

He paced.

When she entered the ResidenceDen, she didn't have Princess. "I left Princess in the kitchen. I've come. I've quit cowering. You say we're HeartMates. I accept that. Offer me the new HeartGift." She hesitated a moment and another smile flashed across her face. "Even offer me the necklace. I'll accept."

She closed her eyes and her expression dimmed. "It has been awful without you, T'Ash. I've been excruciatingly lonely, even with my friends, both old and new, and the Clovers."

He should have felt exultant. She had come to him, and he wouldn't have to reveal himself. He wouldn't have to test her love with the darkness inside of him.

She would be HeartBound to him, linked with him forever, before she learned his deepest secrets. Easy, just the way he'd always expected.

But wrong. Not fair, and not honorable. And despite the fact that he wanted to take her, bond with her on all levels, he would not take her without letting her know his real self.

T'Ash spoke. "I was wrong. You weren't the cowardly one. I was. I never let you into my past. I never left myself vulnerable to you." He felt as if he were wide open to her gaze.

He held out the book in both hands. The Ash Family History, the book he'd been reading when the men came to destroy his House. The book he'd written in during all the dark and wonderful moments of his life. She deserved to see it, to know him. She needed to see it. He hoped it wouldn't drive her away.

She grasped it and he let it go. Then, suddenly, he knew just giving her the book was not enough. It could show her where he'd been, how he'd lived, but not what was important now. What he was now. And the best way to reveal everything was to simply remove all his internal barriers and link with her. She would know all of him, then. And he would know, immediately and intimately what she thought, believed, felt for him. If he dared.

"Wait," he said, sounding rusty. He took the book from her and put it on the desk. Lifting her hand to his chest, he placed it over his heart and captured her gaze with his own.

He flung down all his defenses, leaving himself completely open to her. "See me, Danith, HeartMate. See me and know Rand, and the young Downwind scruff, and T'Ash."

He felt her mental touch. Long minutes shuffled away as she softly turned over certain memories, some he'd prefer her never to know. He stopped the instinctive withdrawal and let her look where she would.

She looked deep.

She found his bottommost secrets.

She grasped his heart, and the dark and dreary fear harbored by Rand was extinguished under her touch, replaced by a rapidly growing tenderness and love.

He moaned with love and sparking desire. He was hers. His power, status, wealth, Flair, were nothing. All that mattered was Danith and her love for him.

Her telepathic touch disappeared.

He shuddered with emotion and saw tracks of tears on her face.

"Rand," she said, raising her hand to slip her fingers in his hair, and comb through it. "My love."

His heart jolted, his wits spun. With everything he had, he wanted to take her, bind her to him. He fisted his hands and kept them at his sides. He wanted more, but she deserved to set the pace.

She blinked rapidly. "You were right. I ran away from problems. I was afraid of all the new things that were changing my life so quickly. Afraid of our life together. Afraid of your Flair and Noble status. But mostly, I was afraid I would never be able to match you, that your power and Flair would overwhelm me. My real self would be lost."

"My match. My HeartMate."

She tugged at his hair. "I know that now. With my mind as well as my heart."

She let him go and ran out the open door.

His insides pinched. What was happening?

Her footsteps stopped. "Come, Rand. Follow me. To the bedroom."

He caught up with her in seconds.

By the time they reached his bedroom in the Master-Suite, he'd teleported his two HeartGifts there. A simple glisten tray floated in midair, holding the necklace and the earrings in it.

Danith gasped, placed a hand over her heart. Her cheeks flushed with desire, and he felt blood pool heavily in his groin, making his sex harder than ever.

She touched the necklace, put it over her head, and lifted the roseamber heart to turn it back and forth. She licked her lips, swallowed, looked at him.

Her eyes were wide with yearning. For him. His breathing matched the unsteady tempo of her own. He gazed at the necklace, then at her breasts, and saw her pointed nipples.

"The flaw." She cleared her throat and spoke again, her voice low and slow. "What does the flaw look like to you?"

He felt a smile spread, knew it warmed his eyes because her question made a tenderness he'd rarely experienced well up inside him. She understood. Everyone saw the flaw differently. Only he, only she, as HeartMates, would see the flaw deep in the roseamber heart as it truly appeared.

"Entwined lovers," he replied, not daring to touch the necklace.

"Yes," she whispered.

"You and me," he said. He took the thin wire redgold knotted earrings and inserted them in her ears, clamping his teeth tight to restrain his passion. He inhaled deeply and smelled the fragrance of womanly readiness. His woman. His HeartMate. His hands trembled.

"And these," he said, dropping his hands and stepping away. "These are the HeartBond knots, they are etched on our marriage armbands, too."

Her entire body quivered before him. She closed her eyes.

He watched her for a moment. Nothing in his entire life was as beautiful as she, awaiting him. She had accepted his HeartGifts, she was legally his. But he wanted the words.

"Danith?"

She opened her eyes, licked her lips.

He remembered how she tasted. His shaft ached, strained against his trous. He didn't want his clothes. So he let the heat from his skin, from all his inner desire, burn them away.

Danith stared at him. He felt large, ugly, scarred, but her eyes widened and when she raised her gaze to his he only saw a soul-deep longing. And tenderness.

She swallowed again, then lifted her chin. She locked her stare with his. "Rand Ash, HeartBond with me."

He closed his eyes and shuddered.

Danith watched her love's eyes flutter open. An intense blue gaze enveloped her.

Now it was time for her to open herself to him—her body, her heart, her mind, her soul. Now it was time for the HeartBond.

The necklace pulsed desire between them. The earrings, encompassing the emotions of Rand as well as T'Ash, vibrated to the beat of the necklace.

In dazed desire she slipped from her gown, took off the necklace, and placed it on the side table. She lay naked on the bed, awaiting him, legs slightly spread. She was his and his alone, forever. She stretched out an inviting hand.

A feral, desperate groan tore from his throat. He pounced, making room for himself between her legs. She felt the heated, throbbing tip of him and gasped, passion and anticipation spiking.

"Now. Can't wait. Not gentle!" His voice held both desire and despair.

"Don't wait. Come to me, Rand."

He forged into her. They rocked in thrusting passion together, bodies rubbing, hands caressing, hearts beating as one, minds and emotions coming ever closer.

They shattered together and through the ecstasy, Danith heard a distant clang. A reverberating sound of warm comfort, of everlasting love. The HeartBond, chaining them together stronger than marriage cuffs.

She would always be loved.

She would never be alone again.

She would always love him.

He would never suffer a solitary life without her.

She looked up. He looked at her with love.

"Mine. My HeartMate."

"Yes."

"My woman."

"Yes."

"My wife."

"Yes."

"My GreatLady D'Ash."

"Yes."

He smiled, a gleeful, boyish smile she'd never seen before. "I like 'yes.'"

She giggled, then stopped abruptly as he smoothly began to stroke his renewed hardness inside her. Then she whimpered. Before pleasure swept her away, she sighed, "My Rand."

"Yes," he replied between gritted teeth, wildness held in check in his gaze. "Yes. Yes. Yes. Yes. Yes." He obviously wanted to extend the sweet delight as long as possible.

Danith endured the acutely pleasurable torture for as long as she could, but she broke first, wanting all of his power thrusting into her, bringing her to the fabulous peak. Wanting his body hard and heavy on hers. Wanting their Flair to mix and mingle and explode around them in a shower of fireballs.

He groaned at her pumping hips, cried out as she grabbed him close and took what she wanted.

They fell together.

They landed in soft comfort and love.

His long hair tangled around his face, his light blue eyes looked wide, unguarded, exposed in his need. He hid nothing.

She cradled his body on hers and wrapped her arms around him.

After a long while he drew away and rolled over.

Danith lay limp. She felt as if she'd melted into the bed.

T'Ash stroked her head. "We will have a marriage ceremony within the week. This Ioho, a good omen that it is so near Summer Solstice. I purchased that land I saw in your mind, where you had your lonesome rituals. We will marry there. The Clovers and the Hollys will be invited. No one else."

Danith didn't have the energy to utter a sound.

T'Ash leaned over her, tracing a finger over her face, down her neck, around her breasts, to place his palm over her still-thumping heart.

"I made us marriage cuffs."

"Uhhhn."

He laughed. Rand actually laughed. Free and easily and his smile was so enchanting Danith sniffed and swallowed tears.

"I know how to control this wild woman of mine," he rumbled, leaning closer. "I love you."

She saw it in his eyes. "I love you, too."

Family, Zanth trilled, bounding through the cat door and leaving the flap swinging noisily behind him.

"Greetyou, Zanth," T'Ash said.

Zanth cocked his head at his person. *You happy. Never see you happy. Good. Good. Good.*

The cat looked at Danith. *You happy too. D'Ash.* He grinned. *Life is good.*

"Zanth, what do you want?" she asked, pulling a cover over her breasts.

Want Mate for Self.
Danith gasped.
Zanth flicked his tail back and forth.
Want Holly hunting Cat.
Rand shouted with laughter.
And, Zanth smiled smugly. *Want last word.*

RITA Award-Winning Author

Robin D. Owens

Get swept away to the planet
Celta—where one's psychic talents
are the key to life...and to love.

"Exciting and magical."
—*Romance Reviews Today*